Joseph Wambaugh is world renowned as the author of *The New Centurions*, *The Blue Knight*, *The Onion Field* and *The Choirboys*, four major bestsellers which have established him as the unequalled chronicler of the police story. After fourteen years with the Los Angeles Police Department, he resigned in 1974 to concentrate on writing and he is now about to start a career as a film producer. He lives near Los Angeles with his wife and three children.

D1136293

Also by Joseph Wambaugh and
published by Futura:

THE ONION FIELD
THE CHOIRBOYS
THE BLACK MARBLE
THE NEW CENTURIONS
THE BLUE KNIGHT
THE DELTA STAR
THE SECRETS OF HARRY BRIGHT
LINES AND SHADOWS

Joseph Wambaugh

The Glitter Dome

Futura

A Futura Book

First published in Great Britain in 1981 by
George Weidenfeld & Nicolson Limited

First Futura edition 1982
Reprinted 1982, 1984, 1991

Copyright © Joseph Wambaugh 1981

The right of Joseph Wambaugh to be identified as author of
this work has been asserted by him in accordance with the
Copyright, Designs and Patents Act 1988.

*All characters in this publication are fictitious
and any resemblance to real persons, living or dead,
is purely coincidental.*

All rights reserved.
No part of this publication may be reproduced,
stored in a retrieval system, or transmitted, in any
form or by any means without the prior
permission in writing of the publisher, nor be
otherwise circulated in any form of binding or
cover other than that in which it is published and
without a similar condition including this
condition being imposed on the subsequent
purchaser.

ISBN 0 7088 2161 8

Printed and bound in Great Britain by
BPCC Hazell Books
Aylesbury, Bucks, England
Member of BPCC Ltd.

Futura Publications
A Division of
Macdonald & Co (Publishers) Ltd
Orbit House
1 New Fetter Lane
London EC4A 1AR

A member of Maxwell Macmillan Pergamon Publishing Corporation

A perverse thank you to those in The Business, who, during a two-year Passage To Hollywood, imbued the author with sufficient venom to produce this book.

and

A humble thank you to Jay Allen, Harold Becker, Jeanne Bernkopf, Jack Herron, John Sturgeon, who helped the author complete the Passage, relatively intact.

Grateful acknowledgment is made for permission to reprint the following:

On the epigraph page, the entire lyrics of the song 'In Hollywood!' – words and music by Ian Whitcomb. Copyright © 1977 by IAN WHITCOMB SONGS, A BMI Company, c/o The Elaine Markson Literary Agency, Inc., 44 Greenwich Avenue, New York, N.Y. 10011

On page 66, lines from the song 'Shall We Dance' from 'The King and I', music by Richard Rodgers and words by Oscar Hammerstein II Copyright 1951 by Richard Rodgers & Oscar Hammerstein II Copyright Renewed Williamson Music, Inc., owner of publication and allied rights throughout the Western Hemisphere & Japan International Copyright Secured British publisher Williamson Music Ltd.

IN HOLLYWOOD!

Where is the place that they all like to go?
   It's Hollywood.
Jack 'n' Jill, Bruce and Bill, Farrah and Bo
   Go Hollywood.
Down on the boulevard Saturday night,
You've never seen such a colorful sight,
But make sure that you roll up your windows real tight
   In Hollywood.

Where are there so many hustling stars?
   In Hollywood.
Stuck in the sidewalk or parking your cars –
   That's Hollywood.
Most every moment you'll hear sirens scream;
Follow the cop cars – you'll soon reach the scene
And you're bound to end up on the big or small screen
   In Hollywood.

In the tradition of countless marines
   Go Hollywood.
Tuck your equipment in super-tight jeans,
   Go Hollywood.
Saunter the boulevard, you're out for hire,
Milk all you can out of old men's desire,
'Cause in just a few years you'll find *you* are the buyer –
   That's Hollywood!

— SONG BY IAN WHITCOMB

1

The Glitter Dome

It was six inches long. He stroked it lightly, but he could not conjure an appropriate response: eroticism, revulsion, fascination, *terror*. He had read it described in a hundred melodramatic and pathetic suicide notes. Technology had even infiltrated death messages: So far this year four farewells were transmitted on taped cassettes, the ultimate proof of declining literacy.

It was dark and cool in the tiny kitchen. The formica tabletop was greasy and wet from the spillage of Tullamore Dew. He stroked the thing again. It had hung on his body for too long. More of a cock than the other one. He used it once a month as required by the Los Angeles Police Department. He had *tried* to use the other one this very night. The fifth of Tullamore Dew was nearly empty. He should be anesthetized. He'd nearly died and all he could think of was his cock. But the memory of the misfire *hurt*.

Even the Pacific Ocean had the sweats that night. The offshore breeze was hot and wet. He ought to have turned and left The Glitter Dome the moment he entered. It was just nine o'clock, yet there they were, perched at the long bar like Mother Carey's chickens.

Chinatown gave him a headache, especially on those two nights a month when The Glitter Dome was jammed with chickens, yet that was why he was here. Police payday.

He had retreated utterly to the bosom of the cop 'family'. To The Glitter Dome. To kaleidoscopic colors: greens, yellows, reds, all of which he hated. To chaotic winking lights and leering neon messages. To winking groupies (seldom at him) and leering young cops plucking the chickens from their tentative perches at that long, long bar.

The hysteria was palpable. The Glitter Dome was teeming, smoky, loud. A dozen couples bumped and banged together on a parqueted dance floor hardly larger than a king-size bed. And it may as well have been a bed: Three of the groping, licking, grinding pairs of cops and chickens had managed everything but penetration.

He had known he should leave. He thought about leaving. But his legs were hurting from a game of handball at the police academy. *His* stupid idea, to provide some badly needed diversion for his partner, Martin Welborn, who, after his marital separation, had become morose, distant, burned out, *eerie*. They'd been partners for three years and he was suddenly scared for Marty Welborn.

So if it hadn't been for his friendship with Marty Welborn, and the handball, and the sore legs, he would not have almost *died* this night. He was ready to leave when one of the chickens (this one more of a vulture) was plucked from her stool by a cop he knew, a street monster named Buckmore Phipps who patrolled Hollywood Boulevard with the subtlety of a Russian gunship.

'Whaddaya know, whaddaya say?' Buckmore Phipps grinned, baring thirty-two donkey teeth, amazingly still intact, given the way *this* street monster did business on the boulevard. 'If it ain't Aloysius Mackey. Welcome to the Bay of Pigs.'

Then Buckmore Phipps was off to the dance floor with his boozy vulture, probably a record clerk. Al Mackey had gotten so he could tell the record clerks from the communications operators even before they opened their mouths. The policewomen were most easily identifiable: They evinced all the cynicism of their male counterparts.

So there was an empty barstool, and his legs hurt, and he had a sudden yen for three fingers of Tullamore Dew. He pointed to the bottle of Irish whiskey and nodded to Wing, the proprietor. With his overlong neck, and hollow eyes, and small head with sparse tufts of slicked-down hair sprung loose on each side like antennae, Wing looked for all the world like a praying mantis hopping around behind the long bar, his bony arms extending from his emerald mandarin jacket. Wing was a third-generation American who affected a Chinese accent and obsequious demeanor for daytime tourists. Nothing was as it seemed in The Glitter Dome.

'Double?' Wing winked, pouring a triple.

Before the night was over he would shortchange the detective to more than make up for it. Nothing was free in The Glitter Dome either. The perfect microcosm for Al Mackey. Thank God Marty Welborn didn't come here. He'd probably go home and swallow his Smith & Wesson. The Glitter Dome was a death wish of a saloon.

Al Mackey tossed it down at once and Wing skipped over with another. Three triples of Tullamore Dew and the warlord of The Glitter Dome could give the uncomplaining detective change for ten and drop his *twenty* into the mysterious box made of monkeypod which sat beside an abacus to accommodate the 'tips' which never passed through the cash register. Wing called the 'tips' a tribute to his honored ancestors who, among the huddled masses, came to these golden shores and prospered. There was an American flag on the front and Chinese characters painted on the back of the box. The message on the back, roughly translated, read: 'Uncle Sam's taxes suck. It's every Chink for himself.'

Another thing that Al Mackey hated about The Glitter Dome was the cascade of fruity drinks they poured over that bamboo long bar: Scorpions, Zombies, Fog Cutters. They all delivered a throat full of phlegm and a world-class hangover. And they were expensive.

'What division you work?'

She was rather young, something between a chicken and a vulture. But why did they all have phony lacquered nails? The one that Buckmore Phipps had plucked loose from the bamboo had actually left claw marks in the varnished bar top.

'Hollywood Detectives.' He said it to the Tullamore Dew, figuring it would be all over the second one of those virile, healthy young authority symbols from Central Patrol came swashbuckling in, full of juice and energy and hope, with the balance of a City of L.A. paycheck causing the *other* bulge in his jeans. We may not be the best cops in the world, honey, but we're the best paid!

And in they came. Look-alikes. Polyester body shirts, tight pants, hairstyles trimmed just short enough to keep the sergeants happy, the inevitable sideburns and moustaches. Why do all cops love sideburns except Al Mackey and Marty Welborn? God, it was so predictable, but not as predictable as the barroom greeting:

'Roll call!' bellowed one young cop, spotting a clutch of pals, and friendly groupies. 'Marcus!'

'Here!' a voice shouted from the smoky darkness. The goddamn place was starting to smell like incense. Al Mackey's head throbbed. A perverted Chinese church.

'Cedric!' the young cop bellowed, and a voice answered 'Present!'

'Sweet stuff!' the cop yelled, and three chickens from the corner pocket tittered and screamed, 'Here! Over *here*!'

The chicken-vulture next to him surprised him by not letting it drop.

'I work communications.'

'I woulda guessed.'

'How?'

'Nice voice,' he said. Big ass, he thought.

'My name's Grace,' she said. 'Some a the fellas call me Amazing Grace.'

'Al Mackey,' he said, giving her clammy hand a squeeze. Stress. Tension. So familiar, all of it. *Déjà vu.*

He became even more depressed when the door burst open again. (They *never* entered without a flourish.) Three more twenty-two-year-old father surrogates, fresh from a nightwatch radio car, came swaggering through the plastic-beaded curtains, doing a momentary freeze-frame for the queue of fatherless Glitter Dome chickens.

12

To Al Mackey they all looked like John Travolta. Good-bye to the operator. Catch your number some other time. Maybe around two A.M. when you haven't been nested and you're ready for the middle-aged casualties even more hysterical than you are. The kind you wake up with in a Chinatown motel (the *walls* are yellow, green and red), all sour and boozy in a lumpy bed, having left those desperate claw marks in the ass of a sad, blowsy stranger.

Just then Al Mackey got the passing bittersweet idea of going home and shooting himself. Surprise, Marty! Old Kamikaze Mackey beat you to it.

He knew he was extra loaded tonight. The chicken-vulture had begun to look vulnerable and lovely. He wanted to touch her hand. Then she opened her mouth.

'I reeeeel-ly like mature detectives as opposed to cocky young bluesuits. In fact I despise *them*. My girlfriend says if they couldn't eat poontang there'd be a bounty on them.'

She giggled into her Mai Tai just as he'd talked into his Tullamore Dew. They hadn't yet tried talking to each other. Perhaps they never would. What's the difference? The clanging of glasses sounded like the tolling of bells. A dark omen. He saw that she was at least as drunk as he.

'I despise that cheating Chinaman,' he said to his Irish whiskey. 'He's a thief.'

Then Al Mackey signaled to the thief, who hopped down the long bar and warmed Al Mackey's cockles by pouring *four* fingers without shortchanging him yet.

'I'll tell you who I hate worse than any Chinaman,' she said to the Mai Tai. Then she sucked the empty straw loudly enough to drown out the music of Fleetwood Mac any old day.

Al Mackey got the clue and nodded to the ever-watchful Wing, who skipped in with a premixed $3.50 special. This time Wing cadged fifty cents from Al Mackey's change.

Amazing Grace didn't thank Al Mackey. Apparently, the information about whom she hated worse than any Chinaman was worth three and a half scoots. 'I hate that

13

big ugly cop you talked to when you came in. You know, whatzisname with the big teeth?'

'Phipps. His name's Buckmore Phipps.'

'Yeah, that piece a cancer. I hate him. Only good thing about him, he's such a lushwell his liver's probably big as his ass. Can't last much longer, way he does it. About a year. Canceled check. End of Watch. Bye bye, Bucko.' Then, for the first time, she stopped talking to the Mai Tai. She turned to Al Mackey: 'Do you know he has a drippy faucet?'

'A what?' Al Mackey was trying to concentrate on her dancing eyebrows. Was she a blonde? Was she *gray*? He looked down and saw that her ass was *bigger* than Buckmore Phipps' liver. The fact is, she was somewhat repulsive. He was getting aroused.

'I happen to know that in Hollywood patrol right now the clap's as common as a head cold. Your friend, Buckmore Phipps . . .'

'He's *not* my friend,' Al Mackey protested boozily. 'I hate him too.'

Wing, never one to miss a conversation heating up, slid in with another triple of Tullamore Dew, took the correct amount from Al Mackey, and managed to steal a dollar from Amazing Grace's bar cash before drifting away.

'Your friend Buckmore . . . excuse me.' She hiccupped wetly and wiped her mouth with a damp cocktail napkin, smearing orange lipstick over her chin. 'He'd like to jump on my bones like a new trampoline. Tried to penetrate my knickers one night right here in The Glitter Dome! That's the kind a animal he is.'

'I hate him,' Al Mackey said fervently. 'I really hate him.'

'And I'll tell you something else.' She leaned closer to say it. 'I happen to know he's practically *raising* crabs. A steno works Hollywood nightwatch told me. He has them in his armpits even.'

'A goddamn crab ranch,' Al Mackey said, seeing two

14

Mai Tais in front of the hefty operator when logic told him there was one. Double vision meant it was now or never.

'Say, listen . . .' He didn't remember her name. 'Listen . . . Miss.'

'That's nice,' she said. 'I told you my name's Grace. You'd rather call me Miss. You don't hear such politeness from those young bluecoats. I think that's awful sweet, Art.'

'Al.'

'That's sweet, Al.'

'Grace, how about I take you home?'

'I got a car.'

'Okay, you take *me* home.' Al Mackey touched her hand.

'Where you live, Al?' She stroked his finger. It was getting hotter by the minute. Wing sidled by, nicking two quarters with utter impunity.

'I don't live far, Grace,' Al Mackey murmured. Their faces were inches apart.

'Where you live, Al?' she belched.

'The Chinatown Motel.'

'Oh, Al!' she squealed. 'That's funny!' Grace pushed him playfully, which caused him to pitch backwards, stool and all. Only the return of Buckmore Phipps kept him from crashing to the floor on his head.

'Hold on there, Aloysius.' Buckmore Phipps easily caught the frail detective in midflight. 'Kee-rist, Mackey, I got a water ski bigger than you. You get any skinnier you're gonna *disappear*.'

When Al Mackey was safely back on his stool and Amazing Grace was sending frantic signals by sucking air through the empty straw, Buckmore Phipps said, 'It's this Glitter Dome piss you're drinkin. Irish whiskey, my dick. Wing has it brewed on the shores a Lake Mojave by a gang a bootleggers. Stuff they can't ferment they use for moorings.'

'My right eye just slammed shut. I'm getting bored,' said Buckmore Phipps' vulture, now clinging to the huge shoulder of the cop. 'We cutting out or not?'

'We sure are, Babycakes,' the big cop cooed. 'Daddy's gonna take his Babycakes home and we're gonna . . . Let's see, first we're gonna . . . *fight*!'

'Oh, Daddy! Daddy!' she squealed, and Al Mackey's depression worsened. Talk about father surrogates!

'Babycakes gives Daddy a bust in the mouth and a crack in the teeth and the fight's aaaaalllll over. Then it's *peace*, Babycakes.' He made a peace sign with fingers as thick as shotgun shells.

'What a hunk!' The vulture ran her claws down the big cop's chest, raking the plunging nylon shirt.

'Listen, Grace,' Al Mackey said, 'what say you and me . . .'

But it was no use. The rum-filled operator was staring at Buckmore Phipps' mean and massive body as the other vulture bit his shoulder and said, 'Will Daddy tell Babycakes cops 'n' robbers stories?'

Buckmore Phipps had been here a time or two. 'Sure I will, Babycakes. Tell you about how I got shot last year. Had a slug in my bladder floatin in piss for a week till they got it out. Gave me *all* new plumbin, though. Now I fire *tracers*! Burny, burny, burny!'

And so forth. Babycakes couldn't keep her hands off him as they pushed through the crowd. Al Mackey heard Buckmore Phipps' superfluous parting shot. The big cop said to his vulture: 'I'm the *best* man in this saloon.'

Amazing Grace sighed and watched Buckmore Phipps all the way through the beaded curtains. Crab ranch and all.

'Well, she can have him,' Amazing Grace announced after they were gone. 'The way he talks to ladies. Calls her every kind a douche bag from full to empty. Still, she'd go along if he said he was driving to Hawaii. Huh! Best man in this saloon. Sure.'

'I'm about the seventeenth best man in this saloon,' Al Mackey said earnestly. Honesty *might* win the day.

But honesty had nothing to do with it, finally. Economics decided things. He wasn't as skinny as he looked before her fifth Mai Tai. And he was actually pretty young. No more than forty-six, forty-seven, maybe. One of those guys that probably looked old in high school. Probably no ass at all, but a nice guy. This Art Mackey was reeeeel-ly a nice guy. Economics. Supply and demand.

Ten minutes later they held each other upright and pushed through the madding crowd, much to the sorrow of Wing, who hated to see rummies get away with a few bucks left in their kick.

Perhaps the second saddest moment of the evening for Al Mackey was the snatch of conversation he heard at the far end of the long bar as he swayed past poor old Cal Greenberg, a thirty-five-year detective from his own division, who was desperately trying to make his point over the din of snaky hard rock to a lethargic young cop from Newton Street Station who couldn't care less.

'I wouldn't mind,' poor old Cal Greenberg shouted. 'If it was music, I wouldn't mind. You call this music?'

'You know that record clerk works the Badcat Detail,' the young cop answered. 'Maggie something? Tits from here to San Diego? That one?'

'Well, do you? Do you call it music?'

'Tits from here to Texas? Maggie I think it is?'

'Tits! That's all you want out of life? Would you rather have brains or tits?' poor old Cal Greenberg demanded.

'Shit,' the young cop said drily. 'If I had brains I could *buy* the tits.'

'But you call this music?' poor old Cal Greenberg insisted. 'This is *not* music. You ever heard of Glenn Miller? *He* made music. Glenn Miller. You ever *heard* of him?'

Wing ended poor old Cal Greenberg's imminent crying jag by pouring him a double. He let his furtive emerald sleeve slither across the pile of bills in front of the old detective. Wing managed to steal two bucks along with the price of the double to add to the box of mad money.

'Tell him, Wing,' poor old Cal Greenberg pleaded. 'Tell this kid. Glenn Miller was a hero!'

'Hero, my tush,' Wing giggled, turning the hard rock two decibels louder. 'He couldn't even *fly*.'

Wing dropped the booty in the box made of monkeypod, gave the abacus a sprightly fingering, and hopped down the bar toward a bombed-out kiddy cop from Hollenbeck who had at least thirty bucks in front of him.

Perhaps Al Mackey's misfire at the Chinatown motel was inevitable. Her flesh collapsed when she took off the bra and panty girdle. She fell out in sections: gelatinous thighs, varicosed greenish calves, stomach crisscrossed by a network of wrinkles and stretch marks. The gray belly of an aged seal.

'Well, goddamn!' she said finally, sweat-drenched and panting, not from lust but exhaustion. 'You a fag or what? I suck my goddamn teeth loose! For what?'

'I'm sorry,' he belched. The combination of booze and tension had him incredibly flatulent.

'It takes a stiff rod to catch the *big* fish, boy!'

'I know. I *know*!'

'Just my goddamn luck! A bar full a real men and I get some kind a *fag*.'

'Maybe we should leave.' He tried to sit up but the ceiling spun. Not in the same direction that it had when he lay down. It was the first time he could remember the ceiling ever spinning in different directions. Amazing Grace. He needed a Saving Grace!

'Okay, okay,' she said soothingly. 'I didn't mean that. That was wrong for me to say. Lord, what's the matter with me? You're havin a little trouble and I call you a fag? Lord, what's wrong with me? I should be *helpin* you.'

'It's my fault. It's not you.'

'No, no, sweetie. Here, come to Mama.' She pulled the skinny detective to her soft sagging breasts and shoved one in his mouth. 'There, there. You'll be okay in a minute. It was wrong of Mama to scold and call nasty names. There, there.'

Spittle was drooling from the corner of Al Mackey's

18

mouth. His right eye was closed, the left nearly so. He was unaware of her fondling his flaccid whanger. He was unaware that he had fallen asleep. *She* was unaware that he had fallen asleep. Then she noticed.

Al Mackey's elbow cracked against the night table when his body hit the floor like a bag of sticks.

'I suck my teeth loose!' Amazing Grace shrieked. 'For what? A fuckin FAG!'

Al Mackey didn't know if she had taken him back to The Glitter Dome. He didn't know what time it was. He didn't know *where* he was, except that he was driving his five-year-old Pinto on the Hollywood Freeway. The next thing he *did* know was that a very strange thing happened: A California Highway Patrol motor cop was traveling beside him on the driver's side, motioning for Al Mackey to come his way.

Al Mackey thought it exceedingly dangerous for the motor cop to be cruising so close to his car, so he held the steering wheel firmly in his right hand and with the left tried in vain to roll down the window. He couldn't understand what the Chippy wanted. Maybe he'd better pull over.

Then an extraordinary thing happened. The Chip yelled at him so loudly it hurt. The motor cop said: 'Get outa that fuckin wreck, asshole!'

Al Mackey decided to pull over. He could hardly see the freeway in front of him. Where were his headlights? He was suddenly aware that cars were passing him as though he was standing still.

He *was* standing still.

The door was opened by the enraged Chip, who grabbed the detective by the torn coat sleeve and jerked him out of the car. Al Mackey bumped his head. The roof seemed lower.

The roof *was* lower.

Al Mackey was standing on the freeway. There was a flare pattern behind him and several rubberneckers slowed to see what happened. The motor cop waved them past, holding Al Mackey erect by the scruff of the neck. An L.A.P.D. radio car rolled up behind them. Two cops came forward with flashlights.

'Need some help?' the younger one asked the motor cop, who at last released his hold and let Al Mackey slump against the demolished Pinto.

'I was tooling along when I see this drunk run up on the embankment,' the Chip said. 'His Pinto climbs the embankment *after* crossing three traffic lanes. Then he rolls over a hundred and eighty degrees and comes back down on the wheels. He thinks he's still driving when I walk up to the car!'

Al Mackey was starting to come around a bit and sensed he was in some trouble. He stepped back from the Pinto and examined it. The roof was six inches lower all the way around. The entire car was more than a *foot* lower since all four tires were flat. Every window was shattered and the windshield was gone. The right passenger door was lying in the lush ice plant beside the freeway. Al Mackey was unmarked except for the bump on the head he got when the motor cop pulled him out.

'Hey! It's Sergeant Mackey!' the younger cop said. He turned to his partner. 'Ron, it's Mackey from the dicks bureau!'

'Oh shit. A cop.' The motor cop's eyeballs rolled back under his helmet. He'd been here before. *Déjà vu*.

Al Mackey just couldn't quite fit it all together. It was like the first moment of dream awakening. Things made sense and yet they didn't. The truth was more elusive than usual at those moments.

'I think I can explain,' Al Mackey began, but he had to stop. Each step he took made him rattle. He tinkled and crunched as he walked. Windshield glass was falling from his clothing like snow. His hair was full of shattered glass. it was even in his pockets.

'Look here,' the young bluecoat said to the Chip, 'we'll

20

call tow service for the car and get him home. He's an okay guy. Give him a break?'

'Asshole!' the motor cop said to Al Mackey, as he stormed back to his bike, kicking up sparks with his cleated boots. He drove his fist into his saddle before climbing on and roaring away.

Al Mackey was absolutely certain that this could be explained, given a few moments to put it all together.

He stroked it again. This was the *real* whanger. This one he held in his hand, not the one that misfired in the Chinatown motel. And look at it, the cylinder so crusty with powder rings it could hardly turn. He couldn't even remember the last time he had cleaned his unfailing surrogate cock. Yet this baby *never* misfired. If he treated the other one like this, what? Terminal scabies? More likely, treatment from some unlicensed Chinese croaker (compliments of Wing after a finder's fee) so the Department wouldn't charge him with Conduct Unbecoming an Officer for coming up with some kind of venereal Red Death. But it couldn't happen. He regularly cleaned and lubricated and pampered the one that misfired.

The glass was empty. He didn't even remember draining it. He put the six-inch Smith & Wesson service revolver on the table in front of him. Lots of people are scared of their cocks. He was only afraid of the one that *didn't* work. Marty Welborn confessed that occasionally his didn't work these days. With Marty it was probably not booze but religion. Maybe they were one and the same? In any case, he was not afraid of the surrogate on the table. He'd carried it too long.

Al Mackey staggered to his feet. The bump on his head was now marble-sized. He weaved his way across the kitchen and through the cramped boxy living room. He kicked his way through the litter: newspapers, magazines, an empty bottle of Tullamore Dew on the three-legged coffee table, which sagged whimsically, propped up by a stack of useless books on criminal law, criminal evidence, and criminal procedure. Books he had never been able to bring himself to study in all the years he had never troubled to take the lieutenant's exam.

He looked at those books, performing their first useful function, supporting the table he had broken two weeks ago when, even drunker than tonight, he had tripped over the goddamn cat.

How he hated that ugly table. How he hated those books he'd never studied. How he would have hated being a lieutenant and sitting at a desk and sucking some captain's ass. How he'd have hated the humiliation of failing the lieutenant's exam. God, how he hated that fucking *cat*.

The tomcat was standing on top of the couch hissing at him, as mean and spiteful as ever – unblinking, glaring. Then the no-name cat turned away and began sharpening his claws on top of the already shredded sofa back, just as he had every day since that rainy night five months ago when the detective took in this nasty, skulking alley cat during a bout of drunken Yuletide sentimentality.

Al Mackey watched the cat and smiled malevolently. It was perfect. It suited the mood, this blatant display of haughty destruction.

'Maybe you want to go *with* me?' Al Mackey said to the cat, who looked up and arrogantly ripped deeper into the fabric. Tufts of cotton began to ball up and leak out. Al Mackey turned and staggered the few steps back into the kitchen. When he returned to the ruined living room he pointed the six-inch Smith & Wesson at the blazing yellow eye.

'Right between your frigging horns,' said Al Mackey.

The striped pearly tomcat narrowed the yellow eye and responded by insolently ripping the fabric yet deeper.

'You miserable prick!' Al Mackey said.

The cat *yawned*. That did it.

Al Mackey kicked the lawbooks from under the coffee table. The cat arched and screamed. The Bottle of Tullamore Dew went flying. Al Mackey kicked the wrecked table again and the *cat* went flying.

Al Mackey watched the remnant of Irish whiskey dribble out on the matted filthy Oriental rug, which like everything else in the bachelor apartment belonged to the landlady. Al Mackey heard the cat snarling as it retreated to its bed in the corner of the bathroom.

Al Mackey was ready to show the world. He went straight to the closet. He pulled a sweat shirt and two pairs of jogging shoes onto the floor. He hadn't done any running in two years. He kicked the jogging shoes across the room. He felt the leather. He took it down from the shelf and lurched back into the kitchen, to the formica table.

This wasn't *anybody's* cock. He slid the two-inch Colt revolver from the black leather holster.

An 'off-duty' gun. It was the first thing they all did twenty-two years ago, those slick-sleeved, scrubbed, and hard-muscled rookies with their big eyes and crewcuts and bags full of hope. They ran out and bought 'off-duty' guns. Dodge City. The John Wayne syndrome. They wouldn't go to the grocery store without an off-duty gun in a pocket or strapped to the armpit or ankle or at least under the seat of the family car. Never know when they might stumble onto a pursesnatch in progress. Or a burglar climbing out a neighbor's window. Or (dare they hope?) a bandit holding up the teller in the local bank while they're in mufti at the next window, clutching their City of Los Angeles paycheck. Then, a shoot-out! (They win, of course.) The L.A. *Times*. A television interview. The Medal of Valor maybe? An accelerated transfer to plainclothes. *Glory*.

The syndrome passes. The off-duty gun is sold, or traded for a more useful revolver, or put away into closets with youthful fantasies.

Al Mackey was such a poor marksman he always shot the pistol range with his six-inch. And though it was unwieldy, he carried it through all the years of detective duty. Not that he still expected fantasy shoot-outs – it's just that he hated these pig-snouted, inaccurate, bullet-spraying off-duty guns, which in fact got so many Los

23

Angeles cops into so much off-duty trouble in barrooms and bedrooms from Sunland to San Pedro.

Suddenly he pointed it at his face. This isn't *anybody's* cock. Don't try play-sucking on *this* baby. This one *wasn't* familiar. This one was a terrifying *machine*, which, if properly used, could take a three-inch shard of glistening skull and deposit it across the kitchen on the windowsill. Would that filthy cat drink his blood?

His hand began trembling. That's why the really serious ones chew on it. Eat it. *Chew* on it. Put it in your mouth because the hand's shaking too much to hold it at the eye or temple. But point it upward. He remembered so many failures: slugs lodged in the soft palate, in the jawbone, in the neck, in the ear. Every goddamn place but in the brain, where they were meant to go. Then: agony, paralysis, deterioration. *Consummate* failure.

He opened his mouth. He moved the two-inch closer. Chew on *this* baby. But the rounds are twenty-two years old. He'd never bothered to replace them. He'd never used the gun. It was dust-covered. The cylinder might be frozen. He'd wiped it off from time to time but he'd never fired it. The rounds were twenty-two years old! They probably wouldn't ignite. The firing pin would make a nice big gouge in a dud cartridge. They'd *never* fire. He was only playing a *game*.

Okay, test it. *Pull*. He was drenched. The sweat slid down his cheeks. Al Mackey was only forty-three years old, but his cheeks were gray and hollow and lined. The oily rivulets followed the premature creases in his face. His hand began to steady a bit. He thought about cocking it. No, do it double action just like on the firing line. It's only a few pounds of trigger pull. He used his thumb. These old rounds won't fire. Possibly.

Chew on it! Eat it! Mercy!

Then he felt it. The gun slid from his fist and clattered on the formica tabletop. A warm puddle under his ass. He jumped up in horror.

'I pissed my pants!' he wailed.

24

The cat hissed. The phone rang.

'I pissed my pants!' he cried, in shame, degradation, *disbelief.*

The phone rang and rang. Gradually he heard it. He lurched into the bathroom. The cat was in bed licking his balls. It caused Al Mackey to look down at his own dripping crotch.

He moved into the bedroom with the Frankenstein gait of a man who'd pissed his pants, in slow motion toward the incessant telephone.

'Sergeant Mackey!' the landlady screamed in his ear. 'It's four o'clock in the morning!'

'Please, Mrs Donatello.' He could only talk in an unrelenting monotone.

'I thought I could at least trust a policeman to respect my property!'

'Please, Mrs Donatello.'

'It wouldn't be so bad if you was a lover boy or a queer or something, but you! You make all this noise and destroy my property when you're all alone! I never seen nothing like this before! You get in these terrible fights with your own self!'

'Please, Mrs Donatello.'

'I'm telling you, Sergeant Mackey. I felt sorry for you. I begged you to go to the A.A. meeting. They can help alcoholics.'

'I don't think I'm an alcoholic, Mrs Donatello.'

'You're an alcoholic, Sergeant Mackey. You're the fourth detective I had as a tenant. Three of you was alcoholics. No more cops!'

'Yes, Mrs Donatello.'

'What did you break this time?'

'I just broke the coffee table again.'

'That's something to be grateful for at least. Did you fall down again?'

'Yes, I fell down.'

'Do you want me to call a doctor?'

'No, an exorcist maybe.'

25

'What?'

'Nothing.'

'I want you out, Sergeant Mackey. Your apartment is filthy. And I don't allow cats. You got too many fleas and roaches in your apartment.'

'How many fleas and roaches am I allowed, Mrs Donatello?'

'What?'

'Nothing, Mrs Donatello.'

'I'll give you thirty days to find another apartment. Thirty days is enough time.'

'All the time in the world, Mrs Donatello. More time than *I'm* going to need, that's for sure.'

It grew into an enormous wet balloon of a sob. Then it exploded. He hung up the phone and began to heave. His narrow, rounded shoulders shuddered and lurched. He looked like an armless man trying to swim. He heaved desperately, unable to hold back the huge wet balloons. Each balloon burst. The tears scalded.

He stripped off his pants. The urine was already beginning to chafe and burn. He wasn't wearing underwear.

'Where's my underwear!' Al Mackey cried. 'I left my shorts in Chinatown!' Sing *that* one, Tony Bennett! Oh God, for a man to *lose* his underwear!

The cat looked at him blankly. Much the same as Wing had looked at poor old Cal Greenberg, who couldn't make them understand that Glenn Miller made *music*. The pitiless cat licked his genitals contentedly and never again glanced up at the weeping man. Even when he cried so hard he vomited in his bath water.

2

The Altar Boy

The last sun shafts cut through the stained glass like venerable swords, but quickly retreated in the face of iniquitous coppery thunderclouds. The lingering smell of incense and charcoal made him nauseous. He actually felt faint, so acrid was the cloud of smoke from the censer during the procession. Father Dominic loved plenty of smoke. Easy on the wine you poured over his tapered fingernails into the chalice, heavy on the charcoal you put in the censer. The altar boy always got dizzy blowing on the coals to get them glowing hot for the pall of somber smoke. But worse than the procession down the narrow aisle was kneeling during the Forty Hours Devotion, in an empty church, cold and shadow-shrouded, during the twilight hours when the wounded, tortured saints and martyrs loomed like bloody phantoms in the gloom. No matter how much personal pain the altar boy endured from the hours on those wooden kneelers, he could of course never begin to appreciate the awful agony suffered by those enshrined forever in paint and plaster and leaded glass.

And each time he sat for a few moments to relieve the muscle cramps, wouldn't Sister Helen or Father Dominic appear black-robed from the dusk and remind him of an altar boy's special obligation to endure that pain and to offer those tiny, insignificant moments of suffering as a special sacrifice to Our Lord and His Mother. Agony was a privilege, if endured without complaint and offered to Them.

The tall priest, frail as a secretary bird, would point a bony finger toward those bleeding martyrs who had been consumed by fire, stripped of flesh, ripped asunder, blinded, mutilated, buried alive. Remember Mother Superior's tale of the candidate's corpse disinterred by the Vatican in search for Miraculous Signs? They found hairs in the hands of the skeleton! Proof that he'd been buried alive, and despairingly ripped his hair from his own head instead of dying serenely, six feet beneath that black earth, triumphantly awaiting his last breath of air with eternal salvation guaranteed. But they found hairs in the skeleton's hand. Not only would he never be canonized a saint, but Mother Superior feared for his very salvation, he of little faith.

'Agony is a privilege, Martin.' The priest's penetrating tenor echoed fearfully through the ever-darkening church. 'You should be grateful, Martin. Do you understand, Martin? Well? Do you? Martin? Martin?'

'Martin! Martin! Goddamnit, Martin!'

Al Mackey was loosening buckles and straps, straining at his partner's heavier body. 'Marty, you goddamned idiot!'

Then Martin Welborn was lying on the floor of his bedroom, unable to raise his head for a moment. He was uncertain where he was. He was uncertain *who* he was. It might be a dream or it might not, this hovering specter who was pulling him into a sitting position.

At last Martin Welborn smiled. 'Tell me, Al, am I a man dreaming I'm a butterfly or a butterfly dreaming I'm a man?'

'You're a freaking idiot, Marty, is what you are! God damn!'

'It's remotely possible,' Martin Welborn answered.

'What the hell're you trying to do?'

'Help me up, Al.'

The skinny detective reached under the armpits of the naked man and hoisted him to his feet. Martin Welborn put his hands out to brace against the wall, misjudged the wall's location, staggered, and sat down on the bed.

'Marty, what *is* this thing?' Al Mackey demanded, pointing to the aluminum stanchions and crossbars and dangling straps standing like a gallows in Martin Welborn's tidy bedroom.

'It's a spine straightener. You know I have back problems.'

'Back problems. Marty, you have *head* problems. Worse than I guessed even.'

28

'Al, Al' – Martin Welborn smiled serenely, standing and slipping into underwear and pants that had been neatly placed on the bed – 'this has been terrific for my lower back. I hang upside down twice a day, morning and night. I straighten out my spine and never have a moment's fear of back pain.'

'Marty, I was banging on your door for nearly *five* minutes. I could hear the shower going. I figured you'd fallen in the tub. Christ, I slipped the lock!' Al Mackey held up his laminated police ID card, the corners chewed by the door latch.

'At least those cards are good for something,' Martin Welborn said, taking a starched white shirt from the mahogany chest. His cotton shirts, professionally laundered, lay folded, stacked in exact rows.

The police identification cards couldn't even get a check cashed. *Sorry, sir, my boss says drivers' licenses only*. But at least they could slip a lock better than most shims. Al Mackey's hands were trembling. He could hardly get his card back in the wallet. 'Do you realize you were passed out? Your face looks like raw sirloin! If I hadn't come in . . .'

'You have a flair for hyperbole, Al, my lad.' Martin Welborn grinned.

It was always 'my lad, my son, my boy', though Martin Welborn was only two years older than Al Mackey. He removed his socks from the second drawer. The pairs of socks were stacked by color shades. It looked to Al Mackey as though Martin Welborn had segregated each stack with a micrometer. When did he start this shit? Marty was never this orderly. *Nobody* was this orderly. Eerie. It was all getting *eerie*.

And it was affecting Al Mackey profoundly. Now *he* was getting drunk and even chewing on his gunsights! Al Mackey got a chill and shivered noticeably.

'How long you had that instrument of torture, Marty?'

'It's a spine straightener, Al. They sell them to people with back problems.'

'Yeah, you said. I say they oughtta put them in the freak

29

shops on Hollywood Boulevard, along with the leather masks, chains and thumbscrews. Goddamn, Marty, if I hadn't come in . . .'

'Al, I hang for exactly three minutes. I was watching the time on the clock by my bed.'

'I was at the door for almost five minutes.'

'You look terrible, Al. Were you at The Glitter Dome again last night?'

'Jesus, your color's just now coming back.'

'You should stay away from The Glitter Dome, Al.' Martin Welborn adjusted an impeccable knot in his paisley tie. 'Can't you find a happier place to drink?'

So Al Mackey gave up. He knew the non sequiturs would continue until his surrender was inevitable. He went into the kitchen of the one-bedroom apartment and opened the refrigerator. He shakily withdrew a bottle of orange juice and three eggs. He wasn't hungry but his vitamin-starved, whiskey-ravaged body demanded food. It was different from a feeling of hunger, this relentless demand. He cracked three eggs, lost one in the sink, but managed to get the other two into a glass of orange juice.

Al Mackey pulled open the drawers looking for a spoon. Jesus! Each drawer was divided by plastic trays. Each spoon was stacked so that it could not stray from its assigned place. Ditto for forks and butter knives. Al Mackey opened the cutlery drawer: steak knives in a row pointed toward the wall. Larger cutlery pointed toward the gas range. Spoons and ladles toward the wall. Tiny blocks of wood kept every utensil in its assigned place.

Al Mackey jerked open every cupboard in the immaculate little kitchen. Each glass was polished. Not a water mark anywhere. Each rested in a specifically assigned position, from the tallest water tumbler down to the stubby whiskey glasses. The spices in the cabinet were lined up by graduating height. The symmetry was perfect.

Martin Welborn walked briskly into the kitchen. He wore a gray three-piece suit with black loafers and gray socks. Tiny patterns of red in the gray silk paisley were the

30

only release of restraint. His heavy black hair was brushed back from a forehead not yet age-lined.

'New suit, Al. How do you like it? Do I glitter when I walk?'

'You glitter, Marty.' Al Mackey finished the glass of orange juice and egg, and studied the composure of Martin Welborn. *I was watching the clock, Al.*

A drop of juice glistened on Al Mackey's chin. Martin Welborn hurried to the sink, opened a drawer, and removed a paper cocktail napkin. The dinner and cocktail napkins were stacked and arranged by size and color.

Martin Welborn dabbed the drop of juice from Al Mackey's chin. Then he showed Al Mackey his handsome, boyish smile and said, 'We'd better hurry, my lad. Captain Woofer's just a wee bit testy these days.'

Captain Woofer had reason to be testy. It had been a very bad year in many ways. One L.A. cop had been arrested in a foreign country, charged with smuggling cocaine. Another had been shot, but not by a bad guy. The wounded cop *was* the bad guy and had been shot down trying to escape capture. Then there was a new scandal involving vice cops accused of providing protection for bookmakers. And last, but by no means least, there was an extraordinary number of controversial cases involving the shooting of unarmed suspects by police, along with mis-taken-identity shootings.

This was reputed to be the most professional police force in America. The media demanded explanations. Deputy Chief Julian Francis decided he had the explanation, at least for police corruption. He had decided to visit every Los Angeles police station personally and try it out on both uniformed and plain-clothes personnel before asking the Super Chief's permission to call a press conference.

Deputy Chief Francis was already getting up a head of steam when Al Mackey and Martin Welborn tiptoed into the squadroom of Hollywood Detectives, five minutes late.

'The cause of our misfortune is apparent,' Deputy Chief

Francis was saying. 'The breakdown of family, church, and patriotism is at the root of *all* these misfortunes.'

So, while thirty detectives let their chins drop on their collarbones, or failed to control the eyeballs sliding back into pain-ravaged skulls (thirteen detectives had hangovers, last night being payday), Al Mackey and Martin Welborn crept to the table belonging to the homicide teams and braced for the family-church-country speech.

Deputy Chief Francis was not about to alter that one. He'd been making the same speech for twenty-nine years. It had impressed the selection board when he applied to become a policeman, just as it had every promotion board since he'd made sergeant twenty-one years ago without having worked more than two months on the street. It hadn't been easy convincing a triumvirate of cigar-mangling, potbellied inspectors in those early days that he should be promoted over the street cops, even though as the speech writer for the chief of police he had composed some of the finest hell-and-sulphur ditties this side of J. Edgar Hoover. But even with those hard-drinking promotion boards of bygone days, the family-church-country oratory had never failed. It put a lump in the throat and tears in men's eyes, or so Deputy Chief Francis was convinced.

It made poor old Cal Greenberg want to puke. His hangover was worse than Al Mackey's. The old burglary detective had his head in both hands and stared past Deputy Chief Francis. The curse of The Glitter Dome. He looked like he couldn't frost a mirror. Al Mackey reached over and sympathetically patted poor old Cal Greenberg's shoulder. There, there.

The seemingly comatose detective never felt it. He was listening to his own private Glenn Miller concert. He had but to blink his eyes to switch from *String of Pearls* to *Little Brown Jug*.

The only variation in the theme of Deputy Chief Francis this year was that he had fallen in love with the buzzword 'impacted'. Everything was either 'impacted on' or 'impacted by'. The immorality of the outlaw cops, exploited by the media, came as the direct result of the cops being *impacted by* the deterioration of family, church, country. And so forth.

Also, the deputy chief's wardrobe had changed this year. Usually he preferred banker's attire, much like that always worn by Martin Welborn. But he'd consciously decided to dress like a working detective until the series of morale-building speeches was finished. Deputy Chief Francis' choice of clothing was perfect: double-knit plaid pants – flared of course, now that flares were out and straight legs in, a detective always being three years outdated. A pale blue polyester sportcoat with extra-wide lapels, a dark brown dress shirt with a stitched collar, topped off by a fat yellow-print necktie. He was careful to keep the double-knit plaids an inch too short and he wore green and yellow argyles to exaggerate the fact. He let his sideburns grow longer, preparatory to his tour of the stations. He had considered a moustache, but there *were* limits. Finally, he topped off his costume with a brass tie tack in the shape of numbers 187, the California Penal Code section for murder. It was perfect. He looked for all the world like a working homicide dick.

Deputy Chief Julian Francis knew that some of the older men might remember the hated nickname Fuzznuts, given to him in 1965 during the Watts riot when he had become separated from his driver and bodyguard in the chaos of burning and looting on Central Avenue. It was rumored that he had waved a handkerchief and tried to *surrender* to a small army of looters near Ninety-second Street, saying he'd always been kind to Negroes. It was a scurrilous story, never substantiated, but he felt the '187' tie tack went a long way to dispel the rumor and suggest he was one of the guys.

Two bearded narcs, dressed like boulevard bikers and known as the Weasel and the Ferret because of their slippery ways, began sliding notes down the line of tables. The notes were actually betting markers. They were offering three to one that Fuzznuts Francis would use the word 'impacted' twelve more times during the remainder of his morale-building speech. It seemed excessive even for Deputy Chief Francis, so several markers were slipped back down the table to the young narcs. They were on a three-month loan to Captain Woofer from narcotics division downtown to help with the outrageous drug problem that the Hollywood business community was always complaining about.

Deputy Chief Francis concluded by saying: 'It will take a strong religious faith to sustain the Los Angeles Police Department *and* the United States of America from the enemy lurking within the human heart.'

Captain Roger (Whipdick) Woofer was genuinely moved. He started *applauding*.

The Weasel and the Ferret were outraged. The number of 'impacteds' had only totaled eleven. One more!

The Weasel raised his hand frantically. 'Sir! Chief!' cried the Weasel. 'What effect has the Vietnam generation of policemen had on the general decline of morality among today's officers?'

The other gamblers knew of course what the Weasel was up to. Poor old Cal Greenberg jumped to his feet. He was holding a marker for two dollars. (All that Wing hadn't stolen last night.) 'Just a goddamn minute, Weasel! He's *finished*.' Then he turned toward the shocked deputy chief. 'You *are* finished, aren't you . . . sir?'

'Well . . .' the deputy chief stammered. The greasy leather covered biker frightened him. (*He's* what's become of the Department these days!) But the menacing old detective with the raw bloody eyes was even more frightening.

Captain Woofer blanched and bellowed, 'Greenberg! What in the world's wrong with you?'

'Nothing, Captain,' poor old Cal Greenberg cried. 'It's just that we shouldn't keep the chief here all day. He's got other duties and . . .'

That reassured Deputy Chief Francis. He smiled and

34

held up his hands. 'Gentlemen,' he said, 'I've got all day. My time is your time.'

'Rudy Vallee, for chrissake!' poor old Cal Greenberg moaned, his bloody eyes rolling back under his veiny lids. My time is your time!

'Greenberg, what in the world is the *matter* with you?' Captain Woofer demanded.

'He's sick,' Al Mackey volunteered. 'He isn't feeling well. Maybe we should take poor old Cal out for some air?' Al Mackey had *three* bucks down. 'Maybe we should let the chief go?'

But all was lost. Deputy Chief Francis smiled paternally and said, 'You've been a damn attentive audience. And I should answer the question of the . . . officer.' It was hell referring to a slimy hippie in a black leather jacket as an *officer*. 'Yes, I do think that the influx of Vietnam veterans, who may not have properly withstood the immoral influences they encountered in that unfortunate part of our world, has indeed *impacted* on the . . .'

He couldn't finish. Twenty-one men and women (those who had some action down) were lowing like cattle while the Weasel and the Ferret were grinning like hyenas. They had won thirty-three bucks.

The chorus of groans startled the desk officer downstairs who had been reading of foreign terrorists attacking police departments with nerve gas which caused involuntary moans before immobilizing the victims. The panicky desk officer was ready to sound an alarm.

Captain Woofer apologized to Deputy Chief Francis for the bizarre behavior of some of his detectives. It could only be that the string of notorious crimes involving Los Angeles police officers was even taking its toll on the morale of veterans like poor old Cal Greenberg. Deputy Chief Francis concurred. He shook hands warmly and called Captain Woofer 'Roger', just as in the old days when they were sergeants together doing public relations work. Captain Woofer blushed and softly responded, 'Thank you . . . Julian,' not loudly enough for the others to hear.

35

Except for the Ferret, who looked at them and said, 'Whipdick Woofer's sucking around Fuzznuts like a pilot fish. Police pansies is what I think.'

Then the Weasel took the last two dollars from poor old Cal Greenberg and said, 'Fuzznuts can't get out the door. Every time he stops, Woofer gets a snootful a shit. Department daffodils is what I think.'

The Ferret, leering like a coyote, was counting his loot and said, 'I needed this. I got in a dice game last night and crapped out three times in a row. I felt awful all morning.'

Poor old Cal Greenberg reached in his drawer for a box of Ex-Lax, as his stomach rocked and rolled. 'At my age if I can crap *once* in a row I'm satisfied.'

Five minutes later Al Mackey and Martin Welborn were called to a private meeting with Captain Woofer, who was even more constipated than poor old Cal Greenberg.

3

The Business

The reason for Captain Woofer's bowel obstruction was that it had been four weeks since the unsolved murder of Nigel St Claire, president of the film division of a major studio, who, like everyone who was anyone in show business, would never have been caught dead east of La Cienega Boulevard unless doing business at Goldwyn, or Paramount, or Hollywood General.

One might visit Hollywood proper to have lunch at St Germaine or go to Ma Maison for dinner, since it was one of the *in* places, what with Beverly Hills overrun by Arabs, Iranians, Texans, and other wogs with megabucks. (A wog could, however, become as instantly acceptable as any German steel exporter or Italian shipping magnate by merely saying 'maybe' to the Ultimate Question in these parts. The Ultimate Question might be uttered during cocktail hour in the Polo Lounge of the Beverly Hills Hotel, or over lunch or dinner in any one of the Six Famous Restaurants.) There were never more than half a dozen truly 'in' restaurants during any particular time warp, not as far as the Truly Successful of The Business were concerned, the Truly Successful being an incestuous group too small to support more than half a dozen.

The Ultimate Question – that which stopped lethargic waiters (off-duty SAG members) dead in their tracks, along with table-hopping mannequins (ditto), and even busboys literally scraping at table crumbs (the Screen Extras Guild for these shmucks), and caused the rest of the eavesdropping clientele to cease all shop-talk, ice-cube rattling, furtive coke whiffing, thigh stroking of either sex by either sex, sometimes simultaneously – that which produced the frozen take reminiscent of the E. F. Hutton television commercial: 'My broker is E. F. Hutton and E. F. Hutton says . . .'

The Ultimate Question, delivered through clenched teeth to keep the jaw from trembling, was: 'Now that I've explained the incredible potential of this film, do you think you might like to get in on the project, for a substantial part of our rather modest budget of . . . *eight* million?' It was always a 'film' or a 'project', never a 'picture' or, God forbid, a '*movie*'. And if the Arab, Iranian, Texan, or other wog simply said 'maybe', this outlander would ascend from the ranks of the great unwashed and become eligible for a 'B' table at any one of the Six Famous Restaurants. (The 'A' table was his *when* the movie started shooting. Talk is cheap.)

All of this was only vaguely understood by Captain Woofer but had led indirectly to his constipation. For the late Nigel St Claire had been found shot to death in the parking lot at a bowling alley near Sunset Boulevard in downtown Hollywood at eleven P.M. Everyone knew that a man like Nigel St Claire, one of the Truly Successful in The Business, would not be caught dead in such a place at such an hour. But he *was* caught dead, and it got great news coverage, and helped to induce Captain Woofer's internal blockage.

Both Al Mackey and Martin Welborn thought it prudent to let Captain Woofer take his good old time getting around to it, and so he did. He settled comfortably on the rubber ring cushion he used for his inflamed hemorrhoids, lit his briar, sucking on it for thirty seconds to get it cooking. Then he fiddled with the stack of papers in his incoming basket and toyed with a plastic paperweight the size of a building brick which had entombed within it a set of gold captain's bars. (They said that even Mrs Woofer called him Captain.) Finally, he looked at the two detectives and said, 'I suppose you men wonder why I called you in here?'

Oh, God! Al Mackey was too hung over for this shit.

First Fuzznuts Francis' lecture, then losing the bucks to the Weasel on the 'impact' bet, and with it the fearful image of Marty hanging upside down like a dead marlin. *Three minutes, Al.* Sure. And barely able to keep last night's debacle repressed. If he started thinking about last night, there'd be a successful reprise tonight and Mrs Donatello could stop worrying so much about fleas and roaches and deal with the problem of scraping Al Mackey's brains off her wallpaper with a putty knife.

But he'd been a cop for twenty-two years. And something within him required that he give someone of captain's rank a response, even someone like Whipdick Woofer. So he nodded tightly and said, 'Yes, Captain, I *was* wondering why you called us in here.'

Captain Woofer sucked on the briar some more and put his feet up on the desk *very* carefully, since elevated legs were good for common cop hemorrhoids but bad for painful police tummies.

'It's because of Nigel St Claire,' he said.

'That's not our case, sir,' Martin Welborn responded gently.

'It hasn't been,' Captain Woofer nodded. 'But it's been four weeks. Schultz and Simon don't have a single lead. They've interviewed more than fifty people.'

'We don't know any more about the case than what's in the newspapers.' Al Mackey looked at Martin Welborn and shrugged. 'Schultz and Simon aren't exactly the gabby type. They haven't asked us for any help.'

'*I'm* asking for your help,' Captain Woofer said, taking the pipe out of his little teeth. He'd begun to look rather old of late. He'd become more bald and he'd shrunk a bit.

'What do you need, Skipper?' Martin Welborn asked.

'I need you two to take over the case,' Captain Woofer said. 'St Claire was a famous man. This case stays in the news. The department's taking a beating these days. Questionable shootings. Outlaw cops. That third-rate television station skewering us all the time. I retire in September. You think I·can take so much heat at this time of life? Every day a hack from *that* TV station asks for a progress report on the murder. I have to go out of my way to be obliging.' Captain Woofer's eyes got soft and moist. He looked exceptionally small and old.

'But we're not supersleuths,' Al Mackey said.

'What would Schultz and Simon think if we took their case?' Martin Welborn said.

'I know only *too* well you're not supersleuths,' Captain Woofer reminded them. 'And I don't give a shit what Schultz and Simon think. They've had their chance. There's only one other homicide team available and you're it. Besides, you're the *ideal* team for this one.'

Before either puzzled detective could ask why, Captain Woofer's eyes narrowed and he said, 'You solved Clyde Barrington's murder, didn't you?' Captain Woofer gave them his craftiest look and chewed on his pipestem, letting the two detectives chew on the remark.

The character actor Clyde Barrington was of show biz, true, but what other similarity? Al Mackey said, 'Skipper, Clyde Barrington wasn't murdered. We didn't *solve* his murder because there wasn't one. We cleared the case by showing he murdered his girlfriend and committed suicide.'

'Nobody's asking anybody to *solve* anything. I just like the way you two seem to *clear* every homicide that might make me more . . .' He sighed and didn't finish. At that instant he exactly shared the same longing as poor old Cal Greenberg, minus the Glenn Miller concert.

So they didn't have to *solve* the crime, only clear it? Al Mackey and Martin Welborn looked at each other again.

'Captain,' Al Mackey began, 'this is a bit different. It would be pretty hard to suggest he committed suicide, what with two ·38-caliber bullets in his face and no gun found.'

'You resourceful boys handled that death two years ago where the coke dealer killed himself with the hatchet, didn't you?' Captain Woofer looked at them craftily. 'You haven't lost your nimble inventive ways, have you?'

'Uh, no, sir,' Al Mackey said, 'but the hatchet was right there.'

Through a videotaped demonstration, Al Mackey, using the 'suicide' weapon, performed convincingly for the camera and persuaded the ever-persuadable Captain Woofer that a man of average strength like the cocaine dealer Dilly O'Rourke, given utter dedication to self-destruction, could actually strike a fatal blow to the front of the skull. It took some doing, including expert opinion from a pathologist regarding the fragility of the human skull at the point of violent contact with the hatchet.

The mushy hole in the *back* of his skull was another story. Martin Welborn, in his youth a Jesuit seminarian, had suggested wryly after three weeks of fruitless investigation that it was time to *pray* for the answer. And lo, within the hour their prayers were answered, not by the God of failed seminarians but by Lord Buddha.

While they were going over Dilly's former digs for the thirteenth time, a sandwich vendor with her hair full of dandelions came tripping in from Hollywood Boulevard carrying a thirty-pound brass Buddha in her track-marked, tattooed little arms. She apologized for having removed it the night Dilly O'Rourke was taken off to become part of the Eternal Force. Someone said she might get in trouble and should bring it back.

She was startled right out of her place in space when the two detectives, with grins a yard wide, grabbed her and sat her down and pumped her shallow well of memories until she recalled that Lord Buddha had always rested over by the Ouija board where Dilly's dead body was visited by every coked-out tenant of the building before someone stopped chanting mantras and called the cops.

Al Mackey's performance was spectacular. The videotape showed him miming the self-inflicted blow to the front of the skull, after which he dropped the hatchet, held the back of his wrist to his forehead like a damsel on a train track, and staggered exactly nine feet five inches across the room, keeling over and feigning a bone-popping collision with the unyielding brass bean of the chubby Chinese deity.

Martin Welborn whistled, applauded, and cheered when the performance was over.

Captain Woofer showed the videotape to the commander and accepted his praise with becoming humility. Another whodunit *cleared*. It became official. Dilly O'Rourke left this vale of tears on his own steam.

The tattooed junkie with the head full of dandelions to this day never failed to wave at the detectives when she spotted them on Hollywood Boulevard while she was selling avocados to buy heroin – a swap, they called it, of deciduous fruit for insidious fruit. She often gave the detectives whole-grain sandwiches filled with parsley and peanut butter in gratitude for not hassling all the tenant-customers of the bloodsucking, coke-stealing little fuck. Now admitting that the tenant-customers had been over-joyed to see him lying dead in his own blood.

The implied message was coming through loud and clear with every suck of Whipdick Woofer's ugly old pipe: Remember the Plato Jones case. *Nimble inventive ways*.

That was a particularly difficult homicide for Captain Woofer. Plato Jones had made and lost three fortunes in the record industry and was now riding high on a hot roll. During his losing spells he supplied a few girls (or boys as the case might be) and roughly two tons of Colombian over the years to his out-of-town customers, which brought him smack into the L.A.P.D. Intelligence files.

But when he managed to bounce back into big bucks with real zippo, as they say, he'd stocked the campaign larders of front-runners in state and local elections. He was embraced by the Truly Successful in The Business. He attended most 'B' premieres and all 'A' charitable functions. He sailed in yacht races with a United States senator. He greased Sacramento lobbyists. He loved baby seals and whales and American Indians. He hated big oil and nuclear plants. So the guy *had* a few bad habits, who's to cast the first stone?

But there was considerable giggling, backslapping and hee-hawing around Hollywood Station the day they found Plato Jones shot through the temple in a trick-pad near Sunset and La Brea, the death weapon beside his body. Of course there wasn't a whore in sight when the corpse was found. There wasn't a fingerprint of a whore, nor anyone else's for that matter – this despite the discovery of a half-drunk glass of Pouilly-Fuissé, bearing *no* fingerprints, resting beside the corpse. It caused considerable damage to the suicide theory, but not as much as the expended shell from the death-dealing ·32 automatic. The shell was found on top of a seven-foot armoire, an eighteenth-century French piece the likes of which was seldom seen in a trick-pad. But then, Plato Jones had nothing if not style, a sentiment echoed at his funeral by two congressmen, three city council members, one consumer activist, two dozen recording stars, a Lebanese opium runner, and thirteen whores.

After a six-week investigation which was getting on everyone's nerves, particularly Captain Woofer's because of the incessant calls from City Hall by a support-your-local-police councilman who was sweating out a $10,000 campaign donation from Plato Jones and wanted this goddamn case put to *bed*, the deft and artful team of Al Mackey and Martin Welborn were handed the investigation and ordered to retrace the steps of the crestfallen failures Detectives Schultz and Simon, who couldn't solve it.

It took Al Mackey and Martin Welborn exactly three days. First, the half-drunk glass of wine was a cinch. Three of Plato's whores were located through a snitch and freely admitted to being in and out of the trick-pad on the night in question. Two of them couldn't remember, but 'might' have had a glass of white wine. And, Lord be praised, Plato thought that black velvet gloves were a super turn-on. Ergo, *no* fingerprints! No lipstick on the glass? Baby, do you think you have *any* lipstick left on your mouth after three or four of those flossy fatcats from Brentwood with

43

those limp little peters make you suck your eyes crossed? (The memory of *that* remark struck Al Mackey where he lived.)

The problem was, of course, the expended ·32 cartridge shell resting in an upright position on top of the armoire. The solution came in a flash to Al Mackey. The *proof* of the solution came after three sweaty hours with Al Mackey standing where Plato Jones received one shot through his right temple. Martin Welborn videotaped Al Mackey, the death weapon at temple height, ejecting an empty cartridge, which due to the angle of the chamber was kicked high in the air and, *voila!* came down on the top of the armoire in an upright position, just as if someone had placed it there.

What the tape *didn't* show was the 231 times the shell was ejected and *didn't* land in an upright position. Had anyone checked closely they would have found gaps in those videotapes ten times bigger than any attributed to former President Nixon. Al Mackey and Martin Welborn decided privately that the odds, therefore, were 232 to 1 that the pimp blew his own brains out. That was close enough. Certainly better odds than Plato Jones ever gave. The deputy chief was happy. Captain Woofer was thrilled. The city councilman was ecstatic. The case was cleared.

'I'd like you to take over the Nigel St Claire case. I already advised Schultz and Simon this morning before you two arrived. *Ten minutes late.*'

'Car trouble, Cap,' Al Mackey said.

'Why should you have car trouble? The Department has mechanics, you know. Why do you think I let you take a city car home? Do you realize how much personal gasoline money you save by taking a Department car home?' Captain Woofer was extra whiny today.

'Well, we *are* on call twenty-four hours, Skipper,' Al Mackey offered.

'Homicide investigators are *supposed* to be on call, Mackey.' Captain Woofer shifted painfully on his rubber gasket.

44

Martin Welborn said nothing. He just sat and smiled serenely, his eyes a bit vacant, going in and out of focus. Al Mackey watched Marty's long brown eyes more than he watched Captain Woofer, who bore watching at *all* times. Captain Woofer had sabotaged two promotions so far this year and transferred one detective, because of sticky investigations that went on too long and caused the captain discomfiture. Whipdick Woofer could be a real sneaky ball whacker, they said. Martin Welborn didn't seem to mind any of this, which caused Al Mackey to worry all the more.

'We *do* have some other cases we're working on, Captain.' It was Al Mackey's last shot.

'Like what?'

'Well, there's that Cuban woman whose husband blew her eight feet out of her wig with that old ·45 British Army revolver. We're still tying up that one,' Al Mackey said.

'A *Cuban* woman,' Captain Woofer sighed.

'Then there's that Korean girl who got shot on the drive-by homicide. The one where the car full of lowrider gang members were getting even with another gang by shooting *anyone* on the street. And she happened to get off a bus at the wrong stop.'

'A *Korean* girl,' Captain Woofer sighed.

'It was a double,' Al Mackey reminded him. 'The bullet passed through the baby she was carrying in her arms before it killed her.'

'A *Korean* baby,' Captain Woofer sighed.

So it was no use. Captain Woofer had his mind made up. They were going to inherit a bad-news homicide, and though Al Mackey didn't have any illusions about getting promoted, he had always wanted to finish his career here at Hollywood Detectives. It was getting too late in life to have his balls whacked and transferred to Watts.

Then Captain Woofer accidentally pushed what Al Mackey knew to be absolutely, unequivocally, positively the *wrong* button for Martin Welborn. Captain Woofer said, 'I can't see anything you're working on now that's time-consuming. That Meadows case is finished, isn't it?'

45

Al Mackey jerked his face toward Martin Welborn. Marty's long brown eyes dropped lower at the corners. They leaped out of focus. Marty stopped smiling serenely. He looked confused.

'Danny Meadows isn't finished,' Martin Welborn said.

'Well, what's left to do with the case?' Captain Woofer asked. 'I thought mommy and daddy were going to cop a plea?'

'Danny Meadows isn't finished,' Martin Welborn said.

'Damn, I can't get comfortable,' Captain Woofer whined. He never noticed the lack of focus in Martin Welborn's eyes. 'You still have more testimony to give, or what?'

'Danny Meadows isn't finished,' Martin Welborn said.

'They've got it wrapped,' Al Mackey said quickly, with darting glances toward Marty. 'Yeah, they're copping a plea. Probably probation for mom, a little jail time for dad.'

'Then the case *is* finished?' Captain Woofer said, glancing toward the unfocused eyes of Martin Welborn.

'Yes, Captain, it's *finished*,' Al Mackey said to Martin Welborn, who didn't seem to hear him.

'It wasn't as though it was some big-deal homicide anyway,' Captain Woofer observed. 'Kid would've been better off if it *was* a homicide. Anyway, I think you could tidy up your pending cases and go talk with Schultz and Simon about the ground they've covered on the St Claire thing. I've got some theories that . . .'

Danny Meadows isn't finished.

Martin Welborn could hardly hear Captain Woofer. His voice came from a cavern somewhere far away. As though from a catacomb. They told him in seminary that strange phenomena often occurred in catacombs. Voices ceased to communicate properly, they were perceived as though coming from places distant, perhaps echoing the voices of the dead holy men in the crypts.

It wasn't as though it was a big-deal homicide anyway, Captain Woofer said.

It wasn't any kind of homicide. And it wasn't often that veteran

46

homicide detectives rolled on a call unless it was a code three call. This was only a code two broadcast. The next-door neighbor who heard the boy whimpering on the service porch had been too hysterical to respond hysterically. She had simply told the communications operator that someone had been hurt by someone else, and to send the police and an ambulance. Then she hung up and couldn't stop screaming even after the police arrivèd.

Martin Welborn remembered exactly what he and Al had been talking about when they heard the radio call. They had been discussing Paula's agreement not to seek a divorce, thus remaining his spouse and heir as far as the Department was concerned. He was willing to pay her far more than she could have gotten in spousal support. A marriage was not dead without an official seal. Not in the eyes of man. God no longer mattered. But a bitter call from Paula for more money had precipitated a night of haunting loneliness. Martin Welborn did not sleep a moment the night before. He replayed sad and happy and hurtful scenes over and over in his mind. Mostly he thought of his two daughters, Sally and Babs. Al Mackey had been through it twice and said the second time was no easier. Al said they were statistics in a divorce-plagued profession in a divorce-plagued city in a divorce-plagued country.

Perhaps if Paula hadn't called the night before. It had exhausted him physically as well as spiritually. He was in no condition to accommodate the meeting with Danny Meadows.

Perhaps if the radio call hadn't been broadcast at that precise moment. Two minutes later they'd have been back at the station. The crime wasn't even in his area. It would have been given to other detectives. Martin Welborn distinctly remembered what he had said when Al asked if he wanted to roll on the call since they were so close. He'd said, 'I'm tired, Al. Do what you like.' The words were etched like a steel engraving. He remembered precisely. What if he hadn't said the last part? Al Mackey would have shrugged and driven to the station, and Danny Meadows would never have become that unrelenting little specter rising to torment Martin Welborn in the night.

Captain Woofer and Al Mackey were staring at him. Al Mackey looked alarmed.

'I asked if you were feeling okay, Welborn,' Captain

Woofer said. 'You're sweating, and you're trembling like a goat shitting soup cans. Do you have the flu?'

'He might be getting the flu,' Al Mackey said quickly. 'I was saying this morning on the way to work that Marty looks like he's getting the flu. Why don't you take a walk, Marty? Get some air. If you're not feeling well, you better go off sick.'

Martin Welborn stared at them for a moment and then focused on Al Mackey's gaunt face.

'I said take a walk and get some air, Marty,' Al Mackey repeated.

Martin Welborn nodded, got up, and walked out of the captain's office. He looked around blankly for a moment, then left the squadroom.

'Your partner's a little shaky,' Captain Woofer said, relighting the briar for the third time.

'The flu, I think,' Al Mackey said. 'Also he's gone through a marital separation.'

'Haven't we all?' Captain Woofer shrugged. 'If I had a buck for every divorced cop, I could've retired ten years ago instead of ruining my health going for thirty.'

'Maybe Marty's been working too hard. Maybe . . .'

'He should take a vacation.' Captain Woofer nodded. '*After* you two clear the Nigel St Claire homicide.'

'Maybe he should take the vacation *now*, Cap.'

'After. He's got troubles, you've got troubles, I've got troubles. It's a troubled world.' The captain suddenly didn't look so old. He smiled as he got the pipe cooking.

And Al Mackey decided that Whipdick Woofer had the crafty reptile eyes of a *real* ball whacker. The detective sighed and said, 'You're the boss . . . Boss.'

Martin Welborn returned to his chair at the table belonging to the homicide teams. He looked composed as he read last night's reports, oblivious to the scowling faces of Schultz and Simon.

Al Mackey approached the homicide table with outstretched conciliatory hands. Al Mackey was big on body language.

'Listen, we didn't ask for this,' he said, knowing what was on the minds of the huge detectives who were stuffing their notes and follow-up reports into the case envelope bearing the name of Nigel St Claire.

'Sure,' said Schultz. 'We're just the junior varsity is all we are. Well, good luck.'

'Here it is, Mackey, all of it,' said Simon. 'The follow-ups are up-to-date: Suspect unknown, investigation continued, arrest is imminent. That's all we got. Good luck to the first team and fuck you very much.'

'We didn't ask for this,' Al Mackey said, with lots of squirming and shrugging. 'You think we want this case?'

The Weasel and the Ferret were jazzed up from winning all the loot, and they particularly enjoyed seeing Schultz and Simon suffer. The giant homicide detectives were possibly the only team of officers in the L.A.P.D. who still wore their hair in crewcuts. They had to drive all the way downtown to City Hall to find a barber who remembered how to cut them. Occasionally, when Schultz was feeling particularly militant, he'd ask for medium whitewalls and come off looking like a *Wehrmacht* tank commander. The Weasel said the two hunkers blotted out the sun when they entered the squadroom. The Ferret said the mastodons registered 5·3 on the Cal Tech Richter when they walked down the stairs.

Hearing the behemoths bitching and moaning to Al Mackey for taking over the Nigel St Claire case, the Weasel said, 'I don't know why Mackey and Welborn should get that hot homicide. After all, Schultz and Simon solved three and a half homicides last month.'

'What do you mean, three and a half?' asked the Ferret, always anxious to play Mr Bones to the Weasel's inter-locutor.

'The fourth one refused to die.'

'Yeah, but if he had, who woulda told Schultz and Simon who killed him?'

49

'That's true. They ain't *never* found a bad guy unless somebody pointed him out.'

And so forth. But even though he was a daredevil who carried a long knife in his motorcycle boot, the Ferret was wise enough to keep his voice down when he was dumping on Schultz and Simon, who had once threatened to squeeze both narcs into little hair balls and hang them from his rearview mirror.

The Weasel decided to console the big detectives with some hot information. Schultz and Simon had been distraught of late since losing a murder case wherein a boulevard cowboy named William Bonney Anderson, a.k.a. Billy the Kid, had blown away three good citizens of Hollywood, two for money, one for fun, and was found not guilty by reason of diminished capacity, after two psychiatrists (it was always the same shrinks the defense dug up in these cases) convinced the jury that Billy the Kid's destiny was preordained the moment his mother laid on him the name of the notorious outlaw.

The Weasel slipped Schultz and Simon the address and phone number of a former and present Hollywood mental case named Pat Garrett Williams, who, the Weasel was convinced, would consider himself officially deputized if given one of those 'Have you hugged a vice cop today?' buttons that the gay community was recently flaunting. Then he could be shown a mug shot, given a throwaway gun, and programmed to relive the century-old killing of the Kid by blowing William Bonney Anderson right out from under his fucking Stetson the next time he went to the coffee shop on McCadden Place to pick up a drag queen.

'It might work!' Schultz said.

'Sounds feasible,' Simon said. 'You two hairballs come up with a good idea once in a while.'

Schultz even let the Weasel rub his crewcut for luck before hitting the bricks today, since the narcs hoped to culminate a big hash bust in the Hollywood hills. In fact, Schultz and Simon seemed so enthusiastic about owning their own certifiably psycho vigilante that they didn't even look up when Al Mackey and Martin Welborn stuffed the story of Nigel St Claire into its final resting place in a case envelope and set out toward square one.

Square one was not necessarily the scene of the crime. Square one was where the body was found. If they were going to clear this one for Captain Woofer, the crime scene might have to be the goddamn French Riviera, Al Mackey said. It was going to take more than their *nimble inventive ways* to clear this killing. They might actually have to solve this one.

When they got close to the parking lot of the bowling alley on Gower Street, Al Mackey looked around and said, 'We're going to have one hell of a time finding a skinny junkie with a fat Buddha *this* time, partner.'

Martin Welborn seemed more or less back to normal after reading the crime and follow-up reports while Al Mackey drove through the morning smog. 'What was a man like St Claire doing at a bowling alley at that time of night?'

'I say we start by assuming the body was dumped here,' Al Mackey said.

'The pathologist was doubtful on that score. The posting indicates he was killed here.'

It always amazed Al Mackey how quickly Marty could read and digest a police report, especially something as convoluted as a Schultz-Simon report, which drove district attorneys mad but seldom resulted in complaint to Captain Woofer. There was something about their combined bulk of 560 pounds which discouraged complaints from *anyone*. Even the doctors at the police physicals failed to send their 'fat-man notices' to the department. Schultz and Simon were overweight the way grizzlies are overweight during hibernation: too heavy for their own good but everyone decided not to tell them about it.

'Let's start at his place of business,' Al Mackey said. 'Might see some movie stars!'

4

The Baby Mogul

It was nearly noon. The windy speech from Deputy
Chief Francis had cost them time in addition to money.
And then there were Captain Woofer's theories as to what
Nigel St Claire was doing in a bowling alley parking lot
when his car was found three miles away on the Sunset
Strip. Al Mackey had taken semi-elaborate notes during
the theorizing and the notes were now in his coat pocket.
The notes said:

1. Call Emmy about alimony payment. Ask for another
ten days. Grovel if necessary.
2. Call Emmy's lawyer if Emmy says to fuck off.
3. Tell Emmy's lawyer that putting an ex-husband in
jail for not paying spousal support never solved anything.
Money, not vengeance, is the name of the game.
4. Call Thelma (or Thelma's lawyer) and tell her that
it's very hard paying spousal support to *two* women.
Plead for understanding since Thelma always had more
heart than that other bitch.
5. Call Johnny and Petey when they get home from
school and say that we'll go to a Dodger game *next*
weekend for sure. Tell them that they might mention to
their mom that their ex-stepfather could take them more
places if he wasn't so broke all the time.
6. When Emmy calls to scream about using her kids as
an economic weapon, tell her that the crybaby baseball
players and greedy team owners have forced the price of
seats right through the roof. And has she tried buying
hot dogs and peanuts at Dodger Stadium these days for
two teenagers with appetites like timber wolves?

Al Mackey momentarily put aside his alimony dilemma when he pulled up to the gate of the famous studio. While he flashed his badge and signed in with the gate guards, Martin Welborn studied the photographs in the case envelope. He instantly disagreed with the supposition of Schultz and Simon that Nigel St Claire was shot first in the temple and then in the forehead.

'Look at the caboose on that one, Marty,' Al Mackey said as they passed a harried extra in the mock-buckskin garb of an Indian squaw. She was scurrying toward a gigantic sound stage marked Stage 2, and Al Mackey was disappointed to see her turn left at the next street when he had to make a right turn to find the surprisingly modest three-story building that housed the Truly Successful moguls. Al Mackey had expected something like a Playboy Mansion-on-the-back-lot.

'I think he was shot in the forehead first,' Martin Welborn said when Al Mackey stopped for a parade of extras dressed like Keystone cops.

'Reinforcements,' Al Mackey observed, but Martin Welborn never glanced up.

'Look at this, my lad,' Martin Welborn said. He could still find some electric current somewhere. It had been a long time since a police investigation had given Al Mackey a charge. It had been a long time since *anything* had given Al Mackey a charge.

Martin Welborn held a morgue photo of Nigel St Claire in front of Al Mackey's sunken eyes. The corpse leered at him through broken dentures. The blood had not been scrubbed away, and filigreed his brow like scarlet lace. The eyes were open and staring. He died with a panic mask preserved.

'I think he saw what was coming, Aloysius, my boy.'

'I think *I* see what's coming,' Al Mackey said, watching a six-foot redhead in French designer jeans and a green tube top sashay toward a door that said Casting. Maybe he could get a job as a studio cop when he retired? Maybe he should put in an application. Just then another auburn beauty moved like a cheetah in front of the car, smiled at the cadaverous detective, and strolled toward the same doorway. Maybe he should put in his application for studio cop *today*. Who *cared* what they paid!

The inside of the building was a little less disappointing than the outside. At least there were movie posters all over the walls – some old, baroque and elaborate – some vivid, eye-catching and new. Posters from the famous films the studio had distributed for three generations. Some bore likenesses of dead movie stars Al Mackey had nearly forgotten. Some showed cinema stars of the present. But other than that, it wasn't much different from corporate offices belonging to the huge parent conglomerate. This studio was merely one of the spider's legs, though its most glamorous leg to be sure.

Another studio guard directed them to the third floor (there wasn't even an elevator. What's this shit? Even police stations have elevators!) where they found the seat of power, the offices of the late Nigel St Claire, bachelor and *bon vivant*, president of the film division. His name had been removed from the office directory in the glass by the stairway. He would be off the stationery by the end of the week. His name had been painted out of the parking lot twenty-six hours after his gutted corpse had been posted by the morgue pathologist and released to a mortuary. (Parking, not pussy, is at a premium around *these* parts, they said.)

Nigel St Claire's funeral had been top drawer. His eulogy was written by an Oscar-winning screenwriter. It was delivered by an Oscar-winning actress in a brilliant move to counter complaints that Nigel St Claire's studio seldom made women's movies. The funeral entourage was choreographed by an Oscar-winning director.

In addition to filmdom's most famous funeral-goers, the choreographer was resourceful enough to employ three SAG 'weepers', two female, one male, the kind who could turn on the waterworks the second anyone yelled 'action'.

Famous mourners had come from all over the world.

54

Nigel St Claire was greatly loved and had been at the fore of all the humanitarian causes in the film community. He had personally organized and promoted the highly publicized Beverly Hills Banquet to Protest World Hunger, at $2,000 a plate. The black caviar was delivered to the party in a wheelbarrow by two ermine-clad starlets. The Soviet consul sent a laudatory telegram saying that such a caviar purchase went a long way toward patching things up after all those hard hats smashed the cases of vodka during the Afghan incident.

Nigel St Claire was likewise the prime mover of the Fund to Preserve Artistic Freedom, not to mention the numerous Save the Dolphins parties. Once he held two parties simultaneously at his three-acre Bel-Air estate, during which Jacques Cousteau specials *and* famous films that promoted First Amendment guarantees were shown together. It was lots of fun tooting coke and watching Jacques Cousteau pointing toward something on camera left, causing the audience to turn to the next screen where he seemed to be looking at Linda Lovelace with her nasal drip, beating her tonsils on an eight-inch salami in the most famous and commercially successful of the Preserve Artistic Freedom movies championed by Nigel St Claire.

So his credentials were impeccable. They talked of his accomplishments in hushed tones from Malibu Colony to St Moritz, when they downed Quaaludes and Perrier by candlelight. It was beyond comprehension that anyone would want to kill such a decent human being. Was he not a man of compassion? He was first publicly to espouse amnesty for the other Truly Successful studio boss who had been charged by a disgruntled sorehead with embezzling studio funds. All the district attorney's office could prove was that he'd stolen less than $100,000. Yet he had been fired from his job! People in The Business were shocked. Furious. Ads were taken in the trade papers to vent their anger. It was absolutely outrageous that the law was persecuting a guy like this for a lousy hundred G's!

55

This is a man who could get into The Bistro *without* a reservation.

Hollywood threw parties in the former mogul's honor. He intensified his sessions with his therapist, who promised the judge that the patient would be cured of his annoying habit within a few months. Pretty soon *all* Six Famous Restaurants were giving him tables without a reservation. French and Italian maître d's started fighting over him, calling each other frogs and wops. Everyone wanted him. They didn't give a shit if he stole the goddamn silverware! He was more famous than Clint Eastwood. He was more beloved than the Thief of Baghdad.

He was promoted to president of worldwide productions in a *bigger* studio than the one that fired him. It was a Hollywood fable come true. The stuff movies are made of. The film colony got misty in his presence. He was kissed by men and women with compassion in their eyes.

In a sense, Nigel St Claire made it all happen the day the errant mogul was rudely jerked out of his Rolls-Royce on Sunset Boulevard by none other than Buckmore Phipps, the street monster, who heard from a girlfriend at the D.A.'s office that a felony warrant had been issued for this famous personage, and the cop that arrested him might get on television. After bail was arranged that very night, it was Nigel St Claire who put together a quick coming-out party for the fallen colleague and started the crusade to save him from doing time in the slammer.

Nigel St Claire had personally given the chairman of the board the solution for keeping pinkies out of the cookie jar. It was a workable plan, the chairman agreed, although he privately admitted to Nigel he'd love to set fire to the little bastard and let him drown in deep water. Which is what would happen, since both the chairman and Nigel St Claire knew that, along with no integrity, he lacked brains, talent, loyalty, industry, and in fact had better clean up his act or his senile grandfather (the chairman's father) would disinherit the little schmuck and he could go on welfare like a nigger.

It was a thorny problem, everyone knew, what with the L.A. *Times* running malicious articles practically every Sunday about how studios that grossed hundreds of millions in film rentals had never shown a nickel's profit. (So *what* if the studio accountants ordered red ink in ten-gallon drums?) And now the chairman's putz of a son had to get himself nailed like some wetback stealing hubcaps!

And wasn't it Nigel St Claire, the Henry Kissinger of The Business, who devised that workable plan for the chairman? There was only one thing to do with the thieving little fuck: place him so high up in the studio he couldn't *use* those sticky mitts. He'd have to go through too many other pirates and freebooters to do much embezzling, and a lot of those old dudes were too tough to let him slash away at *their* boodle. It was a brilliant plan, actually.

So it was Nigel St Claire, more than anyone else, who was the Starmaker of The Business. Several other studio executives began to hope that *their* embezzling might get discovered after seeing what Nigel St Claire's diplomacy had wrought.

Nigel St Claire publicly argued that his cousin deserved a second chance. After all, it was this cousin who had the guts to organize the first Hollywood dinner to demand the impeachment and imprisonment of that crook Richard Nixon.

But now Nigel St Claire was not even a name on the asphalt. In fact, when Al Mackey and Martin Welborn entered his former office suite, his former secretary was standing at the window peering down into the parking lot at a lethargic studio sign painter who was painting in a new name.

She sighed and dabbed at a sparkling drop on her cheek when Al Mackey showed his badge and asked to talk with Herman St Claire III, the new temporary president of the film division.

'I think we told those other detectives just about everything we know,' she said, returning to her desk to blow her nose in a Kleenex.

She was nubile, with an ass like a melon and eyes like an ocelot. Al Mackey was enchanted. 'We've had the case turned over to us,' Al Mackey said. 'Sorry, but we have to talk to everyone a second time.'

'It's such a sad, sad thing,' the secretary said. 'I just haven't got any sleep for days and days. We all loved old Mister St Claire.' Then she added quickly, 'Not that we don't love the *new* Mister St Claire as much as the old one. It's just so . . . *unbearable* to see his name painted right off the parking lot. That's when you realize he might just as well never have lived. Know what I mean?'

'It's tragic, all right,' Al Mackey said, noting that her name was Tiffany Charles and that her phone number was on Schultz and Simon's reports.

'Well, that's life, I guess,' said Tiffany Charles, as Martin Welborn looked around the rather plain office a the pictures of other St Claires of the past and present who were big and little studio bosses.

Tiffany Charles took a pillbox covered with gemstones from her desk drawer, popped two Libriums, gulped them down with Diet-Rite, and said, 'The only thing sadder I can think of would be if they broke your star right out of the sidewalk on Hollywood Boulevard.'

The thought of it made her shudder, until she pictured two big sweating construction workers sexily banging away with jackhammers and she recovered a bit. Then she noticed how Martin Welborn's long, sad eyes got sensual when he looked right at you. He wasn't very old, about the same as Tiffany Charles' dad, which was a turn-on in itself. And he was a pretty big guy with a good body. She wondered what his ass looked like. Tiffany Charles was a sucker for young-looking older guys like this, or else for big sweaty animals that socked it to you and no bullshitting around. Which reminded her: 'What happened to those other two detectives? You know, those big, *big* ones? They didn't get shot or something, did they?'

'Detectives only get shot in movies,' Martin Welborn

said, and his boyish smile made Tiffany Charles almost forget about big sweaty animals.

'Who did your teeth?' she asked. 'They're beautiful.'

'God,' Martin Welborn said.

'You mean they're not capped?'

'Nope.'

'Wow!' said Tiffany Charles, breaking Al Mackey's heart.

'Back to the deceased Mister St Claire,' Al Mackey said, all business now.

'Oh well,' Tiffany Charles said philosophically, 'we can't dwell on the past, can we? Mister St Claire wouldn't have wanted it. He always said you're only as hot as your last gig.'

Which was about the last mention of Nigel St Claire ever heard in those offices.

When they were admitted to the inner office of Nigel St Claire's successor, Herman St Claire III, a twenty-five-year-old UCLA film school graduate with lots of top spin, he was dictating a letter to his steno, Gilda Latour. Be ready for lots of dick-tation, they told her, this one's a lot younger than Uncle Nigel.

But they dressed the same. In fact, Herman St Claire dressed much like Martin Welborn. He looked like a Pasadena stockbroker. And he was tan. Not that phony sunlamp tan. Not tan like the rest of the world's idea of a California tan, but tanner than George Hamilton ever *thought* of being. Tanner than from holding a reflector under your chin six hours a day by the pool at the very top of Trousdale Estates, which was the only place in Beverly Hills to get a *real* tan. In the silent film days, the Truly Successful had schemed of throwing a Great Wall up around Beverly Hills, but had been foiled by the rest of the citizenry. Now Beverly Hills had more traffic problems than downtown L.A., and only at hilltop elevation could you escape the smog which congested the lungs, scalded the eyes, and broke up more tennis games than a thousand phone calls from theatrical agents. And now the Great

Wall idea of yore didn't seem so zany. Why did the so-called community leaders always fail to listen to the Truly Successful in The Business until it was too late? The Truly Successful had continued to warn them: Vietnam. Three Mile Island. And Ronald Reagan? Christ, he couldn't get in The Brown Derby when *real* stars still went there. If they'd stacked those bricks and built the Great Wall, you'd be able to get a decent tan in Beverly Hills without going to a mountaintop like a fucking California condor.

'Take a break, Gilda,' Herman III said to his steno.

Al Mackey couldn't believe it. She's a nine and a half, at least, and she can take a letter? A miraculous place!

And the office was more like it. Lots of European antiques (recycled furniture, they called it around here), photos of Herman III with stars and statesmen, some original movie posters of studio classics, and a forest of hanging ferns to cast mysterious shadows across the sculptured jaw of Herman III.

The baby mogul had a crushing handshake. 'Glad to meet you.' He beamed, making Al Mackey wonder who did *his* teeth.

'Sorry to have to ask you questions all over again,' Al Mackey said, as the two detectives were nudged toward an eight-foot sofa done in soft slate-gray leather, in front of which were two coffee tables covered end to end with copies of *Daily Variety*, *The Hollywood Reporter*, and *Box Office*.

The Hollywood Reporter was open to a full-page ad of an aspiring actress, nude from the waist up. She was a beauty, but seemed flat-chested. Al Mackey leaned over for a closer look. The copy said: 'Would You Believe I'm Only 10?'

'Cute idea, don't you think?' said Herman III.

Al Mackey looked at Martin Welborn. The aspiring actress was ten years old.

Al Mackey then noticed two open volumes the size of telephone books containing pictures of male and female actors. Then there was a smaller book containing the names of directors and their agents along with notations beside the names which seemed to be in some kind of code. 'Got to know the enemy's weaknesses' — Herman III winked — 'if you wanna do a deal. Hey, do you know Ralph Wisehart, works homicide at Beverly Hills P.D.?'

'No,' said Martin Welborn.

'Can't say I do,' said Al Mackey.

'No? That's peculiar. I thought all the guys that worked the Stinker Squads knew each other.' He chuckled at that one, got no response, and said, 'I often go to the pistol range with Ralph. Met him when he used to work burglary. He handled a four-five-nine at my house. Channel-lock job. They were going down twice a week until Ralph and I found this latent on the louvered window and convicted some East Side junkie. The print only had eight points, so it was really my testimony that sent the sucker to Big Q.'

Hermann III had exhausted every piece of police jargon he had learned from his father's six cop movies and still had gotten no smiles. 'How about a drink?' he said finally.

'Bourbon.' Al Mackey smiled.

'Vodka, if you have it.' Martin Welborn smiled.

Having gotten a friendly response at last, Herman III cheerily buzzed for Tiffany Charles, ordering booze for the cops and Perrier for himself. Herman Jr., as well as Herman The Original, had both been globetrotting moguls who pretty much ignored their offspring during the children's formative years. Herman III was never able to begin any conversation unless he felt his listener either liked him or might *learn* to like him. The cops' smiles were reassuring.

While the detectives sat on the slate-gray sofa and put away two drinks each, and ate corned beef sandwiches from the comissary, he told them all he knew about his bachelor uncle's last night on earth. This took one and a half minutes: 'What the hell was my uncle doing at a bowling alley? My grandfather had a bowling alley in his *house* and Uncle Nigel never used it. Uncle Nigel told the houseboy he was going out for an hour and never came back.'

Then he talked about himself. Which took forty-five minutes and might never have ended until he started thinking of jungle animals. 'Do you dig karate, Al?' Herman III asked while Al Mackey wondered whether or not he should put away the third bourbon. It was only two o'clock.

'Can't say as I do, Herman. Actually, I'm in lousy shape.'

'Yeah? That's too bad. I run in all the ten K races. Actually, I do six miles a day. Pulse rate, fifty-two. This is a tough and dangerous business, Marty. You got to stay in shape. These fuckers go for your *throat*. Just last week some midget of an agent tried to hold me up for a million out front and ten points from the first dollar! It's a fucking *jungle*, Marty. You can't believe it. They're animals!'

'I can believe it, Herman,' Martin Welborn said, serenely sipping at his vodka.

'Know what they say these days, Al?' Herman III said. 'They say a million is *scale*! That's what these fucking agents say. A million is *scale*. Can you see why we're all starving to death in The Business these days? Nobody can make a dime anymore. Greedy pricks! What kind of gun you carry, Marty?'

'Gun? Uh, just a four-inch Smith ·38,' Martin Welborn shrugged.

'That's all?' Herman III was visibly disappointed. 'I dig a ·357 magnum.' Then he pointed his imaginary magnum and yelled, 'Bloo-ee!' which startled the crap out of Al Mackey and made him spill the third drink.

'I know how much your uncle Nigel was revered,' Martin Welborn said, 'but can you think of anyone who might want to kill him?'

'Ugh!' Herman III said. 'That was *so* crude. My dad did a film about a killing like that. I never would. I don't like that kind of violence. All that gore, I just don't get off on it. I get stoked on clean shootings, not in the face. You know, Al, you have to get a really good makeup artist to do the blood bags or no one will buy it when you do a tight

closeup of a ·357 blowing holes. Audiences are sophisti-
cated these days.'

'I can believe it,' said Al Mackey.

'See those naked little guys?' Herman III pointed to a
bookshelf behind his desk holding three Oscars. 'You don't
make the audience happy with bullshit bullet holes. That's
what it's all about. See what I mean, Marty?'

Both detectives nodded. Herman III was buying the
drinks.

His caps sparkled through the suntan. He was sure these
guys liked him. He was sure they were okay guys. He
would love to solve a murder case with okay guys like this.
Imagine what everyone would say if he helped solve the
murder of Uncle Nigel. It'd blow their minds. It blew *his*
mind just thinking about it. Imagine having the killer of
Uncle Nigel in his gunsights!

'Blooo-eee!' Herman III yelled, this time scaring the
living crap out of Al Mackey *and* Martin Welborn.

'Listen, guys,' Herman III said, 'a week from Friday my
cousin Syd's having a party at my granddad's place in
Holmby Hills. I got a killer of an idea! How about if you
two come . . . *undercover*? Everyone in The Business is
gonna be there. We might make a list of suspects. I can
introduce you as, say, environmental lobbyists from Wash-
ington. The party's to raise funds to save the pine trees
from the greedy lumber interests.'

The detectives promised to come to the party. Al Mackey
wouldn't have missed it after he heard that Herman III
was inviting both his secretaries. Al Mackey was almost
positive that Gilda Latour winked at him when she brought
his fourth bourbon on the rocks.

And actually, he had begun to have a warm feeling for
the suntanned baby mogul. Herman III was obviously a
big spender and might see to the detectives' *every* need.
Besides, he was kind of a sweet kid and had a voice like
Donald Duck.

5

The Street Monsters

When Al Mackey was to look back on the Nigel St Claire case, he would ponder if it all had significance, those seemingly unrelated incidents which somehow link all men in the Endless Chain. Otherwise, how could the first break in the Nigel St Claire case have come because a marine pissed in a clay pot?

While Al Mackey and Martin Welborn were saying good-bye to Herman III, and while a marine was pissing in a clay pot, a Hollywood Boulevard fruit-hustler was lurking around the corner of McCadden Place observing that Tyrannosaurus was alive and well and strolling down the boulevard dressed in blue. He was referring, of course, to the street monster Buckmore Phipps, who was perfectly ecstatic today. The reason for Buckmore Phipps' delight was strolling along beside him: his old partner, Gibson Hand. And the fruit-hustler had only to take one look at *that* bad news nigger to know it was time to go pushin. Actually, Buckmore Phipps never even noticed anymore that Gibson Hand was a nigger. Buckmore Phipps hated all niggers. He also hated greasers, slopeheads, kikes, judges, lawyers, fags, dopers, reporters, politicians in general, Democrats for sure, his brother and sisters, the chief of police, his ex-wife *most* assuredly, and all but a handful of other cops. Gibson Hand was one of the few people he didn't hate. The reason he didn't hate Gibson Hand is that Gibson Hand hated *everybody*.

Buckmore Phipps had first met Gibson Hand when they had both been in on the famous siege wherein the Symbionese Liberation Army was cooked by a tear gas grenade that set fire to their house. Buckmore Phipps sensed a kindred spirit in Gibson Hand when Gibson Hand's snarling brown face brightened as he strained to hear fat frying and screams of terror. Then, when Gibson Hand spoke to him, he was *sure* they were soul mates. The black cop turned to him and said, 'Guess what S.L.A. stands for?'

Before Buckmore Phipps could reply, Gibson Hand grabbed a bullhorn and became a police folk hero by shouting: 'S.L.A. means So Long, Assholes!'

Buckmore Phipps had decided then and there that he had to work with Gibson Hand. They tried a month together in a radio car and Buckmore Phipps was to enjoy some of his warmest memories.

Gibson Hand sensed from the start that his partner had the stuff of which police folklore is made. He was proved correct on the night they found a dismembered corpse in the trash bin of a department store. The stock boy thought it was a mannequin at first, since it was missing its legs. Then he saw the legs behind the trash bin being eaten by rats. After he stopped retching he called the cops.

The deceased was an eighteen-year-old cheerleader from Pomona who thought it was culturally enriching to hitch-hike until she was picked up and hacksawed into pieces by one of the numerous motor maniacs who prowl the freeways for fun and profit. The girl's corpse was drained of blood when Buckmore Phipps and Gibson Hand rolled up in their black-and-white. The stock boy, his blue eyes swimming, a hand holding his heaving stomach, pointed to the trash bin and tried to run back to the store.

What happened next is anybody's guess. What Gibson Hand *said* happened is what propelled Buckmore Phipps into song and legend. Though everyone knew that Gibson Hand was an even bigger liar than Buckmore Phipps, and that both of them would tell any lie to be enshrined in cop folklore, the story spread that when Buckmore Phipps saw the legless, bloodless remains of the cheerleader, he turned to the stock boy while baring at least twenty-eight donkey teeth and said, 'Hey, kid, you like to boogie?'

And then, according to Gibson Hand, Buckmore Phipps leaned inside and lifted the alabaster torso out of the bin, and holding the bloodless torso under the armpits with those hands big as shovels – the cadaver's head lolling, tongue distended and blue as Buckmore Phipps' uniform – the giant street monster did a spritely Yul Brynner polka in the headlights of the police car, singing: 'Shaaaaall we dance? (do do do) On a bright cloud of music shall we fly? (do do do) . . .'

Gibson Hand said that both he and Buckmore Phipps collapsed into such a fit of laughter that they almost didn't get the stiff back in the bin and the fainted stock boy slapped to his senses before the first detective cars arrived in the lonely parking lot.

Buckmore Phipps and Gibson Hand finally transferred to Hollywood Division together. They began doing everything together. It was as close as either would ever come to love. They were meant for each other.

But, as often happens, fate intervened to thwart the blossoming affection of the two street monsters. Gibson Hand received a long-awaited assignment to the surveillance detail. He was almost tearful when he said good-bye to Buckmore Phipps. He swore he would return some day. He explained to Buckmore Phipps how he just couldn't pass up a chance to work surveillance. There was nowhere else in the Department where a guy could get a chance to kill people as often as you could by working surveillance. Buckmore Phipps promised Gibson Hand he'd never forget him. They punched each other's shoulders and came close to an unmanly scene out there in the parking lot of Hollywood Station that night.

Gibson Hand went to work surveillance and drew a hot assignment and got to ding some people his first week. They had put him in a big liquor store on Olympic Boulevard. The Oreo bandit teams were popular for a while. If they hit in a white neighborhood, the white bandit

66

would be wheel man and his black partner would hide on the floor of the car. Vice versa in a black neighborhood. The liquor stores in the ghetto paid off better, but were riskier to take off because of the arsenals the proprietors maintained.

Gibson Hand was sitting alone behind a two-way mirror in the back room of the store watching *Days of Our Lives*. The door was open a crack when he heard, 'Up against the wall, motherfuckers!'

Jesus Christ, they *all* said that! He turned down the television, picked up the Ithaca shotgun, and released the safety, using his thumb and forefinger to avoid even a tiny click.

The white bandit wore a Porky Pig rubber mask that covered his entire head. He also wore gray cotton work gloves. The mask was too big. It sucked in and out against his face with every breath. He held an old U.S. Army automatic in his right hand and waved it back and forth at the faces of the two petrified store clerks.

Gibson Hand knew the stakeout team outside must be moving in by now. He waited for the bandit to get the loot. Get the bread, white boy! Quit wavin that big ol motherfucker around like that. Get the money, boy. Get the *money*.

Gibson Hand was sweating, holding the shotgun at port arms, waiting until they got it and headed for the door. Then the clerks are safe. Then the gunman's back is to you. Then you can 'shoot the money'. Right through the asshole's *back*. And *then* you can yell: 'Stop! Police!' After he's safely dead.

Gibson Hand knew that the cops who yelled *first* and gave their crazy fuckin selves a chance to get wasted did their work on celluloid, not in real life. Where the fuck *is* the brother?

And there he was. Damn! The brother was one of those dumb old raghead niggers, probably been in jail the last twenty years and didn't notice nobody wore silky-straights anymore, not even pimps. He wore a face mask only. It was Dracula. He wore his hair processed and had his marcelled hairdo wrapped up in a rag. And he wore those old-fashioned wingtips with all the holes. Shoes with a thousand eyes, they used to say. Where the fuck did he get *those* old shoes? Nobody wears do-rags no more, you dumb nigger! Gibson Hand wiped his sweaty eyes on his sleeve.

The black half of the Oreo team walked over to the two-way mirror and looked at himself through the eyeholes of the Dracula mask. It was plastic, not rubber. It didn't suck in and out when he breathed. He just looked dumb. A dumb nigger with a vampire face and a rag on his dumb fuckin head. Holding a sawed-off ten-gauge. Looking right into the sweat-bathed face of Gibson Hand, whom he could not see.

Now the paddy had the loot. The brother was looking in the mirror. He was still looking when Gibson Hand impulsively pressed the gun muzzle to the glass and unleashed a dozen massive pellets of double-aught buckshot. The mirror blew up in the vampire's face.

The white Oreo bandit started screaming in shock and terror when his partner, minus his mask and most of his head, hurtled across the floor of the liquor store spilling blood so fast it greased the skids. The dead body slid all the way, crashing against the liquor counter.

The white Oreo bandit was still screaming in shock and terror when Gibson Hand leaped out of the back room, his Ithaca exploding the second Oreo bandit literally out of his penny loafers and into eternity. (Even *he* wore outdated shoes. They were both parolees from Folsom and still dressed for the early '6os. Poor old Cal Greenberg was the only one who felt sorry for them, wondering if *they* still listened to Glenn Miller.)

Then Gibson Hand went over to his second kill and pulled the Porky Pig mask from the twitching cadaver. When his backup team came running into the store, they found Gibson Hand holding the mask up beside his face, saying, 'Th-th-th-th-that's *all*, folks!'

It was the locker room story of the month. But unfortunately, a news team from the scurrilous television station that Captain Woofer hated happened by while monitoring police calls, and caught Gibson Hand doing a reprise of the Porky Pig impression for a surprised group of detectives. The bastards did an editorial on the eleven o'clock news saying that Gibson Hand's only competitor was Iran's Ayatollah Blood who had chortled over the remains of the dead Americans. And Gibson Hand had been transferred right back to Hollywood Patrol, in despair, since there wouldn't be nearly as many opportunities to kill people and do other good police work.

So Gibson Hand was back walking Hollywood Boulevard with Buckmore Phipps. And unknown to the two street monsters, the first break in the Nigel St Claire murder case was about to occur. A marine was pissing in a clay pot.

The marine in question was an eighteen-year-old private first class from Minneapolis named Gladstone Cooley. A second-generation Swede on his mother's side, he had inherited the best of the Viking bloodline. He was tall, and, as they said in the modeling studios, built like Michelangelo *wished* David had been built. His hair and skin were gold and his eyes were cobalt blue. His only physical defect was an occasional pimple on the torso from applying too much scented baby oil for his posing sessions. He had a room-temperature I.Q., which made him extremely obliging, hence an excellent artist's model and a pretty fair marine.

On his three-day passes from Camp Pendleton he made up to four hundred dollars posing for artists and photographers in Hollywood. He made an additional two hundred as a call boy for discriminating gay customers, got free accommodations in a North Hollywood motel for simply *being* on call, and had seen *American Gigolo* twenty-two times. He was planning a twenty-third viewing the day he was pissing in the clay pot.

Actually, it wasn't the first time he had been called upon to piss in a clay pot. It wasn't *that* uncommon around

Hollywood. The artists' studio was a small one on the second floor, over a head shop where they sold water pipes, roach holders, and star-spangled cigarette papers. Gladstone Cooley had to drink a quart of Pepsi-Cola every twelve minutes when called upon for this particular modeling service. The sculpting instructor who hired him claimed that the uric acid added vitality to the clay and made the sculptures come to life. But even with his I.Q., Gladstone Cooley figured they were just Golden Shower Kids, and if they wanted to pay him fifty bucks an hour, he'd keep pissing in their pot of modeling clay.

Except that inevitably one of the eleven artists who sculpted clay on the long table upon which the marine posed nude except for a Navajo headband would ask Gladstone to be a dear and give a few squirts to the artist's *personal* clay heap on the table before him.

Gladstone was an obliging boy and always tried, as long as they kept him supplied with bottles of Pepsi-Cola. (A company which hurt his feelings by refusing to let him endorse their product with his modeling work and help them win the war against Coca-Cola.)

On this particular day he had pissed in three individual clay heaps in addition to the common vat. Then an argument broke out between an artist who didn't get any individual service and another who did. And try as he might, Gladstone Cooley couldn't squeeze out a drop for the angry artist, even after guzzling two quarts of Pepsi back to back. It was, of course, the pressure of performance. Given the vicious argument and shrill threats flying back and forth, he had simply dried up.

The jealous artist who didn't get his clay pissed on got so mad he picked up his clay pile and threw it at the one who did. This caused a fight which the instructor couldn't quell, and which made Gladstone Cooley want to go back to his peaceful rifle platoon. And he would have, except that the one who had received more piss than he deserved responded to the thrown clay by picking up a drenched clay ball and hurling it at his antagonist. It missed and

sailed out the open window and down to Hollywood
Boulevard, where it knocked Buckmore Phipps' hat off.
The Endless Chain.

When Buckmore Phipps' hat went sailing, he was
standing on the boulevard laying a parking ticket on a
purple Cadillac convertible owned by a despondent black
pimp who was trying in vain to convince Gibson Hand, as
a brother, to give him a break. He was going to jail in two
days anyway, after sentencing on a case where some whore
claimed he broke her leg. Who would believe that anybody
would ruin good merchandise like that except some dumb
fuckin women's libbers on the jury?

Gibson Hand sucked on his cigar and nodded sympathetically at the pimp. And every time the pimp would scurry
back to plead with the implacable Buckmore Phipps,
Gibson Hand would take the cigar out of his mouth and
continue his surreptitious burning of the pimp's convertible
top. By the time the pimp was ready to drive away, and
Buckmore Phipps' hat was knocked off his block-shaped
head, Gibson Hand had managed to burn a hole the size
of a Susan B. Anthony dollar in the pimp's convertible
top, striking a blow for the libbers on the jury.

'Who the fuck knocked my hat off?' Buckmore Phipps
cried when his blue police cap went flying into the street
and was run over by the departing pimp in his Cadillac.

Buckmore Phipps picked up the squashed lid and said,
'Gibson, who knocked my fuckin hat off?'

Gibson Hand hadn't seen the clay missile and thought
Buckmore Phipps' hat had simply fallen off when he stuck
the traffic ticket on the pimp's window.

'I didn't seen nobody knock your hat off, Buckmore. The
pimp couldn't a did it.'

'Gibson, *somebody* knocked my fuckin hat off,' Buckmore
Phipps said, his face crimson, his eyes narrowing murder-
ously. 'AND LOOK AT THE FUCKIN THING!'

The pimp's Cadillac had turned it into one flat hat, all
right. The visor was torn loose. The gleaming hat piece

71

was bent and dangling. The grommet was twisted like a pretzel.

'That is a bummed-out bonnet, Buckmore,' Gibson Hand clucked sadly.

'Some motherfucker's gonna pay!' Buckmore Phipps said, looking around wildly. Just as another slimy clay ball came flying out of the second-story window.

There was a real donnybrook going on upstairs now. Gladstone Cooley had jumped off the table and was already slipping into his black bikini underwear when they *all* started throwing things. The piss and Pepsi were dripping down the walls and everyone was screaming and yelling too much to hear Buckmore Phipps and Gibson Hand taking the stairs three at a time with vengeance in their hearts.

It was Buckmore Phipps who quelled the pandemonium by yelling: 'WHO THE FUCK BUSTED ME IN THE BEAN?'

A silent covey of artists scurried around picking up their berets, locating their sculpting tools, gathering their courage for one quick dash out the door. Except that a black cop with a face like a rabid Doberman was blocking the doorway jamb to jamb with the spread of his shoulders.

'I can explain, Officers,' said a mincing black artist in a lime ascot. 'It was just . . .'

'Up against the wall, you gay-rilla!' Buckmore Phipps snarled. 'Nobody's explainin nothin until I find out who knocked my hat off!'

It was fortunate that neither Buckmore Phipps nor Gibson Hand suspected what was used to moisten the clay ball or there probably would have been screaming sculptors falling from the windows like confetti that day.

'Who the fuck're you?' Gibson Hand demanded of the quivering marine, who was desperately trying to squeeze into his French jeans. He wore them so tight he had to lie down to zip up. He usually stuffed the crotch of his bikinis with sponge rubber to look more valuable on the street, but today he wasn't bothering. He was just sweating to get into those goddamn jeans. At last he prevailed, jumped to his feet, and said, 'Private First Class Gladstone Cooley, sir! United States Marine Corps!'

Then both Buckmore Phipps and Gibson Hand started lowing like cattle. *Another* marine! Buckmore Phipps and Gibson Hand had served with the Fifth Marines and were mortified that Selma Avenue and the gay bars were *full* of them.

'You know, Buckmore, they oughtta jist do their recruitin for the Corps at the Hollywood Y.M.C.A., the way things are these days,' Gibson Hand said.

As all the sculptors were standing in terror against the dripping walls awaiting orders from the street monsters, Gibson Hand spotted a fourteen-year-old girl trembling in the closet where the clay pots were stacked. She was a dayworker whose job it was to mop up the excess piss from the floor and to make Pepsi runs as required.

'Get your ass outa there, lil sis,' he said, and the freckled runaway crept out with her gaze locked on her battered moccasins.

'Where you from, kid?' Buckmore Phipps asked.

'Culver City,' she squeaked.

'When you run away from home?' Gibson Hand asked.

'Two days ago. I been staying in this apartment over in East Hollywood with a *friend*.'

Gibson Hand offered a rare glimpse of his paternal side. 'Well, you go ahead on and stay in East Hollywood with your friends. But if you do, I'd just go and O.D. right now, I was you, before some a those East Hollywood dudes bust in your pad. That way, you won't feel them cuttin your fuckin throat with a beer opener. And they'll have to settle for rapin your slimy body *after* you're dead, which they don't like to do nearly so much cause they like to hear you kick and scream. Now GIT YOUR SCUM SUCKIN ASS ON OUTA HERE AND BACK TO CULVER CITY!'

When the runaway was running hell-bent down the staircase, Buckmore Phipps turned to Gibson Hand and said sincerely, 'That was sweet, Gibson. It takes heart to counsel a runaway kid.'

Then they got down to business. Two of the sculptors, one a Greek, the other a Turk, naturally blamed each other for the errant clay ball that had knocked Buckmore Phipps' hat into the gutter. Buckmore Phipps asked Gibson Hand which one they should book.

'I don't give a shit,' he shrugged. 'They're both grease-balls, ain't they?'

They were about to drag *both* greaseballs down the steps while they tried to figure out a booking charge when Gladstone Cooley said, 'Sir, I hope you don't have to report me to my commanding officer or anything.'

'Lemme see your marine ID card,' Gibson Hand said impulsively.

Buckmore Phipps scowled at the Pfc. and said, 'If they had jarheads like you back in the big war, they'd a had to take that flag and suck it or fuck it *to get it up* on Iwo Jima.'

And when Gibson Hand snatched the marine liberty card from Gladstone Cooley, a scrap of paper came with it.

'This name's familiar, Buckmore,' he said, looking at the paper. 'I can't remember where I heard it, but I heard it somewheres.'

Buckmore Phipps read the note, which said 'Nigel St Claire' and gave a phone number. 'Yeah, I heard that name somewheres lately. Who is this?' he asked the marine.

But then a vagary of fortune not only saved the Greek and the Turk from bunking in the slam, but prompted an incident which made Buckmore Phipps and Gibson Hand not police legends as they'd always dreamed, but police laughingstocks.

They heard a burglar alarm ringing loud and clear from outside the artists' studio. Buckmore Phipps looked at Gibson Hand and at his watch and said, 'It's only three o'clock. Somebody's testin his burglar alarm, is all.'

'Pardon me, Officers,' said the Greek, who certainly didn't want to share accommodations at the graybar hotel with a Turk. 'If you'll just look out the back window, it might be the Batbite Specialty Shop. He closed at noon today. I happened to be there and . . .'

Gibson Hand strolled to the window, peeked out into the back alley, and saw the rear door of the Batbite Specialty Shop kicked off the hinges.

'It's a four-five-nine in progress, Buckmore! Let's hit it!'

So the sculpting class breathed a collective sigh of relief and pushed on out of there, along with Pfc. Gladstone Cooley, who was hastily handed his papers by the snarling black cop. The street monsters were already thundering down the rear stairway, about to catch a burglar with his mitts in the candy.

Except that they didn't sell candy at the Batbite Specialty Shop. They sold leather masks for slaves, ventilated leather paddles for masters, police nightsticks for slaves *and* masters. They sold handcuffs, scourges, and even iron maidens (it costs big bucks for *some* pleasures), and assorted other instruments which Buckmore Phipps and Gibson Hand had to admit would come in handy during some of their back alley interrogations.

They caught a horsed-out junkie named Jukebox Johnson – a former disc jockey fallen on hard times – with a load of sadomasochistic magazines, making his second trip to a junkyard Chevy. Jukebox Johnson was one of those unfortunate thieves who always ran from the cops, even though he couldn't run that fast, even when he was facing drawn weapons and spotlights in the darkness. He'd been shot five times by cops over a fifteen-year span of unsuccessful burglaries.

He was one of those crooks the cops talked about: 'You know old Jukebox?'

'Oh, sure, I shot him a couple times.'

But today there was no need to shoot Jukebox Johnson. He was traveling at slow motion speed and thought he was highballing it. He had decided to pull the job *after* he got mellowed out on two grams of good heroin, and he was seeing flying giraffes and big colored bugs eating each other, when Gibson Hand picked him off the ground by the collar.

'Jukebox, what in the fuck are you doin?' Buckmore Phipps said disgustedly. 'I mean, this is broad fuckin daylight!'

'Hi, Buckmore. Hi, Gibson.' Jukebox Johnson smiled sheepishly through a row of crooked black stumps. 'I can explain. See, I met up with these S and M freaks. They carry a huge stick. Call it their board of education. The big one beats on his boyfriend all the time whether he needs it or not. They seem like a nice couple, though. They commissioned me to do this job. Told me they needed some more equipment for a party tonight. Offered me a whole piece of unstepped-on China white. What could I say?'

'Damn! In broad daylight? I oughtta let you run down the alley and shoot you a couple times,' Gibson Hand said disgustedly.

'What's the trouble, Officers?' a man said, hurrying toward them from a Lincoln he'd just parked in the alley.

'I'm sorry I did it, Buckmore,' Jukebox Johnson whined. 'I get nervous around these freaks with all their whips and stuff. I been thinking about working for these *other* guys who're into mugging and stickups, just to get my head straightened ou?.'

'I'm Harvey H. Fairchild,' the man announced, presenting Gibson Hand with his business card. 'One of my fellow shop-keepers told me the alarm had been set off and I got here as fast as I could.'

So, while Gibson Hand kept the handcuffed Jukebox Johnson near their radio car, Buckmore Phipps took a burglary report from Harvey H. Fairchild and helped turn off the burglar alarm. Harvey H. Fairchild was friendly and pink, shaped like a teardrop. He sported lots of jewelry and a silk suit that Buckmore Phipps wouldn't mind owning for his big nights at The Glitter Dome. Harvey H. Fairchild told Buckmore Phipps that he found selling the S & M toys lucrative but disgusting, and vowed that just

76

as soon as he had a nest egg he was cutting out for a chicken ranch in Saugus.

He was really a swell guy, all in all. He smoked real Cuban cigars and gave Buckmore Phipps one when the cops left him to secure his broken door.

Except that it wasn't *his* door. It wasn't his shop. As far as the detectives could piece it together, after entering through the broken rear door of the Batbite Specialty Shop, he eventually tunneled through the wall into the neighboring jewelry store, and made off with $275,000 in watches, rings and necklaces.

When the *real* owner of the Batbite Specialty Shop showed up at the police station along with the jewelry store proprietor, both screaming and yelling about the mentality of cops, and when Buckmore Phipps and Gibson Hand were called code-two into the detective bureau with their worthless business card belonging to a pretty good tunnel man, the street monsters figured out right away that Jukebox Johnson had been in cahoots with Harvey H. Fairchild. It was all the detectives could do to keep the two street monsters from breaking into Jukebox Johnson's cell and lynching the little traitor on the spot, except that he had already been writted out of jail by a lawyer who said he was retained by one Jules P. Laidlaw, a fat pink guy with lots of jewelry and a groovy silk suit.

So it was woe to the boulevard denizens for the next few weeks while Buckmore Phipps and Gibson Hand worked at exorcising the memory of their Waterloo at the hands of Jukebox Johnson and a future corpse who called himself Harvey H. Fairchild and Jules P. Laidlaw. During those humiliating days Buckmore Phipps broke two molars grinding his teeth in frustration, and Gibson Hand accidentally snapped a police nightstick in two, whacking a telephone pole. There was scarcely a word passed between the two street monsters on their fruitless manhunt. Instead of asking each other whether one wanted to drive or write reports, Buckmore Phipps or Gibson Hand would turn a

77

rabid face toward another rabid face and say: 'How about today you write and I *fight*.'

So, knowing that Buckmore Phipps and Gibson Hand were cutting a swath across Hollywood not seen since the Hillside Strangler manhunt (like rogue elephants they foraged through every addict haunt and hole-in-the-wall for the needle-scarred carcass of Jukebox Johnson), the little junkie decided it was time to take a Greyhound with part of his score from Harvey H. Fairchild's tunnel job, and head on back to Little Rock for a permanent family reunion. Jukebox Johnson knew full well that life was harder for ex-disc-jockey, junkie burglars in Little Rock, but he also knew that as far as *he* was concerned, Buckmore Phipps and Gibson Hand just weren't about to be taking any prisoners.

6

Just Plain Bill

'I've thrown more freaking passes the last two days than Roger Staubach threw in his whole career,' the Ferret moaned.

'Then take a little off them,' the Weasel complained. 'My ribs look like I just fought ten rounds with Larry Holmes.'

'I start lobbing the ball to you and I'll lose control and bust another window. That's all we need. Screw it, let's take a break.'

So the two narcs, dressed today in sweat shirts and jeans and tennis shoes instead of leather jackets and boots, took their football and retreated half a block down Oxford Avenue to the green Toyota where they kept their other props.

They'd been street football jocks the last two days while watching a certain house south of Los Feliz Boulevard. Two days before that they were gardeners, after having been lucky enough to find a house on the street with the residents on vacation. The Ferret mowed the lawn seven times. The Weasel dug up all the crabgrass, pruned the roses, snipped back the ivy, and when they'd run out of things to do, started all over again. It gave them a splendid vantage point from which to observe the house in question, but after two days of overzealous gardening there wasn't enough left for a hungry snail. They packed up their gardening tools after it looked like a horde of locusts had hit the yard. Then they started playing the endless game of catch football.

The resident of the house under surveillance was, according to a usually reliable snitch named Sox Wilson, dealing chunks of hash as big as cucumbers, and had bragged that this very week he was going to wheel his silver Mercedes 450SL out of his garage and make a fresh buy from his Asian connection on the waterfronts of San Pedro.

The county recorder's office showed the property deed to belong to a Randolph Waterman, who had leased the house to a vacationing couple, who had subleased the property, apparently to the hash dealer or one of his friends. The narcs couldn't find out the name of the dealer except that everyone called him Bill.

'Bill what, for chrissake?' the Weasel demanded of Sox Wilson.

'I dunno, I dunno, Weasel,' Sox Wilson whined. 'If I'm lyin, I'm flyin.'

'If you're lyin, you're fryin,' the Weasel corrected him.

'If you're lyin, you're dyin,' the Ferret corrected them both, cleaning his fingernails with his stiletto.

'They call him Bill,' Sox Wilson pleaded. 'Just plain Bill.'

It wasn't that a hash bust was worth mowing blisters on your hands, or facing heat exhaustion from throwing footballs all day, but Captain Woofer happened to *live* on the street, and when he heard that dope was being dealt there (Weasel's dumb mistake in *telling* him) he ordered the two narcs to crawl out of all their leather, look as respectable as they were capable of looking without cutting their beards and ponytails, and get that son of a bitch who *dared* to sully the street where the captain had resided for twenty-three years. It was almost the only investigation going on at present that Captain Woofer gave a damn about except the one involving Nigel St Claire. The Weasel and the Ferret expected to get their balls whacked good if they didn't nail Just Plain Bill in the next few days.

There *was* another investigation going on which concerned Captain Woofer more than Just Plain Bill and Nigel St Claire put together. It was an ultra-secret investigation being conducted by Internal Affairs Division. The fact was that someone was trying to drive Captain Woofer bonzo. It had been going on for over three months. Although neither Captain Woofer nor the Internal Affairs headhunters had been able to put it together, it all began the morning after a local television showing of *Gaslight*, where Charles Boyer tried to drive Ingrid Bergman bonzo and nearly succeeded.

As all policemen learn: Life imitates not art but melodrama.

During the month of February, when the captain and his wife, Sybil, went for a weekend fishing trip in San Diego, someone listed their home with a local realtor for such a ridiculously low price that it was sold before the Woofers returned from the holiday. The listing party's description could have fit a thousand sleazeballs from the boulevard. Captain Woofer looked at over five hundred mug shots of known confidence men to no avail. The Woofers got sick and tired of realtors showing up with prospective buyers for the next two weeks, and finally put a Not For Sale sign in the front yard. The transaction was nullified and the whole incident was dismissed by bunco detectives as an obvious prank.

The investigation was revived and Internal Affairs Division was brought into the picture when, three weeks later, the license number of Captain Woofer's family car was plugged into the statewide computer as a stolen vehicle containing armed and dangerous occupants. It wasn't a damn bit funny when Sybil Woofer and her best friend, Mrs Commander Peterson, were jacked-up by two cops with shotguns and ordered out of the 'stolen' station wagon in front of the Hermès store in Beverly Hills.

While the two women screamed and cried, with their hands planted firmly on top of their coiffured blue hair, a crowd of ogling Arabs, Iranians, Texans and other wogs quickly gathered and shook their heads and spoke to each other in their exotic tongues about the anarchy in California where female desperadoes disguised themselves to look like window-shoppers from Van Nuys.

81

The most despicable incident had occurred one week before Al Mackey and Martin Welborn were given the Nigel St Claire case. It happened when Captain Woofer, echoing Deputy Chief Julian Francis' call for better police relations with the swelling tide of ethnic minorities in Los Angeles, mentioned to the squad-room full of bored detectives that he too had always been *kind to Negroes*. Which caused the Weasel and Ferret to exchange knowing looks. Within a week, two things happened: First, someone forged Captain Woofer's signature on a payroll deduction card requesting that five percent of Captain Woofer's police salary be deducted and sent as a charitable contribution to the United Negro College Fund. Second, an ad appeared the following Monday in the classifieds of Los Angeles' largest underground newspaper. It said: 'Male, white, 59 years old, pipesmoker, neat, obedient, always kind to Negroes, seeks young virile Negro with whom to *be* kind. Willing to pay handsomely if pipestem exceeds seven inches.' The deplorable ad listed Captain Woofer's home telephone number, which began ringing every three and a half minutes, erasing any doubt in the minds of the headhunters from Internal Affairs Division that the swine who was trying (with some success) to drive Captain Woofer bonzo had to be an insider. The girl who took the ad from the cash customer was unable to provide any kind of helpful description. The man who placed the ad had worn a scuba diving mask and a wet suit when he strolled into the office.

When the incredulous headhunters asked if she didn't think the man's costume was a bit unusual, the girl said, 'Where the fuck you think this is – Wahoo, Nebraska? This is *Hollywood*, U.S.A.!'

It began to look like the vicious attacks on Captain Woofer had run their course when yet another incident occurred, this one the most direct and personal, literally under Captain Woofer's stopped-up nose. It had to be someone very close, someone who knew that Captain Woofer had a corker of a head cold that week. His adenoids were mushrooming, his eyes watering, his nose was absolutely useless, and two bottles of spray hadn't unclogged it. Captain Woofer had been leaning back in his swivel chair, his sore tail planted in his rubber ring, legs up to relieve the inflammation, squirting drops in his nostrils. Nothing worked. He had caught a cold by sitting in his rhododendrons all night watching the house of the mysterious neighbor on Oxford Avenue.

He was suffering and miserable when he ordered the Weasel and Ferret to get that son of a bitch of a dope dealer, and left no doubt that he would whack their balls if they failed. It made *them* downright hostile. And not toward Just Plain Bill, the alleged hash dealer.

The very afternoon that the Weasel and the Ferret were working the stakeout on Oxford Avenue, Captain Woofer strolled out of his office into the squadroom, made a strange statement to his troops, and keeled over into the lap of poor old Cal Greenberg.

The paramedics were called and Captain Woofer was rushed to the receiving hospital, where there was a physician on duty who did *not* have the sniffles and could detect a powerful odor on Captain Woofer's breath. That, coupled with the fact that his distended pupils looked like black dimes, caused the physician to put in a call to the police department which resulted in Captain Woofer's being the *suspect* in an investigation by Internal Affairs Division.

The headhunters, who had not watched *Gaslight*, were nevertheless able to absolve Captain Woofer of any charge of misconduct. It was apparent that he was the victim of yet another attempt to drive him bonzo. And it had temporarily succeeded.

They discovered that Captain Woofer's beloved briar had been tampered with, probably when Captain Woofer went to the toilet to make his futile morning attempt, and undoubtedly by someone who knew that Captain Woofer had the habit of leaving his pipe on the towel tray in the restroom, along with his coat and gunbelt. The gun stayed on the floor beside the toilet. What with all the raids against him these days he didn't feel safe *anywhere*.

It seemed likely that someone had crept into the men's restroom and unloaded Captain Woofer's tamped and loaded briar, reloading it with very high grade hashish or Thai stick, according to the crime lab. Then a layer of tobacco was spread over the potent pipe which was tamped and replaced. With Captain Woofer's head cold, he smelled nothing. With his sniffer out of commission it was difficult to *taste* anything, but he did think upon reflection that the smoke seemed extra harsh. After he'd smoked half a pipe load, Captain Woofer felt that something was wrong. Still, he smoked. Then he stood up unsteadily and strolled out of the squadroom, and made a singularly bizarre announcement, even for him.

Before he keeled over into poor old Cal Greenberg's lap he pointed to a sixty-year-old clerk typist named Gladys Bruckmeyer who was just trying to do her time and get her pension and retire to a mobile home in Apple Valley. Captain Woofer aimed an accusing finger at her and, his voice full of righteous indignation, cried: 'You! IT's YOUR FAULT, GLADYS BRUCKMEYER!'

Gladys Bruckmeyer snapped out of her Apple Valley reverie so fast she tore her pantyhose jumping up. And, as the senior clerk typist wondered what mistake she could have possibly made on Captain Woofer's progress reports to spur *this* kind of rage, he repeated it: 'IT's YOUR FAULT, GLADYS BRUCKMEYER!'

The entire squadroom, of course, grew deathly still. Detectives hung up on callers in midsentence. Pencil lead broke in midstroke. It was a frozen tableau unique in the history of Hollywood Detectives.

Then Captain Woofer, still puffing on the pipe, in the presence of nearly the entire squadroom of astonished detectives (two were off throwing footballs with peculiar smiles on their faces this morning) unequivocally accused Gladys Bruckmeyer and challenged her to deny it.

And in her shock and fear of losing her pension and

never living in Apple Valley, Gladys Bruckmeyer became disoriented and confused.

'WELL?' Captain Woofer thundered at the top of his ragged lungs. 'DO YOU DENY LETTING THE CATERPILLARS CONQUER THE KINGDOM?'

Just before Captain Woofer did his nose dive into poor old Cal Greenberg's lap, Gladys Bruckmeyer tearfully admitted that she *couldn't* deny it.

'But can't you give me another chance, Captain?' she sobbed. 'I've already got my mobile home picked out!'

While the Weasel decided to pop a can of beer and take it laid-back and easy, because this hash dealer, if he *was* a hash dealer, was *never* going to make a move, and while the Ferret prowled around what was left of the yard on Oxford Avenue, morosely throwing his stiletto into an olive tree, the only piece of vegetation they hadn't demolished, Just Plain Bill made his move.

If the Weasel hadn't reached into the back seat of the green Toyota for the beer, he might never have noticed the little silver Mercedes wheeling out of the driveway and turning north toward Fern Dell Park. Before the Weasel got the Toyota fired up and pointed in the right direction the Mercedes was already out of sight. The happy Ferret leaped into the nark ark as the Weasel yelled, 'Let's get *on* it!' and careened toward the park.

The two narcs thus began a tail which ultimately resulted in the Weasel and the Ferret helping to coach the Los Angeles Lakers toward a world basketball championship. And only incidentally resulted in yet another break in the Nigel St Claire murder case.

The thirteen hours with Just Plain Bill almost ended before it all began. The Mercedes made a right, and yet another right on Franklin Avenue, heading back to the Oxford address like a homing pigeon. But before reaching Oxford, the Mercedes made a fancy U-turn on Franklin Avenue and then another, almost running smack into the

85

green Toyota, causing the Weasel to yell: 'Eat the floormat! The asshole's looking for a tail!'

Then, with the Ferret down on the floor of the Toyota, the Weasel turned east on Franklin Avenue, certain that Just Plain Bill had not seen the Toyota and, if he had, would have seen only one head in the car rather than the ever more suspicious two-man tailing team.

They only had to wait thirty minutes. The silver Mercedes pulled out of the Oxford driveway a second time. The driver seemed more satisfied that there was no one watching the house and he made a southbound turn, passing the Toyota, which was jammed parallel between two neighborhood cars, and *both* narcs ate the floormat until the Mercedes turned west on Franklin. Then they roared after him, taking Just Plain Bill more seriously.

'This sucker's for real,' the Ferret observed. 'Why didn't we believe Sox Wilson this time? We should have two more cars on this tail.'

'Why did I open my big mouth to Woofer about the doper on his street?'

'Why don't those *unknown suspects* have a little more imagination next time and come up with a surefire scheme to get Woofer in the ding ward at the Veterans' Hospital *before* he knocks our dicks down? I got a bad feeling this is gonna be an all-nighter.'

'I got a bad feeling I ain't gonna meet whatzerface with the four nipples at The Glitter Dome tonight.'

'Shit, neither one of us is gonna be touching pee pees tonight and . . . FOUR NIPPLES?'

Just then the Mercedes gunned it on the yellow and busted the light on Gower Street.

'Son of a bitch! He's *still* hinky about a tail!'

The Weasel slid the Toyota over to the eastbound lane, causing a laundry truck to jam on his brakes, turned south, jumping the curb in a service station, crossed the sidewalk, and after two other cars were behind the Mercedes, risked getting back into the westbound lane to continue following. If they had run the stoplight behind the watchful driver, it would have been all over. The Ferret's pulse was kicking in at 130 beats a minute, and he glanced repeatedly at the bulging green eyes of the bearded Weasel with his death grip on the steering wheel.

'Goddamn, Ferret, watch the fucking road! We're gonna *lose* him. Shit, where *is* he? We *lost* him!'

Both narcs swiveled every which way, squinting down side streets against the smoggy rays of the setting sun that made every pale car look silver.

'I blinked. I just blinked for a second.'

'Well, do your goddamn blinking when this tail is *finished*! Do your . . . There he *is*!'

The silver Mercedes was parked on Vine Street in front of a liquor store. The Weasel kept the Toyota lost in the number one traffic lane, and while the Ferret hit the floor, drove past the store until he could safely turn left. He parked on the first street south, where the Ferret leaped out of the car and ran to the corner to act as point man. While the Weasel kept the Toyota ready at the curb, the Ferret stood peeking around the corner at the silver Mercedes. Suddenly the Ferret ran back to the Toyota, and the Weasel dropped it in low gear.

'Is he moving?'

'No. He's still inside. Does she *really* have four nipples?'

'FERRET, GET THE FUCK BACK TO THE POINT! THIS IS BUSINESS! WE'RE GONNA GET OUR DICKS KNOCKED OFF!'

So the Ferret loped back to his point position and sulked, and vowed to move in on the chicken with four nipples *if* the Weasel would only reveal her identity the next time he got drunk at The Glitter Dome. *Four* nipples!

Then Just Plain Bill strolled out of the liquor store, glanced lazily both ways on the street, lit a cigarette, and got back into the 450SL, heading north again.

The nark ark tailed him north on the Hollywood Freeway. They were resorting to props now. On the outbound trip the Weasel tucked his pony tail up under a construction worker's hard hat. The Ferret kept down in the seat, only raising up when the Weasel's eyes were drifting.

Then the Mercedes took an off-ramp and an on-ramp and headed back *inbound* on the Hollywood Freeway, and the Ferret put on his blond Farrah Fawcett wig and slid over close to the Weasel, as they both sweated in what was left of a very hot afternoon.

'I think your deodorant's failed you,' the Weasel said when the Ferret cuddled up.

'You were expecting Bo Derek?' the Ferret answered. 'Oh, no! The asshole's going back *home!*'

There was no traffic between the Mercedes and the Toyota when they took the off-ramp. Just Plain Bill seemed to be looking in his rearview mirror. The Ferret had to put both arms around the Weasel and snuggle.

'God damn, Ferret! I'm taking you to the morgue. They may as well start the autopsy right now.'

'How you think *you* smell after throwing footballs for two days? You ain't used deodorant since Christ was a carpenter. You . . .'

'There he goes! *Back* on the goddamn freeway!' the Weasel yelled, and the Ferret threw his Farrah Fawcett wig in the back seat and jumped huffily to his side of the car.

Just Plain Bill continued back inbound on the freeway, this time heading directly toward downtown Los Angeles, toward the Harbor Freeway, toward the waterfronts of San Pedro.

Except that by now the outbound freeways were jammed with afternoon commuters, so the Weasel and the Ferret settled in six cars behind the silver Mercedes, which they assumed would stay on the freeway all the way to the harbor.

'I wish Just Plain Bill was a broad. It's *so* much easier to tail a broad,' the Ferret said, looking cagily at the Weasel, who had dumped his prop hard hat in favor of a prop cowboy hat in case Just Plain Bill was looking.

'Broad or not, he's one tough mother to tail,' the Weasel

said, rubbing his distended eyeballs. Do all your blinking *before* you start the tail.

'A broad spots some guy tailing her, it's no problem,' the Ferret said, casting sidelong glances toward the Weasel. 'She's flattered, in fact. She thinks her Maidenform's working. Which reminds me . . .'

'Yes, she has *four* fucking nipples, and you could give me the entire balance a your paycheck that you *don't* have to surrender to your ex-wife's lawyer, and I still wouldn't tell you her name,' the Weasel said.

'Come *on*, Weasel, I shared that stewardess with you that time!'

'Whadda you mean, *shared* her? You gave me her phone number and address is what you did, and you didn't tell me she had a thing for Samoan longshoremen, and I nearly got my throat torn out when I tripped-on into that little beer party where guys were so big they made Schultz and Simon look like the Captain and Tenille. And *that's* what you did for me by way a sharing her.'

'Are all four nipples actually developed? Are they pink or more brownish? Are they two by two or sort of scattered? Just tell me if her first name is Trudy, Shirley or Rosie? It's one a the three, ain't it?'

And so forth. It passed the long tedious ride down the Harbor Freeway in bumper-to-bumper, creeping lines of traffic. The exhaust fumes mingled with the dusk to produce that peculiar, deadly, beautiful Los Angeles sunset.

And while the Ferret pondered four nipples, two up and two down, Just Plain Bill waited until the very last second at the Santa Barbara Avenue turnoff and jerked the wheel to the right, gunning the Mercedes down the ramp. The number three traffic lane, containing a green Toyota and a pair of bearded narcs, ground to a stop.

'We lost him! He's gone!' the Weasel yelled.

'I told you we shouldn't be so far back!' the Ferret yelled back at him.

'Did you want me to bumper-lock him? You wanted me to tip our mitt, maybe?'

'You get too cute and careful and this is what happens! I mowed that lawn seven times! Why didn't you get in the *center* lane?'

'You *never* use the center lane in busy traffic, you dumb shit. You get hung up in the center lane!'

'So you had to be cute and now we're jammed up, and might as well take a trip to the fucking ocean and see if the grunions are running, or dig for clams, or scrape abalone off the fucking rocks, or . . .'

'Ferret, he's *behind* us!'

And he was. Just Plain Bill had come back onto the freeway at Slauson Avenue. The Weasel could see him six cars back through the rearview mirror.

'Jesus Christ! Don't turn around,' the Ferret said.

'You think I'm crazy? Get your wig.'

'You said my deodorant failed,' the Ferret reminded him.

'Stop pouting, and slide *over* here!'

So they cuddled again for another five miles, with Just Plain Bill behind them. It wouldn't have been a bad way to tail him actually, since most people use their turn signals well in advance for a turnoff, and could be seen in the mirror, thus allowing the Weasel to turn off *first*. Except that Just Plain Bill didn't drive like most people. He didn't even drive like most hash dealers. He drove like he was delivering the secret of the neutron bomb to the goddamn Russians, and the Weasel was getting sick and tired of it. The Weasel lost his patience totally when the Mercedes managed to slide through an opening in traffic and get into the number one lane, pulling quickly ahead.

'He's in the *fast* lane, Weasel!' the Ferret said.

'I see him.'

'Well, get the fuck outa this lane!'

'I *can't* get out. Can't you see I'm blocked?'

Then the Weasel leaned out the window and waved frantically at an old man beside him in a Buick who grinned toothlessly and waved back. And blocked them in more completely.

'I live my whole fucking *life* in the slow lane!' the Ferret whined.

Then the Weasel leaned out the window and screamed at a Triumph TR-7 in front of him, and pressed on the horn. The driver responded by flipping them the middle digit and viciously stepping on his brakes, causing the Weasel to jump on *his* brakes which sent the Ferret's head bumping into the windshield, knocking his Farrah Fawcett wig askew.

The Weasel reacted by playing bumper cars with the TR-7, whanging the rear of the roadster, jetting the Triumph forward with each clang of the bumpers until the driver's head was whiplashing like a metronome. The driver held up both hands in abject surrender and pulled off the freeway into the ivy, letting the Weasel careen madly down the shoulder of the freeway some half a mile, where they spotted the Mercedes cruising smoothly in the number two lane. Traffic was lighter this far from downtown and darkness had dissolved the mauve and crimson beauty of the ominous smoggy sunset.

By the time they reached San Pedro the Ferret had knocked back a six pack of beer, the prerogative of the passenger, and was getting beery enough to wax philosophical. He said, 'I think my horoscope's all wrong lately. Can you still see Just Plain Bill?'

'*I* can still see,' the Weasel said disgustedly. 'Which is more than I can say for *you*.'

'I think I'm gonna move from Venice,' the Ferret said. 'You can't find love on a surfboard at my age.'

'You got gills,' the Weasel grumbled, watching the Mercedes switch gradually to the slower lanes. 'You can't move inland. You wouldn't live that long.'

'I don't care,' the Ferret said, popping open the last can of beer, making the Weasel curse. 'My karma's bad. I think I'll take a leave of absence, go to the Himalayas, and worship some Chinese guru in Katmandu or wherever the hell.'

'I think that's the wrong place for those Chinese gurus.'

'Wherever. I think I'll live with a monk and a mongoose and maybe I can find nirvana. Which is *a woman with four nipples.*'

That caused the Weasel's eyeballs to click back under a hard hat, now that he'd switched props again. 'All *right*, if you'll stop getting sloshed, since we got business to attend to. I'll tell you who she is. But only *after* we do our business and only if you stop swilling the suds.'

The Weasel hadn't finished his sentence before the full can of beer went flying out the window. The Ferret was all business. 'I've got my eye on him, Weasel!'

'Good.'

'I wish we had a chopper. We coulda knocked out his taillight to make him easier to tail.'

'We coulda, yeah.'

'We coulda put phosphorescent paint on the roof of his car if we had a chopper to spot him.'

'I suppose so.'

'Don't worry, Weasel, we're gonna sandbag this bastard!' The Ferret now sat ramrod straight, watching the Mercedes through binoculars. He looked like Charlton Heston on the bridge of a destroyer. It was amazing what some men would do for four nipples.

Just Plain Bill, meanwhile, seemed to be taking a leisurely harbor tour for himself. He cruised into the parking lot of Redbeard's Saloon, where cops and longshoremen had had some legendary punch-outs over the decades.

It was said that when Redbeard died, his funeral was attended by half of San Pedro and *all* of the winos, pugs, and street fighters from the Main Street gym to Terminal Island prison. Redbeard Mahoney in his time had been a merchant seaman, a renowned arm wrestler, and a pretty good professional boxer, except for his crystal chin. So they *all* came, after Redbeard Mahoney bought it by drinking a quart and a half of Jamaican rum in one hour, thus winning a $500 bet but losing his life from alcohol poisoning. He went out with such flair that every Los Angeles wino from skid row to the waterfront spoke of his exit in hushed tones.

The waterfront had looked like Mardi Gras the day of his funeral. There were two Dixieland bands, a troop of boy scouts, a platoon of uniformed cops who had earned their battle scars in Redbeard's Saloon, and a busload of ragtag winos let out of Central Jail by a sentimental watch commander who had lost three teeth to a sailor in Redbeard's Saloon in 1948, but had had the pleasure of seeing Redbeard Mahoney dislodge *all* the teeth of the cop's adversary and then hold the sailor's arms so the cop could personally play a little catch-up. Redbeard Mahoney was that kind of guy.

Except that his name wasn't Redbeard Mahoney. It was Moses Mankowitz. And in his will he asked that a rabbi be present to oversee the modern Viking funeral. At the fateful moment when the mortician's powerboat was about to depart the wharf with the urn full of Moses Mankowitz, a.k.a. Redbeard Mahoney, an Orthodox rabbi squared his black hat, smoothed his long black coat, adjusted his horn-rimmed glasses, and courageously marched through that mob of winos, pugilists, longshoremen, merchant seamen, commercial fishermen, veteran detectives, over-the-hill harness cops, weeping whores, and motley seafarers from Long Island to Long Beach. The multitudes got strangely silent when the little man in the black clothes and long black beard stepped forward to read in an ancient tongue. And then they heard it. Moses Mankowitz?

At first it spread through the crowd like shared moonshine. Each passed it on to the other: Moses Mankowitz? Seventy-year-old B-girls began wiping tears and scowling. What did it all mean? Moses Mankowitz?

And then it descended on the crowd like a pall of tear gas! They grimaced. They gagged. They howled. They *choked* on it. Moses Mankowitz? Redbeard Mahoney? The Irish son of a bitch *was a fucking hebe!*

When the crowd started to surge like the scum-crested waves lapping that wharf, the rabbi was warned by a uniformed cop that discretion was advised. Just then an incredulous Italian tuna skipper with a skinful of 80-proof bourbon from Redbeard's own saloon came charging forward, leaped on the deck of the funeral boat, climbed the flying bridge, and wrestled the urn from the terrified mortician.

'Say it ain't so, Moe!' the wop screamed to the urn, proving that he *did* believe it.

The police honor guard pounced on the distraught dago, wrestled the remains from his craggy claws, and threw Redbeard Mahoney's earthly remains into the boat like a hand grenade, after which the seafaring mortician gratefully gunned both diesels and left a wake eighty yards wide as he headed out to open sea to scuttle the Jew in the jar before somebody scuttled *him*.

But now Redbeard's Saloon was just a tourist trap. The Weasel and Ferret had to take turns running to the alley to take a leak while the other kept watch. Christ, *nobody* would deal hash in a corny tourist trap like Redbeard's Saloon!

'I ain't going for this,' the Weasel finally said, as they sat in the dark, slouched down in the Toyota watching Just Plain Bill's Mercedes for over an hour. 'This guy's wearing me down. It just don't make sense. This joint is where you find busloads a bluehairs when they get off the freaking cruise ships!'

Then they both got a rush. Just Plain Bill sauntered out of the tourist trap with two wizened men carrying brief-cases, and a spindle-shanked woman who looked only a week away from Gladys Bruckmeyer's mobile-home fantasy.

'I'm about to break out in spots,' the Ferret said. 'I don't know where this guy's coming from!'

But they soon found out where they were *going*. They

were going for a ride over the Vincent Thomas Bridge. The new threesome got in a forest-green Cadillac and followed Just Plain Bill's Mercedes to the toll gate and across the bridge while the Weasel and Ferret cursed and swore and argued with the toll collector, who didn't believe they were cops. What kind of cops didn't have enough change for a ride on a toll bridge? Then the Ferret remembered there was a five-dollar bill stashed in his tennis bag in the trunk and they paid, swearing at the collector while he wrote their license number down to report them to the *real* cops.

The slavering narcs were deciding what revenge to wreak on the toll collector when the Ferret yelled: 'I *am* breaking out in spots!'

Coming the *other* way on the bridge was the silver Mercedes, followed at a two-car interval by the nervous trio in the green Cadillac. So it was off the bridge, a squealing U-turn, and back on again. The Ferret was ready to give up, deciding that this was just some kind of nutty scavenger hunt.

After leaving the Vincent Thomas Bridge, Just Plain Bill decided it was safe enough to get down to his real business, and he drove toward a row of warehouses near the harbor with the Cadillac close behind. Two blocks behind the Cadillac, the green Toyota was forced to maneuver without lights through the narrow deserted alleys and streets.

When the Weasel saw the brake lights on the Cadillac stay lit after it stopped near a side door ominously close to the ocean, he made a decision.

'Screw it,' the Weasel said. 'I get any closer, lights or no lights, Just Plain Bill's gonna make us. If he's got any pals around here we might be made already. Let's take a chance.'

So he pulled the Toyota into the nearest alley, up to a wall behind a trash heap, and they took their flashlights and guns from under the car seat and crept along the walls toward the smell of brine and dead fish and gull shit, toward the unlovely smell of the harbor of Los Angeles.

They stopped and hunkered deeper into the darkness when the Cadillac's brake lights went out and the two men left the woman in the car and, minus the briefcases, walked toward the wharf and out of sight.

Now the Weasel and Ferret were sucking air, all right. This wasn't a hash buy going down.

'We're lip-deep in horseshit,' the Weasel whispered.

'We're up to our ass in alligators,' the Ferret whispered.

They crept ever closer, and now they didn't even notice the chilly sea air. They were both sweating like a ten-mile run. They were silently cursing the three-quarter moon and wishing for cloud banks, or fog. Suddenly a gull screamed. Then a *man* screamed.

The woman in the car heard it, or thought she did. Was it just another gull? She got out and said, 'Rodney?'

The Weasel and the Ferret were padding along now at a trot, running up behind the quivering woman who was standing beside the Cadillac with the door open. Then the cry of a gull was drowned out by a man screaming, 'Don't! Please! Nooooooo!'

And the woman beside the Cadillac outscreamed a squadron of gulls when lean shadows flew by her in the darkness and the two narcs rounded the corner, their hearts banging out the sound of everything but the woman's screams. The Weasel literally ran into Just Plain Bill, knocking him flat on his face and sending his ·32 Browning clattering across the brick tarmac where a new member of the cast, an Asian, had one of the old men on the ground, taping his mouth and tying wrists and ankles preparatory to cutting his throat and dropping him into the water.

The other old man, who had been kneeling face-to-muzzle with Just Plain Bill's automatic pistol, was already taped and tied when the gunman went flying and the Weasel hit the ground just behind him.

The Asian was on his feet, scrambling for his knife, when

96.

the Ferret came on them with his beam of light. While he began to understand what the hell was happening, the Asian accomplice was off and running, away from the dock straight toward the old woman in the Cadillac. The Ferret fired three times at the dodging figure, missed all three and went after him, leaping over the scuffling figure of the Weasel, who was pistol-whipping Just Plain Bill's noggin into a pile of tapioca.

The Asian hit the old woman so hard her dentures popped out and rattled to the street before she did. Then he grabbed one of the leather briefcases out of the car, and was silhouetted beautifully in the Ferret's sights twenty yards down the alley when the Ferret skidded on those fractured dentures and involuntarily fired a shot into the quickly descending fogbanks. *Now* the fog had settled when they needed light.

The old lady was still on the ground, yelling 'Rodney!' which sounded mushy without her dentures, and the Ferret was limping after the fleeing figure with the briefcase. The chase ended against a chain-link fence around a boatyard full of engines. Inside was a frothing Doberman perfectly willing to eat the Asian, who slammed against the fence, dropped the briefcase, spilled bundles of money, and was about to surrender. But the exhausted Ferret (who would never again drink ten cans of beer on duty) stumbled on the curb and went ass over tennis shoes. And *his* gun went clattering.

The Asian killer cried out joyfully, picked up the Ferret's gun, turned, and fired one shot point-blank through the fence into the open mouth of the Doberman, who dropped like a brick, his snarl frozen forever.

Then, while the Ferret started to weep for his mother and wish he'd been an accountant like his father, and had all sorts of incoherent thoughts he would later not remember, the Asian killer pointed the gun at the Ferret's mouth just as he had at the Doberman's, and pulled the trigger. And it clicked. The two-inch Smith & Wesson was a *five*-shot revolver.

The assassin screamed like a gull, picked up the brief-case, and started up the fence, but before he did he pulled a knife from nowhere and slashed at the Ferret, who raised his hand, getting a defense wound across the palm which would later require a dozen stitches. When the killer reached the top of the chain-link fence, the Ferret, weeping now out of fury, snarling like the deceased Doberman, took out his stiletto and threw it at the climbing figure. But since knife throwing only works in movies, the weapon struck the killer in the shoulder, handle first, and dropped harmlessly at the Ferret's feet. While the bleeding narc roared helplessly and would have given four nipples for *one* bullet, the limping assassin stepped over the dead dog and made his way through the boatyard to freedom. The Ferret scrambled about on the wrong side of the fence and threw *rocks* at the assassin with his bloody hand.

By the time the Ferret got back to the would-be corpses, the Weasel had things reasonably well sorted out. The two old geezers were goldbugs from Spring Street in downtown Los Angeles. They had been buying and hoarding gold in their store long before the precious metal went soaring and bouncing up and down on the exchange. Just Plain Bill had sold them a considerable quantity of gold Krugerrands over the last two years, no questions asked. He'd finally set them up for a big buy of bullion from an Oriental 'fisherman', also no questions asked.

The goldbugs were more than a little frightened about a waterfront liaison, but Just Plain Bill was a trusted customer, and one goldbug decided to bring his wife along, feeling certain that the dear old doll would add a measure of safety if there was some kind of double cross planned. Just Plain Bill knew and liked her and would never hurt such a nice old dame. And so forth.

The three never were convinced that the Weasel and the Ferret were correct in their assessment that Just Plain Bill and the gook who boogied were going to cut her, from her sagging gullet right down to her chilly old giz, the second they had the two larcenous goldbugs safely trussed up and ripped open like baby hogs, to be dumped into the bay with all the unwanted fetuses, unloved hoodlums, savagely raped runaways, and suicidal wretches of every stripe who ended up there.

In fact, when one of the goldbugs pulled himself together sufficiently to begin thinking about the satchel crammed with $50,000 that the Ferret *let get away*, he began getting churlish with the lieutenant in charge of the twenty-five policemen who eventually swarmed all over the scene, searching in vain for any clues to the identity of the escaped assassin. (It was apparent that Just Plain Bill was an old pro who was going to do all his talking through a lawyer from one of those Century City law firms with about a hundred names. The Mercedes was registered to him under his true name of William Bozwell.)

While a paramedic was binding the Ferret's hand and getting ready to transport him to the hospital for suturing, the place was overrun by big-footed bluesuits running amok and trampling any evidence there *might* be.

The snippier of the two goldbugs turned toward the Ferret and said, 'If you just could have gotten the briefcase! I don't care about the guy getting away! If you just could have gotten the *briefcase*! Do you know how hard I *worked* for that money?'

And the Weasel got *very* worried, because the Ferret's eyes got that blue agate look to them and started pinwheeling as he said very quietly to the goldbug: 'Do you have *any* friends who would risk their lives for you? No? Well, I just *did*. And I don't even *know* you. And *furthermore* . . .'

The Weasel thought it prudent to remove the Ferret before he squashed that goldbug on the spot. But the Weasel wanted to make sure the prisoner and money were being attended to by the pair of uniformed cops who had Just Plain Bill handcuffed and standing off down the alley with his face to the wall in front of the nark ark. One of the bluecoats, a lanky cop with acne, was keeping an eye on the briefcases, which the Weasel had opened and thrown into the back seat of the Toyota along with the four

99

packages of currency the Ferret had retrieved when he nearly got dinged with the Doberman. The cop standing by the Toyota used his flashlight beam to stare in rapture at the contents of the car, while the other one worked out on a wad of gum and kept his shotgun pointed at the back of Just Plain Bill, who was dripping blood from his head, and sweating from the pain of the tight handcuffs. But he wasn't complaining.

The Ferret was really starting to tremble now, as the image of himself lying dead with the dog began to crystalize. And the more he trembled the more crazed he looked.

When they got near the Toyota the Weasel saw that the tall cop with acne was actually *fondling* the packages of money in the back seat. Suddenly the tall cop turned, looking temporarily as bughouse as the Ferret, and said: 'No one knows how many packages he dropped! No one knows how many you picked up! No one knows . . .'

He stopped babbling when the Ferret nodded eagerly with his brand-new lunatic smile and said, 'That's right, pal. You got it all figured out.'

Both the tall cop with acne and the Weasel watched in confusion as the Ferret limped over to the other bluesuit who was guarding Just Plain Bill and, before anyone could speak, snatched the shotgun out of the cop's grasp with his bandaged hand. The Weasel feared that Just Plain Bill was about to lose the need for lawyers and writs and bail bonds and Asian assassins, but instead of blowing Just Plain Bill all over the brick wall of the warehouse, the Ferret spun around and pointed the shotgun at the tall cop with acne and said: 'Okay, pus pockets, why don't you just get over there against the wall? WITH THE OTHER FUCKING THIEF!'

'Maintain, partner, maintain!' the Weasel coaxed, as the tall cop stopped fondling the money and reached for the lowest cloud bank, saying: 'I was just jiving ya! Hey, can't ya take a joke? It was just a joke!'

But the Ferret couldn't take a joke, not after looking at

his own gun in the hands of the ecstatic assassin who heard the Ferret cry for his mommy.

'Main-tain, Ferret! Mellow *out*!' the Weasel pleaded.

Then the Ferret slowly uncoiled and let the Weasel take the shotgun from his bleeding hand and give it back to the petrified young cop, who had swallowed his gum and had all but forgotten Just Plain Bill, who was hoping to get out of this alive and into a nice safe jail cell.

As the narcs drove off in their Toyota with the loot intact, the tall cop with acne was still saying, 'It was just a joke! Can't ya take a joke?'

Then the television news team showed up, the one that had busted more blue balls of working cops than a whole binful of captains and deputy chiefs. Leading the pack was a well-known Los Angeles television reporter who had, some months earlier, heard that a suspect in a police shooting was shot approximately a dozen times in the lower body by a small-caliber gun. Certain that he had the ultimate story of police brutality, he announced it on the eleven o'clock news, implying that the wounds had been inflicted while the victim was in police custody after he had been wounded during a fight with a shotgun-wielding cop. Which of course had every cop hater in town straining at the leash like the now dead Doberman, until it was later explained that *one* round of ·oo buckshot produces just that many holes.

Tonight, the reporter gave this story one minute of on-screen coverage. A cop got cut up and let a bad guy get away. And they *lost* $50,000 of the victim's hard-earned bread. And television shots of the cops made it hard to tell the players without a program, since Just Plain Bill looked like Pat Boone and the narcs looked like Manson Family rejects. It was a boring story.

The Weasel was genuinely sorry for the Ferret's slashed and painful wound and had a pretty good idea that his partner had aged three or four years during those moments of abject terror when he was calling for his mother and wished he'd listened to old dad. So he suggested they go to the Fabulous Forum and catch the Lakers' playoff game. Except they were both broke (after paying at the toll bridge and buying a pint of Scotch to stop their hands from shaking), so the next day they went to the Los Angeles Lakers' office, badges in hand, and reported that the Department had received a serious threat to detonate a concussion grenade near the Laker bench if the team should beat Dr J and the Philadelphia 76ers.

The team officials and stadium security placed the two narcs at court-side, where they gassed with all the show biz celebrities. Finally, in the last quarter of the game, the Ferret moved right down on the Laker bench to guard the team from the fictitious Mad Bomber, and during the heat of action he jumped in with a play that he guaranteed would leave Kareem open for a left-handed skyhook, and fake Dr J and his entire team clear into the parking lot.

No one will ever know if the astonished Laker coach took the advice about Dr J from the bearded young cop with boozy breath who babbled something about just winning a one-on-one with Dr D, the grim reaper. But the Weasel and Ferret were convinced that it was the narc's brilliantly designed play which helped the Lakers win the world championship of professional basketball.

A footnote to the entire evening came when one of the goldbugs was given back his belongings, which the Asian assassin had dropped when the Ferret was blazing away at him on the docks. The goldbug found everything intact: his keys, his wristwatch and rings, his money, his wallet containing credit cards and driver's license. But there was something else. It must have been dropped by the assassin, who Just Plain Bill said was a stranger he'd hired after a brief meeting in a Hollywood Boulevard massage parlor. (Just Plain Bill denied they were going to *harm* the old duffers. Just tape them up and leave them on the tarmac for dockworkers to find while washing away the morning gull shit.)

The objects that the goldbug said did not come from *his* pockets and must have been dropped by the fleeing assassin, were: an ordinary house key, and a scrap of paper bearing the business telephone number of a famous Hollywood movie studio.

7

The Empty Cathedral

It was turning into a very tense and nervous week. The street monsters hadn't yet figured out where they had heard the name of Nigel St Claire. The robbery detectives from downtown who were wrapping up Just Plain Bill Bozwell were now learning from the goldbug that the house key and the movie studio phone number didn't belong to him. Therefore the Hollywood homicide team of Al Mackey and Martin Welborn were making no progress at all and devoting their time to going through the motions with a few other cases in their pending file. A clean-desk policy is bad news in any bureaucracy.

And with Captain Woofer so recently returned to duty after learning that the caterpillars hadn't really conquered the kingdom, the squadroom was visited by headhunters from Internal Affairs who had been questioning all personnel who might have slipped the load of dope into the captain's pipe. The suspect list included Gladys Bruckmeyer, who was still on sick leave from the emotional effects of that fateful day. The headhunters were sick and tired of the failure of the Weasel and Ferret to keep appointments for their interrogation, but after the narcs made the big-deal bust of Just Plain Bill Bozwell (who quickly got out on bail) they were station-house celebrities. Even Captain Woofer had excused their failure to keep the dates with Internal Affairs. But Captain Woofer was still monomaniacal, and would have gladly nailed a gold piece to the mast if he thought a reward would harpoon the swine who had been tormenting him so mercilessly.

So, until they either got a break in the Nigel St Claire case or experienced a major epiphany whereby it would be revealed how they could turn this one into a suicide, Al Mackey and Martin Welborn decided to dab a little ointment on open sores. One of the most painful to Martin Welborn was the Bonnie Lee Brewster case.

The most efficient and certainly the happiest detectives were able to keep every case apart from themselves and sectioned off, with all fences intact. They worked hardest on the cases that the boss *said* were most important, collected their paychecks twice a month, and only worried about their own backyards. They got their miniature badges and gold ID cards and enjoyed retirement parties where they all knocked back lots of booze and gossiped about the retired detectives who got those cushy jobs as corporate security chiefs where they took down eighty grand a year.

But Martin Welborn was one of those self-proclaimed fair-to-middling detectives who never constructed fences, and often lost his perspective, and now was in danger of losing his sense of humor as well. Which is why Al Mackey was so tense lately, and had a nearly irresistible urge to go to Marty's apartment and mix up his paprika and cinnamon, or maybe throw his socks into his underwear drawer just to see if Marty could handle it.

There was something else bothering Al Mackey: the obsessive stops at St Vibiana's Cathedral damn near every time they went downtown to the police building. In more than twenty years Al Mackey had never had a partner want to visit a church. It was unnatural.

Martin Welborn knew he shouldn't stay long. Al would be anxious to get back to Hollywood. It was amazing how quickly time passed in St Vibiana's Cathedral. He remembered attending mass here in the early reign of John XXIII, when he would have walked with a sickbed strapped to his back before missing mass. Before the vernacular masses, and guitar masses, and charismatic priests, and the groping and pawing at the end of these secularized services: 'Let us offer each other the sign of peace!' When strangers turned with embarrassed or forlorn or beatific faces toward one another, depending upon their degree of intelligence, and shook hands. And Martin Welborn wanted to run away.

How dare they intrude between him and his God? How dare these benighted priests fail to see that by emasculating the ritual and mystery and guilt, they castrated The Faith. All the Catholic Church ever had been was ritual and mystery and guilt. And that was Everything. That was Order. Who could wish for more from God or man? Perfect Order.

It was time to go and he hadn't found it yet. He stood up to look over the second pew in front of him in the empty cathedral. Then he saw it. It had been left in a different pew today. This was the third visit he'd made this week. He'd even made a visit one evening after work. It was written in pencil on lined notebook paper. The hand that wrote the note was unsteady and light. The note said: 'Never Fail Novena. Most Sacred Heart of Jesus be praised and glorified now and forever. Most Sacred Heart of Jesus pray for us. Mother of God, Mary most holy, pray for us. Good Saint Theresa pray for us. Saint Jude, help of the hopeless, pray for us. One Our Father, one Hail Mary, one Glory be. Nine days novena. Leave a copy each day at church. At end of nine days your prayer will be answered.'

Martin Welborn read it twice, was tempted to say the Our Father, Hail Mary, and Glory be, but didn't. He hadn't said a prayer in a long time. He placed the note back on the pew where he found it and left the cathedral to join Al Mackey.

Before he left, he had a fleeting memory of the old cardinal, now dead so many years. When he was a young policeman in uniform, before the total devastation wrought by Vatican II, he loved to attend the solemn high masses and hear the Gregorian choir. The old cardinal was a rock, but the legacy of Vatican II would have eventually killed him if age hadn't. Martin Welborn would never forget the majesty of the old man as he chanted the ancient Latin rite. Martin Welborn once got to kneel and kiss the old man's ring. The cardinal wore lovely crimson slippers.

'You were in there twenty minutes this time,' Al Mackey said when Martin Welborn trotted down the steps of St Vibiana's, dodging two sleeping winos who were about to be carried into the big blue drunk wagon which was making its rounds.

'Was I? I couldn't have been in there that long.'

'I'm telling you, Marty. Twenty minutes. What do you *do* in there?'

'Nothing. It's peaceful.'

'Do you pray or what?'

'Not hardly.'

'Then what do you *do* in there? Burgle the poor box? What?'

'I sit.'

Al Mackey shook his head and sighed and drove up Los Angeles Street onto the Hollywood Freeway. They rode quietly for a few minutes and Al Mackey said, 'I don't know how to say this . . . You see, I think . . . Marty, I'd like to talk to you about something.'

'Of course, my son.' Martin Welborn smiled. He looked exceptionally tranquil. He always looked exceptionally tranquil lately. And that's what was making Al Mackey exceptionally nervous.

'We've been partners a long time, Marty. I got the right.'

'What right, Al?'

'I got the right to jam into your business.'

'Jam away.'

'I, uh, I have an opinion. I'm not pretending to be an expert, but I have an opinion. My opinion is that you oughtta go talk to somebody.'

'Somebody?'

'A doctor, maybe. Like that doctor we met on that Simpson case. He was a nice guy.'

'The psychiatrist?'

'Yeah. Somebody like that.'

'What would I tell a psychiatrist?'

'Goddamn it, Marty, I don't know!' Al Mackey had to hit the brakes as the freeway motorists slowed to ogle some poor bastard getting a speeding ticket. Better him than me!

'I wouldn't know either, Al,' Martin Welborn said serenely.

'Okay, you could start by telling him why you like to hang upside down like a freaking dead fish!'

'I have a sore back, Al. I've had a whiplash injury, remember?'

'Okay, then tell him why you go to church more than the Pope, why don't you?'

'It's peculiar to make occasional visits to a church? I told you I don't pray, if that's troubling you. I like the architecture. I wanted to be married there but we couldn't arrange it.'

'Okay, then talk to him about your marriage. Tell him how hard you took it when Paula walked out. Talk about how tough the separation has been for you.'

'Haven't both your divorces been tough on you, Al? Separation? Isn't it tough on everybody? Remorse. Guilt. Recriminations. Rather common, wouldn't you say?'

Al Mackey was losing patience with the stalled traffic and started blasting the horn. 'Why don't you write a letter?' he yelled out the window at the car in front.

'Calm yourself, my lad,' Martin Welborn chuckled. 'Maybe *you* should visit the good doctor.' Martin Welborn looked at an ancient Filipino with an aluminum walker, moving down Temple Street at a rate of six inches per step. 'Imagine how it is to go back *up*,' he said.

Al Mackey took a deep breath, wiped his brow with his hand, and looked at the surprising amount of moisture he found there. Then he said, 'Okay, Marty, I've got something you can discuss with the shrink. You can discuss the fact that your drinking glasses are lined up like a goddamn chess game. And your spice cabinet looks like three rows of checkers. And your socks and underwear and shirts look like you're waiting for the inspector general.'

'Is there something wrong with being neat?'

'You were never that neat. *Nobody* was ever that neat. You've just been getting a bit . . . *too* neat lately.'

108

'I'll try to be a little sloppier if it'll make you happier, Al,' Martin Welborn said good-naturedly.

'Oh, screw it!' Al Mackey said.

'Let's make another follow-up on Bonnie Lee Brewster, Al,' Martin Welborn said. 'Just one more time.'

Just one more time. It had been just one more time at least once a week for the past three months. That was another thing he'd like Marty to talk to the shrink about, Bonnie Lee Brewster and these crazy 'follow-ups' that Marty insisted on making to that psycho old woman, Auntie Rosa.

She lived up above Franklin Avenue in one of those spooky old houses that suited her style and business. Palm reading and crystal gazing and looking into one's *past* was legal enough in the city of Los Angeles and one could even get paid for it, but the second a psychic or medium took one step into the future and made a prediction for money, the medium or psychic would be wearing bracelets of steel instead of gold, and find herself charged with a bunco crime. Auntie Rosa broke the law from time to time, but the police had pretty much let her be since she had come in very handy on a few cases involving missing and murdered children. So far, she wasn't hitting the mark on ten-year-old Bonnie Lee Brewster, but she called Martin Welborn regularly. Sometimes she wept during the calls. It was right there, swimming in a mist over her bed, the figure of Bonnie Lee Brewster in a blue dress with white knee socks and a yellow Snoopy pin on her white collar. And no one told Auntie Rosa. The press didn't know because there was an incorrect clothing description broadcast on the police frequencies the day Bonnie Lee Brewster disappeared. The child had changed clothes and her mother didn't even know it for twenty-four hours. But Auntie Rosa called Hollywood Detectives and talked to Martin Welborn and *she* knew.

The little girl was last seen talking to a man two blocks from her home on Ivar Avenue. There was blood found near the alley. There was no ransom demand. Nothing. In the past Auntie Rosa had 'found' the sodomized, butchered body of an eleven-year-old boy in a culvert near the Los Angeles River. On another occasion, she 'heard' a five-year-old girl crying out for help in the attic of a stucco cottage in Eagle Rock. Auntie Rosa described the house and street so minutely that police found the house and the lunatic child chained in the attic by her parents.

So, even though cops are generally skeptics, not many laughed overtly at Auntie Rosa, and nobody was tossing her in the hoosegow for occasionally making a few bucks by looking into the future of the ladies of the neighborhood.

Al Mackey couldn't stand the smell of the sniffling old hag. She smelled like fish and garlic and onions and cats. Al Mackey thought she must have a hundred cats, and he started his psychosomatic sneezing when they got within a block of the corny old house with all the theatrical trappings.

Martin Welborn was very respectful of Auntie Rosa and she was always glad to see them. She had a goiter hanging from her neck and limped painfully on thick wrapped legs. Auntie Rosa was ageless, and they were never certain whether or not she was a Causasian. Al Mackey suspected she was some kind of Eurasian. But with a blue-black dye job and double face-lift it was hard to tell.

'You know, Sergeant Welborn,' the old woman said, when they sat down in the musty parlor, 'I saw Bonnie very clearly Tuesday night. I cried myself to sleep. She was calling for me, my darling Bonnie.'

Auntie Rosa always referred to missing children as her darlings.

'That child's dead,' Al Mackey said. 'There was blood.'

'She's not, Sergeant Mackey! Oh, she's not!' Auntie Rosa cried, and her head began a palsied bounce, a legacy of her last stroke. The goiter danced and bobbed.

'Now, now, Auntie Rosa, I agree with you,' Martin Welborn said. 'I think Bonnie's alive somewhere.'

'She *is*, Sergeant Welborn! She's alive and she knows we're searching for her!'

As she said it a cat chased a kitten across Al Mackey's feet, making him shiver. Goddamn spooky old dame!

'Is she . . . being harmed, Auntie Rosa?' Martin Welborn asked quietly.

Then the old woman started to cry. She wheezed and sniffled and wiped her nose on her sleeve. 'I believe she's being harmed, Sergeant Welborn. She calls, but it's like a very strange siren's song. Like . . . like she *wants* us to come, but there's *danger* all around her. Like there's a breathing burning force that lurks. That waits for *us*, Sergeant Welborn!'

'That child's dead,' Al Mackey said, but they didn't seem to hear.

'Now, now, Auntie Rosa,' Martin Welborn said, when the old woman's palsy got so violent she started spilling her tea.

'The devil is a raging lion, Sergeant Welborn!'

'I don't know, Auntie Rosa,' Martin Welborn said soothingly, as he patted her liver-spotted hand. 'I think he may just be a dumb little coyote. *If* he exists at all.'

'Oh, he's real, Sergeant Welborn. He's *real!*'

'Let's hope so,' Martin Welborn said, still patting the old woman's hand. 'Life would be unbearable if we didn't have the devil, now wouldn't it?'

The old woman oozed a raspy wheeze of a laugh, and said, 'You're absolutely right, Sergeant Welborn. Life would be *hell* without the devil.'

'If you hear or see anything, just *anything* of Bonnie Lee Brewster, you call me, Auntie Rosa. At the station or at home. Day or night. Anytime.'

'You're a fine boy, Sergeant Welborn,' Auntie Rosa said. The palsy diminished as the detectives rose to leave.

'Thanks, but I'm just a fair-to-middling detective. I need your help.'

'We'll find Bonnie, Sergeant Welborn,' Auntie Rosa said, her goiter buttery in the lamplight. 'No . . . she'll find us!'

When they were driving back toward the station, Al

Mackey said, 'Anyplace else you'd like to go now, Marty? The ding ward at the Veterans' Hospital, maybe? Course even there we might not find anybody as nutty as Auntie Rosa to talk to. Maybe we should see an astrologer? How about we go on *The Gong Show*?'

'I'd like to go to the bowling alley parking lot one more time, Al. I want to pace it off. I want to talk to the employees.'

'The employees? They've been interviewed and reinterviewed. They closed early. They saw nothing, Marty. Nigel St Claire didn't know bowling balls from elephant's nuts, for chrissake!'

'Okay, let's just pace off the parking lot. Let's just . . . get a *smell* of the area.'

And that's the kind of detective Marty had become, and that was exactly the *wrong* kind of detective to be, in Al Mackey's opinion. He said, 'Marty, deductive thinkers solve crimes. You and Basil Rathbone always agreed on that. Mystics belong in dark bedrooms up in Laurel Canyon floating in homemade tanks of Jello with all those out-of-work actors looking for their life force. The only cop I know that solves crimes sniffing the air works with the airport detail and has four legs, a bushy tail, and bad breath.'

But Martin Welborn just chuckled in his good-humored way, and Al Mackey looked at his partner's smooth boyish jaw and barely graying hair and dry steady hands, and realized that Marty looked maybe ten years younger than *he* did. And maybe it was he, not Marty, who was going to end up in Laurel Canyon with his saffron nightgown and his hair full of forget-me-nots. Christ, he and Marty were turning into the yin and yang of mental health!

The buildings hung against the sky in what looked like lovely storm light. But it was only the deadly silver particles of smog. Martin Welborn paced off the bowling alley parking lot, taking copious notes, pausing to examine cars, pedestrians, traffic volume, while Al Mackey dodged the flying squads of roller skaters who float about the street of Hollywood like the ghosts in Auntie Rosa's visions. Some of the skaters wore transistor headsets and boogied to new-wave or punk rock. In fact, some of the skaters were dressing punk. A young man with an earphone radio wore satin skating shorts and his torso gleamed with play knife-wounds that must have taken hours of makeup work. He flew across the parking lot, disco skating with a partner who wasn't there. The young man wore nothing on his upper body except feathers and a leather bra.

Another skater, this one a woman, suddenly appeared from the west side of the parking lot, a shaggy blur in the sunlight, and jumped over a Suzuki motorbike that was chained to the perimeter fence. Of course, the skate-boarders around town did all kinds of leaping tricks, but Al Mackey had not thought it possible to make those leaps with heavy shoe skates. She wore a leotard with one leg zebra-striped and the other hot pink. Her top, a see-through plastic that made her sweat like a pig, had two daisy-shaped pasties over her nipples, making her one of the more modestly attired of the parking lot new-wave skaters.

Al Mackey was starting to get hunger pangs when he noticed that fifty yards away across the vast parking lot Marty was talking to a group of more conventional skaters. The conversation lasted a surprisingly long time and several others joined the group to talk with Marty.

Al Mackey had never particularly understood his partner in the years they'd worked together. But before Marty's separation from Paula they had seen each other socially at least once a week.

Since he had never had children with either ex-wife, Al Mackey realized that now, in early middle age (God, he hated the sound of it), Martin Welborn was probably the only person in the world he gave a damn about. Marty was one of those people you could never imagine anyone *not* liking. Even Marty's ex-wife, Paula, must have cared for him at one time. Paula Welborn was an intelligent, handsome woman. Al Mackey hated her guts.

Al Mackey saw Paula Welborn as one of those cunts who figured she'd married beneath her, finding herself as she did with a diffident young cop who was overtrained by Jesuits in dead languages, mummified philosophy, and dying theology, all stirred into a nice steaming mulch. Water it daily with a cauldron of guilt and let's see what grows in God's Garden.

Of course, if Paula had grown up in Plains, Georgia, and managed to hook up with old Teeth and Prayers himself, she'd still have thought that she'd married beneath her. She was that kind of bitch.

Al Mackey sweltered in the sunshine, and wiped his smog-inflamed eyes, and thought that Paula Welborn was one of those broads who flirted with half the men at a cocktail party (never with Al Mackey – is *that* why he hated her from the start?) and then, when a drunken lieutenant or captain or commander made a play (she seldom wasted time turning sergeants' dicks hard), would run to Marty and cuddle up next to him like a big cat, and show the gang that they may as well go to The Glitter Dome or settle for their momma's old bones.

She was also one of those who, on infrequent nights between Al Mackey's first divorce and his oh-so-brief marriage number two – when Al Mackey was a tetherfall of rage and confusion getting slapped around the financial maypole by lawyers – would *concede* to Marty's dinner invitations to Al Mackey. And she'd make the concession clear enough at some point during the night when Marty was out of the room tending to the homework problems of their teenaged daughters, Babs and Sally.

And even though she made sure Al Mackey knew how she felt about Marty's invitations, wouldn't she often have to go to the john, and start unzipping her jeans in front of Al as she walked out of the room? She was just that kind of bitch, all right. But, on the rare occasions he even mentioned her, Marty claimed they were relatively happy until her mid-life crisis blew the ship of wedlock right out of the freaking water.

And there was the other thing: Marty's religious crisis, which Al Mackey could only guess at. Marty had left the seminary three years before he would have been ordained, but he never talked about it and he never talked about his mother's response to the Quantum Leap over the wall. In fact, he never talked about religion, although Al Mackey's parents were from Ireland and he had some curiosity about The Faith. Thankfully, they were from the North. He hated priests. Imagine if he was a guilt-ridden mick, what with a genetic enzyme dysfunction that made all Celts latent alcoholics. Al Mackey had recently become involved in morbid studies of *that* disease.

Marty would never talk about those bad old days with the Jesuits and resisted any efforts on Al Mackey's part to learn about his past. Al Mackey might broach the subject by saying, 'You know I like the way this new Pope carries himself. He's the first priest I haven't figured to be a rest-area Romeo.'

And Marty would smile and say, 'He has a moosh that belongs on a leg-breaker, all right.'

And Al Mackey would say, 'Yeah, and he's in direct line with Jesus Christ.'

And Marty would say, 'Yeah, and he's *Polish*.'

And that was all. There would be no more talk of the Pope's moosh, or Marty's religious crisis, which Al Mackey guessed was severe. And only once did Martin Welborn refer to his family in Ohio. It was on Mother's Day, and Al Mackey was just finishing up the second oh-so-quick marriage to that cunt who not only busted his balls but jumped up and down on them with cleats, leaving him as bankrupt as Chrysler Corporation.

Al Mackey brought a bouquet of carnations to the Welborns that day and explained to Paula that it was customary to wear a pink one in your lapel if your mother is alive. If she's dead, you wear white. Al Mackey would never forget that day, because when he and Marty were waiting for Paula and the two girls to get ready for their big Mother's Day outing on Restaurant Row, Al Mackey broke a pink carnation from the bouquet and offered it to Marty. Al Mackey knew that Marty's mother was alive and well in Ohio, yet Marty looked at him with those long brown eyes just for an instant, and Marty broke off a white carnation and pinned it to the lapel of his suit coat.

Al Mackey never asked another question about Martin Welborn's mother.

Marty seemed to be finishing his talk with the skaters. He waved to Al Mackey, who was leaning against the fence on the other side of the parking lot watching a black kid skate between the rows of parked cars. *Backwards.*

Martin Welborn started toward his partner, but another skater whizzed by behind him and he only caught a glimpse peripherally as the boy disappeared below the roof line of the cars. He was smaller and younger than the rest. He was blond, and Martin Welborn found himself running around the car for a look. The boy was gone. The boy looked like Danny Meadows.

Danny Meadows called him Daddy. He said: Daddy? It was the only word Danny Meadows ever spoke to him: Daddy?

Babs still called him Daddy. Sally would call him Daddy forever. He was sure of that. Although she was older than Babs, she would never call him Dad. She would never call him Father.

No one would ever call him Father. It was unthinkable: Father Welborn. But clergymen had the lowest suicide rate in the nation, along with social workers. Doing good deeds apparently keeps people from chewing on guns. Policemen and doctors had the highest rate. Apparently being as useless as policemen and physicians is not good for longevity. Ninety percent of suicidal policemen use guns. Doctors use their own familiar weapons. To each his own. Most policemen who did it were passive men with inadequate personalities, they said. It seemed strange because police work does not attract passive men. He didn't know about the inadequate personalities.

Martin Welborn had known three Los Angeles policewomen who did it. All three policewomen went out like real guys. They ate their gun muzzles. They proved their machismo at the end.

116

One of the most ironic things about those few older officers — those very few who survived their attempts, those failures who survived and therefore were exceptionally inadequate policemen, because no adequate policeman should ever survive a manly attempt — those survivors invariably stated that they experienced a strange and overwhelming anxiety. The anxiety was that at any moment one might have to deal with unknown or terrible situations. It was most ironic because it was the thrill of meeting the unknown which drew young men to the job. Yet it was the thing that most terrified the older policemen when they were well on their way to a dreadful destiny. It was very ironic.

One of the policewomen who did it was a former partner of Martin Welborn. She was a passive personality, now that he thought of it. She was shy and beautiful. She had enormous eyes. Just like Danny Meadows.

'Will you snap out of it, Marty, for chrissake,' Al Mackey said to him. 'Marty!'

'Huh?'

A skater brazenly sailed between them, saying, 'Hop back, Jack.'

'I'm starving to death,' Al Mackey said. 'Let's go get something to eat. Jesus, you were just standing there with that thousand-yard stare again. You don't even *hear* anybody when they're talking to you. Jesus Christ, Marty!'

'I'm sorry, Al,' Martin Welborn said. 'I was just thinking . . .'

'Lemme guess. You figured out how I can turn this Nigel St Claire ballbreaker into a suicide. Tell me, quick. How?'

'That's not at all what I was thinking.' Martin Welborn smiled. 'Those skaters told me something interesting.'

'I like the guy with the checkerboard hair the best.' Al Mackey snorted. 'I saw him on *Batman* once.'

'They told me some things,' Martin Welborn said. 'Al, there's someone who might know what Nigel St Claire was *doing* in this parking lot the night he died.'

8

Gloria La Marr

Poor old Cal Greenberg was doing everyone's work today. Just his luck to come in the squadroom when everybody was out jerking off. All the brass was at some goddamn retirement luncheon for a commander in the valley. The sex detail, Ozzie Moon and Thelma Bernbaum, get sick on the same day and have to go home. (A likely frigging story!) Everyone but the chief of the police and Walter Cronkite knew that Ozzie and Thelma spent more time together wrestling with her panty girdle in Griffith Park than they *ever* spent working on their cases. Some sex detail. They were qualified experts, all right.

And then two bluesuits had to go and bring in a bubblegummer. 'I ain't no kiddy cop,' poor old Cal Greenberg moaned. 'Can't you put him somewheres till somebody *else* comes in?'

'Sure, Sarge,' said Buckmore Phipps. 'I can drop the little turd off the Capitol Records Building, you want me to.'

'I can dump the little turd on the Hollywood Freeway, you want me to,' said Gibson Hand.

Meanwhile the little turd, a twelve-year-old cookie bandit named Zorro Garcia, sat down and decided it was a toss-up between the big white cop and the big black cop as to which one would be likely to keep the vow they both made to grind him up in the big cement mixer over by the Cahuenga Hardware Store.

But it became readily apparent to Zorro Garcia that the detective had more authority than the two street monsters and that he had more or less slid in safe at home. Zorro Garcia was a peewee member of the Black Spider Gang.

When he was old enough he hoped to be a *cherry*, then a *cutdown*, then finally, after he'd been shot and stabbed ten times and was too old to fight, a *veterano*.

As with many barrio youngsters, his buzzword was *barely*. Zorro Garcia decided to flex his macho little muscles with an opening statement to poor old Cal Greenberg: 'Sir, these officers barely advised me of my rights. And I barely had time to pay for the Life Savers. And I barely got in the store when this dude started hassling me. And he barely gimme a chance to talk. I couldn't barely say nothing. I don't think the dude likes Met-sicans. Cause I go to him, I go: "Do you like Met-sicans?" And he goes, "Not too much." So then I just barely made up my mind.'

Poor old Cal Greenberg sighed and leaned forward over the table, stretching his suspenders, and said, 'What, may I ask, did you just *barely* decide to do?'

'I barely decided to file a class action lawsuit for all Met-sicans in the Black Spiders against that store and against the Los Angeles Police Department.'

'How old are you?' poor old Cal Greenberg asked.

'Twelve. Barely.'

'Why are you a cookie bandit?' poor old Cal Greenberg asked. 'Are you hungry?'

'I was. I ain't now.'

Buckmore Phipps sat down at the vacant table of the sex detail and absently leafed through a book of photographs, hoping to find some shots of naked women.

Gibson Hand stuck three sticks of gum in his mouth and said, 'Zorro goes in the gud-damn market every day and pulls the same scam.' Then Gibson Hand produced a beer opener and a tablespoon which he had confiscated from the cookie bandit. 'He roams through that store and eats about a thousand bucks worth a cupcakes and ice cream, and especially Famous Amos chocolate chip cookies cause he's got expensive tastes. And then he washes it down with about two cases a Seven-Up and then comes burpin and fartin through the checkstand with his little belly poochin out and spends a few dimes on some Life Savers.'

119

'Only reason the dumb shits at the checkstands ever catch these cookie bandits is they eat so much they turn chartreuse and kinda stand out in the crowd,' Buckmore Phipps added.

And the little outlaw logged *that* one away in his book of experience. Don't be a pig and turn weird colors. It's quality, not quantity.

'Oh, I wish you wouldn't do these things,' poor old Cal Greenberg said. 'Because I'm too old to play like a kiddy cop. Tell me, do you do well in school?'

'Sure,' Zorro Garcia said. 'Joo think I want to grow up to be a co . . .' And then he stopped and looked at Buckmore Phipps' jaws tighten and Gibson Hand's nostrils flare. 'Joo think I want to grow up to be a . . . *con*vict or something?'

'If I let you go home, do you promise not to go in that store and barely eat half a ton of groceries again?' poor old Cal Greenberg asked. It was the music. When *In the Mood* and *Tuxedo Junction* were on the Hit Parade, *nobody* went into stores and gobbled a thousand bucks worth of chocolate chip cookies.

'I don't get to go to Juvenile Hall?' the cookie bandit cried dejectedly. *All* the midgets and tinys in the Black Spiders had been to the Hall. Most of the peewees even! It was getting embarrassing.

'If I do send you to Juvenile Hall will you promise not to go in that store and eat a ton of groceries?' poor old Cal Greenberg asked.

'I'll think it over,' the cookie bandit said. 'I wooden mind a *weekend* in the Hall.'

'And we get to take you there, you little *turd*,' Buckmore Phipps leered, and the bandit decided then and there who Buckmore Phipps reminded him of: that dude on *The Incredible Hulk*. The green one. 'I don't think I want to go to Juvenile Hall after all,' the cookie bandit said. 'I won't go in *that* store no more.'

Poor old Cal Greenberg was old enough to know that

life is, after all, one big compromise. He settled. 'Okay, it's a deal. We're gonna let you go home.'

'Home? Home? Gud-damn!' Gibson Hand roared, jumping to his feet and towering over the now quivering cookie bandit, who gaped up at that snarling black face. 'Home, my ass! I wanna take this little turd over to the Cahuenga Hardware Store. And grind him up in the cement mixer until he's taco meat! And put him in a manure bag and send him to those wetback farmworkers to spread on all that boycotted lettuce. I wonder how that spic prick Cesar Chavez would like that?' Then he lowered his scowling face until they were nose to nose. 'And every . . . fuckin . . . time I eat a tostada I could think a this little turd when I grind up that lettuce in my teeth!'

Poor old Cal Greenberg knew that the trembling cookie bandit hadn't a clue as to who the hell Cesar Chavez was, but the fact that the street monster was scaring the cupcakes out of him was good enough. 'There's just one more thing,' the detective added. 'If I let you go home, you also gotta promise not to pursue a class action lawsuit against the police department. We got enough troubles these days.'

And while that further condition was being considered, the door burst open, and Schultz and Simon came thundering in with a much bigger problem. 'Greenberg, are you the acting watch commander today?'

'I guess so,' poor old Cal Greenberg moaned. The only reason he hadn't taken his thirty-year pension long ago was that he'd have to be home all the time with his second wife, and not be able to sneak off to the senior citizens' dances and fool around with his first wife, who had turned into a firecracker after she dumped him.

'This here's Gloria La Marr,' Schultz said. 'And we got a big problem for ya.'

Their problem was a big one all right, about six foot six. Gloria La Marr was a transsexual whom Schultz and Simon had just extradited from Nevada as a favor for the vacationing robbery team. She was a natural blonde (she claimed) and had good-sized breast implants, but not nearly big enough to go with her height. She did, however, have excellent legs, and Schultz, who was six foot five himself, had told Gloria La Marr on the airplane that he always looked for nice pins on tall girls and found them very seldom. Gloria La Marr had blushed and asked Schultz if he'd order her another Bloody Mary from the stewardess, and Simon sat across the aisle, squeezing his 280 pounds into an economy class seat, and decided that Schultz should retire on a medical pension now that he had gone fruitcake.

But even Simon had to admit one thing: Gloria La Marr *did* have a groovy pair of wheels.

The problem was where to book her. And when Schultz escorted Gloria La Marr out of the squadroom and down the hall to the women's restroom, it was heaped on poor old Cal Greenberg.

'I don't see no problem,' poor old Cal Greenberg said to Simon, as the elephantine detective took off his plaid sportcoat, scratched his wrinkled crotch, and gave his crewcut a massage to return the circulation after the miserable plane ride.

'It's a problem, Cal,' Simon whispered, making sure that Schultz and Gloria La Marr were well out of earshot. 'The first problem came when we went to the airport. Gloria refused to fly unless she could wear that black evening gown and Dolly Parton wig!'

'I think the dress is rather attractive,' poor old Cal Greenberg shrugged. Age. Wisdom. *Compromise*.

'Yeah, well how would *you* like to lay over for two hours in Vegas with Gloria La Marr, and everybody staring at ya? And the airlines, a course, won't let you handcuff prisoners, and the airport security won't let you make no fuss when Gloria La Marr has to go to the john, and you don't know *which* john! How would you like to make those decisions?'

'So what did you do?'

'Everything Gloria demanded, is what we did. It was

better than taking a bus clear from Vegas! Or renting a car and running into the same problems every time she had to take a leak somewhere along the trip. That broad's got a bad bladder.'

'I still don't see the big problem,' poor old Cal Greenberg said, noting that the crotch of Simon's double knits was ripping out from his ordeal. Those sweaty tree-trunk thighs couldn't be contained in one pair of pants for two days.

'I just ask you how would you like to be walking through airports with big Gloria swishing around in that black gown and Dolly Parton wig and those spike heels which make her about seven feet tall? Schultz walked ten paces in front and I walked fifteen feet behind.'

'Sounds like you pulled it off admirably,' poor old Cal Greenberg said. 'I still don't see . . .'

'But Schultz started getting *chummy* with Gloria on the airplane!' Now Simon pulled his chair close to poor old Cal Greenberg's and whispered, which frustrated Buckmore Phipps, and Gibson Hand, and especially Zorro Garcia.

'So? Schultz can get her phone number for when she gets out of the joint,' poor old Cal Greenberg said. Nothing surprised him these days. A cop asking a transsexual for her phone number. *Pennsylvania 6-5000*. Where *are* you, Glenn Miller?

'But that ain't the problem!' Simon cried in frustration.

'Well, before I qualify for social security, which ain't gonna be long, I would like you to *try* to tell me what *is* the problem.'

'The problem is *where* to book her?'

'Well that ain't no problem at all,' poor old Cal Greenberg said. 'Is *that* what's troubling you? Look, Simon, this is modern times. I don't care if Gloria La Marr used to be Slug MacGuire. I don't care if she was a linebacker for the Green Bay Packers. I don't care if she fought Joe Frazier. And won. That was when she was a man. Far as I'm concerned, she's just a tall broad now. Vanessa Redgrave's a tall broad. My ex-wife is a tall broad.' (He paused and thought of that hot number igniting all those other gray panthers at the Stardust Ballroom.) 'Gloria is . . . *peculiar*-looking, I admit. But all you gotta remember is that she's just a tall, funny-looking *broad*. So you take her and book her at S.B.I.'

The Los Angeles women's jail, Sybil Brand Institute, is perched high up over the San Bernardino Freeway. The cops called it Fanny Hill.

Simon listened patiently, but pained. When poor old Cal Greenberg was finished he said, 'Now I'm gonna give you the good news and bad news. The good news is that Gloria has a pretty nice set a knockers, all right. And dynamite legs. And she ain't got no balls. The *bad* news is, she ain't had her *second* operation yet. She still has her dick!'

'Oh,' poor old Cal Greenberg said. 'Are you sure?'

'Sure? Well I didn't get down there and look! But the jailer in Nevada told me.'

'Goddamnit, why is she doing it *that* way?'

'Why?' Simon sputtered. 'Why?'

'Yeah, *why*?' Zorro Garcia piped up from the corner of the squadroom. Buckmore Phipps and Gibson Hand were likewise staring at Simon. *Everyone* demanded an answer.

'Why?' Simon fumed. 'I don't *know* why! How the fuck could I find out *anything*? Schultz monopolized her on the airplane. Buying her those Bloody Marys. I bet she's in there pissing tomato juice right now! Seated, a course.'

'In the *ladies'* room,' poor old Cal Greenberg mumbled. Why didn't Gloria have the whole operation done at once? Did the croaker discover in the middle of surgery that she hadn't paid his last bill? Did Gloria hate to part with it? Did she want the *worst* of both worlds? *The White Cliffs of Dover. Pennsylvania six, five, oh oh oh.*

'They ain't gonna accept nobody up on Fanny Hill with a cock, even if it don't work,' Gibson Hand observed.

'That's true,' poor old Cal Greenberg agreed.

'But you put her down in the men's lockup, she'll end up

with all the cigarettes in the jail,' Buckmore Phipps observed.

'That's also true,' poor old Cal Greenberg agreed.

When Schultz and Gloria La Marr came back from the restroom, she settled the problem. She said she preferred the men's jail because she was so tall that women tended to stare at her.

'But Gloria, there's a lot a *animals* down there,' Schultz cried, and Simon decided to take Schultz up to the police academy for a jog around the track and a steam bath, and maybe beat the shit out of him on the wrestling mat to get his head straightened out.

When two bluesuits came to take her down to the men's jail Gloria was fluttering like a big hummingbird, and calling Schultz by his Christian name, and promising she'd plead guilty in court to the strong-arm robbery (which had occurred *before* her transsexual period), so as not to cause him any more trouble. She shook hands warmly with Schultz before the bluecoats handcuffed her and took her away.

'Bye, Gloria,' Schultz said sadly.

'Bye, Gunther,' Gloria said demurely.

'Joo know something?' Zorro Garcia observed. 'If those two get married they could have some kids big as King Kong, barely.'

After Schultz and Simon processed their extradition waiver and other paper work on Gloria La Marr, they were shocked to discover they still had three hours until end of watch. Simon told Schultz this goddamn efficiency had to stop. It was making for a long day.

But Schultz, who was usually Simon's equal in bitching, whining and complaining, was strangely quiet as they drove back to Hollywood from downtown.

'What's the problem – you thinking about Gloria?' Simon sneered, looking up from the traffic at his partner.

'I'm thinking about the Billings case,' Schultz said.

'Why'd you have to bring that up, for chrissake?'

'It won't go away,' Schultz said.

Samuel Billings was a gas station owner. He had a swell location right on Cole Avenue. Schultz and Simon knew him slightly from having handled a prior robbery where he was held up by a gentle gunman who only motherfucked him and pushed him around, but didn't pistol-whip him or kick him or stab him or shoot him. He was netting nearly two thousand dollars a month, and seldom got beaten out of it by the hordes of Hollywood marauders with guns who understood Samuel Billings perfectly.

Samuel Billings had been a Little League father, an Optimist, a PTA member. He had two boys in college, supported his mother-in-law, and had it by the tail. Until he started feeling guilty about all that good fortune, which wasn't fortune at all but came as a result of his working sixteen hours a day on days he thought he was taking it easy.

So he joined the local Give-a-Con-a-Break Program and hired Wilfred James Boyle, who was only six months out of Soledad and was already sick and tired of this eight-to-five bullshit on the grease rack. How could he kick back when he had to worry about things like paying utility bills? Or getting a driver's license? How could a dude mellow out when he had to remember to give his landlady a money order once a month? How could he stand even *buying* that fucking money order once a month? And income tax! This year (if he stayed on the street long enough) he would have to file his first W-2. The thought of it filled him with such frustration and rage that he felt like screaming and yelling and maybe running right down Cole Avenue with his stuff hanging out. Or maybe grab the cunt of the next woman who came in to ask for two dollars and fifty cents worth of gas. Or punch out the next sissy that wheeled in on his bicycle and came sashaying up to ask if he would blow up his tire.

Wilfred James Boyle had cut out from *his* boring working-class family scene in Tulsa when he was fifteen years old. He'd been in eleven jails and prisons in the

126

intervening eighteen years, and the worst of them, Folsom, was better than that boring fucking house in Glendale where Samuel Billings lived with his boring wife and his boring kids and thought he was in hog heaven. And, in that he was an intelligent sociopath, Wilfred James Boyle understood the handicap that Samuel Billingses of this world are so proud of: conscience. To Wilfred James Boyle it was like being born with a clubfoot, and Samuel Billings *bored* him by preaching about how lucky a guy is to have it!

Like three quarters of recidivist sociopaths who live most of their lives behind stone walls and barbed wire, Wilfred James Boyle needed his own kind of Perfect Order. Which prison provided. And when he was on the streets during his 'leaves of absence' – that is, between convictions – he needed *action*. And it was as simple and as complicated as that: Take my liberty or give me . . . action. A high. A rush. A kick.

Schultz and Simon believed that initially he had never intended to shoot Samuel Billings. He probably had just come in from changing three tires, giving four lube jobs, helping with a minor tune-up, and said fuck it, his own motor was out of tune. He had to get his head straight.

He probably just took a look at Samuel Billings' own ·38 revolver, which he stupidly kept locked in the office cabinet where they stashed the oil filters and spark plugs. Stupid, because even though Samuel Billings had been a quarter-master on Guam during the big war and was a loyal Legionnaire who attended most of the meetings and all the conventions, he would probably just have gotten himself killed sooner if he'd tried shooting it out with the gentle junkie who had robbed him on the other occasion.

So Schultz and Simon figured that Samuel Billings, splattered with crank-case oil, thinking of the meat loaf and mashed potatoes he was going to stuff in that ample belly, just couldn't believe it when he found Wilfred James Boyle about to clean out his safe and say bye-bye Billings.

Samuel Billings had probably tried to reason with the younger man, and even if Wilfred James Boyle had been able to articulate his feelings about institutional life, and action, it's doubtful that Samuel Billings would have been able to believe that his faithful employee, his protégé, his friend, would ever hurt him. Since Wilfred James Boyle had been a student in eleven schools of very hard knocks, he wasn't about to ever reveal to the cops what did happen. But perhaps when Samuel Billings saw that persuasion was useless he made a grab for his own gun in the young man's hand. Probably not to save the three thousand dollars, but to save the young man.

When Schultz and Simon arrived on the scene, the money and Wilfred James Boyle were well on their way to Tijuana, where Wilfred James Boyle discovered in two weeks that when Mexicans catch you robbing somebody they throw you in prisons that make Folsom look like the Bel-Air Hotel. And if you blow away the Mexican counterpart of Samuel Billings, they offer you a cigarette and a blindfold. So Wilfred James Boyle crossed back into San Diego, robbed another gas station, got caught by the C.H.P., and ended up in the frustrated paws of Schultz and Simon.

The gun that had been left next to Samuel Billings' dying body by Wilfred James Boyle was picked up by the first policeman on the scene, who, out of curiosity, opened the cylinder and closed it again. Which wouldn't have been a calamity except that since Samuel Billings expired thirty minutes into surgery, Wilfred James Boyle, being the only living witness, claimed he was just planning to rob his employer. The boss grabbed the gun and he tussled with Samuel Billings and one shot was fired accidentally into Samuel Billings' belly. What Wilfred James Boyle forgot in the excitement was that the old ammunition *misfired*. There were two misfires and one round fired. However, since the first bluecoat on the scene had opened and closed that cylinder, obscuring the firing order, Schultz and Simon could never prove that on some other occasion Samuel Billings hadn't tried to pop a couple of caps at a cat or a rat (the hypothesis of the defense), leaving two misfires in the gun. Thus the defense destroyed Schultz and Simon's contention that Wilfred James Boyle ruthlessly pulled the trigger *three* times, and three times is *no* accident, Wilfred baby.

But as juries are wont to do, they bought Wilfred James Boyle's story, and he was acquitted of the murder of Samuel Billings. And he plea-bargained his robbery down to a grand theft after the judge, who had only gotten senile in the last few years, agreed that the revolver might easily have been used by Samuel Billings on a prior occasion to shoot at rats on Cole Avenue, even though Schultz got on the stand and pleaded with the jury to believe that the rats hanging around Cole Avenue that time of night didn't necessarily have whiskers and big ears, almost causing the judge to declare a mistrial on the spot.

And this was the same judge that Schultz used to admire so much. In fact, many's the time he fondly remembered a day when the judge slapped a thousand-dollar fine on a Sunset Boulevard player just for kicking the crap out of his main momma, even though she appeared in court and told the judge she kind of liked it once in a while to keep her in line. The pimp grinned that day and shuffled around on his platforms and pulled open that plum velvet vest and reached inside to the pocket on that $150 Gianni Versace linen shirt, saying, 'Shee-it, Judge. I got that much in my puck-it!'

And the judge grinned back at him and said: 'Now reach in that other puck-it and give me thirty days!'

But now the judge was senile and another of Schultz's heroes had bitten the dust. The thing that Schultz took away from the Billings case, and which even Simon thought of from time to time, was Samuel Billings lying on the floor of the gas station. Maybe knowing him from the first robbery made it . . . different. He was bleeding from the mouth and turning gray, but he kept looking at that little hole in that big belly with fear and grief in his eyes. And then he'd look at Schultz with The Question unspoken.

Schultz knew that bullet had kicked around and done

severe damage, with all that blood coming out of Samuel Billings' mouth, but he kept patting him on the shoulder and answering The Question with a lie: 'You got nothing to worry about, Sam. Hell, you're gonna be on your feet tomorrow morning. Just a scratch. Yes, sir.'

The thing that Schultz seemed unable to let go of was the look on Samuel Billings' face just before he faded into the coma. The look that said: You're a liar.

'I don't wanna try to explain to Mrs Billings why Wilfred James Boyle only got convicted of grand theft,' Shultz said. 'I'm too tired.'

Simon glanced quickly at his partner and he *did* seem tired. His crewcut was growing out and he was losing his militant look.

'You'll feel better after you get a couple drinks down at The Glitter Dome after work,' said Simon, driving off the freeway ramp in moderate afternoon smog.

'I also been feeling bad lately that we couldn't a done better on the Nigel St Claire case. I hated having a case taken away from us like that.'

'I don't feel bad about nothing,' said Simon. 'Nothing. I still get my paycheck twice a month. You just need . . .'

'I need a pension,' Schultz said. 'I wish I had my twenty in. I don't know if I can wait two more years.'

'You gotta get your head straightened out, boy.'

'Know what I saw in today's paper?' Schultz said, his voice flat and empty. 'The Alphabet Bomber is defending himself at his trial. He had a minister on the stand. Him and the minister got in a *theological* discussion, the paper said. Nothing makes sense no more. The minister was one a the guys had his leg blown off by the bomber.'

'So?'

'So what *difference* does it make if Wilfred James Boyle got three years for offing Sam Billings? I ain't got nothing to say to Mrs Billings.'

'Then don't *say* nothing,' Simon scowled. 'I'm getting sick a all this sob-sister shit anyway. You gotta get your head straightened out. You keep up this crybaby crap you're gonna be a fruitcake like Gloria. I'm warning ya, boy.'

So Schultz decided to keep the confusion and crybaby crap to himself, and suggested to Simon that they spend the last three hours of their duty tour in The Glitter Dome. Hell, they deserved it after the arduous extradition of Gloria La Marr.

And so they did. And they were *six* hours overtime when they checked in that night. Five minutes after they entered the empty squadroom a reporter at the Parker Center pressroom received a rather incoherent telephone call from someone identifying himself as Sgt. Schultz of Hollywood Detectives. The caller reported sighting an unidentified flying object hovering three hundred feet over the famous Hollywood sign on the hill.

When a young reporter came bitching to Captain Woofer the next morning about his wild-goose chase in Hollywood hills, a bleary-eyed Schultz denied any knowledge of the phone call and threatened to sue the newspaper for libel.

The Weasel shrugged and said, 'Shit, this ain't no biggy. Schultz sees a UFO *every* time he leaves The Glitter Dome. What's the press gonna say when they find *that* out?'

9

Mr Wheels

The roller rink on Friday night was even more garish than The Glitter Dome. Al Mackey got a headache the second they walked in the door. Someone kept alternating the stereo volume until you couldn't tell Kool and the Gang from the B-52's, and Al Mackey wished they'd just let it all out. The decibel fluctuation was more unbearable than the shattering level they eventually settled on.

The strobe lights were dumb and the fragmented mirrors were predictable, but what wasn't predictable was the skill of the skaters. They skated alone, they skated in pairs: boys with girls, girls with girls, boys with boys. They skated in trios and foursomes, same mixture. They skated in sinewy queues, and snake dances, and even cracked the whip like skaters of yore. But McCartney and Wings or Ambrosia kept everything frantic. The skaters had to stay electric or perish in the crush, so they got rewired every thirty minutes. The carpeted lobby was littered with fallen rainbows, dexis, bennies, ludes, speed, even some dust, though it had a bad rep these days, what with cops claiming that every dude they blew away was loaded on angel dust. It was getting so the people on the boulevard were saying when life gets too tough and you want to check out, just do a little dust and go out on the street – some cop'll obligingly shoot you.

And of course the smell of pot was everywhere. Al Mackey was getting high just sitting next to a skater who had been smoking joints nonstop since they arrived. But he wasn't about to change seats in the gallery. She wore velour shorts and a yellow tank top that was cut off about an inch below the natural drop of her breasts when standing. Now she was sitting. Al Mackey wasn't *about* to change seats.

Martin Welborn was roaming around the rink. Of course, he and Al Mackey looked like cops, being the only two men in business suits among the hundreds of skaters and spectators. But nobody seemed to mind. If they were narcs they *wouldn't* look like detectives, they'd look like the Weasel and Ferret, everyone knew that. And since most of the roller disco gang only did dope, they had no fear of the two detectives who were maybe Feds looking for somebody special.

It was hard to say how special he would be. When Martin Welborn had announced yesterday that he thought he knew of someone who might have seen Nigel St Claire in the bowling alley parking lot the night he expired, Al Mackey thought Marty had really pulled a good one from the old clues closet. It had made a lot of sense at the moment, but like so many good ideas it seemed to have outlived its time now that he sat here and saw at least a hundred skaters who could easily be their man.

According to the skaters at the bowling alley, the parking lot at night was a fabulous place to skate after ten o'clock when the lot emptied of cars. Even with poor lighting from the street, the new asphalt surface let you fly. And they said no one flew faster or later at night than *Mr Wheels*. He was a fearless skater (no knee pads, no elbow pads, no wrist braces) who would come wheeling through that lot backwards, his radio going full-out, singing loud enough with Boz Scaggs to draw frequent complaints from neighbors. And causing police cars to come by and make him tone it down. The field interrogation cards and moniker file had already been checked by Al Mackey and Martin Welborn for the nickname Mr Wheels. There were three 'Mr Wheels', none of them even close to the description of *their* Mr Wheels, who was about fifty-five years old, skinhead bald on top, and thinner than Al Mackey. Which meant that apparently none of the cops who got the complaints from residents near the bowling alley (and warned *their* Mr Wheels to keep the noise down) ever bothered to fill out an F.I. card on the midnight flash. The lazy pricks!

Of course Al Mackey and Marty could get on the horn at the rink and ask all the flyers to take off their wigs and hats, Al Mackey thought, and that would have been just about everybody in the place. If there was ever a wig and hat heaven, it was Hollywood, U.S.A., especially in a place as unisex as a rocking-out roller rink.

Just then the skater next to him turned to her left and passed a joint to a skater sitting in the seat behind her. She stayed twisted until he finished his second hit, and her *entire* right tit wobbled out the bottom of her tank top. Al Mackey decided Marty could roam around the rink all night.

Whether it was the air or what, Al Mackey started appreciating the flying circus. One slovenly skater in 1960s lowlife funk came blazing by doing flips right before his eyes. Others in Rodeo Drive pastel silks with coordinated knee pads and mint leather boots made incredible throws, catching their partners in mid-flight, somehow avoiding a trio of black hot dogs in black-on-black with black boots unlaced and turned down, letting their ankles move as though on ball bearings. They grooved and jived and danced through the others, hot-dogging at speeds that would have produced maiming or death if they had collided. It was absolutely amazing to Al Mackey. Nobody even got bumped by the black lightning bolts. They skated, flipped, twirled, leaped, spun, zigged in, zagged out, so close the satin sizzled when they flew by and almost sucked the old turtles into their jet stream.

And there were old turtles, all right. Some of them broke Al Mackey's heart. Middle-aged novices with lots of gold chains and slave bracelets, five years out of date, maybe recently divorced like Al Mackey, maybe from the San Fernando Valley like Al Mackey, maybe with a sex life as sad as Al Mackey's (though he doubted that), down here trying to beat the clock. Martin Welborn always said he didn't get frustrated with Latino witnesses like other detectives did when the witnesses screwed up court cases because of a cultural inability to grasp the concept of time. Martin Welborn said he envied Latinos their stubborn refusal to be *intimidated* by time.

But some of these old turtles were surely intimidated by it. And they were intimidated by the death squads hurtling by at blurring speeds, and Al Mackey was saddened, watching a rolling turtle gamely trying to skate backwards to impress some coked-out raspberry rocket in a molded-plastic Wonder Woman breastplate with her shorts sliding all the way up the valley of dreams. She didn't even *see* the old turtle when one of his jerky backward turns almost resulted in a bolt of black lightning striking him at thirty miles an hour. Which would have sailed him over the railing, crashing him into the walls of mirrors, and that would have taken his mind off hills and valleys and nylon wheels and put him into dental reconstruction and plastic surgery. It was fascinating but frightening to watch after a while, when you considered the possibilities.

Martin Welborn had momentarily stopped his search for the bald beanpole and was captivated with one of the solo skaters who held the center of the rink, all but oblivious to the giddy kaleidoscope encircling her. Her hair was pulled back into ropes of ash and pinned to stay put when she did her figures and slides. Ballet on roller skates. Martin Welborn hadn't thought it possible. She wore a champagne leotard and stockings and buff boots. She seemed to be skating for herself, deep in concentration. When she came to the rail to speak to someone in the gallery she smiled, and her teeth were as white as Martin Welborn's, which meant they were probably capped, but he could see she was nearly without makeup and her heavy eyebrows and matted lashes were her own. The body said twenty-five years old. The laugh, the voice, the lines by the eyes and mouth and on that lovely neck said thirty-five at least. Like all policemen, Martin Welborn looked straight at the hands.

The hands told many things and couldn't be camouflaged. They revealed the sex when it was in doubt, the age, and especially the intention. Watch the hands, the old-timers always said. Nobody can hurt you if you watch the hands.

And once, when Martin Welborn was a rookie walking a beat on Pico Boulevard, he broke up a fight in an Indian bar and watched the hands of a drunken brave so closely the Indian kicked him in the balls and put him in the hospital for two days, the exception that proved the rule. However, hands did reveal sex and age, and *usually* the intention.

Her hands were forty years old, but they were long and lovely. She looked at Martin Welborn, but didn't see him. He wondered what she did, if she was married, if she was alone. He hadn't been attracted to a woman so strongly since Paula had gone. He had never ceased being overwhelmingly attracted to Paula. She was the most desirable woman he had ever known, and now that she was gone every sexual fantasy, awake or asleep (and they were few), involved Paula. Strangely, he did not torture himself with fantasies of Paula with other men. He only thought of her with himself, where she belonged. Yet he had no illusions. She had left him forever.

There was something about this skater. She glided back to the center of the rink and resumed her difficult exercises.

At that moment Al Mackey jumped out of his seat and hustled toward the railing. He'd spotted a hairless scarecrow in magenta skates weaving in and out of a stream of girls who were dangerously cracking the whip. He was agile enough to skate under the arms of each girl, who held the waist of the girl in front of her. Only occasionally did he make a girl break her hold as he shot in and out. They all seemed to know him and held their little asses back, allowing him to make the seemingly impossible maneuver. Several of the people in the crowd applauded.

Al Mackey was wondering if Marty had spotted the skater, when another fifty-five-year-old stringbean flew by

Al Mackey's face in a russet-colored, Ted Nugent wild-man wig that trailed behind him like flames. Al Mackey realized that the russet rover could also be bald under there. It was futile.

When Al Mackey got up close to the railing and away from the obliterating cloud of marijuana smoke and the wobbly tits next door, there were dozens of them who *could* be Mr Wheels. Super-thin is in. Everyone was nearly as skinny as Al Mackey. After having sand kicked in his face all these years, he was in *style*. As long as he spent his life in Hollywood, U.S.A.

Then he saw Marty waving at him from across the gallery. They went up to the snack bar and had a cup of coffee and agreed it was hopeless.

'I asked the manager and at least a dozen of the hottest skaters if they knew Mr Wheels,' Martin Welborn said. 'No luck.'

'I talked to a few who knew a "Wheels" or a "Wheely" and even one who knew a "Mr Wheels", but he didn't come close to the description,' Al Mackey said.

'You want to go bowling?' Martin Welborn smiled.

'Marty, you don't wanna start hanging around that bowling alley parking lot every night, *do* you?'

'Just a couple nights?' Martin Welborn said. '*One* night, maybe?'

'For what? It's a long shot that Mr Wheels even *saw* anything.'

'There might be a connection. He's the only thing living and breathing in that parking lot at that time of night. Except for Nigel St Claire on *one* night.'

'We haven't determined for sure that Nigel St Claire *was* living and breathing when he arrived in that parking lot,' Al Mackey reminded him.

'You're going to have a *very* tough time proving he committed suicide.' Martin Welborn grinned.

'I'm working on it! I'm working on it!' Al Mackey said, as the girl with the tank top wiggled by. 'Jesus, let's get outa here, Marty, before I go bonzo and rent me a pair of skates and go down in flames the first trip around the floor chasing some coked-out cookie in cutoffs!'

'Okay, let's go home, my boy,' Martin Welborn said. 'But let's just stop by the parking lot for a few minutes.'

'Christ.'

'Just for a few minutes? We might get lucky.'

A few minutes turned into half an hour. And then an hour, as Al Mackey knew it would. They sat in the dark of the detective car and watched the empty parking lot.

'You know, Marty, you gotta stop taking police work so seriously,' he said. 'After all, you've got twenty years on the job. You're supposed to know better.'

'Nineteen years and eleven months,' Martin Welborn corrected him.

'I'm ready to go home. I've had it.'

'You've got a weekend to recuperate,' Martin Welborn said.

'What're you doing this weekend?'

'Oh, I think I'll just take it easy this weekend,' Martin Welborn said. 'Nice and easy.'

And though he did not know it at this moment, that was as far from the truth as a telephone call could take him. The telephone call would make it the most agonizing weekend of his recent life. It would be worse than the weekend when Paula moved out.

They saw the skater enter the parking lot from Gower Street. Or rather they saw a shadow moving faster than a man on foot could move. Both detectives got out of the car. The shadow moved closer and it was not shaped like Al Mackey and Mr Wheels. The shadow was shaped like Orson Welles.

The rotund skater did a few figure eights and puffed back out onto Gower, disappearing at Hollywood Boulevard.

'Let's *go*, Marty!' Al Mackey said, and Martin Welborn reluctantly nodded.

But when they arrived at the station Martin Welborn

got an idea. 'One minute, Al. Hang around just for a minute, okay?'

'*One* minute. If I don't get to The Glitter Dome before eleven o'clock on Friday, Wing gets nervous. Guys like Buckmore Phipps are more dangerous to steal from.'

'Just give me a minute,' Martin Welborn said, leaving Al Mackey in the empty squadroom, where he began putting away his cheap plastic briefcase and making the closing entries in the log. He was about to write their time in the sign-out sheet when Martin Welborn came running into the squadroom with that kid grin of his, which Al Mackey knew would make Wing very unhappy, forcing him to steal from somebody else tonight.

'Look at this, Al!' he said, showing him two F.I. cards, forcing Al Mackey to admit that the cops who were called to tell 'Mr Wheels' to keep the noise down weren't lazy pricks after all.

'I don't think it would've occurred to me,' Al Mackey admitted.

The skater's name was Griswold Weils. He had no moniker of Mr Wheels. It was just the natural mistake of skaters who, during casual nocturnal introductions while flying backwards through life in a bowling alley parking lot, thought he said *Wheels*, a natural handle for a skater. Hence, Mr Wheels.

They found Griswold Weils in a likely place: his apartment on Catalina Street, as correctly listed on the F.I. card. It was a typical Hollywood two-roomer which said that the unemployment compensation had nearly run out. He was indeed bald, as skinny as Al Mackey, and was exceedingly agitated at having *Friday Night at the Movies* interrupted by two cops who dropped in to talk about a murder. In fact, he was scared shitless and sat reeking of fear on the daybed while the detectives straddled kitchen chairs.

'I woulda called the cops, if I knew something to help ya!' Griswold Weils gnawed on smoke-brown knuckle

139

calluses. 'I never saw a body, honest I didn't. If I'd gone to the bowling alley that night and skated over Mister St Claire's corpse, don't you know I'd a called the cops!'

'You read about it?' Martin Welborn asked.

'A course I read about it,' Griswold Weils said. 'And I saw it on TV and everything.'

'Why are you so *scared*, Griswold?' Al Mackcy asked.

'I'm scared a cops.'

'How many times you been in jail?' Al Mackey asked.

'A couple times. Nothing much. Never in prison or anything.'

'What were you arrested for?'

'I did some . . . photography once. Twice.'

'What? Porn?' Al Mackey asked. 'Kiddy porn?'

'Yeah. Vice nailed me both times. I quit for good. Never made no money at it anyway.'

'What do you do for a living?' Martin Welborn asked.

'Cinematographer. I used to be. Made a few movies. Real movies, I mean. Features. Did some television. Got drinking too much.'

'Is that when you got involved making kiddy porn?'

'Twice,' Griswold Weils groaned. '*Twice*. I got busted both times. It was the booze. I been off the stuff for over a year. I been into skating. I discovered a talent I didn't know I had. At the age a fifty-two I discovered I'm a flyer! You should see me on skates. It's changed my life. I'm trying to get back into television. I was wonderful with a camera. I did three features! I was on my way before the booze got me. I'm making a comeback.'

When they *reek* of fear, a detective runs a bluff: 'How well did you know Nigel St Claire?' Martin Welborn asked suddenly.

'Officer! I swear to you. I never met Mister St Claire in my whole life. I swear to you!'

'You're lying,' Al Mackey said. And then, embellishing Marty's bluff, he added, 'Partner, I think it's time to advise Mister Weils of his constitutional rights.'

'For what?' Griswold Weils asked. 'For what?'

'We have to take you to the station,' Al Mackey said. 'We're investigating a murder. We have a witness who says that you know something about it. You're lying, so maybe you know *a lot* about it.'

'Witness? *What* witness?'

'Your mind's going, Griswold,' Al Mackey said. 'You think you're *me*. You're asking me the questions now.'

And then Griswold Weils got up off the daybed and sat down again. Got up and sat down yet another time. He looked as though he could skate right through the window. It was easy to imagine a man like Griswold Weils flying blissfully through empty parking lots in the black of night, outdistancing all the goblins chasing him in and out of bottles. He *reeked* of fear.

'Stop . . . your . . . *lying*!' Al Mackey said, more confidently now.

'I don't wanna go to the station,' Griswold Weils said. 'I last seen Mister St Claire, oh, maybe five years ago. About the time I shot my last feature. I never did see him when I was shooting TV commercials.'

'Why don't you just tell us *everything* and you'll feel lots better and you can catch the end of the movie after we go,' Martin Welborn said, getting up and turning off the portable set that Griswold Weils must have gotten in a Western Avenue junk shop.

'Well, I . . . it's *possible* I talked to him recently on the phone.'

'It's *possible* you talked to him,' Al Mackey said.

'I talked to *somebody*.' Griswold Weils was doing enough eye blinking, lip chewing, fist clenching, to make even the detectives fidgety. 'What did the witness *say* about me?'

'Let's just skate on down to the station,' Al Mackey said. 'You can talk plainer there. In a little room. No windows. No distractions.'

'Wait a minute, wait a minute!' Griswold Weils cried. 'I mean I talked to *somebody* on the phone who *might* a been Nigel St Claire. Kee-rist, I don't even remember what Mister St Claire's voice sounded like! Five years since I heard his voice. I only made the one feature at his studio. I was at the wrap party when he made us a speech. He came on the set maybe two, three times because it was a twelve-million-dollar show and that was a big feature five years ago. Today, they blow twenty million like I blow a deuce at the two dollar window. The business is ruined by the kid wonders.'

'Griswold, did the person who *could* have been Nigel St Claire telephone you here at your apartment?' Martin Welborn asked.

'Yes . . . no . . . kee-rist, I'm all mixed up! First, I got a letter through my guild and they forwarded it to me. No letterhead. Some so-called producer called himself . . . let's see, Mister Gold.'

'What's your guild called?'

'The International Photographers' Union, local six five nine.'

'Did you save the letter?' Al Mackey asked.

'No, then . . . let's see, the call came about three days later. I was here in the afternoon when *someone* called. He said he had a job for me. He told me that my work was the finest he'd seen in over forty years in the business. He said he was Mister Gold.'

'You said you once heard Nigel St Claire's voice five years ago,' Martin Welborn said.

'Yeah, at the wrap party for that one show I shot at his studio. No way I can say if his voice sounded like Mister Gold. Five years?'

'What else did he say?'

'He said he heard I had some hard times and he talked about the hard times.'

'What did he say *exactly*?' Martin Welborn asked.

Griswold Weils had stopped the blinking and biting, but he was still squirming around on the clammy daybed, sliding in and out of his ragged bedroom slippers. 'He talked about, you know, hearing I had some troubles with booze and that he hoped I licked it and I told him yes.

And then he mentioned, you know, the troubles I had with the law.'

'He talked about your arrests for making kiddy porn,' Al Mackey said.

'He knew. Course, lots a people knew. It was in the papers. Kept me from getting some jobs. I was drinking so much then I didn't know anamorphic from anaconda. Fact, I think I *saw* a few snakes one time looking through a lens. Roller skating saved my life.'

'What was the job he had for you?' Al Mackey asked.

'He never did say. He said he wanted to talk to me about it in person. Okay, I figured it *might* be kiddy porn but I can't even pay my rent!'

'Did he give you an appointment?'

'No, he said he'd meet me somewhere and talk about it.'

'Where?'

'I told him my address but he said he didn't want to come here. Then I . . . I told him, let's meet in the bowling alley parking lot across the street where I skate most every night.'

'You met the night that Nigel St Claire was found dead,' Martin Welborn said, and there was no concealing the excitement now. Even Al Mackey was catching it.

'I *swear* to you I never saw nobody! I showed up just like the telephone voice said, after the bowling alley closed. I skated in and nobody was there. Living or dead, nobody was there. There was no car there. I listened to my radio and skated, oh, maybe half an hour and nobody showed up. I thought maybe it was some kind a sick joke. I just figured some prick was playing a sick joke and kicking me when I was down.'

'Who would kick you when you were down?' Martin Welborn asked.

'Nobody I can think of,' Griswold Weils said. 'I thought maybe Pete Flowers, the guy I shot the porn shows for. I go to jail and *he* gets mad about it cause he lost some money. But that don't make sense. Pete ain't been around for a while. And then Mister St Claire's body is found the next day! And I figure, my God! what if it was Nigel St Claire on the phone who made that date with me? Or what if he was with the guy who called? But I thought the best thing for me is to shut up and mind my own business cause I don't know nothing about it anyway, and I'm just getting my chance to get back in The Business. I might get to shoot a commercial next month, everything works out right.'

'Would Nigel St Claire be involved in kiddy porn?'

'No way!' Griswold Weils said. 'For what? Mister St Claire is a big man. A millionaire! What's he need with those kind a problems? He could buy a whole boatload a kiddy porn he wanted it for himself. Is a man like Mister St Claire gonna risk his position to make a few bucks in kiddy porn? You believe that, how about him dealing dope? Maybe he's gonna start running opium outa Pakistan? Mister St Claire? Does it make sense?'

'Not much,' Martin Welborn agreed. 'So what do you suppose he was doing in the parking lot?'

'I *can't* figure it!' Griswold Weils cried. 'All I can do is shoot movies and skate! He wanted skating lessons, he could buy his own rink! I can't figure it. So I decided to stay out of it. I never been involved in anything like this and I'm too old to start. But you know what? I *never* went back to that bowling alley parking lot to skate. I just can't go there and think about Mister St Claire laying there like they described it in the papers. And whoever killed him, I don't want to know nothing about, or have him know about me. Please don't let anybody know I talked to you!'

'You must be curious to know what Mister Gold wanted,' Al Mackey said.

'Not that curious,' Griswold Weils said. 'But I'm curious who the witness is that said I was connected with Mister St Claire's dead body. Who told you I was there that night?'

'Tell me,' said Martin Welborn, 'when you got in trouble making the kiddy porn . . .'

'They were *seventeen* years old, for chrissake!' Griswold

Weils said. 'One a those sluts looked thirty! Kiddies, my . . .'

'When you got arrested,' Martin Welborn continued, 'who did the technical work with you? I mean, when you make films don't you need lighting men and so forth?'

'A gaffer. I used to be a gaffer before I got into photography. Then I was a focus puller, then a camera operator. I was even a grip for a while in the old days. Hell, you don't need a real crew to make the kind a shit that got me busted. I did everything. We just rented the camera and lights. The so-called director was a pimp. My hands were shaking so much from the booze you could see the boom mike in every frame. I did terrible work. I'm glad they busted me both times, tell you the truth. Even without my real name on the credits I wouldn't want anybody to see that kind a bad photography. If I shot *real* kiddy porn I'd want it to be right. I'm an artist. First, last, always.'

'An artist,' Al Mackey said.

'And that's all I know about Mister St Claire's death. Now can I turn the movie back on? I used to work with the director of photography who shot it. I'm making a comeback in The Business, I can promise you. I'm coming *back*.'

'On roller skates,' Al Mackey said.

And when both detectives got ready to leave, Griswold Weils said, 'Am I ordered not to leave town?' which caused Al Mackey and Martin Welborn to look painfully at each other.

'How much money do you have, Griswold?' Al Mackey asked.

'Now? Oh, three or four bucks, I guess. Unemployment check comes next week.'

'Well, unless you take a bus, I guess that wouldn't get you past the city limits, would it?' Al Mackey said.

Martin Welborn, ever the more compassionate soul, satisfied the cinematographer's B-movie needs: 'Griswold, we'd like to advise you not to leave town,' he said, and Griswold Weils nodded grimly.

At last, Al Mackey thought, he was going to get to The Glitter Dome after all. He hoped Amazing Grace wasn't there. She might tell everyone about his miserable performance, unworthy of even a B movie. Maybe *he* should take up roller skating and try for a comeback.

The call, which would make the coming weekend the worst in Martin Welborn's life since Paula Welborn walked out for good, was waiting at the desk when the detectives started toward the deserted squadroom. The young uniformed policeman at the desk said, 'Sergeant Welborn, I got a message for you.'

The message was from Sgt Hal Dickey of Wilshire Detectives. It simply said, 'Call me as soon as you can. Dickey.'

'Wonder what Hal Dickey has for us?' Martin Welborn said.

'Let's split,' Al Mackey said. 'Call him Monday.'

'It says to call as soon as I can. Maybe it's urgent.'

'Okay, okay, you sign us out. I'll call Dickey.'

'All right, my lad,' Martin Welborn said. 'You'll get to The Glitter Dome before it closes. Stop worrying.'

But Martin Welborn was dead wrong. And Elliott Robles was just dead.

Al Mackey used the desk phone and talked a few moments to Hal Dickey while Martin Welborn was upstairs in the squadroom. After he hung up, Al Mackey started pacing the corridor of Hollywood Station, showing more tension than Griswold Weils. He didn't know whether to go upstairs and tell Marty there or wait for him to come down. He thought about not telling him at all. That was crazy. Marty would find out soon enough. He thought about *how* to tell him.

Elliott Robles was a snitch. Not a very good snitch, but a snitch nonetheless. He was a former heroin addict whom they cured at an addiction center by introducing him to methadone. Now he was a meth head, totally addicted to that drug.

146

He was a comical little twenty-seven-year-old Mexican with an Anglo name. He loved being the only Chicano in Hollywood with such an unlikely name: Elliott. He probably dreamed up the name the first time he was booked and it stayed in the computer as his 'key name'. Al Mackey never bothered to find out. He was a snitch and gave them information leading to the clearance of two gang killings, so they didn't want to know too much about him for fear he'd be burned as a material witness at a murder trial. Know as little as possible and one can truthfully say 'I don't know' to the relentless questions of defense counsel who want to identify and impeach one's 'anonymous' informants.

They'd paid Elliott Robles no more than two hundred dollars in the six months they'd known him. He'd showed them his tattoos. The Virgin of Guadalupe on one inner arm, The Sacred Heart of Jesus on the other. *Both* were covered with old and new scar tissue from his thousands of drug injections. He said he'd decided to become a paid informant to get enough money to have skin grafts. He'd converted, and was now a Jehovah's Witness, and didn't like the tattoos anymore. Al Mackey had promised to introduce him to some Feds in case Elliott came up with some bigtime narcotics dealer he could turn for enough money to get the skin grafts. But Elliott Robles never came up with a big-time anything. Even his death was very small-time, and Al Mackey didn't know how to tell Martin Welborn.

When Elliott Robles snitched off the trigger man in a lowrider, drive-by gang shooting, Martin Welborn had interrogated the killer, Chuey Verdugo, while Al Mackey booked the ·22-caliber rifle that the young man had used to shoot down a sixteen-year-old paperboy making an early morning delivery on the wrong gang turf during wartime. (Any blood will avenge the honor, just so it's spilled in the right place.) Elliott Robles, in his zeal to earn some money for turning the shooter, had told everything he knew and everything he'd heard about the shooter, hoping to impress the cops to the tune of a hundred scoots, at least. Among other things, he told Martin Welborn that the shooter was wanted for a hit-and-run killing in Tucson, where he ran over some dude who raped his girlfriend.

And Martin Welborn, perhaps because that was the week prior to Paula's leaving, perhaps because they'd been working forty-two hours without sleep on the drive-by shootings, perhaps because he just got sloppy during the interrogation, ran a very careless bluff and said to the shooter: 'Now let's talk about the guy you ran down in Tucson. Did you know the cops there have information about you?'

And the shooter looked at him quizzically for a moment. And took off his black woolen watch cap and wiped the sweat from his face with it, and drew very deeply on the cigarette Martin Welborn had given him, and began to *think*. And it came to him. Chuey Verdugo scratched his scraggly goatee and smoothed his Fu Manchu and dropped his head and started to shake.

It took a few seconds for Martin Welborn to realize that he wasn't shaking from fear. It was laughter. It began like heavy breathing, and grew into a chuckle, and finally the young man, who had just fired a shot through the head of a paperboy who happened to be on the wrong side of an imaginary line in East Hollywood, was roaring, and Al Mackey ran into the interrogation room.

'You gotta tell me that one, Marty,' Al Mackey said. 'Is it the one about the whore and the peanut?'

Martin Welborn shrugged, and both detectives waited until the shooter settled down and wiped the tears from his eyes with the watch cap, and when he was finished he said, 'I never ran over nobody in Tucson. I never even drove a car in Tucson. But one night when I was talking to this Mexican with the funny name a Elliott, I *told* him I ran over a dude in Tucson. He was passing out joints in the poolroom and wanted to hear some bad talk, so I made some up.' Chuey Verdugo wet his chops and laughed

148

again and said, '*Now* I know who told you I shot the paperboy.'

And for several months, whenever the subject arose, Al Mackey would try to reassure Martin Welborn that anyone could make a mistake during an interrogation, and that if he'd been in that room he would've said the same thing, and the shooter was going to be in jail for a long time in any case, and Elliott Robles had been warned that Martin Welborn had made the mistake.

Elliott Robles was burned. Al Mackey told him that he should think about moving out of town. But the Mexican with the funny name had just looked at Martin Welborn and said, 'You took my business out on the street, Sergeant! Where would I go? How far is El Monte?'

'About twenty miles,' Martin Welborn told him.

'I never been further away from my barrio than twenty miles,' Elliott Robles said.

And that was it. Elliott Robles quite understandably went out of the snitch business and contented himself with stealing car stereos, although that was getting tough in his part of town, what with everyone taking their stereos out of their cars at night. And finally he got nailed on a daytime residential burglary and did ninety days in the county jail, where he was safe enough. But eventually Elliott got out, and received the biggest surprise of his life when he learned that Chuey Verdugo had won an appeal and had been ordered released from custody on his *own recognizance* when his mother pleaded to the court that she desperately needed the boy to support her and the other eight children, which, of course, he'd never done even before he went to the California Youth Authority penal camp.

Chuey Verdugo, two days after his release, shot Elliott Robles nineteen times at about the same moment Martin Welborn was watching the champagne skater gliding through her floor exercises. Sgt Hal Dickey of Wilshire Detectives already had the shooter in jail and wanted to inform Al Mackey and Martin Welborn. Chuey Verdugo had used a ·22-caliber revolver. It took quite a bit of time to reload enough rounds to fire nineteen slugs into the corpse, and the noise and the loss of time led to his capture by a passing radio car. The shooter said it was worth it.

Martin Welborn didn't react at all when Al Mackey told him in the parking lot. He simply said he'd like to walk for a while.

'How about coming for a drink at The Glitter Dome?' Al Mackey urged afterwards.

'I don't think so,' Martin Welborn said.

'How about going *anywhere* for a drink?' Al Mackey said.

'I'm a little tired. It's been a very long day.'

'How about coming to my place and having a drink?' a very worried Al Mackey said.

'Elliott was a nice goofy kid, wasn't he?' Martin Welborn said.

'Marty, it is *not* your fault.'

'See you Monday, Al.'

'Anybody could've asked the same question during that interrogation, Marty.'

'That's kind of an *unforgivable* mistake, though,' Martin Welborn said. 'At least as far as Elliott was concerned.'

'We told Elliott about it as soon as it happened, Marty. Elliott knew the risk. We told him to get out of town. He *knew* the risk.'

'How many times did you say, Al?'

'How many times what?'

'How many times did Chuey Verdugo shoot him?'

'What *difference* does it make, Marty?'

'No difference. Good night, Al.'

'Want me to come to *your* place for a drink, Marty?' Al Mackey said to Martin Welborn, who was walking into the darkness.

'See you Monday, Al,' Martin Welborn said, without looking back.

10

Tuna Can Tommy

The Weasel and the Ferret were going after Tuna Can
Tommy. It wasn't their idea of course. Every time those
lazy pricks on the vice detail couldn't catch some minor
pain in the ass they'd paint a portrait of the pain in the ass
as a dope dealer and turn it over to narcotics. Probably
Tuna Can Tommy smoked a couple of lids a week. If they
iced down everybody who smoked a couple of lids a week
they'd have half of Hollywood in the cooler and the other
half waiting their turn. Many are chilled, but few are
frozen, the two narcs always said.

They'd thought that Captain Woofer would still be
tickled to death with the way they brought down Just Plain
Bill. But no, a short weekend to recuperate and they get
handed some other guy's problem. (The Ferret had night
sweats on Friday and Saturday from dreams where the
Asian Assassin was chasing *him*.) Thirteen more years for
their pensions. Why in hell did guys like poor old Cal
Greenberg hang around so long?

It seemed that Tuna Can Tommy made lewd telephone
calls to Hollywood housewives. And he occasionally left
Polaroids of himself on the windshields of cars parked near
the Hollywood Ranch Market. In the photographs he wore
a cowboy hat, cowboy boots, a Lone Ranger mask and
nothing else. He apparently staked out the area and
usually selected cars belonging to women reasonably
young and attractive, although sometimes he wasn't so
particular. At least one massive momma came wallumping
into the Hollywood vice office bitching about a Tuna Can
Tommy Polaroid she found on her windshield. She weighed
in at two hundred pounds and was surging out of her

shorts and tube top, yelling loud enough to scare Gladys Bruckmeyer clear up in the detective squadroom.

Gladys Bruckmeyer was back to duty after her encounter with caterpillars who conquer the kingdom, but was still spooky when it came to sudden changes in decibel level. The detectives pretended not to notice that Gladys Bruckmeyer would cry out every time Captain Woofer called her name. 'He'd call, 'Gladys!' and she'd scream and hit the tab bar which sent the carriage flying, ringing the margin bell.

It was, 'Gladys!' ding! 'Gladys!' ding! Which was driving everybody crazy until poor old Cal Greenberg sabotaged the typewriter bell when Gladys took one of her frequent trips down the hall to gobble some Miltowns.

So the Weasel and the Ferret were ordered by Captain Woofer to quit basking in celebrity for capturing Just Plain Bill, and get out there and rid the Hollywood citizens of Tuna Can Tommy. All theirs because the squirrel is suddenly transformed into a dope dealer by an 'anonymous informant' who talked with the vice sergeant. Times are pretty goddamn bad, the Weasel complained, when cops started using the same lame lies to each other that they should save for the real Enemies in the judiciary. But the Weasel and the Ferret had to spend most of Monday morning in a fruitless stakeout near the Hollywood Ranch Market for a fruitcake with Polaroids who signed each photograph 'Love from Tommy', and who ended his lewd phone calls with, 'Love ya! It's Tommy!'

'In the first place, what's he doing so bad in leaving his own personal valentine on these cars?' the Weasel whined, during the second hour of their stakeout.

'Guy doesn't ask for nothing,' the Ferret moaned. 'Just to show these broads how he looks naked in his Lone Ranger mask and boots. What the hell. How many strangers you run into these days who leave an *I love ya!* on your car?'

'Most people just say, "have a nice day",' the Weasel agreed.

'Those lazy pricks on the vice detail,' the Ferret groused.

'They probably couldn't catch him if he left his last name,' the Weasel bitched. 'We'll have to pick up a Polaroid. See what his chubby body looks like.'

'Vice couldn't catch him if he left his telephone number and address,' the Ferret said. 'I'll be so glad when this loan-out is over. I wanna get back downtown and away from Woofer.'

'Wonder why vice calls the squirrel Tuna Can Tommy?' the Weasel mused. 'And I wonder how *we* got picked for this whole Hollywood assignment in the first place?'

The way the Weasel and Ferret were picked was elementary. Captain Woofer simply begged Deputy Chief Francis to loan him a team of narcs to help mollify the merchants and politicians constantly harping about Hollywood becoming a slum. And when Fuzznuts Francis asked what kind of narcs he wanted, Captain Woofer said to send him a pair of grungy, ugly, filthy, hairy, disgusting, creepy scumbags who would fit in with the run-of-the-mill Hollywood street folks.

The scumbags were sitting in their battered Toyota by the Hollywood Ranch Market, sharing these woes, when they received the radio call which would plunge them yet deeper into the Nigel St Claire murder case. The radio call was to phone the station. The Ferret went to a telephone booth and after a few minutes came hurrying back to the Weasel with a happy smile in his beard.

'Huzzah!' the Ferret cried. 'We may wrap up Tuna Can Tommy even faster than Just Plain Bill!'

'He give himself up?'

'He made another lewd phone call last night, only *this* victim says she thinks she recognizes the voice!'

'Yeah?' The Weasel was already firing up the Toyota. 'Where we going?'

Rita Roundtree was reading *Daily Variety* when the two narcs entered the fast-food famous-name restaurant, and took their seats at the counter. She glanced at the two hairballs in leather jackets and took her time finishing the column about a 25-million-dollar movie that was boffo in six openings. Then she looked at the extravagant ads that *some* talent agencies took for their clients and wondered why she'd hooked up with such a low-rent agent, and no wonder she hadn't had a job since four months ago when she had *one* line in a pizza commercial. It was so discouraging she let out a big sigh.

Her sigh took her high-riding 38D cups even higher than the hairballs' hopes. They of course knew who *she* was from her telephone call to the vice unit. When she finally decided the two leather-covered creepos wouldn't go away she moved sluggishly down the counter, one of an army of Hollywood waitresses seduced not by dreams of streets paved with gold but of sidewalks paved with *stars* in solid brass.

'What can I get you?' she asked lethargically.

'You Rita Roundtree?' The Weasel grinned.

'How'd you know?' She was suspicious.

'We're from Hollywood Station,' the Ferret said.

'You're cops!'

They were used to it. The Ferret slipped his badge from under the shoulder of his leather jacket, showed it to her, and put it back. He didn't bother with the identification card. She'd never recognize the clean-cut young kisser on that old card anyway.

'It's just like in the movies,' the Ferret said. 'When does Tommy come in here?'

'I don't *know* his name's Tommy,' Rita Roundtree said, disappointed that the cops they sent didn't look like Starsky and Hutch.

'He *calls* himself Tommy, right? You told the lieutenant you recognized his voice?'

'He comes in here for breakfast, maybe four, five times a week. He was trying to disguise his voice but I know it was him.'

'What'd he say?'

'Same thing every one a those heavy breathers says when they get on the line.'

'Specifically,' the Ferret said, looking at those high risers.

She caught him ogling. 'Would you like me to whisper all the dirty words in your ear, Officer?' she said, and it was clear the Ferret was not her type.

Which let the Weasel know they might as well forget the fantasies and get down to business. 'We'll have you make a crime report if we get him,' the Weasel said. 'We have to know the exact words so we can make a case in court.'

'He said he hoped I wore bikini panties cause he'd like to get a mouthful of the crotch and suck them right off my cunt like spaghetti off a spoon, is what he said if you gotta know.'

'Yeah?' cried the Weasel, pretty damned impressed with this Tuna Can Tommy.

'Really?' cried the Ferret, deciding it was a neat idea if you think about it.

'He's a goofy fat guy,' Rita Roundtree said, pouring them coffee. 'Got these tufts a red hair growing out his ears and nose. Yuk! I hate tufts a hair growing out ears and noses.'

The Weasel and Ferret immediately looked at each other's ears and noses, but they both had such long hair and bushy beards it was impossible to tell.

'How come the lieutenant told us you wanted to see us right away, if he comes in for *breakfast*?' the Ferret asked.

'He eats his breakfast at noon, that's why,' Rita Roundtree answered. 'Same thing every time. Two over easy, hashbrowns, bacon, ham *and* steak. A real geeky porker.'

They only had to wait twenty minutes for the porker. Several other noontime customers had entered but the clump of red hair on the head of the fat man told them even without her nod. Tuna Can Tommy made a little small talk with Rita Roundtree, and eyed her ass when she gave his order to the fry cook. Of course so did every other man at the lunch counter, except for two body builders who were holding hands and sharing a chocolate malt.

Tuna Can Tommy drank three cups of coffee after

breakfast and left Rita Roundtree a two-dollar tip which made her somewhat regret calling the cops. With all the cheap fucks around here, a lewd phone call from a big tipper who wants to suck your drawers off isn't too high a price.

The Ferret went for the Toyota and the Weasel tailed Tuna Can Tommy on foot. It was a piece of cake. A big-time Hollywood dope dealer? Those lazy pricks on the vice squad.

They tailed Tuna Can Tommy to an apartment building just two blocks from the famous Chinese Theater. The throngs of tourists nosing around the concrete footprints (John Wayne's look so *small*, they invariably cried) made it that much easier to do the surveillance on foot. The Weasel found it so simple, he practically walked into the apartment building and up to the third floor *with* the fat man. He spotted the apartment number, returned to the mailbox, and saw that Tuna Can Tommy's real name was Dudley Small. He rejoined the Ferret, who had parked the nark ark and was hotfooting it toward the apartment house, wiping his ever-sensitive smog-filled eyes.

It was a 1920s Spanish-style apartment building, which meant it had a basement for sure. Ten minutes later the two young narcs were in the basement with their home-made resistors, wires and alligator clips, perfectly willing to risk a few years in the slam for illegal wiretapping.

Poor old Cal Greenberg had said it best: An unlucky policeman's life passes through four phases – cockiness, care, compromise, despair. The lucky ones don't reach phase four. The Weasel and Ferret were still in phase one. Swashbucklers.

But the telephone box was practically inaccessible with all the furniture and piles of junk stacked everywhere. Besides, the guy wasn't worth all this trouble. The Ferret went back to the car and returned with a stethoscope from their bag of tricks. Then they were in the upstairs hallway, the Ferret watching the stairway and the Weasel with his stethoscope pressed to the door, listening for hot talk from Tuna Can Tommy. But the telephone was too far away.

After fifteen minutes Tuna Can Tommy made a call. All the Weasel could hear was a brief muffled monologue. The Weasel took the stethoscope out of his ears, signaled to the Ferret, and both narcs then went to the window leading out onto the fire escape. Tuna Can Tommy's draped window was four feet from the railing, close enough to hang on with one hand, reach across the brick wall with the other, and raise the window if it was unlocked. The entire illegal maneuver if mismanaged could result in a three-story fall to the alley below. They didn't hesitate. After a quick huddle, the Ferret, being the most agile, climbed over the railing and the Weasel went to distract Tuna Can Tommy. Dare-devils.

The Weasel knocked at the door, and after a moment Tuna Can Tommy opened it with the chain lock holding.

'Pardon me,' the Weasel said. 'I'm looking for Martha Beaglelump. Does she live here?'

'Never heard of her,' Tuna Can Tommy said.

'Oh, that's odd. I was *sure* this was the right apartment.'

'No, you have the wrong apartment.'

'Do you know a lady about fifty years old in this building? Lives alone? Wears butterfly glasses? Sort of walks like a rabbit? Hippety hop?'

'No, not in this apartment,' Tuna Can Tommy insisted.

'Thanks anyway,' the Weasel said cheerfully, as the fat man closed the door.

Two minutes later he joined the Ferret on the fire escape, where the heavily draped window was now opened eight inches.

'Hello, lemme talk to Flameout,' they heard him say on the telephone. After a pause he said, 'Flameout? It's me, Dudley. How's Tarnished Gem look in the fifth? Yeah? Okay, get me down for five across. Yeah, that's all. Thanks.'

Shit. He was calling his *bookie*. It was a goddamn vice case all the way. Lewd phone calls. Gambling. Next thing he'd turn into a whore or something. Heavyweight drug dealer? Bullshit!

Then Tuna Can Tommy dialed the telephone again and he said, very officiously: 'Hello, is this Roberta Philbert? Yes? Mrs Philbert, I'm calling for the Santa Monica Research Institute of Consumer Affairs. We're trying to determine what kind of laundry detergent the average housewife uses. We'll be happy to send you, with our compliments, a gift certificate for fifty dollars' worth of the detergent of your choice if you'll just answer a few simple questions.'

There was a pause, and the Ferret and Weasel began grinning like cats. *This* sounded like old Tuna Can Tommy, all right.

'Yes, that's right,' said Tuna Can Tommy. 'First, I'd like to know which detergent you're using now. Yes. Uh huh, and is it strong enough to get the dirt out of your kids' playclothes? Yes? How about your husband's shirts? Does he wear white shirts? No? How does it perform on white? Say, underwear? Your husband's underwear? Yes? and the kids' underwear? Does it perform adequately? And *your* underwear? Uh huh, and can you tell me, what kind of underwear? No, not theirs. Yours. Do you wear *white* underwear? Uh huh, and do you wear other colors? How about red? Do you wear bikini underwear? Hello? Hello!'

The Weasel and Ferret held a quick conversation outside Tuna Can Tommy's door.

'We got nothing to bust him for,' said the Ferret. 'Nothing that'll hold up in court.'

'This is *bull* shit anyway,' the Ferret said. 'We're narcs!'

'Let's jack him up a little bit. We could spend a month sticking to his wall like freaking mosquitoes. If he confesses and throws himself on the mercy of the cop, we'll take him down and book him. Otherwise we'll terrorize him a little bit and tell him to take his Polaroids to Malibu. Virgin territory and all that.'

'Go for it,' the Ferret agreed, and this time it was he

who knocked on the door, yelling, 'Mr Small! It's the mailman! I have a registered letter for you!'

And when Tuna Can Tommy unslid his chain and turned the latch, the door burst open and he was caught in a wristlock and choke hold by what *had* to be a Hell's Angels enforcement squad and he had a passing panicky wish that he'd given away *all* the Polaroids. When the mortician gave his mother his remains and personal things, he didn't want her to know about the other life.

Tuna Can Tommy could have kissed both of them after they pushed him down on the couch and told him to stop screaming or they'd cut his fucking throat and that they were Los Angeles police officers. He examined the badge closely.

'You *are* cops! You *are* cops!' Tuna Can Tommy cried. That badge is *just* like the one on *Dragnet*!'

'Jesus, you're a real screamer, ain't ya,' the Weasel said. 'Can't you talk in an ordinary tone a voice?'

'I'm sorry,' Tuna Can Tommy said. 'I was so frightened! I'm so *happy* you're cops!'

'Yeah, yeah,' the Ferret said. 'Listen, we can't dick around with ya. We got information you're the masked man leaving his nudie pictures around town. No sense lying about it. Our crime lab is the best in the world. Interpol and Scotland Yard come to us. Our scientists subjected your pictures to a spectograph, monograph, and polygraph. There's no point in lying and denyin. They got every freckle and mole on your tubby little frame pinpointed by a fluoroscope and gyroscope.'

'All we gotta do is get a court order, make you pull your pants down, bingo, it's all over,' the Weasel said. 'I don't see how you can get outa this one.'

'Ain't no way,' the Ferret said. 'You might as well tell us all about it, make you feel better.'

'Can't say I blame you for what you done,' the Weasel said. 'I got a thing for sucking their pants off myself. And I don't care what kind a detergent they use.'

'You know *everything*!'·Tuna Can Tommy sobbed.

'A course we know everything,' the Weasel said. 'Ya said ya watch *Dragnet*, for chrissake!'

'I'm sorry I did it,' Tuna Can Tommy blubbered. 'Can't you give me another chance? I never been arrested.'

'Well, we *might*, but we heard some other tidbits lately. Oh, by the way, they been directing sound waves at your house for about a month now. You feel funny sometimes when you go to bed? Itchy in the crotch maybe? Funny sort a wiggly feeling in your tummy? Maybe after one a your phone calls? Maybe your dork gets hard?'

'Yes! Yes!' Tuna Can Tommy said, weeping openly.

'That's from the sound waves,' the Ferret said. 'We learned it from the Russians. They do it to our embassies. Makes you goofy after a while. Half the fucking ambassadors in Europe end up making phone calls late at night asking broads about their underwear. It ain't *all* your fault, Tommy.'

'My name's Dudley,' the fat man cried. 'Tommy's my alias!'

'Well, we gotta tell ya, your bad habits know no limits, Tommy,' the Weasel said, but Tuna Can Tommy was crying so hard he could hardly hear him. 'We discovered through our latest sound waves that you're also involved with bookmakers. Christ, I like underwear too, but I try to control *some* bad habits: Polaroids, bookmakers, flogging your dummy. You gotta stop *somewhere*, Tommy.'

'I only bet on horses once in a while,' Tuna Can Tommy wailed. 'I won't do it anymore!'

'And the last thing is, we know you're a doper, Tommy,' the Ferret said. 'Now just turn over your stash to me and it'll go a lot easier on ya.'

'I'm *not*!' Tuna Can Tommy wailed. 'I'm *not*. I work every night at the Swifty Messenger Service. I'm the best and speediest deliveryman they have. Speedy messengers *can't* be dope fiends!'

'You can't give some people a break,' the Weasel said to the Ferret. 'Get your coat, Tommy, we ain't gonna stand here and watch your sinuses drain.'

'Wait, please!' Tuna Can Tommy cried, getting up and running into the bedroom toward the nightstand drawer.

Both startled narcs drew their guns, and after they got Tuna Can Tommy's renewed burst of terror under control, they sat him on the bed and removed the package from the drawer. He had exactly fifteen dexis and twelve reds, depending upon whether he wanted to go up or down. 'That's all the dope I've got,' Tuna Can Tommy sobbed. 'I got it at Flameout Farrell's place. You probably know he's my bookie.'

'We know everything.' The Weasel nodded.

Then the Weasel said, 'Bookies don't usually offer uppers and downers to their clients.'

'Flameout didn't sell them to me. In fact, nobody *sold* them. Some guy came in Flameout's restaurant and *gave* them to me one day. Drives a Bentley. I think he's a big coke connection!'

'Another big connection,' the Ferret groaned. 'What makes you think that?'

'Somebody mentioned it. He's also a big horseplayer. I heard he drops maybe a thousand a day at the track and thinks nothing about it!'

'Yeah?' the Weasel said. A grand day. Maybe this could turn into a drug case after all. The Ferret nodded at him. They were getting sick and tired of dicking around with Tuna Can Tommy.

'Okay, Tommy, now you listen to me,' the Weasel said. 'We might be able to let you slide this time *if* you're cooperative. It's called trading up. Little fish for big fish. You understand?'

'No.'

'What's this dude's name, the flash who gave you the uppers and downers?'

'Lemme think,' Tuna Can Tommy said. 'You got me so scared I *can't* think!'

'Aw right, aw right,' the Ferret said, 'get your act together. Mellow out. Lay down on the bed.'

'What're you gonna do?'

'Gang-bang ya, whadda ya think? LAY DOWN ON THE FUCKIN BED!'

Whereupon Tuna Can Tommy plopped down, belly up to prevent the gang bang as long as possible. He stared at the two ferocious narcs with terror in his eyes.

'You got any spit left, or you scared spitless?' the Ferret asked.

'I don't know!' Tuna Can Tommy wailed.

'Open your mouth,' the Ferret commanded.

Tuna Can Tommy, sweating buckets, his gelatinous body quivering from neck to knee, opened his mouth and closed his eyes, and gagged when something hit the back of his throat.

'Now swallow it, you got any spit left,' the Ferret ordered.

Tuna Can Tommy gulped once, twice, and got it down. He smiled. It was one of the reds.

'Hey, lemme try that!' the Weasel said, taking a capsule from the Ferret's hand. 'Open up again.'

This time Tommy nodded eagerly and opened his rubber lips. (God, he *did* have ugly tufts of red hair hanging out his snoot. Gross!)

The Weasel stood at the foot of the bed and hit him in the eye with the first Seconal capsule. 'Leave it!' he ordered, when Tuna Can Tommy tried to gobble it up. The second one was a bull's-eye landing right in that big pink mouth and the fat man swallowed it easily. Less fear, more spit.

The Ferret and the Weasel, who were now starting to enjoy themselves, each got one more in Tommy's gaping maw, missing a few, but getting better with each toss.

'Now, goddamnit, you starting to kick back?' the Weasel wanted to know.

'I feel *better*, Officer.' Tuna Can Tommy smiled.

'Okay, what's the name of the big player, might be a coke dealer?'

'Lloyd,' Tuna Can Tommy said without hesitation.

'Lloyd. I wasn't told his last name. Drives a black Bentley. I've never even *seen* coke. I don't have *every* bad habit.'

'Okay, where's Flameout Farrell work out of?' the Ferret asked.

'You know that dirty-book store on Hollywood Boulevard?'

'*Which* dirty-book store, for chrissake?'

'The one with the big Greek statue? Where the statue's urinating in the pond? That one. The one near the freeway.'

'He owns the bookstore?'

'No. He owns the little restaurant three doors down. Stays open till nine. I eat my supper there sometimes. I don't think he's much of a bookmaker. The phone doesn't ring that much. You won't tell him I told on him, will ya?'

'Now if we didn't protect the confidentiality of our . . . *agents*, we couldn't trade little ones for big ones, could we?'

'An agent!' Tuna Can Tommy beamed. This was a better fantasy than sucking underwear. He boldly opened his mouth and pointed. Now that he was an agent he could make certain demands.

The Weasel flipped one more in there and said that is fucking *it*. Any more downers and he'd be the *late* secret agent. Which reminded Tuna Can Tommy of the mortician and the personal belongings. He glanced involuntarily toward the other drawer, and the Ferret noticed.

The Ferret reached inside and found four self-photographed portraits in cowboy boots, hat and mask.

The Ferret cried, 'Out of freaking *sight*!'

'Those are *real* ostrich boots,' Tuna Can Tommy said proudly.

The Weasel, who was writing in his notebook, mumbled, 'You wear five-hundred-dollar ostrich, I wear thirty-dollar shit kickers. There's gotta be a moral somewheres.'

'It ain't your *boots*, masked man!' the Ferret cried to Tuna Can Tommy. 'Now I know how you got your nickname!'

'What nickname? I always sign the picture Tommy.'

'The vice cops didn't show us your Polaroids. Now I know why *they* call you Tuna Can Tommy!'

'Do they call me that? Oh, that's mean!' He looked as though he might start crying again. 'I can't help the way I'm *built*!'

The Weasel stopped making notes about Flameout Farrell and Lloyd the alleged coke dealer and took the pictures from the Ferret.

'My God!' the Weasel cried. 'Your putz! It's nearly three inches in *diameter*!'

But, alas, it was less than two inches in length. It was shaped exactly like a tuna can.

11

The Gunfighter

Tuesday morning was a bad day in the squadroom. The United States Supreme Court had just decreed that it was not fair if the cops used a third-party conversation to 'trick' a murderer into confessing. Henceforth, Schultz had to watch what he said to Simon in the presence of any more stranglers they arrested *if* what he said somehow persuaded the strangler that the jig was up and he might as well confess where he buried his corpses and piano wire. It was a very black Tuesday.

In fact, the nine old pussies of the Potomac had made Schultz so mad he couldn't take a joke when the call came in from Gloria La Marr down at the county lockup. The Weasel said they write lots of songs about lovers parted by prison walls, and Schultz informed the Weasel that the health plan includes dental care now, so go ahead and keep dumping on him.

'Hello, Gunther, how *are* you?' Gloria La Marr purred.

'Hi, Gloria,' Schultz said, then turned his bearish body toward the pin map on the wall and put his hand over the mouthpiece, since the entire squadroom was eavesdropping.

'I told them at my arraignment that I just wanted to plead guilty so as not to be no more trouble,' Gloria La Marr said.

'That's the right thing to do, Gloria,' Schultz said.

'This is a *very* confidential call. You were awful nice to me, buying me drinks and all, and never making fun of me like other people sometimes do.'

'You're a nice person, Gloria,' Schultz said.

'Thank you, Gunther. Well, they have me in the sissy

tank with all the gay people so I don't think I have to worry about being . . . attacked or nothing like that.'

'That's good, Gloria,' Schultz said. 'I'm glad to hear that.'

'I'm going to have the rest of my operation just as soon as I get out.'

'That's good too, Gloria,' Schultz said.

'Reason I called you is, well, I know I can trust you and I know nobody in jail will ever find out and . . . well, if *anything* good should happen as a result of what I'm going to tell you, well, I just know you'd talk to the judge and . . .'

'I'll help you any way I can, you know that.'

'Thank you, Gunther,' Gloria said. And then she knocked off the cooing and her voice became more tense and masculine. 'I never snitched off nobody before, you understand. I never gave nobody up, but . . . well, there's a boss queen down here named Violet. She read all about the thing where two of your cops started following a silver Mercedes in Hollywood and ended up in San Pedro. Violet was in the army ten years ago and she spent a year in Vietnam and she knows a little of the language. She *swears* she tricked with Bozwell, that guy the cops arrested. Him and a Vietnamese guy picked her up on the street in that Mercedes a few nights before she read about the bust. The guy Bozwell was drunk and talked to the other guy in rice-paddy lingo. About *gold*. She caught *that* word, all right. She says Bozwell offered to take her to a restaurant on Melrose near Western that looked Chinese. They dropped the Vietnamese guy there and she never saw them after that night.'

'I'll pass it on,' Schultz said.

'It probably don't mean much, Gunther, but if something good should come out of it, you'll put in a word for me, won't you?'

'Sure I will, Gloria.'

Then Gloria La Marr sounded feminine again. She started to weep. 'Now that I'm . . . *almost* a woman, I . . .

I hate jail. I just *hate* it now. It's different for a . . . a *woman*!'

'If anything comes of it, I'll put in a word, kid. I promise.'

When Schultz hung up and turned his grizzly shape around in the chair, everyone started shuffling paper, dialing phones, drinking coffee, and generally averting the eyes. Would Gloria La Marr come to Schultz's retirement party someday? As his *date*?

Then Schultz took Simon, the Weasel and the Ferret into an interrogation room and closed the door. Which worried the Weasel no end. 'I was only joking about Gloria, Gunther!'

'Might not amount to nothing,' Schultz said. 'But how would you two like to take down that gook that tried to kill you down there in San Pedro last week?'

'Would I like to take down the gook!' the Ferret cried. 'Would I like a broad with four tits?' And he glared knowingly at the Weasel.

'Okay, might not be much, but Gloria La Marr says there's some queen down in the fruit tank who tricked with your boy Bozwell. Somebody called Violet. Don't go talk to Violet or Gloria's gonna get burned. Anyways, Violet saw the picture of Bozwell in the paper. Bozwell was with a dink the night Violet met him and they talked a few words of gook. About *gold*. That woulda been two nights before he tried to shoot your eyes out, Ferret. Maybe it's nothing. It's worth a check, is all. She said the gook went to some restaurant on Melrose near Western. Maybe a Chinese restaurant.'

'Just Plain Bill Bozwell *did* serve in Vietnam for two years,' the Ferret said. 'It was on an old five-ten in his package. Maybe that's where he learned to cut throats. Old habits?'

'Can't ya make him a deal if he turns the gook for ya?' Schultz asked.

'He's saying nothing more,' the Weasel said. 'Wouldn't talk much to the robbery dicks from downtown. Told the dicks from the Harbor to go dance in eel shit. Had enough money to get a lawyer and writ out the next day. Anyway, he just might be telling the truth about not knowing the slope too well. Maybe they *did* just meet in a massage parlor, and Just Plain Bill started practicing his Vietnamese, and . . . birds of a feather?'

'Well' – Schultz shrugged – 'want me to give it to robbery? After all, they're handling the case.'

'No, let *us* check it out,' the Ferret said. 'I got a personal interest in finding that boy.' His heart started beating irregularly. Don't kill me! Mother! 'A *personal* interest.'

'Got any leads at all?' Simon asked.

'Naw,' the Weasel said. 'The dink dropped a few things outa his pocket when he was ripping himself up on the fence. A key and piece a paper with a phone number.'

'Where's the number come back to?'

'Nowhere that means anything. Main switchboard of a big movie studio. Probably five thousand people in and out a those places every day. They even film TV shows there. Probably trying to get on a game show or something.'

'Which studio?' Schultz asked.

'The one where that guy was the boss, the one that got dusted in the bowling alley parking lot.'

'Nigel St Claire,' Schultz said, looking at Simon. 'And how about the key? They make it?'

'Just an ordinary key,' the Ferret said. 'Nothing.'

'Maybe it's a key they *use* at the movie studio,' Schultz said.

'First thing they checked after they ran the telephone number. Wrong brand a key.'

'*Somebody* oughtta find the Chinese restaurant and stake it out,' Schultz said. 'Somebody has to be *you*, Ferret. You're the only one knows what the gook looks like. You'd know him, wouldn't ya?'

The Ferret remembered him. The bastard *grinned* when he pulled the trigger. Then the grin disappeared when it clicked. The Ferret remembered him, all right.

'We don't have much going on anyway,' the Weasel said, knowing how badly the Ferret wanted the assassin.

Although they were still sore about having the murder case taken away from them, Schultz and Simon were policemen enough to report the slim lead to Al Mackey and Martin Welborn.

'The Oriental bandit had the number of the studio? Must be a thousand extensions and private numbers there,' Al Mackey said when he was told.

'Just thought I'd tell ya,' Schultz said. 'It's *your* case now.'

'That wasn't by choice.'

'Yeah, I know, I know.'

'Maybe they're doing another thirty-million-dollar war epic and he wants to play a Vietcong. Maybe . . .'

'Just thought I'd *tell* ya,' Schultz said.

'If anything comes of it, I'll be sure to put in a word for Gloria La Marr,' Al Mackey said, sending Schultz scowling back to his table.

The *whole* fucking world knew! 'Just because the broad's serving time,' Schultz moaned to Simon when he sat down. 'Gordon Liddy did *more* time and he's on the *talk* shows!'

That did it. Gordon Liddy was Simon's hero. Comparing Gloria La Marr to Gordon Liddy! This was the day to take Schultz to the police academy and thump him on his noggin and hope it wasn't too late to get his head all straightened out.

That afternoon while Simon had Schultz on the police academy wrestling mat trying to make Schultz see that he was going bughouse, the Weasel and the Ferret were intently watching the entrance of the only restaurant in the general vicinity described by Violet. It was not Chinese but Thai. They were staked out on the rooftop of a secondhand store on Melrose Avenue, wearing cowboy hats to shade them from the sun while they ate the world's driest burritos, served by an Arab in a Mexican restaurant owned by a Korean.

Al Mackey and Martin Welborn went about their ordinary business, which involved two aggravated assaults, one domestic shooting, and a lover's stabbing of a gay. The stabbee ended up with more sympathy for the knife wielder than he had for himself, which was not unusual. The detectives decided to get a rejection of a criminal complaint and let them work it out themselves over wine and linguini.

It was up to the street monsters, Buckmore Phipps and Gibson Hand, to open the next door into the mysterious murder of Nigel St Claire.

Buckmore Phipps was mad today because the roller derby and the $1.98 *Beauty Contest* got preempted by a presidential address. Gibson Hand was irritated because a bunch of celebrity pussies were trying to put his favorite newspaper, *The National Enquirer*, out of business. There was trouble in their world.

So they were in no mood for bullshit while cruising up La Brea on the way back from Gibson Hand's favorite barbecue grill, when they spotted two drunks having it out on the sidewalk in the presence of three other winos and a moaning basset hound.

The lackluster combatants, who were pounding each other wearily with a length of two-by-four and a piece of lead pipe, didn't even notice the cops gliding up in the black-and-white. Finally one of the winos in the gallery saw the street monsters.

'Uh óh,' he said, elbowing the wino who was sitting next to him on the curb, who elbowed the next wino, who elbowed the moaning basset hound and said, 'Shut the fuck up, dog.'

When the street fighters finally saw the street monsters, each dropped his weapon and waited meekly for the bracelets. However, Buckmore Phipps and Gibson Hand were out of their divisional boundaries and full of ribs and black-eyed peas. They weren't *about* to get out of their car.

The basset hound moaned even louder when all the yelling and fighting ceased.

'Why is that dog groanin like that?' Gibson Hand asked lazily.

'Got hit by a car bout a hour ago,' a wino answered.

'Country dog,' another wino added. 'Jist brought him in from a farm. Not used to cars. Jist stood there and watched the car run over hisself.'

'Either shoot him or shut him up,' Gibson Hand said.

'*You* kin shoot him, you want to,' a wino said. 'Course he was jumpin around a minute ago. I think he jist liked the attention he got when he was run over.'

'Why are you two beatin on your heads with that two-by-four and piece a pipe?' Buckmore Phipps asked wearily, as Gibson Hand leaned back on the headrest and picked his teeth with a matchbook.

'Motherfucker went to git some wine and chicken goblets and ate it *all* for he got back,' one fighter said.

The other one made a terrible mistake. He said to the cops, 'I know my rights. I ain't got nothin to say to *you*.'

Gibson Hand rolled his head slowly toward Buckmore Phipps, wondering if he should take the shotgun out of the rack and turn it into a pistol by busting the stock across the fighter's noodle, but decided he'd eaten too many ribs for all that.

Buckmore Phipps said 'You!' to the fighter who had made the big mistake. 'Get in the car. We're bookin you for ADW.'

'What's that?'

'Assault with a deadly weapon.'

'Deadly weapon? Shee-it! I on'y hit the motherfucker with a pipe!'

Gibson Hand knew they were not going to book the wino for ADW or anything else, because when the drunk got in the car they headed out of the city and into the jurisdiction of the county sheriff.

Buckmore Phipps, driving leisurely, looked at the surly

combatant and said, 'Maybe we oughtta just book him for drunk instead?'

'I ain't drunk *either*,' the fighter said, adding insult to injury.

'We're gonna let our sergeant check you,' said Buckmore Phipps. 'He's a qualified expert. Drinks a fifth a day. He says you're drunk, you're drunk. He says you ain't, you ain't.'

Gibson Hand was getting curious when they pulled up in front of the West Hollywood Sheriff's Station. Buckmore Phipps jotted something in laboriously disguised handwriting. He folded it carefully, but the fighter was so bagged he couldn't have read it anyway, and after sobering up he said he wouldn't know those two cops from Cheech and Chong.

Buckmore Phipps said, 'Take this note *and* your lead pipe inside and hand the note to the desk officer. If the sergeant thinks you're sober enough and wants to let you go, it's up to him. I explained everything on the note as I saw it. We'll wait here.'

The wino staggered around the sidewalk, tucked his shirt in, zipped up his fly, rehearsed walking a straight line. When he was convinced he could pull it off, he weaved his way up the steps and into the sheriff's station with his note and lead pipe.

The deputy on the desk was reading a *Penthouse* magazine and was pissed off at being interrupted. The length of pipe in the asshole's hand got his attention, however. The fighter handed the deputy the note and said, 'Lemme see the sergeant right away.'

The deputy unfolded the note. It said: 'This pipe is loaded with plastic explosives. I want twenty thousand dollars, a helicopter, and the Big Sheriff himself as a hostage or I'm blowing this fucking place into the ocean.'

The street monsters waited until they heard the terrified shouts and running feet and frantic deputies whomping on the fighter with sticks before they sped back to Hollywood. It made their day a *little* more tolerable, all in all.

*

But while the day of Buckmore Phipps and Gibson Hand had improved somewhat, the Weasel and the Ferret had nothing to be thankful for except that low brassy clouds made the rooftop more bearable. The Ferret was getting irritated because the Weasel was catching a nap up there, lying on the air-conditioning unit, using his battered cowboy hat as a pillow.

'Goddamn! I gotta wear out my peepers with these freaking binoculars while you sleep,' the Ferret whined.

'I wouldn't know the dink if I saw him,' the Weasel mumbled. 'One of us might as well stack a few Z's.'

'Least you could do is run down and buy a couple six packs,' the Ferret said.

'Maybe you hadn't a drank a couple six packs, you wouldn't a fallen down that night and you'd a put one right in that gook's ten ring and we wouldn't *be* here,' the Weasel said, closing his eyes and rolling over.

Maybe he was *right*. That grinning face. The Ferret thought about looking for an old Vietcong poster, the kind *he* carried as a war protestor before he was drafted. He'd pin it to a silhouette on the target range. Maybe he'd practice with a couple of boxes of rounds. The gook *grinned* when he pulled that trigger in the Ferret's face.

'Do you suppose they still have any old Ho Chi Minh posters around anywhere?' he asked the Weasel.

'Call Jane Fonda and ask her,' the Weasel mumbled, and within seconds he was snoring.

But the street monsters weren't snoring. They were about to meet the man who died with his boots on.

It was too close to end of watch to be getting a bullshit radio call about somebody disturbing the peace. Especially at a motel on Sunset Boulevard that everyone knew was alive with pimps and whores, and probably nobody ever spent the whole night there since it was built. Or changed the sheets, for that matter.

When they arrived the ambulance was still twenty blocks away. The motel manager, a seventy-year-old

Cambodian hired hand, was guarding a door. His fifteen-year-old grandson was beside him guarding a window. Inside the motel room were two bodies, one very hot and bothered and screaming, the other getting cooler by the minute.

'Okay, what's the problem?' Buckmore Phipps sighed, as both street monsters emerged lazily from the radio car, leaving their hats but taking their sticks.

'Who's that screamin?' Gibson Hand wanted to know.

'A lady's screaming,' the boy said. 'We won't let her out.'

'Why won't you let her out?' Buckmore Phipps asked, belching up some barbecue. He had to cool it with this soul kitchen safari. His GI tract was getting full of little holes. He belched again.

The boy said something to the old man in Cambodian and then answered, 'Because she killed a man in there and we thought you might like to talk to her.'

'SHE WHAT?' Gibson Hand came to life.

'I didn't kill nobody!' the whore wailed, when they got her quieted down and sitting in the only chair in the motel bedroom.

The walls were mirrored and so was the ceiling. There was a mirrored headboard, and a mirrored door to the closet as well as to the bathroom.

'Talk about a wilderness a mirrors!' Buckmore Phipps exclaimed.

'Ever a good-sized earthquake, you'd be a plate a ground round, is what you'd be,' Gibson Hand noted, looking at the ceiling full of glass.

'I didn't kill *nobody*!' the whore screamed.

She was twenty years old, and almost honky white, Gibson Hand noted. She had a medium Afro, very frazzled at the moment, and black mascara streaming from her eyes to her lips to her pips, as Buckmore Phipps noted.

Her pips were hanging there because she was naked to the waist. She didn't even know her wraparound skirt was

174

the only piece of clothing on her body. The only reason it was still on her body is that the trick had said he liked it better when they 'hiked them up'. It reminded him of when he was a kid in the drive-in movies during the '50s. When the girls always 'hiked them up' in case the ushers came along with flashlights. Hiked-up skirts made him as hard as a frozen cod, he had said.

Roland Whipple had aptly selected as his last metaphor a frigid fish, which is what he was starting to resemble. He lay on his back with his dead eyes looking up at the mirrored ceiling that reflected back to his dead eyes a lifeless love muscle, which oddly enough had ceased operation more reluctantly than his overworked heart muscle. When that one stopped banging, so did he. And suddenly. The massive cardiac arrest struck with a seismic jolt. He ran his final mile with a world-class finishing kick. When he convulsed, the whore, who was riding on top, flew two feet off his rigid member and came down on his belly with a squishy plop.

'Talk about a slam dunk!' she exclaimed. 'Baby, that was a motherfucking ex-plosion!'

But Roland Whipple never heard the applause. He was creaking like a bellows. The last of his air was wafting up toward his reflection on the ceiling. The mirrored headboard was wet from their thrashing, but Roland Whipple had fogged his last mirror.

'You could say a lot a last words about a guy checking out like that,' Buckmore Phipps said, looking down at Roland Whipple's corpse.

'Can I go home now?' the whore wailed, still hysterical and unaware that her tits were bobbing around loose, and neither street monster was about to tell her.

The corpse still wore a prophylactic. It was a fancy green one with little red rubber tentacles. He'd bought it in a dirty-book store on Hollywood Boulevard. The girls just loved them, the salesclerk had said.

The whore was about to tell him it felt like she was

being screwed with a can opener and she wanted an extra ten bucks for this shit, when he convulsed.

'How do those funny things work?' Buckmore Phipps asked the whore. 'I always ride bareback myself. Take a chance my way, though. Lots a . . .'

'I wanna go home!' wailed the whore. 'I didn't mean to cause a orgasm like *that*!'

'You have to say that cowboy died with his boots on, so to speak,' Gibson Hand observed.

'Lots a worse ways to go,' Buckmore Phipps clucked. 'It ain't *real* sad. More like a gunfighter on the streets a Laredo.'

'I didn't *kill* him!' wailed the whore.

'Well, in a manner a speakin you did,' Gibson Hand said. 'But nobody's blamin you for it.'

Then the ambulance came and went. The paramedics took one look at the stiff and one of them said, 'You have to admit, the man died with his boots on.'

Five minutes later the homicide team had taken charge and the whore was fully dressed, sitting in the back seat of the detective car with Al Mackey while they all waited for the coroner's meat wagon.

The street monsters were pissed off because Martin Welborn had told them to hang around and try to keep the crowd of curious pimps, whores, tricks, and hustlers down to a hundred or so.

The cause of death went unquestioned by the detectives. It was not an uncommon way to die around these parts.

'Okay, give us a phone number where we can reach you,' said Al Mackey, writing a cursory death report. 'And I don't want the number of some other motel or a massage parlor where you *don't* work, or the goddamn phone booth on the corner. I want a *real* phone number where you can be reached if we have any more questions.'

'Okay, okay,' the whore cried. She was pulling everything out of her purse looking for the phone number of her mother, who had two out of three of her kids to raise. The last one she'd hustled off to her aunt.

The whore was leafing through her trick book with quivering lip and shaking hands. She couldn't *think*. She started dropping things from her purse. There were phone numbers of good tricks to look for, bad tricks to avoid, high rollers and fat cats, good pimps who let you keep some money and bought you nice presents with part of the money they took from you, bad pimps who poured lighter fluid on your clothes and played with unlighted matches when you weren't behaving. There were dozens of telephone numbers in that purse. Al Mackey amused himself by looking through them, hoping to find some movie star names, which most whores wrote in their trick books for prestige whether they banged the celebrities or not.

Then he saw a familiar number. 'Look at this, Marty. It's that number again.' Then to the whore, 'Where did you get this?'

The whore looked at the scrap of paper. She screwed and unscrewed her brow. She put both hands on her Afro and tamped it down. She couldn't *think*. 'Lessee, lessee,' she said. 'A trick? I don't know! I'm still shakin! I don't know my mother's phone number, even!'

Martin Welborn looked at the studio telephone number and said, 'How well did you know . . . Nigel St Claire?'

'Never heard that name,' the whore said, and she seemed truthful enough. She was on one track only: momma's phone number. She was too rattled to be telling lies.

'Whose number *is* this?' Martin Welborn asked.

The whore looked at it again. 'I don't *know*! Gud-damn! It ain't even *my* writin, Officer. It's probably some trick's number, is all it is. Prob'ly some other girl give it to me. I can't *find* momma's number!'

She started crying and Martin Welborn said, 'Calm down. I think we can get along without your mother's number *if* you can remember who gave you *this* number. Do you think you can do that?'

'Am I gonna git to go home? I'm sorry that man's dead. I'll give you back his money. You kin give it to his wife. I never had nothin like this go wrong before!'

'You can go home. Just as soon as you remember who gave you that telephone number.'

The whore looked at the scrap of paper again. She fumbled with a cigarette, and Al Mackey struck a match and lit it. She took a puff, another, and said, 'This here's . . . I think this here's Lulu's writin . . . no . . . it ain't Lulu.' She smoked for a few seconds and stared and then she said, 'I know! It's Jill's handwritin! Yeah! Jill gimme this number. Sure!'

'Is it a trick's number?' Al Mackey asked.

'It ain't no trick. It's a . . . a . . . it's a *movie* studio. Whadda ya call them offices you go to to get in a movie? As an extra?'

'A casting office,' Martin Welborn said.

'Yeah! You got to ask for a certain company. And a certain guy. I forget his name now. Jill knows his name.'

Are you trying to get in the movies?' Martin Welborn asked.

'Honey, everybody's tryin to git in the movies,' the whore said, and *that* was true enough. 'Jill said this dude in a big black car liked her looks and asked would she like to play in a movie. Course *all* the tricks say bullshit like that, but this one, *this* one give her twenny dollars. For nothin. Jist to call the number and make an appointment. Didn't want his dick sucked. Nothin. Said he liked her looks, is all. He was legit, she figgered. Drove one a those 'spensive cars.'

'A Rolls?' Al Mackey asked. Nigel St Claire drove a blue Rolls. It might pass for black.

'No,' she said. 'Not a Rolls. The other one. Same thing almost.'

'A Bentley?' Martin Welborn asked.

'That's it. Guy drove a big black Bentley. The kind with mink floormats, all that. Said she thought he was a pimp at first, 'cept he was a white guy. She gimme the number in case I wanted to try to get in the movie too. I forgot the name a the movie company though.'

'Did Jill call him?' Al Mackey asked.

'I dunno,' the whore said. 'Kin I go home now?'

'Just as soon as you tell us where we can find Jill,' Martin Welborn said calmly.

'Gud-damn!' the whore cried. 'You keep on sayin yes I kin go, no I can't go!'

'This is almost the last question,' Martin Welborn said. 'What's Jill's last name, what's she look like, and where can we find her? Just to talk. She's not in trouble.'

'Well, in the first place, no whore got a last name. She's white. About my age, maybe younger. Long stringy blond hair. Does a lot a dope. Kind of a pretty girl though. Sometimes gives massages up to The Red Valentine on the Strip. But I don't want nobody to know I told you. Promise?'

'We promise,' said Martin Welborn.

And now the whore, realizing she was indeed going home, started getting her shit together. 'Listen, about that money the dead guy gimme? I *earned* it, right? I mean, he drove a big car. I bet his old lady don't need it no worse'n I do, right? Business is business.'

'You earned it all right,' Martin Welborn said.

Just then Buckmore Phipps and Gibson Hand came to the car, griping as usual.

'Look, Mackey, it's gettin dark,' Buckmore Phipps whined, which caused the Cambodian kid to nudge his grandfather and tell him in their mother tongue that the huge cop was afraid of the dark! And here *they* worked every night at the motel among pimps and prostitutes and cutthroats and never gave nightfall a thought!

'We're almost finished,' said Al Mackey. 'A couple more minutes.'

'Couple more minutes,' Gibson Hand moaned. 'I got a date down in The Glitter Dome with a lady.'

'A *lady* at The Glitter Dome,' Al Mackey muttered.

'This one could fuck *three* tricks to death like that one in there,' Gibson Hand bragged. 'Calls herself Amazin Grace.'

Which caused Al Mackey's head to swivel. The Great Chain!

Martin Welborn stepped out of the detective car to mollify the two street monsters. 'Just keep the crowd contained for another minute,' he urged. 'She'll get scared if any pimps or whores start roaming around back here. We might be getting a lead on a very important murder case.'

'Murder case,' Buckmore Phipps snorted. Sure. He figured the two detectives were just trying to line up a hot head job with the foxy little chippie.

Gibson Hand didn't believe the likely story either.

'What's the big murder case, Sarge?' he challenged.

'The one where the movie big shot got murdered,' Martin Welborn said. 'Nigel St Claire.'

'Nigel St Claire!' Both street monsters exclaimed simultaneously.

'That's the name!' Buckmore Phipps said.

'I had it on the tip a my motherfuckin tongue all the time!' Gibson Hand said.

'What do you know about Nigel St Claire?' Martin Welborn asked quickly.

'Nothin,' Gibson Hand said. 'It's jist the name on a note we found on a marine last week. Don't mean nothin. It's jist we *both* knew we heard the name somewheres and we couldn't remember.'

'What about Nigel St Claire?' Al Mackey asked, jumping out of the detective car.

'Nothin. It's nothin,' Buckmore Phipps said. 'Damn, it's gettin dark. I got a hotter date than Gibson's got. Come on, Mackey!'

'Who had his name?' Martin Welborn demanded, and suddenly the street monsters realized the dicks mean business.

'Jist some nudie gy-rene,' Gibson Hand said.

'Jist some fruit-hustler from Camp Pendleton,' Buckmore Phipps added. 'He had a phone number with it.'

'You can go now,' Martin Welborn said to the now

happy hooker. Then he turned to the street monsters and said, 'I hate to disappoint your dates, but let's go back to the office and hear *all* about your nude marine.'

'*She* balls a guy into the grave and gits to go home,' Gibson Hand moaned. 'I ain't had so much as a hand job in a week and I gotta work overtime!'

While the disgruntled street monsters were telling Al Mackey and Martin Welborn all they knew about the marine, the Weasel and the Ferret were about to have their first serious altercation during a two-year partnership.

'We are three fucking *hours* overtime!' the Weasel yelled as the sun was falling into the Pacific Ocean, which they couldn't have seen if they were fifty floors in the air instead of two, given the natural overcast and unnatural smog in the Los Angeles twilight.

'I wanna stay a little longer,' the Ferret said. 'That slope's gonna go in that restaurant. I can *feel* it.'

'You can feel it. Feel it! What the fuck are you now, a Sunset Strip swami!'

'You got a feeling, you go for it. I don't know how to explain it. The karma's right.'

'The karma! The karma!' The Weasel stomped around the rooftop in his motorcycle boots, kicking at any lazy pigeons too dumb to get out of his way. 'Why don't you go out to Malibu and join one a those cults that pray to fat little Indian kids in leisure suits and white shoes. Karma!'

'You can go. I'm staying,' the Ferret said.

'Should I take a cab, maybe?'

'Take the Toyota.'

'How you getting back to the station?'

'I'll take a cab. I'll hitchhike. I'll walk.'

'First place, you ain't got money for a cab. Second place, nobody would pick up anybody as barfy-looking as you. Third place, you ain't walked since Judas flimflammed Jesus fuckin Christ!'

'Get off my roof,' the Ferret said. 'I don't need you.'

'I ain't leaving you alone on this roof,' the Weasel said.

'You gonna *carry* me away?' the Ferret said, and now things were getting very tense.

The ball was in the Weasel's court. There was a semi-pregnant pause, and he said, 'I think I know how you feel. That guy sticking your own piece in your face. This ain't Nam. This is *your* town. It's one thing to be dinged in war. It's one thing to buy it on the freeway. But it's something different when a guy in your own home town is up there against your belly. What I mean is, it's a rotten mean lowlife thing to be *murdered*. Is that how you feel? Something like that?'

The Ferret turned his back to the Weasel and looked down at the Thai restaurant. There was a little man going in. He wore a seersucker suit with black-and-white patents. He was not the assassin. The Ferret kept his back to the Weasel and said, 'I *dream* about him. This was . . . *personal*. In Nam I never wanted to ding somebody *personally*. I'm gonna tell you something cause I know you won't tell. When I went home that night I . . . *cried*. It's the first time in my life I ever realized what a *sorrowful* thing it is to be murdered.'

The Weasel was silent for a moment and then he said, 'I got six bucks hideout money stashed in my boot. I'm gonna buy some beer. Shit, I ain't got nothing to do tonight but watch *Dallas* anyways.'

The Ferret nodded and the Weasel left the rooftop. Another man who was exactly the right size got out of a Ford and walked into the light from the Thai restaurant. He turned toward the street. The binoculars pierced the gloom, and the Ferret could see him perfectly. He was not the assassin.

12

Jackin Jill

Even the Ferret was willing to come down from the roof
after dark. His eyes hurt and he was exhausted. He felt like
going home and falling in bed without his TV dinner. One
thing about his ex-wife, she could cook. Tomato soup and
cheese sandwiches for tonight's gourmet treat?

'I don't have enough energy to fart,' he said on their
drive back to the station.

'I'm certainly glad to hear that,' the Weasel said.

'I think I'll sleep in my clothes like a freaking fireman,'
the Ferret said. 'I bet I couldn't make a move if you set fire
to my beard.'

Nothing could arouse him tonight, he thought. Except
that, in just over an hour, he was going to be darting down
Hollywood Boulevard breaking windows and sounding an
alarm: The Mafia's coming!

Buckmore Phipps and Gibson Hand had just about
wrapped up their story of Gladstone Cooley when the
Weasel and the Ferret got back to the squadroom, surprised
to see the street monsters and the homicide team in the
office at this hour.

'All you gotta do is phone Camp Pendleton tomorra,'
Gibson Hand said. 'Pfc. Cooley. Huh! That's what's wrong
with this fuckin country. Marines in black skivvies. Shit,
gimme a hunnerd-pound gang kid with a twenny-two rifle,
we'll shoot the fuck outa a whole battalion a marines like
that one. One scrawny spic with his Mexican Mauser. And
me!'

'Wasn't no grunts like that when *I* was in the Corps,'
Buckmore Phipps said. 'He's just part a today's youth. It's

the Democrats. Any more Democrats runnin this country and the Libyan navy might decide to capture New York.'

'We'll talk to our young marine tomorrow,' Martin Welborn said. 'And I want to thank you guys for helping out.'

'Whatcha got, big homicide?' the Weasel asked, while the Ferret yawned and made the last log entries of the day.

'Jist a gunfighter died with his boots on,' Gibson Hand said.

'Keep in mind that name and description of the whore they call Jill,' Martin Welborn said to the street monsters. 'The phone number is turning up too often.' Then he turned to the Weasel and Ferret and said, 'I was going to tell you tomorrow, the phone number surfaced again, the number your suspect dropped the night you busted Bozwell.'

'That number of the movie studio?'

'That one,' Al Mackey said. 'Lots of street folks seem to be carrying that number these days.'

As the street monsters were starting out the door Al Mackey said, as an afterthought, 'You might keep an eye out for a high-roller in a black Bentley.'

Which made the Ferret's droopy lids flicker a bit. 'What black Bentley?' he asked the homicide detectives.

'Some guy in a Bentley gave the phone number to a little blond whore named Jill who gave it to another whore who screwed a guy to death in a motel tonight,' Al Mackey explained. 'This is getting complicated. See, it's the number Buckmore's marine was carrying. It's the same . . .'

'A black Bentley?' the Weasel said to the Ferret. 'Tuna Can Tommy's friend?'

'. . . number your gook was carrying,' Al Mackey continued.

'We know about a horseplayer drives a black Bentley,' the Ferret said, wide awake now. 'Might be a coke dealer too, but that's probably bullshit. Yet there ain't *that* many black Bentleys screwing around the boulevard. They don't like to drive them outa Beverly Hills without an armored escort.'

'*Might* be the same guy,' the Weasel said.

'Well, we're goin home,' Buckmore Phipps announced. 'You get a line on this gook, give us a chance to ride along. Gibson ain't killed no one for two, three weeks now, since they kicked him out of surveillance.'

'We'll let you know,' Al Mackey promised.

'I think that people that drive Bentleys are show-offs,' Buckmore Phipps observed to his partner as they exited.

'A course, Buckmore! That's what life's all *about*!' Gibson Hand said. 'Lemme explain it all to ya . . .'

'You think the guy in the black Bentley might be connected with the slope that tried to waste me the other night?' the Ferret asked Martin Welborn.

'I don't know,' Martin Welborn said. 'All we know is everyone keeps popping up with that movie studio phone number. A whore named Jill who got it from the man in the Bentley. A marine male model from Camp Pendleton had the number and *name* of our victim. Your Vietnamese rob-and-cut man had the same number. And another guy who likes to skate was given a mysterious appointment where our victim died. Since we know about *this* many, there might be dozens more carrying that number around. Why *that* studio? What's it got to do with our victim? I'd like to find Jill and the guy in the Bentley for starters.'

'Jill we can't help you with,' said the Ferret. 'But we might be able to find a guy named Lloyd, drives a black Bentley around the boulevard.'

'We just can't stroll into Flameout Farrell's restaurant and ask the bookie to give us a client list,' the Weasel said.

The Ferret got up and started pacing back and forth in the squadroom. He looked at Al Mackey and Martin Welborn. He looked at the Weasel. Then he grinned darkly. 'If this black Bentley leads to the dink, all I want is to *be* there when you take him down. You gotta promise.'

Al Mackey shrugged and said, 'Gibson and Buckmore wanna be there, you two wanna be there. I'd say that gook has about as much chance of being taken alive as Custer's bugler.'

'You promise?' the Ferret demanded. 'Day or night?'

'We promise,' Martin Welborn said.

'Let's go, Weasel!' the Ferret said. 'I'm cooking!'

'Should we know where you're going?' Al Mackey asked.

'Better you don't,' the Ferret assured him. 'When you come in tomorrow morning, we're gonna have you a name to connect with a black Bentley. I only hope it's the right Bentley.'

'Good night, fellas,' Al Mackey said. It was best not to ask too many questions of the Ferrets and Weasels of this world. There was less to deny when the headhunters put you on a polygraph.

'I don't know about this,' the Weasel said as the Ferret careened down Hollywood Boulevard toward the little restaurant owned by the bookmaker Flameout Farrell.

'It'll work, goddamnit,' the Ferret said. 'Don't be a pussy.'

'I don't know.'

'Look, you saw how dumb Tuna Can Tommy was. You think a gook like that is gonna have a *smart* bookie? A smart bookie ain't gonna work outa some greasy spoon on the boulevard in the first place, is he? The damn street's crawling with heat!'

'Maybe we just oughtta go see Tuna Can Tommy. Maybe he could find out Lloyd's last name and address for us. After all, we *did* make him a secret agent.'

'Puh-leeze,' the Ferret said. 'I can see it now. Tommy in his Columbo raincoat and cowboy boots sneaking around a horse parlor? Bet he'd be naked under the coat. Show his stubby putz to every broad he passed on the way. Puh-leeze, Weasel. This'll work, we do it *my* way.'

Doing it the Ferret's way entailed the Toyota being parked on Wilton Place, with all further action on foot.

They operated without flashlights and it was risky climbing the ten-foot fence surrounding the film-processing plant next to the restaurant. Chain-link fences often meant guard dogs, but there was no dog shit close by so they risked it. The problem would be going back over that fence and doing it quickly after they were through with step one. Especially if some Hollywood radio car just happened by and saw two leather-covered thugs climbing fences in the darkness, and let go a couple of rounds from the Ithaca, leaving their bodies draped over the top of the fence. Very few of the Hollywood patrol officers knew the two narcs and there would be no time to get acquainted if they were spotted fleeing at night. But it was all part of it. Even the Weasel, after he resigned himself to the Ferry's dopy plot, was starting to get stoked up.

They crept down the walkway between Flameout Farrell's little restaurant and the film-processing plant. They jumped back into shadows when an old woman in a baseball cap passed by on a bicycle with a raucous white duck riding passenger in the basket. The Ferret looked at the Weasel. The duck wore a yellow sweater. Hollywood.

When the Weasel got near the sidewalk he glanced inside Flameout Farrell's Fancy Eatery and saw a sad pensioner gagging back a fat-laden ham sandwich while a faded little guy in a T-shirt, presumably Flameout himself, was counting the day's take from the cash register. A cigarette with an ash longer than the butt hung from his lower lip and accounted for the argument he'd had with the pensioner when he gave him his ham on white.

'I didn't ask for no pepper on my ham.'

'You didn't *get* no pepper on your ham.'

The Weasel looked at his watch and whispered, 'Tuna Can Tommy said he closes about now.'

'Just our luck he gets a late customer,' the Ferret whispered as they retreated down the alleyway.

'Wonder how long the old guy's gonna suck on that slimy sandwich?'

'Let's just do it anyways,' the Ferret said. 'Might even make it more realistic, there's a customer in there.'

'I don't think that's a good idea,' the Weasel said. 'Uh uh. Bad.'

They crept back up to the corner of the building, waited for a stream of traffic to pass, watched for pedestrians, and peeked around the corner again. 'The old bastard just ordered *another* cup a coffee!'

'Fuck it,' the Weasel said. 'I'm too bummed to be hanging around here like an alley cat. Let's do it, get it over with.'

'After you, weaselly one.' The Ferret grinned.

The Weasel reached inside the deep pocket of his motorcycle jacket and removed an ordinary building brick. He started wiping the brick on the leg of his jeans until the Ferret said, 'They can't get *lifts* off a freaking brick! You been watching *Kojak* reruns or something?'

So the Weasel looked both ways, emerged from the darkness, and nodded to the Ferret, who removed a hefty brick from *his* jacket. Then both narcs stood on the sidewalk, and after a ready, set, hut one, hut two, hauled off and heaved both bricks through the front of Flameout Farrell's glass windows. It sounded like a symphony of cymbals.

Both narcs were darting down the walkway and hitting the first fence before Flameout Farrell even got off the floor. The customer was running around the restaurant in total panic, still holding his ham sandwich, yelling, 'Earthquake! Earthquake!'

And Flameout Farrell, believing it was indeed an eight point sixer, crawled under a table as advised in the civil defense warnings.

'This is the biggy they predicted!' the pensioner screamed. 'California's going to Tahiti!'

Then, when there was no shaking or ominous rumbling and the old man stopped yelling and confusing him, Flameout Farrell, who had bitten his cigarette in two, started spitting tobacco and crawled cautiously out from under the table.

'Somebody threw a *brick* through my windows!' he said,

188

seeing the shattered missile on the floor. 'Somebody threw *two* bricks through my windows!' he said, examining the wreck of a restaurant. Arizona wouldn't get the beachfront bonanza after all. Somebody busted his fucking glass!

The Weasel and Ferret sat two blocks down Hollywood Boulevard and cursed. It took the radio car *twelve* minutes to get there. Lazy pricks.

'The citizens deserve better protection from assholes who destroy your property,' the Ferret said indignantly.

The uniformed cops obviously had other fish to fry and took the world's fastest crime report. They were gone before Flameout Farrell even started sweeping up the glass, trying to decide how he was going to get the place boarded up at this time of night. He was thinking about looking in the phone book for midnight lumber yards when the narcs knocked at the door, holding up police badges. Formalities over with, they entered the little lunch counter by stepping through the ten-by-twelve opening that used to be windows.

'We were sent from downtown as soon as we heard,' the Ferret said.

'Yeah? I didn't expect no detectives till tomorrow or the next day,' Flameout Farrell said. At first he looked white and washed out, his dirty blond hair going to gray. In the light his hair gave his sallowness a translucence.

'We work intelligence,' the Weasel said. 'Undercover.'

'You the vice squad?' Flameout Farrell asked.

'We was the vice squad we'd a busted your ass a month ago, Flameout,' the Ferret said. 'We know you're taking horse action here.'

Flameout Farrell's mouth dropped open and he got more washed out. In fact he blanched white as dry ice. 'Me? Me? Me?'

'Knock off the fucking arias, Flameout,' the Weasel said. 'Me me me, my nuts! Siddown!'

Flameout Farrell would have sat without being commanded. His legs had turned to licorice.

'There's only one reason we're bothering with you tonight, Flameout,' the Ferret began.

'Why's that?' Flameout Farrell looked from one narc to the other. 'I never bought no hot typewriters from boulevard junkies! I never . . .'

'We're here to save your life,' the Ferret said.

'My life!'

'We ain't interested in you. We're interested in Carlo Andrutti.'

'Who's Carlo Andrutti?'

'You really are small-time, Flameout,' the Ferret said disgustedly. 'Carlo Andrutti only owns every back office from here to Malibu, is all he owns! And it just so happens that about the time you got conned into operating a little phone spot in your kitchen . . .'

'That's right!' Flameout Farrell agreed, 'I was *conned* into it. I ain't really interested in horses, and . . .'

'. . . about the time you got into it, a guy, oh, maybe a hundred notches higher in the organization than the guy *you* deal with . . .'

'And we *all* know who that is.' The Weasel nodded.

'About that time Carlo Andrutti notices little poverty palaces like this springing up in Hollywood and he doesn't run a retirement fund for fry cooks, and he . . . doesn't . . . like it!'

'I don't know nothing! Nothing!'

'And since we work on organized crime we gotta figure ways to keep guys like you from wearing cinderblocks tied to your underwear and ending up scaring the surfers at the Santa Monica Pier when you come bobbing up a month from now taken off at the balls by sharks. And that's what we're doing here, Flameout.'

'So who . . . who . . .'

'Flameout, you are a freaking idiot,' the Weasel said, tugging at the gold stud he wore in one ear.

'We were tailing some a Carlo Andrutti's gunsels for two days. They busted out the windows of every phone spot and cash room in town that isn't owned by Carlo Andrutti.'

'They're trying to tell you something, Flameout.'

'They're hoping you get the message, Flameout.'

'And all we're trying to do is stop the button men from hitting the mattresses.' The Ferret liked that. *Mattresses. Button men.* Just like all those dumb gangster movies they dreamed up over lunch at The Rangoon Racquet Club.

'What can I do? I didn't *know* about Mister Andrutti!' Flameout Farrell exclaimed. 'I'll give it up if somebody's gonna get mad at me!'

'First of all, anything we tell you has to remain confidential. This is police business, Flameout.'

'I won't say nothing.'

'And anything *you* tell *us*, which we can use to save your ass from these hoods, will likewise remain confidential.'

'Okay,' the Ferret began, 'first thing is, there's a guy comes in here to get some action down. Drives a black Bentley. Let's start with him.'

'I don't know nobody like that,' Flameout Farrell said.

'Fuck him. Let's go,' the Weasel said. 'Carlo Andrutti's gonna hang him upside down and drain his blood like a rabbi with a chicken.'

'Wait a minute, wait a minute! Okay, I *know* him!' Flameout Farrell cried. 'You gotta protect me till Mister Andrutti knows I'm outa the bookmaking business!'

'The guy in the Bentley's a problem, Flameout,' the Weasel said. 'I'm not at liberty to tell you how or why, but he's a problem for us. Let's start with his name.'

'Lloyd.'

'We *know* that. His last name?'

'I dunno.'

'Where's he live?'

'I dunno. He's a customer. I mean, he got a little action down maybe once, twice, is all. He talks like some kinda player, but he never spent more than a hundred bucks with me.'

'Uh huh. And how did you meet him?' the Ferret asked.

'He knows . . . he, uh, he . . . knows somebody I know.'

'You want us to walk right outa your miserable life right this minute?' the Weasel asked.

'No! He, uh, he knows . . . my daughter,' Flameout Farrell said softly.

'Who's your daughter?'

'Her name's Peggy. She's only seventeen. She's . . .'

And then both narcs were utterly astonished to see Flameout Farrell, the inadequate entrepreneur and failed bookie, look up with eyes overflowing. He put his face in his hands and sobbed like a widow at a wake.

The narcs gave each other puzzled shrugs and waited. The Weasel finally offered Flameout Farrell a cigarette, which he accepted. The Ferret lit it.

'He . . . he . . . he said he's trying to . . . *help* Peggy,' Flameout Farrell sobbed. 'She . . . she ran away thirteen months . . . months ago. She's into . . . into drugs and . . . and maybe . . . other things.'

'Prostitution?' the Ferret asked.

Flameout Farrell nodded and looked at the floor. 'He . . . this guy, Lloyd . . . he came in here one night with Peggy. She said . . . she said she wanted to get some things belonged to her mom. Her mom went off a long time ago. Some rings and . . . stuff. I didn't . . . didn't want no rings. I just . . . I just wanted my Peggy to *stay*!'

'And where did she go?'

'I don't know and neither does Lloyd. He left her on a street corner,' he said, wiping his eyes. 'Lloyd came back two, three times since. Peggy told him about my sideline. He said he came back to get some action down, but he ain't no horseplayer. He sits. He talks to some a the other players that come in. He waits a few minutes. I think he was waiting for my Peggy to come back.'

'What's he talk about?' the Ferret asked.

'He asks about her. Who her friends are. All the things I don't know. He swore to me he never, you know, never took advantage a her. He swore he felt sorry for her and wanted . . . wanted to *help* her.'

Flameout Farrell saw the two cops exchange glances. 'I woulda believed *anybody*, he said he'd help make my Peggy come home!' Flameout Farrell said, breaking into tears again.

'You put your home address and phone number on that police report?' the Weasel asked.

Flameout Farrell nodded and wiped his eyes on the greasy sleeve of his T-shirt. His skin had an ivory cast. He was an odd-looking little man. His flesh was like old china.

'When this guy Lloyd comes back, I want you to find out something about him. Where he lives. A last name. Where he hangs out. And get his license number,' the Ferret said.

'I'll try.' Flameout Farrell nodded.

'What's he look like?' the Ferret asked. 'How old?'

'Maybe thirty-two or thirty-five.'

'Color hair?'

'Dark. Dark eyes. No, blue eyes I think. Shit, I dunno what color eyes. He's maybe six feet. Well-built.'

'Like a body builder?'

'Not that well built. He looks like all these outa-work guys come around and eat two doughnuts and call themselves actors. Nice clothes. A disco-looking guy.'

'Next time you see him, tell him you know where he might find Peggy,' the Weasel said. 'And that you can get in touch with her. Then you make a date for Lloyd to come back, and you call us.' The Weasel gave his police business card to Flameout Farrell.

'What's this got to do with Mr Andrutti?' Flameout Farrell asked pathetically.

'It's gonna save *your* ass, believe me,' the Weasel said.

As the narcs were stepping through the yawning hole they had made, Flameout Farrell said, 'He don't call her Peggy.'

'What?' The Ferret turned.

'He calls her Jill. I guess that's her street name. Jill.' Then Flameout Farrell put his face back in his hands and sobbed desperately.

*

While the Ferret and Weasel were finishing up what had been a very long day, Al Mackey and Martin Welborn were sitting in the detective car off the Sunset Strip. They were parked in the lot of a service station that was closed for the evening, tucked away behind four other cars. The stripped-down detective cars were not meant for undercover work and were as recognizable to the street folks as a black-and-white, minus the Mickey Mouse ears.

'I don't know why I let you run my life, Marty,' Al Mackey said, his head resting on the doorpost while Martin Welborn sat behind the wheel and watched The Red Valentine Massage Parlor through binoculars.

'I'm saving you from The Glitter Dome. Look at it that way, my son.'

'Glitter Dome. The Angels are on TV tonight. I was gonna curl up with a beer and a turkey sandwich and watch the home boys get the crap knocked out of them again. And for extra excitement there's always the challenge of waking up and kicking that sneaky cat out of my bed soon as I fall asleep. God, I *hate* that cat.'

Martin Welborn did not lower the binoculars for an instant. There was quite a bit of foot traffic going in and out at this time of night. There were also four whores hustling motorists on the corner. One was a white girl, but it wasn't 'Jill'. She was a brunette. He wondered if she could be wearing a wig. 'Turkey sandwich, eh?' Martin Welborn said finally. 'Learning to cook *this* time around as a bachelor?'

'You kidding? I wouldn't even *touch* anything in my filthy kitchen, let alone eat. Reason I feed the cat there, I hope he'll get ptomaine and die. I pick up sandwiches from the deli. Stays open late enough to accommodate all the losers of the world.'

'You should learn to cook,' Martin Welborn said. 'It makes living alone ever so much more . . . acceptable.' Then he lowered the binoculars and looked at his partner and Al Mackey saw the eyes drop at the corners and knew he was thinking of Paula Welborn.

But Martin Welborn wasn't thinking about Paula. She flashed through his mind for an instant. Then she was gone. The talk of loneliness triggered more fearful images. They had buried Elliott Robles today. He had thought about going to the funeral. He had thought about sending a mass card. But just because Elliott was Mexican didn't necessarily mean that his family was Catholic. There weren't many Catholics named Elliott. There weren't many Mexicans named Elliott. Except that funny little junkie, Elliott Robles.

'You took my business out on the street,' Elliott Robles had said to him when Martin Welborn made the fatal mistake during the interrogation of Chuey Verdugo. Elliott had terrible fear in his eyes when he said it. And then, after a while, he looked resigned. Was it because of all the drugs he shot? All the stealing he had to do to get the drugs? Perhaps it was acceptance that Martin Welborn saw. Perhaps he didn't hate the detective for his unforgivable, fatal blunder. Perhaps. It was comforting to think so. To make believe.

Martin Welborn thought of another gang member who once told him, 'You take my guns away and get me wasted, I'll come back to haunt you.' Would Elliott Robles come back to haunt him? To haunt him as Danny Meadows had done?

They had arrived at the Meadows' house that day before the radio car. The screaming woman stood in front and never said an intelligible word. She didn't even gesture or point. She just looked at the house and screamed.

'Screamed,' Martin Welborn muttered.

'What?' Al Mackey said. He had been dozing. 'You see something?'

'See something?'

Martin Welborn was trembling. Like the afternoon in the captain's office when they were given the Nigel St Claire case, when Marty's eyes went in and out of focus so strangely. Al Mackey couldn't see those long brown eyes in the darkness of the detective car. Marty had the sweats. The eyes.

'You okay, Marty?'

'Okay?'

'You, uh, think maybe we worked long enough for one

195

day? I think we worked long enough for two days. I don't think we're gonna find a little blond whore named Jill if we sit here for a week.'

Martin Welborn unfolded his handkerchief, wiped his brow, folded it neatly, and put it back in his pocket. 'Must be getting hot flashes.' He grinned. 'Happens in our midforties, they say. Got to get used to it. It's hell growing old, eh, my boy?'

'Yeah, hell,' Al Mackey said, looking at his partner closely. Whatever it was had passed. The only reason he was going along with Marty in this silly stakeout for a whore who was given a phone number that probably had nothing to do with their murder victim was that the Nigel St Claire case had given Marty some fresh juice. For the first time since Paula Welborn left.

'I think we could sit here for a week and not find a blond whore named Jill.'

'I agree with you,' Martin Welborn said finally.

'We just have to slog through it, Marty,' Al Mackey said. 'We're not going to get any breaks in this case. We already know there's no Jill known to Hollywood Vice. Tomorrow we check with Sheriff's Vice. Then Administrative Vice. Then we start calling the Bentley dealers.'

'There are *lots* of Bentleys in California,' Martin Welborn reminded him. 'What do they say? If California seceded from America it would be the seventh richest *nation* in the world?'

'Yeah, and I got a feeling most of those Bentleys are right around here,' Al Mackey sighed. 'And probably *Lloyd* is an alias anyway. Or the car's registered to somebody else. Slog it out, is all we can do.'

'There *is* another possibility,' Martin Welborn said.

'What's that?'

'Go in the massage parlor and ask for her.'

'I'm sure they're gonna be delighted to give us the address and phone numbers of street whores they employ as part-time masseuses.'

'Go in as a *customer*,' Martin Welborn said. 'Con them out of the information.'

'Who we gonna get to go in?' Al Mackey said.

Martin Welborn looked at his partner and smiled. 'You've always been a better con man than I could ever hope to be.'

And that was true enough. A massage parlor john. Al Mackey hadn't had a massage since he was on U.S. Navy liberty in Japan in 1955. She was sixteen years old, as light as a moth with the hands of a wrestler. The massage lasted five minutes, the sex one hour. In those days he could cut it.

'I don't think I got enough money for a massage,' he said, looking through his billfold.

'What do they cost?'

'Damned if I know.'

'Couldn't be more than twenty dollars, could it?'

'For the kind they give around here, I imagine it's more than twenty dollars,' Al Mackey said. Marty *should* have been a priest.

'I've got thirty-five dollars,' Martin Welborn said, handing the money to his partner.

'I've got twenty-three. That should be enough to convince them I'm for real and loosen a tongue.' Loosen a tongue? Maybe this assignment wouldn't be too bad!

'Give me your gun and badge. Better give me your ID card, too, in case somebody looks through your things while you're lying in the spa, or whatever.'

Al Mackey picked up the binoculars for the first time and looked at the unimpressive entrance to The Red Valentine. It was an ordinary storefront except that the windows were totally painted out and the door was framed with blinking light bulbs. Show biz.

'Most of the customers been wearing suits like me?'

'All kinds of dress,' Martin Welborn said. 'You look all right.'

'Don't think I look too much like a cop?'

197

'You look like a not-so-successful insurance man out for a night on the town. You certainly *don't* look like a cop.'

'What's that supposed to mean?'

'I'd say the weight loss since the last divorce has made you look *less* like a cop than before.' Which was a kind way of putting it.

When Al Mackey walked through the blinking doorway into a red-carpeted room with gold velour wallpaper, the receptionist leered at the emaciated customer. 'Welcome, dear. Looking for a relaxing rub?'

'Yeah, business made me kind of tense today.'

'Regular massage is twenty-five. Aphrodite Special is forty-five. Spa and steam is twelve dollars extra. Course you don't look like you need the steam. Some guys sweat off five pounds in there. You don't need to sweat off nothing.'

What is this shit? He came in here to let them guess his weight? He looks *less* like a cop than before? Al Mackey decided it was garbage burgers, fries, and peanuts for the rest of this week. Never mind what it did to his stomach, he was going to put on some *weight*. A guy could only take so many cracks about his body.

'I guess I'll take the regular massage,' he said.

'Oh.' The disappointment was ill-concealed. She pushed her heart-shaped rose-tinted glasses up on her nose. She had the ubiquitous Bo Derek hairdo but she certainly wasn't a ten. Not even a five and a half. 'That'll be twenty-five. You pay now.'

'What's the name of my masseuse?' Al Mackey asked.

'You been here before?'

'Two, three times,' Al Mackey said.

'Well, we have Trixie, we have Gina, and we have Laurel tonight.'

'Don't know them,' he said. 'Last time I was here, I had a girl I really liked. I think her name was . . . let's see . . . Joy?'

'Don't know no Joy,' she said. And *that* looked true enough in her case.

'Wait a minute. Not Joy, uh, it was ... Jill. That's it. Jill. Is she here tonight?'

'Jill? No, she ain't been around for a few weeks. She only works part-time.' Then the receptionist grinned and said, 'You had Jill give you a rub, it was a *romantic rub*, I bet.'

'It was!' Al Mackey cried.

'You didn't get no massage from Jill for twenty-five. You musta got the Aphrodite Special. Maybe even a *extra special*?'

'I sure wish Jill was here,' Al Mackey said.

'Okay, honey, we can take a care a you now I know what you need. We got two other girls for the Aphrodites. We got Laverne. We got Juicy Lucy.'

'I don't know.' Al Mackey hesitated. 'Maybe I oughtta come back some other time. Jill and me really got along.'

'A course, a course. I understand,' the receptionist said impatiently. 'I know what kind a massage you need. Why you think they call her Jackin Jill?'

'Jack and ...'

'Jackin Jill. Jackin Jill! I know what you want. Now, Laverne's a spade. You ain't prejudiced, are ya?'

'No but ...'

'And Juicy Lucy's a Jap. Only been here six months from Tokyo. Speaks pretty good English, though. You won't have no trouble making *her* understand.' The receptionist giggled at that one.

'If only I could get with Jill again.'

'Listen, Juicy Lucy knows all those massage tricks from Japan. In fact, she taught Jill how to give massages.'

'Oh, I see,' Al Mackey said. 'That's different. As good as Jill? She a friend of Jill's, is she?'

'Matter a fact, they are. You still like Jill better after you try Juicy Lucy, you tell me, I'll make an appointment and you can come back and see Jill.'

'Well, I guess I can't go wrong,' Al Mackey said.

'That'll be an extra twenty. Juicy Lucy don't give nothing but the Aphrodite Special.'

Al Mackey hoped Captain Woofer wouldn't balk when they turned in an expense chit for this one. Forty-five bucks!

'You decide on the spa?'

'Hell, no!' Al Mackey said. Forty-five bucks.

It was a tiny room with one table containing oils and lotions, towels and washcloths. There was a massage table covered with clean sheets and a towel folded across the end where his head would go. There was a wooden chair and two wall hooks with a few coat hangers. There was some jazz being piped in on a scratchy little speaker with a loose wire. And that was it. Forty-five bucks.

He was expecting plush pillows, Persian rugs, maybe a little pool with a fake waterfall, some sexy Japanese wall paintings. Where's the goddamn bar? He was starting to get nervous. After all, this *was* his first massage except for the twelve-dollar special in 1955. He needed a drink. He looked outside the little room where the receptionist had directed him. He couldn't hear anything like the revelry he'd expected.

There *is* no goddamn bar! Just half a dozen little cubicles like this! The steam and spa was probably a splash-down with a Water Pik.

At least she was young. She wasn't particularly pretty, not like the one in 1955. She wore shorts and a tank top, like a skater. She said, 'You take off clothes, please. You ray down on table. I be back.' And she was off.

Al Mackey took off his coat and pants and hung them up. He worried about his wallet, but what the hell, how much could they steal? And how could anyone dip into his pants without him knowing? When he didn't feel two little hands on his ass he was going to look for that wallet. He got down to his underwear and faltered. What the hell. Line of duty. He stripped off the ragged jockey shorts and tucked them in the pocket of his suit coat. He didn't want her to see them. That *last* bitch he married never even saw to it that he had decent underwear.

He lay prone on the table and waited. The music was getting more scratchy. Forty-five bucks.

The door opened and Juicy Lucy came back in with some fresh towels. 'You want Aphrodite Special?' she giggled. 'I very good. You rike, I sink.'

'Yeah, last time I had Jill give me one,' Al Mackey said, watching her pour some lotion on her hands and rub them together.

'Jill good girl. I teach her. You want oil or rotion?'

'I think Jill used oil.'

It felt erotic the moment she poured the warm oil down his back. It stopped feeling erotic when she started working on his neck and shoulders. Goddamn! She was brutal!

'You so skinny,' she said. 'Sometimes hurt bony guy. No meat. Bones hurt.'

'Yeah, yeah,' he said. 'I didn't know you had to be Arnold Schwarzenegger to get a massage.' He was getting sick of all these cracks.

'Who?'

'Never mind. Listen, when's Jill coming back?'

'You rike Jill, yes?' she said. 'Jackin Jill. You rike me too. You see.'

'I like you already,' Al Mackey said. 'Oooww! Easy on the spine, will ya?'

Things got better when she did his legs and toes. No pain. He was still on his stomach. Guys paid money for this torture? 'Listen, when did you say Jill's coming back?'

'Okay,' she said in exasperation, 'you want Jackin Jill business quick? I try give good massage first! Okay.' And she dumped half a bottle of scented baby oil down the crack of his buttocks.

'Wow!' Al Mackey cried.

Then, with him still on his belly, both her little hands were all over him. 'You not patient,' she said. 'You wait, it get better. You no wait. Jackin Jill. Jackin Jill. All you want, Jackin Jill!'

'Wow!' Al Mackey cried as she kneaded his buttocks.

The hell with Jill. The hell with Marty. It was 1955 again and he was a young *bull*!

But suddenly, when he was getting semi-stiff, it was over.

'Finish,' she said. 'I give you *super* Aphrodite, for cost twenty dollar more.'

Al Mackey jumped off the table and ran to his pants. Fuck you, Amazing Grace. The answer was in the *hands*. He was a massage parlor junkie!

He only had thirteen dollars and some change.

'I don't *have* twenty dollars,' he cried.

'Massage over.' Juicy Lucy shrugged.

'Wait. Wait. I've got thirteen! And some change!'

'Nope. Twenty dollar,' she said, picking up her towel as Al Mackey's semi died aborning.

'Do you take Master Charge?'

'Cash money.'

Christ, he had a thirty-dollar Timex! 'Listen, I'll come back and pay you . . . tomorrow! You be here with Jackin Jill and I promise I'll give you a hundred dollars for a double massage.'

'You no have twenty now. You have hundred tomorrow. Yes yes.'

'Look, I don't carry cash on the Strip. All these hooligans running around.'

'Okay, I give you super, but you owe Juicy Rucy.'

'All *right*!' Al Mackey sighed, lying back down. The Super!

'Now,' she whispered, 'I show you where Jackin Jill learn her trick.' She leaned over and kissed Al Mackey on the cheek. *Kissed* him. That he didn't expect. 'Oooohhh,' he sighed. My little cherry blossom! Then she started tickling his buttocks and thighs. He felt the hair on his legs stirring. He could hardly feel her hands. Was she going to knead his balls like bread dough? What?

She then tickled him lightly along the spine. She purred and whispered to him in Japanese. She was probably calling him a stinking disgusting round-eyed degenerate, but he didn't care.

'It good?'

'It good!' he sighed.

So far she had not touched his genitals. When she did he was going to inflate like a goddamn life raft. He was ready. Then he felt just *one* fingernail touch the hair on his balls.

'Oh, my God, it's been such a long time!' he cried.

She put two fingers down there and began tickling not just the hair, but the sacs themselves.

Get ready, Lucy-san. Al Mackey's going up like a rocket!

Except that he didn't. She touched them for perhaps ten seconds. She had never even gotten to his cock. He felt something warm and wet on his stomach.

'My God!' he yelled in despair.

'What?' the startled masseuse cried.

Al Mackey turned over and sat up. The telltale deposit told all. She took his semi-limp member and shook it disgustedly. 'This not my fault. This *you* fault.'

'Oh, God!' he cried. Misfires were one thing! But premature ejaculation? Was there no end to the humiliation!

'I earn money. I try to do best.' She gave the drooping whanger another sneering shake. 'This not my fault. This *you* fault.'

'I know, I know!' Al Mackey cried. 'God, I know!'

Al Mackey let himself be led to a prefab plastic shower stall where the masseuse scrubbed the oil off him and sprayed him down with a jet of lukewarm water. So much for the Japanese bath. At least she tried to dry him off, but he took the towel and did it himself. He tried to get back to business despite his desperate depression.

'I meant it about tomorrow night,' he said. 'I'll be here at eight o'clock. I want to see Jill.'

'And me,' she reminded him.

'Right.'

'Hundred dollar.'

'Right, right.' He nodded.

203

'You have this . . . *thing* go wrong with Jackin Jill?' Juicy Lucy asked, while Al Mackey slipped his necktie over his head and zipped his fly.

'Look, I've *never* had trouble with sex in my life!' he said. 'Everything works right!'

'Yes yes,' she said.

Maybe it was the kiss, he thought, as he waited at the traffic signal to cross Sunset with some wired-up Brooke Shields clones. She had blindsided him with that kiss. It was the *last* thing he expected. He couldn't remember the last time he'd been kissed tenderly.

The light turned green and he crossed with the chattering bubblegummers. He felt so old. Maybe sex was over for him. Who needs sex? Does Jerry Brown need it? He's only the fucking *governor*. GOD, IT'S ALL OVER!

'Well, all your little muscles relaxed?' Martin Welborn grinned when Al Mackey got in the car.

'You don't know the half of it,' Al Mackey said sourly. 'And you aren't *going* to. Jill might be there tomorrow night. I didn't want to push it too far, but I think I have a date with her and Juicy Lucy at eight o'clock.'

'Who's Juicy Lucy?'

'Do you have enough change left to buy me a cup of coffee? I need a cup of coffee.'

'You spent it *all*?'

'Massages aren't what they used to be,' Al Mackey said. 'Nothing is.'

13

The Burbank Bomber

The homicide team was twenty minutes late the next morning. Luckily, Captain Woofer was at a coffee klatch with the Chamber of Commerce and wasn't there to catch Al Mackey and Martin Welborn dragging in.

Al Mackey was horribly hung over from an evening of Tullamore Dew and a furious dream-chase of a giggling Japanese masseuse who knew the Truth. After kicking the cat off the bed three times, Al Mackey awoke in the morning to find it had clawed to shreds the underwear he had dropped on the floor. He was forced to admire an animal who could punish with such inspiration. The vicious bastard was better than a set of thumbscrews.

Martin Welborn hadn't chased his ghosts. He'd been chased by them. He had dreamed of Elliott Robles. It was fragmented.

You took my business out on the street, Sergeant Welborn! Where can I go?

The dream awoke him at three A.M. He managed to go back to sleep after an hour of night sweats. He dreamed about Danny Meadows. He awoke crying out. He did not go back to sleep at all after that.

Their morning coffee hadn't yet been touched when they were surrounded by the Weasel and Ferret on one side, Schultz and Simon on the other.

'Okay, Winkie and Blinky, you two got your little peepers open yet?' the Ferret asked. 'We got a few transmissions for ya, somewhat garbled but maybe you can figure em out. A whore named Jill? She's the seventeen-year-old daughter of a nickeldime bookie owns a restaurant on Sunset. Her real name's Peggy Farrell and we already

205

pulled her juvie package this morning while you two were laying in bed playing with pee pees.'

'Both our mommas went south,' Al Mackey said, grimacing from the squadroom coffee. 'No pee pees.'

'Peggy Farrell has two busts for runaway,' the Weasel said. 'Both times released to her daddy, Flameout Farrell, the world's crummiest cook and bummed-out bookie. But get *this*! She's been seen with this dude in the black Bentley at her daddy's place! And dad-o says Lloyd-of-the-Bentley keeps coming back, supposedly to get down on a horse but really to find out where the hell's Jill.'

'I know it ain't our case,' said Simon, 'but we made some calls this morning and found that Just Plain Bill Bozwell moved out, with no forwarding address. And there's nothing in his package about any gook associates.'

'We already knew that.' Al Mackey nodded.

'It's anybody's case,' Martin Welborn said. 'We want you to work on it as much as you care to. We appreciate it.'

'There ain't an F.I. in this department on Bozwell. None at the Sheriff's Office either,' Simon said. 'Maybe he just hired the slopehead for the night, like he claims. Maybe you just should forget him, concentrate on the others?'

'We'll take a crack at him when he shows up for his preliminary hearing,' Martin Welborn said.

'Oh yeah, robbery called and said the preliminary's been continued,' the Weasel said. 'The defense needs two weeks to prepare the case more *adequately*. Sure. Probably try to scare off the goldbugs, something like that. Well, that's robbery's problem.'

'The gook is *my* problem,' the Ferret said, flexing his bandaged hand. 'His case ain't closed in *my* book.'

'*Two* weeks,' Al Mackey said, as the coffee burned his tongue and woke him up a bit. 'Okay, we may as well forget about talking to Just Plain Bill Bozwell.'

'You start on the Bentley yet?' Schultz asked.

'We're getting ready to.' Al Mackey sighed. 'Must be a fleet of them around here.'

'If we help solve the murder of a big shot, do we get interviewed on television?' the Ferret wondered.

'I guarantee it,' Al Mackey said. Young cops. A sporting event. A *game*. Hi, Mom, it's me!

'We ain't got much these days. Couple chickenshit domestic shootings, Want some help?' Simon offered.

'*Do* we?' Al Mackey said, showing the first painful smile of the hung-over morning.

'We're going back to that Thai restaurant and stake it out for a few hours this afternoon,' the Ferret said.

'I thought you were supposed to be destroying all the dopers on Hollywood Boulevard,' said Schultz.

'We'll tell Whipdick Woofer the gook's been positively snitched off by our number one anonymous informant as being the kingpin importer of China white straight down the Ho Chi Minh trail. Or some fantasy like that. He don't think too clear anyway since somebody loaded his pipe.'

The smog roared. The sun screamed. For a hangover victim it was a *long* ride to Oceanside, and neither of them had had three uninterrupted hours of sleep the night before. Loading up on aspirin, Al Mackey had at least quelled the thundering headache. He snoozed for half an hour while Martin Welborn drove to Camp Pendleton, the world's second largest marine base.

A telephone call made before leaving Hollywood had Pfc. Gladstone Cooley cooling his heels in the provost marshal's office before the detectives arrived. He was wearing starched Marine Corps dungarees, bloused over his boots. His T-shirt was dead white against his golden unflawed skin. He was a recruiting poster marine.

After the introduction to the lieutenant on duty the detectives were given private use of Pfc. Cooley, who was literally shaking in those spit-shined boots, not so much in fear of the cops as of the MPs, who didn't cotton to any hint of entanglement with the civilian authorities, and figured they *owned* these young men, who were invariably guilty until proven innocent.

'Is there anything we can get you, son?' Martin Welborn asked. 'A cigarette? Something to drink?'

'No, thank you, sir,' Gladstone Cooley said, sitting at rigid attention, his starched dungaree cap in his lap.

'Do you think you could sit at ease?' Martin Welborn asked. 'You're not in any trouble, you know.'

'Yes, sir. Thank you, sir,' Gladstone Cooley said, opening his knees six inches.

'Do you remember the day the two big uniformed cops came in the modeling studio?' Al Mackey began, as the kid's cobalt-blue eyes roamed around the spartan military office. He settled on a file cabinet upon which rested an MP's helmet, webbed belt and stick.

'I remember the day, yes, sir.'

'You gave the policeman your ID and liberty card, and you also gave him a piece of paper. It had a telephone number on it. Do you remember that number?'

'Number? I usually have a few numbers with me, sir.' The young marine's mouth was so dry he was clicking on all his consonants.

'Would you like some water?' Martin Welborn asked.

'No, sir,' Gladstone Cooley said. 'I'm not sure which number, sir. I was *real* scared a those policemen, sir.'

'Well, it was a number of a movie studio,' Al Mackey said. 'Does that help?'

'Oh, yes, sir. I remember now. Those policemen were . . . monsters, sir.'

'Do you still have that piece of paper?'

'No, sir. I think the black policeman dropped it when they ran out the back door. Then I ran out the front door. So did all the artists. Those policemen looked like . . . like they should have spikes sticking out the sides a their necks. They were *monsters*, sir!'

'Yes, yes, we know,' Al Mackey said. 'Was that phone number written by you?'

'No, sir. It was written down by some man I met. He gave it to me and asked if I had any interest in an acting job.'

'Who was the man?'

'I don't know his name. He came to the modeling studio one day. I model sometimes at a different studio on Sunset. It was a similar kind a job. He just came in and saw me and asked me.'

'What's the name of the studio?'

'I forget. Some gay guy named Malcolm owns it. Near Genesee.'

'Gay guy?'

'Yes, sir. But *I'm* not!'

'Did the man say what kind of acting job it was?' Martin Welborn asked.

'No, he just said it was a movie they was gonna start shooting in June. And they wanted to give me an audition and see was I suitable.'

'Where was the movie being shot?'

'I don't know.'

'What was it about?'

'I don't know.'

'Was it a porn flick?'

'That's what I figgered. I mean, there I was, a . . . model and all and . . .'

'A gay porn flick?'

'That's what I asked him.'

'What did he say?'

'He said it was absolutely not a gay porn flick.'

'Did you ask him if it was a hetero porn flick?'

'I tried to find out things like that and how much they paid and all, but he told me just to call that number and I'd get the details. He said it was big money for three days' work. He asked if I could get a few days' liberty during the week and I said yes.'

'And what was the name of the man you were supposed to call at that number?' Martin Welborn asked.

'I forget,' the kid said. The marine was winding down, flipping his cap around his hand. 'Let's see, it was a Mister . . . Mister . . . I forget now. Fact is, I wasn't sure about calling, more I thought about it. I don't mind posing

209

and all but I didn't wanna be seen in some movie like that back in Minneapolis.'

'Was the name Nigel St Claire?' Al Mackey asked.

'No, that wasn't the name,' the kid answered.

'That's the name that was written on your pieee of paper,' Martin Welborn said. 'Those two policemen remember that.'

'Yes' – the kid nodded – 'I wrote that name down.'

'Why did you write that name down?' Al Mackey asked.

'When the guy gave me the number he said it was gonna be a good movie and that the phone number went to a famous studio. And when he mentioned the studio, I knew it was Mister St Claire's studio. Then I knew the movie couldn't be too bad. So I thought about trying to call Mister St Claire personal and see if he remembered me and find out could he put in a word for me if I auditioned.'

'And how did you know Nigel St Claire?' Al Mackey exclaimed.

'Met him at a screening,' Gladstone Cooley said. 'He was real nice. Paid me lots a compliments. When he heard I was a marine, he said he made three movies about marines. Said the Marines was his favorite branch a service. Said I was the best-looking marine he ever saw.'

'Did he ask you to be in a movie?'

'No, we just talked for a few minutes. I told him I was a part-time model and I'd like to be an actor, but he just smiled and said hang in there, something like that.'

'Did he give you a card? A phone number?'

'No, that was all he said. Then he just walked away and talked to lots a other people. It was after a private screening at the Directors Guild.'

'Who were you with?'

'I was invited by a man, directs television shows. He wouldn't like me to say his name. He's married.'

'What's that got to do with anything?'

'Well, his wife might not like to know he took me there.' Then the kid's room-temperature I.Q. clicked on. 'He's not gay either. We're just friends.'

'When the man came to see you at the modeling studio, did *he* mention Mister St Claire?' Martin Welnorn asked.

'No, sir. He just said he heard from some artist that I was a good prospect for a movie.'

'What did he look like?'

'Six feet, maybe. Gray hair, I think. In his late thirties. Moustache. Nice-looking guy. Wore aviator-type glasses.'

'Think very carefully, son,' Martin Welborn said. 'Did you mention anything to Mister St Claire about where you could be located?'

'I told him I was stationed at Camp Pendleton.'

'You told him you modeled. Could you have mentioned Malcolm's studio to Mister St Claire that night?'

'No, sir.'

'Did you mention any possible way that you could be reached other than at Camp Pendleton? I mean, you were *thinking* about an acting job, weren't you? Meeting an important movie man like Mister St Claire?'

'No. I just mentioned I get jobs from Lonnie's Casting Service in case he ever needed my type as an extra.'

'Good. You mentioned Lonnie's Casting Service,' Martin Welborn said patiently. 'Now, does Lonnie's Casting Service know how to contact you if someone should call?'

'They refer any calls to Malcolm's modeling studio,' the kid said.

'Thank you, my boy,' Martin Welborn sighed.

'Oh, I get it!' the kid said. 'Mister St Claire coulda told the guy who came to see me to call Lonnie's. And Lonnie's coulda referred him to Malcolm's!'

Good-bye, America, Al Mackey thought. Bring back the draft or I'm taking my police pension and highballing it to Cabo San Lucas. Or points south. Before the Russians find out.

'Can you tell us anything more about the guy who contacted you and gave you the number?'

'No, sir.'

'Okay, son, you can go back to your company. We'll

211

explain to the provost marshal that it was just routine and you're not in any trouble.'

'Thank you, sir.' The kid beamed. 'I hope Mister St Claire's not in no trouble? He was real nice.'

'You don't read the papers, son?'

'No, sir.'

'Watch TV?'

'*Dukes of Hazzard.* That's my favorite.'

'Mister St Claire's not in any trouble,' Al Mackey said. 'Not anymore.'

'If you think of anything else, you call us, will you?' Martin Welborn said, giving the marine a business card.

'Yes, sir,' the marine said. Then he looked puzzled, and as he was turning to go, he said, 'You mean if I think of anything else about Mister St Claire? Or the guy in the Bentley?'

'Bentley?' Al Mackey exclaimed.

'Yeah, some a the artists called me when he was driving away. Big black Bentley. They said he's gotta be real and I oughtta call that number. Maybe I shoulda?'

'Son, you keep our business card,' Martin Welborn said. 'If you think of the name of the man you were supposed to contact at the studio for the acting job, you call. Okay?'

'Got it.' Pfc. Gladstone Cooley beamed. 'Bye, sir! Bye to you too, sir!'

While Martin Welborn drove and Al Mackey slept during the trip back to Los Angeles, the Weasel and Ferret were *both* asleep on the roof overlooking the Thai restaurant on Melrose Avenue. And while the two narcs slept a black Bentley pulled up in front of the restaurant. A handsome man in aviator glasses got out, looked in the door of the little restaurant, got back in his Bentley, and left. When the narcs awoke at two o'clock that afternoon, they were covered with pigeon shit.

But while Al Mackey and the Weasel and Ferret slept away the afternoon, the street monsters, who didn't give a damn about the Nigel St Claire murder case and wished the detectives would stop picking on them and making them work overtime thereby missing the *real* action at The Glitter Dome, accidentally found Jackin Jill.

It was a day like all days the way it began. Buckmore Phipps told horror stories to Gibson Hand to get him jazzed up for another run at the boulevard. It was just like before a game when Buckmore Phipps had been a semipro defensive tackle.

The first horror story involved the latest do-gooder scheme he'd heard about on the six o'clock news, the idea being to compel criminal offenders to make restitution to their victims and to the community where their crimes were committed.

'See, Gibson, they don't want these poor dudes rottin away in the slam when they're not *dangerous*. They call them *property* offenders. You know, like all these daytime burglars who ain't dangerous till a housewife happens to come home with her arms full a groceries. When the dude's haulin her goodies off in a pilla case and then he sees she's under seventy-five and she's scared and suddenly this guy who ain't *dangerous* gets a hard-on cause he's such a punk he can't usually scare *nobody*. And she gets his gun up her cunt cause he discovers it's *fun* to overpower somebody. But up till then, he was never *dangerous* cause no housewife ever walked in on him before.'

'How they gonna force him to pay back what he stole?'

'Get this. They charge the cons *five* dollars a day for room and board and get them *jobs* to pay back victims and the state! Can you dig it? They rake leaves for three bucks an hour and the state takes a few bucks a day for restitution and then they can go out every night and steal three hundred bucks' worth a loot to buy new Sevilles which they keep stashed at the girlfriend's house where they also have fine threads and wristwatches and color TVs and enough dope to keep momma happy. And they *still* get meals and a room and a brand-new leaf rake for *five* dollars a day!'

'I'm in the wrong job,' Gibson Hand said. 'You too. Course you ain't a spook. They might not let *you* in these programs so easy, you turned crooked.'

That startled Buckmore Phipps. Once in a while Gibson Hand said something to remind him that Gibson was a nigger. And suddenly Buckmore Phipps came to the realization that he hated white people nearly as much as blacks! Maybe, in a certain sense, *everybody* is a nigger! It was the most frightening philosophical insight he'd ever had.

'Gotta take a leak,' he said shakily, driving the radio car into a service station.

Buckmore Phipps got out from behind the wheel and went to the men's room door. Locked! Every gas station restroom in town was locked. Afraid they'll steal the goddamn toilet paper, no doubt.

'Hey, kid, go get the key to this shithouse,' he said to a teenager who was gassing up a Pontiac and cleaning the rear window.

'Just a second, Officer,' the kid said.

'I gotta piss, boy. Get the key or I'll shoot the fuckin lock off!' Buckmore Phipps was in a foul mood thinking about the terrible possibility that *everyone* was a nigger. Even *him*!

'You might have a couple fruits locked theirselves in there,' Gibson Hand noted. 'You take a piss in these toilets, you gotta hold your cock in one hand, your stick in the other.'

After the kid came hustling back with the key, Buckmore Phipps found there were no fruits locked inside. It was the day that Teddy Kennedy announced that he might withdraw from the presidential race. If there was one thing worse than a Democrat, it was a liberal Democrat.

Impulsively he said, 'Gimme the hand mike, Gibson.'

The radio car was parked just a few feet from the door, so the coiled mike cord stretched from the car into the restroom. Buckmore Phipps pushed the send button on the hand mike and flushed the urinal three times, sending

214

a whoosh of water crashing into the headset of an operator on the complaint board downtown who cried: 'What the hell! Did some cop drive off the Venice boardwalk?'

Buckmore Phipps flushed the urinal again and again, and finally he made an announcement into the mike: 'So long, Teddy!'

'Buckmore, you shouldn't oughtta get into politics so heavy,' Gibson Hand said. 'It ain't good for your head.'

Buckmore Phipps was unstoppable in an election year, but done with politicking for the moment, he proceeded to roger a radio call to Selma Avenue, were two male prostitutes were duking it out over the favors of a customer in a white Jaguar who couldn't decide which boy he wanted for twenty dollars.

The street monsters didn't like fights. Unless *they* were in them. It made them nervous to see all the sissy punches and flabby slaps and face scratching that went on. Not just among Selma Avenue fruits but even in barroom brawls where people were supposed to be better at it. The fact is, most people liked to fight like baseball players. Lots of show and nobody gets hurt. It always made the street monsters want to jump in and kick and gouge and kneedrop and arm strangle and do all the other things that *worked*.

After a few minutes of watching, they got bored with the two fruits bloodying each other's noses. The john in the Jag noticed the black-and-white and said *adios*, roaring away.

'Hey girls, knock it off,' Gibson Hand said without even bothering to get out of the car. 'You *don't* knock it off, I'm gonna tear your lips off and put you right outta business.'

'We ain't got no shakes yet today,' Buckmore Phipps reminded him. 'Maybe we better write a couple F.I.'s?'

'Okay,' Gibson Hand sighed, and both street monsters got out of the car to do a little paper work and keep the sergeant happy. They were writing field interrogation cards when a station wagon drove by and slowed.

The driver put his head out of the window and said,

'You don't have to allow yourself to be detained unless there's probable cause!'

'Who's that?' Gibson Hand said to the two combatants, who were wiping their bloody noses.

'Never saw him before.' One fighter shrugged.

'Nobody I know,' said the other.

Then the car stopped and the man got out. He carried a clipboard. He was bald on top but the fringe around his head hung below his ears. He wore a crisp safari jacket and gold-rimmed sunglasses. He started writing on the clipboard.

'I'd like your names, Officers.'

'What for?' Buckmore Phipps demanded.

'Do you have any reason to be detaining these two men? Or is it simply for walking on Selma Avenue?'

'Jist a gud-damn minute . . .' Gibson Hand sputtered.

'There is *no* crime to be walking, or standing, or sitting on Selma Avenue regardless of what *you* may think. And, as you know, there is no crime in *being* homosexual.'

Buckmore Phipps was turning white around the gills. 'You just better fly on, shitbird,' he warned.

'*You* men!' the intruder said to the combatants. 'You have a right to *be* here on Selma Avenue. You have a right to get *into* cars. At the moment, it is a public offense to engage in sex for money. That's true for either sex. It's a public offense to engage in certain conduct in public. That's true for either sex. But that's all. You do *not* have to let these officers harass you.' He punctuated his statement by a forceful finger thrust. Which accidentally poked Buckmore Phipps right in the *eye*.

The case which eventually ended up in the Los Angeles municipal courtroom involved not the two original combatants who fought for the customer on Selma Avenue. It involved the people versus Thurgood Poole, the gay rights activist, who maintained he was merely trying to protect the freedom of two members of the gay community on Selma Avenue.

What the other witnesses claimed, both street monsters

216

and the two combatants, was that all four of them were perfectly justified in breaking Thurgood Poole's nose and collarbone and dislocating his shoulder and dancing on Thurgood Poole's kidneys.

The gay rights activist went to jail for battery on a police officer and eventually ended up in court facing all four witnesses. The two members of the gay community he was trying to protect told the jury he was just a meddling busybody who shouldn't go around picking on diligent policemen like Officer Phipps and Officer Hand, who both sat in court in double-knit leisure suits and clip-on neckties and smiled sweetly at all the old ladies on the jury.

Thurgood Poole ended up with summary probation, a five-hundred-dollar fine, and more dents, cracks and bruises than both teams in the Super Bowl. The two battling fruit-hustlers ended up with a letter of commendation from the commanding officer of Hollywood Station for doing their civic duty in coming to the assistance of two beleaguered policemen.

All in all, it was a pretty good day for the street monsters, who got rid of tons of tension. It wasn't often these days you got to do good police work like they did on Thurgood Poole. But while they were enjoying the Waterloo of Thurgood Poole, a horny spring-loader in a ball-point pen factory in Burbank was about to deliver Jackin Jill right into their puffy mitts.

His name was Bruno Benson and he was sick and tired of sitting around all day sticking little springs into ball-point pens. In fact, he got so sick of it, and was feeling so horny, he decided to make his fourteenth bomb threat of the month, take the rest of the day off, cruise down the Sunset Strip, and maybe find a cute thirty-dollar hooker who could suck the batteries out of a flashlight.

During his lunch hour he strolled out the back door of the plant, hopped up on the cab of one of the delivery trucks, dropped over the fence into the alley, moseyed down to the gas station on the corner, dialed the plant manager, and told him the same thing he had told him the other thirteen times: There was a bomb planted in one of the cartons in the warehouse and it would go off sometime before the end of shift unless one hundred thousand dollars was left in a package on the bus bench across from NBC Television Studios.

Of course the plant manager never left the package of money, but that didn't bother Bruno Benson a bit. Because each time the manager received the bomb threat he was obliged by union and company policy to call the cops, and then to inform employees of the possibility of a bomb having been planted, giving them the option of leaving for the day or remaining on the job.

During his three weeks of employment Bruno Benson had earned a total of $485 including overtime. He had *cost* the company $230,687, which he figured made him the most expensive employee in Burbank, except for Johnny Carson.

While Bruno Benson was off for another afternoon, sucking on a fifth of Jim Beam, cruising hornily down the Sunset Strip in his pickup truck looking for a hooker, Jackin Jill was telling her pal Juicy Lucy in The Red Valentine Massage Parlor that she didn't want to work at the parlor anymore because the cheapos take too big a cut out of your fees, and she was doing far better on her own at one of the outcall massage services listed in the Yellow Pages. Which meant that she wasn't interested in the hundred-dollar bag of bones who Juicy Lucy said was coming back at eight o'clock for a doubleheader.

Meanwhile, the Weasel and Ferret were amusing themselves by shooting at pigeons on the roof over the Thai restaurant with plastic slingshots and pieces of ·oo buckshot from a police shotgun round. They'd played Frisbee for a while until the Weasel got carried away with a fancy behind-the-back toss and the disc went sailing clear over to Western Avenue into the shopping cart of a wino ragpicker who gave a Thanks, Lord! glance to the sky and sold it to the first roller skater sailing by for enough to buy a pint of Sneaky Pete.

It was while the Ferret was looking at his Frisbee going bye-bye that he glanced down at the restaurant and saw the black Bentley drive slowly up in front and stop.

While both narcs were fighting over the binoculars, the driver, who never emerged from the car, seemed to feel that his man was not inside, and drove off in traffic.

'Son of a bitch ain't going in!' the Ferret cried.

'Fucking bus is blocking me out!' the Weasel cried, frantically adjusting the binoculars.

'Stop, you prick!' the Ferret moaned.

But the Bentley turned right and was gone. They didn't even get the license number.

No crack of wings. No pigeons plummeting. The only creatures going bonzo were the Ferret and Weasel who were stomping around the rooftop in frustration, yelling and firing wildly at the bored and listless birds, who had no fear of these two assholes with slingshots. As the narcs finally decided that their stakeout would have to be moved to the street, where they had access to the Toyota, Bruno Benson was driving by the Whiskey-A-Go-Go.

He had so far spotted five whores hustling afternoon motorists. They were all at least twenty-five years old. Almost as old as his youngest daughter. He didn't go for these old ones. Then he saw a very pale, thin little blonde in tight jeans walking east on Sunset. Now, *she* was young enough for Bruno Benson.

'Hey, honey, how about a lift?' Bruno Benson yelled from the number one lane.

'I can walk,' she said.

'Why walk?'

'Good exercise.'

'I know a better way to exercise,' Bruno Benson giggled, taking a big gulp of Jim Beam.

A redneck drunk in a pickup truck? Poison. 'Catch you later, honey,' she said, crossing to the north side of Sunset.

Bruno Benson circled the block and came roaring up behind the blonde with *both* his engines racing.

'Look, baby,' he yelled. 'I ain't some toaster mechanic from Ventura. I'm a player. I got money!'

She kept walking west on Sunset, but she slowed enough to keep pace with the pickup creeping along beside her.

'How *much* money?'

'Enough.'

'Good-bye,' she said, quickening her pace.

Skinny little bitch. He had half a mind to tell her he was the Burbank Bomber, driving the cops crazy with thirteen, no, *fourteen* calls to the ball-point pen factory. 'I got *fifty* dollars!' he said. 'But I don't know if you're worth it.'

Then the pale blonde stopped, turned, and walked over to the truck that was idling at the curb. Up close she had a quality, all right. Her skin was . . . Bruno Benson later tried to describe the gossamer girl to another spring-loader. She was like those figurines you see down at Farmer's Market. Like that.

She said, 'For fifty dollars, if you'll settle for a short time, I'll *be* worth it.'

Except that she made a very unprofessional error. On the way to the motel, Bruno Benson wanted to substitute her head for the bottle of Jim Beam between his legs.

'Come on, just kiss it a little till we get there. Get me warmed up.'

'We'll be at the motel in a few minutes, sweetie.'

'Come on, just a kiss,' he said, his voice husky with horniness. She was so young!

'Sorry, sweetie,' she said. 'You have to watch the road.'

But when he expansively pulled out the roll of fives and tens and dropped twenty dollars in her lap, saying, 'This is a bonus,' and unzipped his khaki pants, the whore let greed overcome professional reservations.

She hadn't been down on him for ten seconds before Bruno Benson forgot to watch the road and started watching the ceiling of the truck cab and howling like a wolf. His howl was cut short when he slammed into the rear of a school bus and all the kids going home got a good giggle at the expense of the guy running around the street holding his bleeding dick.

And the pale little whore was sitting on the curb, still coughing when the police car pulled up and Gibson Hand said to the howling Bruno Benson, 'Put your joint away, you're causin a traffic jam.'

'I'm hurt, I'm hurt!' Bruno Benson bellowed.

'What happened, your cock go in the cigarette lighter?' Buckmore Phipps asked. 'Never seen a traffic injury where only a cock gets crunched.'

'That howlin's gettin on my nerves,' Gibson Hand said.

Then the street monsters looked from the choking whore to the howling driver and put it together. 'First the whore down at the motel fucks a guy to death,' Gibson Hand observed. 'Now this one almost bites a dude's cock off. You know, we're *safer* gettin our pussy at those Chinatown gin mills, Buckmore.'

Though they didn't want to bother with a traffic accident at *any* time of day, let alone so late in the afternoon (there's never a traffic car around when you need one. Those lazy pricks!), the street monsters were stuck with it.

'Gimme some ID, sis,' Gibson Hand said to the blond whore.

'Don't have none,' she said, starting to get her breath back.

'What's your name?'

'Peggy Farrell,' she said, truthfully.

'How old're you?'

'Twenty,' she lied.

'You wanna go to a doctor?'

'No,' she said. 'I'll just go on home.'

'You got any a his cock stuck in your teeth?'

'No.'

'Awright, jist lemme get your address and phone number.'

Then Buckmore Phipps came over and whispered, 'Think we gotta book this drunk, Gibson? The bus driver's yellin about gettin rear-ended and he can *see* the dude's swacked.'

'Shee-it!' Gibson Hand snarled. 'Means we're gonna be workin overtime again tonight!'

By then Bruno Benson was getting calmed down and had his wounded penis back in his pants, and was worrying about going to jail for drunk driving, and wondering how he was going to get enough money to pay ten percent to a bail bondsman. Then he thought of his twenty-dollar bill. She sure as hell hadn't earned it!

'She has twenty bucks a mine. I want it,' he said to Buckmore Phipps.

'She sucked your dick, didn't she?' Buckmore Phipps shrugged. 'I don't wanna get involved in no business dispute. I got enough problems here.'

'She *stole* twenty bucks from my pocket after we crashed,' Bruno Benson said. 'I want it!'

'That's a goddamn lie!' the blonde yelled raspily, and then started coughing through her swollen throat.

'She stole my money. I want it. Or I'll prosecute!'

'Officer, I've got a bus full of kids,' the bus driver yelled out the window.

'Fuck it!' Gibson Hand snarled. 'Driver, you come to Hollywood Station and make a traffic report after you get rid a those gigglin milk suckers! Buckmore, we gotta take both these people to the station, see what the fuck we got.'

And so the Burbank Bomber and Jackin Jill were *both* in custody and crying when, fifteen minutes later, they were led into the detective squadroom where Jackin Jill would meet the bag of bones who had hoped to be her date that night.

14

Mr Silver

The detectives were cleaning up their paper work for the day, making the last phone calls to crime victims, or girlfriends or wives (Yes, dear, it's just a coincidence that when I have to work overtime it usually happens on payday). Poor old Cal Greenberg wasn't in any hurry to go, but wait till tomorrow: seniors' night at the Stardust Ballroom! And his second wife out of town visiting a niece! Pennsylvania six five, oh! oh! ooohhh!

Then he saw Buckmore Phipps come in with a tearful little blonde in tow and he started getting depressed.

'Hey, Greenberg,' the street monster said. 'Who'd handle a trick roll on Sunset? You?'

'It depends on the circumstances, Buckmore,' poor old Cal Greenberg sighed. He should have moved quicker and been gone. 'Was it a robbery, a plain theft, what?'

The weeping blonde said, 'That man's a liar! I didn't rob nobody!'

'Well, she hurt the dick of a trick, and the bus driver they rear-ended is mad, and the trick's too drunk to walk so I don't know how great a victim he is, and I get it *all* jumped on me!'

'You're not making too much sense, Buckmore,' poor old Cal Greenberg sighed. 'Sit down, my dear, and tell me your name.'

'Peggy Farrell,' the whore cried.

'PEGGY FARRELL!' Simon, Schultz, the Weasel and Ferret, Al Mackey and Martin Welborn, *all* nearly scared the constipation out of poor old Cal Greenberg.

'Jackin Jill!' Al Mackey cried. 'I had a date with you tonight!'

*

223

Peggy Farrell had never had so much attention in her life, what with two scary cops in beards and leather jackets trying to talk to her about Lloyd in the black Bentley, and being overruled by two gigantic detectives in funny haircuts like they wore in the olden days, all finally being overruled by the other pair of detectives. One was the skinny one Juicy Lucy told her about, and the other, the one she didn't mind talking to, was a good-looking man with a gentle smile and beautiful teeth and dark eyes that turned down at the corners and made Peggy Farrell think that with a guy like him she could almost switch back to men for the sex she did apart from business. She sat in the interrogation room for thirty minutes with Martin Welborn and Al Mackey.

'I ain't really a runaway,' she sobbed. 'My dad knows I never left Hollywood. I just didn't want to live with him no more.'

'And where do you live, Peggy?' Martin Welborn asked.

'Around.'

'We could detain you at Juvenile Hall,' Al Mackey said.

'I didn't steal that man's money,' she said.

'But you're technically a runaway.'

'I'll be eighteen the first of next month. It wouldn't make much sense to treat me like a juvenile, would it?'

'No, but we could,' Martin Welborn said. 'Why don't you want to tell us where you live?'

'Cause I live with somebody I don't want to hurt, that's why.'

'Is it a man?' Al Mackey asked. 'The man you work for?'

'I don't have no pimp.'

'All the girls say that.'

'I don't have no pimp. I been bothered by a couple pimps. One said he'd pour acid on me if I didn't work for him, but so far I ain't been hurt.'

'Is the person you live with straight?' Martin Welborn asked.

224

'I live with a woman,' Peggy Farrell said. 'She's an older person.'

'How old?' Martin Welborn asked.

'Old. My mom's age.'

'How old is that?'

'She's forty-two.'

'Is she your lover?' Martin Welborn asked.

'Whadda you think?'

'Does she approve of the fact that you hustle tricks?'

'No. She has a good job. She's been trying to talk me out of it. In fact, I hardly ever do it anymore. This guy in the truck just wouldn't let up. Practically waved the money at me.'

'Let's forget him for the moment,' Al Mackey said. 'Tell us all you can about Lloyd in the black Bentley.'

'He's just a guy offered me an acting job, is all. I didn't know he was some big criminal or something. He was an outcall massage. Asked for me by name. Didn't even take the massage. Just met me, paid me, and gave me the phone number.'

'How old is Lloyd? How tall? What color hair? Describe him,' Al Mackey said.

'It's hard for me to tell when a guy's thirty or forty if he's in good shape like Lloyd. I think he has light hair, maybe even gray. But he's youngish. Like you,' she said to Martin Welborn, which made Al Mackey wince, being two years younger.

'Why don't you know for sure what color hair he has?'

'He never took off his cap both times I saw him. One a those caps like Scotch or Irish people wear in movies. Tweedy like. And he wore it down close to his glasses. He wasn't anxious to be too recognizable, that's for sure. He had a grayish moustache and tinted glasses. Big wire-rimmed goggles.'

'What color tint?'

'Brown. Made his brown eyes harder to see.'

'Good girl,' Martin Welborn said. 'And you only saw him twice?'

'Twice. And I *never* tricked with him. He never asked for it. First, he picked me up at Sunset and La Brea and took me by my dad's restaurant.'

'Why did you ask him to take you there?'

'There were some things a my mother's she left behind when *she* ran away from home. I wanted them. I figured with Lloyd along, my dad wouldn't make no fuss and try to get me to stay. I mean, Lloyd wasn't a guy to fuck with, in that big car and all. And afterwards he dropped me back at Sunset and La Brea and gave me twenty dollars just to call a number and ask for Sapphire Productions. Said to tell the guy that answered who I was and where to meet the next time.'

'That's when you met the producer?' Martin Welborn asked. 'Where did you go and what was his name?'

'His name was Mister Silver. We met at this house clear up on top of Trousdale. I used to have two massage customers up there.'

'Did he live there?' Martin Welborn asked.

'I don't think he did. Once he had to go to the bathroom and he opened the hall closet by mistake.'

'Very good, Peggy,' Martin Welborn said. 'What did you and Mister Silver talk about?'

'About me playing a part in this movie they were making in Mexico. A small part, but Lloyd said they'd pay me a thousand a day for three days' work. Said they'd drive me down and bring me back.'

'*Drive* you down?' Al Mackey said. 'It wasn't far enough to fly?'

'I got the impression it wasn't far from the border.'

'Was anyone else at the house in Trousdale?'

'Just Lloyd. He was assistant producer or something.'

'Was it a porn flick?' Al Mackey asked.

'I guessed it probably was,' she said. 'I didn't ask. But I wondered why they wanted to shoot the movie in Mexico. Unless it was kiddy porn.' Then she added, 'I ain't in favor a kiddy porn, you understand. Makes me wanna barf. Some a those little girls and boys, eight, nine years old. I had some tricks once, *had* to see that stuff before I could make them come off. I almost grossed out. I never take a trick a second time if he makes me watch kiddy porn. They take those little kids and drug them out and make them do . . .'

'Yes?'

'Everything they make *me* do,' she said quietly. '*Everything*. And they're babies.'

'Yes,' Martin Welborn said. 'But you were going to do the movie?'

'I thought maybe it wasn't *real* kiddy porn, you know? Maybe just a bunch a teenage actors. Maybe fourteen, fifteen years old. I don't call that kiddy porn. You're fourteen, you're old enough to do what you want.'

She *looked* fourteen, Martin Welborn thought. Although they knew from Flameout Farrell that she was telling the truth when she said she would legally be an adult on the first of the month. Her skin had the translucence of antique china. She was very frail and had the huge cautious eyes of an antelope. She was so delicate she probably wouldn't be able to order a drink unchallenged until she was thirty years old. She was not pretty in any ordinary way. But she was most peculiarly exquisite.

'You must have asked Mister Silver how you were selected, didn't you?'

'Yeah. He said he didn't know. Then Lloyd said one a my massage customers told him I was special. He didn't say who the customer was. I didn't ask. I musta massaged a thousand guys. He said several other girls and guys were being interviewed. In fact, Lloyd looked at his watch after we were there awhile and said he better take me back, pick up the next girl for Mister Silver to see.'

'Then what happened?' Al Mackey asked.

'Nothing. Lloyd took me back.'

'To Sunset and La Brea?'

'Yeah. I don't want nobody to know where I live.'

And then the detectives exchanged glances. It was time

227

to turn the screw a bit. They had to keep in touch with Peggy Farrell, the only lead they had.

'You know, Peggy, you *are* technically a juvenile until your eighteenth birthday.'

'So?'

'So we have to release you to a parent.'

'You can't call my dad!' she said.

'We have to release you to a responsible adult.'

'I don't *know* no responsible adults!' Peggy Farrell cried, revealing the story of her life in six words.

'I suppose we could release her to the woman she lives with, couldn't we, partner?' Al Mackey said to Martin Welborn.

'Perhaps.'

'I don't wanna embarrass Lorna!' Peggy Farrell said. 'She's the only person cares about me. The only person I care about.'

'Well, we're not permitted to release a juvenile except to a parent or an acceptable adult. I think we could drive you home and maybe leave you with Lorna. That, or your father.'

'Will you have to tell Lorna about, you know, that guy in the pickup? I promised her I'd quit turning tricks.'

'No, we'll just tell her you were . . .'

'Tell her I got caught with some grass in my purse!'

'That's what we'll tell her,' Martin Welborn said. 'What does she do for a living?'

'She's in the movie business.'

Al Mackey gave Martin Welborn another glance and said, 'In what capacity?'

'She's a script supervisor. Worked on millions a movies. They're the people sit there when they're shooting and tell the director which way someone should look. Like camera left, camera right. What color tie the actor had on when they shot the beginning of a scene yesterday. Feed the actors their lines, stuff like that. She took me to see them shooting on a sound stage once. It was terrific.'

'And what studio does she work for?' Martin Welborn asked.

'They work at all the studios, not for any particular one, those script people.'

'What did she think of your movie offer?' Martin Welborn asked.

'She got real mad. Asked me as many questions as you guys. *Real* mad. Said it was kiddy porn for sure. And I'm stupid. And pretty soon I was crying and . . . we made up.'

'Did you promise her you wouldn't do it?' Al Mackey asked.

'That's why I didn't contact them again like I was supposed to,' Peggy Farrell said. 'I figured I had the job if I wanted it. But I promised Lorna. She told me Sapphire Productions was probably some fly-by-night production company into kiddy porn on the side.'

'Could you find the Trousdale house again?'

'It was night. All those winding streets up there? All those white houses that look just the same? No way.'

'And exactly how did you contact Lloyd?'

'I called that number of the studio and asked for Sapphire Productions. Some guy answered and I told him Lloyd gave me the number and for Lloyd to call me back or meet me.'

'Would you know Mister Silver if you saw him again?'

'Maybe. He had bushy black hair and a big beard and glasses that might all have been phony.'

Al Mackey removed a picture of Nigel St Claire from the case envelope in his plastic briefcase. It was a corporate portrait taken just six months before his death. He wore a somber dark suit and tie and was seated on the corner of his desk with a bevy of gleaming Oscars behind him. He looked to Al Mackey like all the glamour in the world. When Al Mackey looked at that man he invariably thought of the Riviera, private jets, limousines, French maids who looked like Bardot used to look.

And violent death. They had *other* pictures of Nigel St

Claire. Peggy Farrell studied the picture for a moment, started to shake her head, but picked it up again.

'It *is* Mister Silver?' Al Mackey exclaimed.

'No,' she said.

'Damn.'

'But I *know* this man.'

And then there was anxious pacing outside the interrogation room while Peggy Farrell was given a bottle of soda pop, and five minutes alone to study the picture of Nigel St Claire to try to remember which 'massage' it was. Because where else would she meet a man who looked as important as this one? The Weasel and Ferret, even Schultz and Simon, had decided to hang around.

Finally the door opened and Peggy Farrell timidly emerged, holding the empty pop bottle.

'Well?' Al Mackey said.

'I gave him a massage. It was an outcall. He tipped me thirty dollars.'

'Where?' Al Mackey asked. 'When?'

'A couple months ago. The Magic Carpet Motel. They don't ask no questions there. Don't even make you register. I don't think they could help you find him, if you're looking.'

'How do you remember him, Peggy?' Martin Welborn asked. 'The thirty-dollar tip?'

'No, not the money,' she said, looking at the picture. 'He said such pretty things to me. He said I had the most beautiful skin he ever saw in his whole life. He said he slept with some a the most beautiful women in the world, but he never saw skin like mine. He said I was something really special. . . .' The girl stopped and looked at the six policemen staring at her. 'A course all tricks bullshit you and all, but . . .'

'Well, we might as well split,' the Weasel said to the Ferret, as Schultz and Simon also decided to call it a day.

'We'll take you home to Lorna now,' Martin Welborn said.

'You won't tell her about the trick?'

'No.'

As they were heading for the door, the Ferret came back and said, 'This guy in the black Bentley, he ever with a partner? A Vietnamese guy?'

'No. He was alone when I was in the Bentley.'

'He ever mention a Thai restaurant?'

'What's that?'

'Thai. You know, Thailand? A restaurant near Melrose and Western?'

'No.'

'Shit!' the Ferret muttered.

'He could speak Chinese though. He *might* go to those restaurants.'

'How do you know?' Martin Welborn asked.

''Cause he said a few words to the houseboy that brought us the drinks up in Trousdale that night.'

'*What* houseboy?' Al Mackey cried. 'You said only Lloyd and Mister Silver were there.'

'I don't count a houseboy,' Peggy Farrell said.

'How do you *know* it was Chinese he talked?' the Ferret demanded.

'I *don't* know. Mighta been Japanese. Whatever.'

'What did he *look* like?' the Ferret yelled.

'I don't know! Stringy Oriental guy, is all. I remember one thing. He smiled when he brought me a martini and he had a *mean* smile.'

And then Peggy Farrell *really* got scared because the bearded cop with the bandaged hand was jumping around and running toward another table and tearing open drawers and muttering.

And Martin Welborn was saying, 'Ferret! Easy, boy. Easy, lad.'

Then the narc came running back with his ponytail flying and shoved a police mug shot in front of Peggy Farrell and said: 'Well?'

'Well what?'

'Is this Lloyd?'

'Easy, Ferret,' Martin Welborn said with more authority in his voice. 'Let *us* handle this, son.'

And the Ferret sat down but drilled holes through Peggy Farrell, who was so astonished she started shaking again. She looked at the mug shot. Police mug shots were scary-looking. The seconds passed. Six detectives were so still the hum of the wall clock sounded like a car engine.

Peggy Farrell held her hand over the hairline. 'Do. you have any more pictures of him?'

'Isn't that enough?' the Ferret cried.

'I mean, can I draw on this one?'

'Draw on it? Sure!' the Ferret exclaimed, and the Weasel put his hand on his partner's shoulder to keep him in orbit. Draw on it! Fold it! Spindle it! Eat it!

Peggy Farrell picked up a felt marker from the table and drew a crude moustache and glasses and hat on Just Plain Bill Bozwell. When she was finished she looked at the picture again, nodded, and said, 'It's really *scary* when you see someone you *know* in one a these police pictures.'

Lorna Dillon had a two-bedroom bungalow in Benedict Canyon, bought years before the real estate boom. She had a garden, two oak trees, an avocado tree, an orange tree and two olive trees. Her home, her garden, her life, were in perfect order. Except for the past six months, after she met Peggy Farrell while having lunch in a sidewalk cafe on the Strip.

She didn't seem particularly surprised to find two detectives with Peggy at her door. She said she'd been expecting it one of these days, and didn't seem to believe their story that Peggy had been picked up by some patrol officers because of a jaywalking offense and was discovered to have marijuana in her purse.

'I'll talk to the officers privately,' she said to Peggy Farrell. 'Go to bed.'

And the girl immediately obeyed the mother she'd never had.

Martin Welborn had no doubt that Peggy Farrell would

usually obey this imposing woman. But Lorna Dillon sometimes had to be on location and was gone for days at a time, and it must be then that Peggy Farrell got sick and tired of the neat little home and neat little garden and the peace and tranquility of the canyon and returned to the old haunts on the Strip, and the chance for not-so-easy money.

Lorna Dillon was not butch, but her voice was deep and her arms and legs were nearly twice the size of Al Mackey's. She wore tennis shorts and a T-shirt and was obviously a jock. Al Mackey later said she looked like a younger Magnani: all woman, but by no means weaker than *anybody*.

'Would you like some coffee?' she asked.

'No thanks,' Martin Welborn said.

'What happened? She get caught hustling johns?'

Martin Welborn nodded. 'I don't think it was all her fault.'

'It never is,' Lorna Dillon said. 'She could live a decent life here.'

Martin Welborn said, 'Ms. Dillon, could you tell us how much you know about this offer Peggy got to make the film?'

'Not much,' she shrugged. 'Did she tell you about the men up in Trousdale?'

'Yes.'

'It's obviously kiddy porn, wouldn't you think?'

'But she's not a *kiddy* in that sense,' Al Mackey said.

'Oh, I don't know. How much kiddy porn have you seen, Sergeant?'

'None,' Al Mackey admitted.

'How about you, Sergeant Welborn?'

'None.'

'Well, I'm in the movie business, so I've seen lots of things in the past twenty-five years. They could take a kid like Peggy and make her look twelve, thirteen. But I suspect they'd spice up their little film with some *real* toddlers, ten years old and *younger*. Pedophiles have a saying: "Eight is too late." '

'What makes you think that this is what they were up to?'

'They went to some trouble to interview Peggy. They offered her three thousand dollars for three days. And they're going to Mexico? This makes it a big production as far as garbage goes. They could shoot their stuff a lot cheaper right here in Los Angeles with a cast of young adult porn actors if it was *legal* porn. They have to be going for the real toddler stuff. Or . . .'

'Or what?'

'Animals. The only thing that's illegal in porn is to use minors under eighteen, or animals. It could have been an animal show in Mexico. Dogs, donkeys, that sort of thing. Have you ever seen a young girl screwing a German shepherd? Or how about a six-year-old child, sedated, but still suffering enough pain to jerk her head back in agony when she's penetrated by a full-grown man?'

'No, I can't say that I've seen any of that,' Martin Welborn said.

'We don't work vice,' Al Mackey said. 'Just nice clean homicides. Usually.'

'Homicide? Then what're you doing with Peggy? I thought you were vice cops.'

'We're working on the Nigel St Claire murder case,' Martin Welborn said. 'She had the telephone number of St Claire's studio. Some other people did too. We're just grasping at straws.'

'Sapphire Productions.' Lorna Dillon nodded. 'Sounds like one of those here-today, gone-forever little companies that move on and off the lots. I made her promise to forget that job.'

'Yes, she told us.'

'Did she tell you that she and I are . . .'

'Yes,' Martin Welborn said.

'Is there anything *else* you need to know?'

Al Mackey said, 'Being in the business, would you be able to guess who they might be? The man Lloyd in the black Bentley? The man who called himself Mister Silver in Trousdale?'

'The filthy vermin who make those kinds of films? We're *not* in the same business at all. I'm afraid I wouldn't know, gentlemen. Is that all?'

When she stood up she was nearly as tall as the detectives and shook hands with a tennis grip. Al Mackey figured *she* could give a massage with those hands.

The detectives drove to Nigel St Claire's studio and ended the day at Sapphire Productions. Which boasted no sapphire and no productions.

'I'm between shows,' they were told by Ellis Goodman, who *was* Sapphire Productions. He didn't even have a secretary. He had a desk, a chair, a sofa, a coffee table. Lots of copies of *Daily Variety* and *The Hollywood Reporter* were lying around. He had a telephone with no extension, and that was *it*, except for a beat-up refrigerator he had bought for thirty bucks from a movie company next door which had just gone out of business.

He was nearly seventy years of age but had frenetic darting eyes which made him seem younger. His hair was dyed black but the roots were showing. If tiny actors didn't buy their wardrobes from production companies, Ellis Goodman did. There just weren't as many tiny actors these days, so his maroon blazer hung on him like a cloak. Alterations didn't come with the wardrobe. And he was 'between shows'.

'Look, I don't really know this guy Lloyd!' he said. 'Sure he gets people to call here, sure! But I don't really *know* him! What did he do, anyway?'

'Nothing illegal that we know of,' Martin Welborn said. 'We'd just like to talk to him.'

He sat down behind the desk and said, 'You wanna drink? I don't know whether cops drink on duty in real life or not? I don't know nothing outside a the movies. Been in the business forty-eight years.'

'We drink outside the movies,' Al Mackey said.

He hardly had the words out before Ellis Goodman ran

235

to the trashed and paint-sprayed refrigerator that had obviously been used on a movie set for 'atmosphere'. Inside the refrigerator was half a bottle of orange juice, two bottles of Perrier, one lemon, two cans of beer, and a box of animal crackers.

'What'll ya have? Beer?' Ellis Goodman asked hopefully, holding up the two cans.

While the detectives drank their beer, Ellis Goodman nervously said, 'Whatever Lloyd did, I don't know *nothing* about it. I only know movies. I been a production manager, assistant producer, associate producer, producer, and excutive producer on seventy-three movies in my time. Seventy-three! That Lloyd was bad news. I never shoulda let him talk me into helping him out. What'd he do?'

'How did you help him out?' Al Mackey asked.

'Letting him use my phone number. An answering service, I was! Dumb! Dumb! You do dumb things, you're between shows and need a few bucks.'

'Where did you meet him!' Martin Welborn asked.

'Lloyd?'

'Yeah, Lloyd,' Al Mackey said.

'Let's see, Lloyd. Oh yeah, I met him at that little joint just outside the main gate. Everybody eats there. I figured he worked on the lot.'

'Who introduced you?'

'Nobody. He asked me if he could share my table. I was alone. We talked.'

'About what?'

'Nothing. Baseball. Politics. And movies. That's when he laid his trip on me.'

'What trip is that?'

'He said he would love to pretend he was a movie producer and be able to have some friends call a big studio like this one and ask for a production company. I said, that's nice, and then he says he'd just like to be able to do this for a few weeks and would I be interested in playing let's-pretend-Lloyd's-a-producer for five hundred bucks?'

'And you said yes?'

'I said no. What the hell, I says. You wanna impress some friends, buy them flowers.'

'Then what?'

'Then he says somebody told him I was between shows and he'd give me a thousand bucks if I just took calls for him for three weeks. Maybe ten calls, no more. And tell the callers that Lloyd wuld meet them when and wherever they said.'

'And then you'd call Lloyd?' Al Mackey asked.

'No way,' Ellis Goodman said, with a tic starting to pull at his mouth. 'No way. Whatever he done, I don't wanna know. And I don't wanna know *him*. He'd call me as late as seven o'clock in the evening cause that's when I leave. Movie people come in late but we stay late. We work long hours in The Business, I can tell you. It ain't all bouquets and blow jobs, like you probably think.'

'And you'd give him his messages,' Martin Welborn said.

'That's right. Some callers were boys, some were girls. You could tell they were all young people. And then I guess he could tell them he was a big-shot movie producer with Sapphire Productions and give them a number of a major studio, and like that. And that's all I know, fellas, and I gotta go home now.'

'Did you ever see him with anyone else?' Al Mackey asked, as Ellis Goodman opened the door for the detectives.

'Nope. I just saw him that time at the restaurant and once again when he had me meet him out on the street by the front gate when he gave me the thousand in cash.'

'Did you see his car?'

'Yeah. He drove a black Bentley.'

'Did you know Nigel St Claire?' Martin Welborn asked.

'Sure, everybody knew Nigel. If they been around The Business long as me.'

'Did you see him socially?'

'Naw, once in a while I'd run into him on the lot. I worked on lots a pictures a his over the years.'

'Did he know you were between shows?'

'*Everybody* knows I'm between shows,' Ellis Goodman sighed.

As Ellis Goodman was locking the door and the detectives walked to their car parked in front of Sapphire Productions, Martin Welborn turned and said, 'Do you have any idea why Lloyd would pay one thousand dollars to play producer?'

'Of course I know!' Ellis Goodman said.

'Why?'

'Blow jobs! What else? *Blow jobs!*'

15

The Screaming Cowbirds

The rest of the week was slogging through it, the ultimate test of any detective being endurance. They learned that there were more than three hundred homes in Trousdale Estates and that half of the residents didn't know the names of the property owner next door, let alone who might be leasing or renting at any given time. And, being part of the show business 'beaten track', as the realtor called it, property often changed hands every time someone was 'between shows'. It was a transient life on the beaten track and their real property was lost like their chips at Caesar's Palace.

The Bentley search was also petering out. The California Department of Motor Vehicles did not have the capability to supply computer runs by make of car. They'd checked virtually every leasing agency in metropolitan Los Angeles which might lease such an expensive car, with not a single lead to follow up. Just Plain Bill Bozwell, a.k.a. Lloyd the Producer, was possibly borrowing someone's car. Perhaps the car and house belonged together, Martin Welborn reasoned.

Schultz and Simon had renewed interest in the case and offered to handle the everyday cuttings, shootings and sluggings for Martin Welborn and Al Mackey, to free them for the Nigel St Claire investigation.

The Ferret, bonzo over the fantasy of finding the Vietnamese partner of Just Plain Bill, had leaped into the case with both motorcycle boots, and drawn the Weasel with him. He could recite from memory every piece of information on Bill Bozwell from L.A.P.D. records, the

F.B.I., C.I.I., and even what he had learned from the U.S. Army.

Bill Bozwell had been arrested nine times, twice in Los Angeles County and seven times in Orange County, where he was born and raised. All arrests came after his return from Vietnam in 1971. He was thirty-four years old, and had served a total of two years and ten months behind jail and prison walls. His specialty was armed robbery and extortion but he was also an occasional hash dealer and once he had been caught inside a two-million-dollar home in Newport Beach, stealing gold coins and jade sculpture. He had no known accomplices, and was regarded as a loner, both in prison and out.

During the last three arrests he listed his occupation as actor, but his name was unknown at any of the local guilds. His mug shots were downtown at Parker Center awaiting an examination by the L.A.P.D.'s foremost expert on pornography who was returning from vacation next Monday. He would determine if Bill Bozwell was an 'actor' he had seen in the voluminous porn material the Department had confiscated in recent years.

In short, Just Plain Bill was a hoodlum, with a tendency toward violent crime when profitable. And even if they knew where to find him while he was out on bail, it was virtually certain that, if he agreed to talk to them about his life as Lloyd the producer, his reason for it would probably be that put forth by Ellis Goodman – blow jobs.

Martin Welborn said if there was a connection between Bill Bozwell and the Nigel St Claire murder case, it might be in that house in Trousdale Estates, if they could only find it. Al Mackey said the hell with Just Plain Bill and the house in Trousdale Estates and the Nigel St Claire murder case because tomorrow night was the party.

'What party?' Martin Welborn asked.

'Kee-rist, Marty. *The* party. Herman St Claire invited us to a party.'

'Oh, *that* party,' Martin Welborn said.

'Yeah, *that* party! You mean you're not going?'

'I hadn't planned to.'

'You what? A real show-biz, honest-to-God, A-rated Hollywood party? The kind where all the girls look like those sultry animals on the Bain de Soleil television commercials? The kind where they look at your hundred-ninety-dollar Gucci loafers and say, "Glad you came casual, honey." *That* kind a party!'

'I really hadn't thought it would help us with the case, but . . .'

'Screw the case. Let's go and do whatever they do there!'

'Might not hurt to meet some of Nigel St Claire's associates,' Martin Welborn said.

'Thank God,' Al Mackey sighed. 'I thought your mind had snapped.'

'My mind hasn't snapped,' Martin Welborn smiled.

There were nine female parking attendants in black satin jackets and jogging shoes careening around the narrow streets of Holmby Hills when Al Mackey and Martin Welborn arrived at nine P.M. (fashionably late, Al Mackey insisted). It looked like the parking lot of an OPEC conference in Caracas. There were nothing but Rolls-Royces, Clenets, Mercedes, several little Volantes at one hundred thou per pop, and yes, three Bentleys (none black), lining the street on both sides, clear to the horizon. Martin Welborn was already thinking about searching the side streets for a *black* Bentley when a perky valette took one look at the detective car and said, 'You guys part a the security, pull in the service entrance.'

Although Al Mackey was miffed at not being treated like a guest, Martin Welborn grinned and said it was a good idea to keep their car available. This was show biz, after all. Maybe somebody would jump up and confess like in all the movie murder mysteries. The valettes kept several crates of red roses handy to give to each departing female guest, and the detectives parked behind the rose mountain.

There was half an acre under tent, in addition to the entire house that was available to roaming guests. The

241

detectives guessed there were several security officers there, probaby off-duty policemen. At the moment, a twelve-piece mariachi band blared away while two hundred guests mingled.

Herman III wasn't hard to find. He stood near the front of the fifty-foot single row of tables heaped with crystal and candle, canapé and caviar. With the trained eyes of investigators the cops spotted the nearest bar in a hurry. A Mexican barman in a white jacket and bow tie was pouring Dom Perignon as though it was plain old Ripple, sloshing it all over the bar as he tried to keep up with the crush of drinkers pressing in on him. There was another bar at the far end of the dance floor and yet another at the back of the tent, and they all seemed to be just as busy, so the detectives lined up at the first one to get their whiskey and vodka. There were none of the bare-chested waiters in bowlers, white gloves and suspenders at *this* party. This was *Old* Hollywood.

Then they paid their respects to the host, who had forsaken his on-the-job Brooks Brothers three-piece and was resplendent in cream-on-cream with a thin antique-fabric nutmeg necktie for contrast. He looked like an eggnog.

Herman III was talking to a Famous Singing Star who had just arrived in a green sweat suit to match her Rolls-Royce. On the sweat shirt was crudely stenciled front and back the name of the movie which had just wrapped that very day. Everyone said the sweat suit was a darling idea and the *paparazzi* on the street took more pictures of her than of anyone else.

At first, Herman St Claire III stared at Al Mackey blankly when he held out his hand. 'Mackey and Welborn, L.A.P.D.? Remember?'

'Oh sure!' he cried. 'Sure. Al and . . .'

'Marty.'

'Of course! So glad you could come! I'd like you to meet . . .'

But the Famous Singer had boogied as soon as she heard

242

who they were. They weren't like the cops at home in Queens. These L.A. cops would bust their mother if she snorted one spoon. And the Famous Singer had a Bull Durham tobacco bag around her neck under her sweat shirt clearly stenciled: 'Nose Candy!' The bag was full of cocaine that cost $150 a gram and was guaranteed to be quality stuff that wouldn't embarrass her at a nice party. Everyone who saw it said it was a darling idea too. No way was she going to let some cop confiscate it.

'Listen, I'll introduce you around if there's anyone you wanna meet. Meanwhile you boys help yourself and mingle.' Then, as an afterthought, Herman III said, 'Oh, by the way, you getting anywhere on my uncle's case?'

'Not much happening yet,' Al Mackey said.

'No? Too bad. Listen, you fellas mingle.'

And so they mingled, drifting from one group to another, mostly admiring the splendid women who had blithely regressed three hundred years. There were miles of ruffles. Tiers of them. Ruffles on hip-belted silk crepe. Twice-ruffled silk jackets over twice-ruffled silk blouses. There were even ruffles on the tailored coatdresses.

And the exotica: jodhpurs, knickers, and gold gold *gold*. Twenty-four-karat dresses glittered like mother lode. Headdresses reflected most of the subcontinent of Asia and the entire continent of Africa, twenty-four karats from the top of the head to the tip of the toe. There were enchanting girls in gold brocade culottes and gold-encrusted jerseys. All in all, it made Al Mackey think of munchkins and monkeys and rainbows. Fabulous!

He saw a bizarre art deco costume of graphic zigzag, red line on white, done in folds and wraps and ending up with a puffy mini over leggings. It was topped off by a hat-helmet with simulated strands of gold brocade hair. And then he recognized the girl: Tiffany Charles!

Martin Welborn began nibbling at one of the ordinary items on the mile-long table, baby shrimp in guacamole sauce, when he turned to see Al Mackey trotting across the dance floor, his second tumbler of whiskey giving him the courage to burrow right through a crowd and say, 'You're Tiffany, Mister St Claire's secretary. It's *me*, Al Mackey? Sergeant Al Mackey? Remember?'

'Oh yeah,' she said. 'I really don't know anything more tonight than I did the other . . .'

'This is a *social* occasion!' Al Mackey cried. 'I *love* your outfit. I've never seen gold hair. Is it real?'

'Uh huh,' she said, seeking rescue. Already her friends were drifting away.

'Fourteen karat?'

'Twenty-four,' she muttered.

'Wow! They pay secretaries pretty well where you work.'

Somebody save her from the scrawny cop! A dress like this he thinks you earn taking dictation? Help!

'Listen, I gotta go talk to some of Mister St Claire's stars,' she said. 'You just *mingle*, huh? Have a good time.'

'I'm *trying* to mingle,' he cried, as she slipped away across the dance floor, which was starting to empty of the clutches of drinkers now that the nondanceable mariachis were leaving and an orchestra was setting up.

While Al Mackey was wandering in the general direction of the bar, Martin Welborn was drifting from group to group, categorizing the people from investigative habit. The screenwriters interested him because they talked so much about grand theft. In fact, it was just about *all* they talked about.

'Don't deal with that shmuck,' a fat writer said. 'The picture did twenty-five million in rentals. I mean U.S. and Canada, baby. I had ten points after break even. Ten! You tell how I never saw a dime. You tell me.'

'Charlie, it wasn't *him*,' a tall writer advised. 'He's only the executive producer. It's that studio.'

'I don't go with a major if I can help it,' a young writer warned.

'That's dumb,' the fat writer said. 'I always go with a major. They know how to fuck you better but they do it in style. You want to be raped by a nice clean cock lubed with K-Y jelly, or you wanna get gang-banged by the L.A. Rams with sandpaper rubbers?'

'Can I think about that awhile?' a slender writer cried.

'Be glad you write for television. There's no prestige in features anymore. It's *all* shit.'

'Shit?'

'Shit?'

'Shit.'

'You think they can't steal television? We made our shows at half a million per. Seven years on the air and they show a deficit of ten million? That's a lot of red ink. *Tell* the S.E.C. that network bookkeepers don't steal.'

And then an ancient screenwriter with a glass of champagne in each hand jumped up and said, 'Maybe you shmucks think you'd have liked working for Cohn, or Goldwyn, or Louis B. Mayer, God forbid?'

'Don't *tell* me the fucking idea!' a woman suddenly screamed to another writer. 'I'll end up in a lawsuit! Somebody says a rowboat sank in the marina, you write *Poseidon Adventure*, they *sue* you for stealing an idea! The Enemy is all around!' She was a severe woman with a voice like Tallulah Bankhead. She looked around fearfully. Looking for The *Enemy*. Shit.

Martin Welborn couldn't wait to tell Al Mackey: They talk more about grand larceny than a convention of burglary detectives.

Meanwhile, Al Mackey had found himself a cluster of directors sitting around the fireplace inside the house. Directors didn't seem to drink much. A little champagne or white wine. Although at least six of them were cruising at five thousand feet on something else, he was sure of that. They had all graduated from the UCLA film school, or were from New York, or were foreigners. For sure, the foreigners talked the most, particularly a Famous French Director who looked like Soupy Sales. He held the other directors spellbound, telling them what Los Angeles was all about.

'It's all about space.' His command of English was

excellent but his words were spidery, and they crept from heavy lips. 'The shape is difficult.'

'There is *no* shape!' a bearded young director dissented, and the others murmured.

'Ah,' the Frenchman corrected, 'space and light can create an *illusion* of shape. I love *that* phenomenon about Los Angeles. It's a . . .'

'. . . a movie set,' another young director said. He too had a beard.

'There is value to that,' the Frenchman warned. 'A feeling of not *being* in time or space. It can be creative. The loneliness of a city of space and light. And the smells! I love the smells of the lost lonely children on the vast, lonely, heartbreaking streets of Beverly Hills.'

'It's the light! It's the light!' a voice interrupted, and a woman hopped into their midst, and up on the hearth. She was tiny and needed the height. She had the huge mouth and sapphire eyes of a flesh-eating bird. Even Al Mackey recognized her. She was a Famous Novelist. The directors might not respect screenwriters, but a Famous Novelist even got the attention of the French Director.

'It's the light!' the novelist cried. 'It's not like New York. The light here is fuchsia and filtered through the pastel gauze of anonymity. There's nothing like it anywhere. The French Impressionists would have perished in delight!' She held her hand up as though to shield herself, but the only light came from an off-lit Picasso drawing over the fireplace.

Al Mackey had read one of her books. She wrote of angst and despair. But he didn't know the light bothered her so much. He was too shy to suggest that maybe she should wear sunglasses all the time?

'Absolutely,' the French director said. 'There is the smell of the anonymous machine. And colors? My God, in this city I could *eat* colors!'

'No, it's the light! It's the light!' the tiny novelist cried, and the Frenchman did not correct her.

Al Mackey finished up his sixth double whiskey and vowed to check out the light tomorrow.

'And *why* did *she* withdraw from your film? And will you finish it?' Yet a third bearded young director, with a Bronx accent, suddenly changed the subject. They all apparently knew who *she* was.

'Artistic differences,' the French director said, smiling. They all nodded knowingly.

'I think she has a certain metaphysical quality,' another director said. He sounded a little different to Al Mackey. Brooklyn?

'Of *course* she has a metaphysical quality,' the testy Frenchman said. 'This role calls for an artist with an *earth* quality!'

'There are times in our medium when the color of earth transcends metaphysics,' a fifth director announced, and Al Mackey was surprised. No beard? What *is* this shit?

'It's *not* the earth tones,' the novelist screamed. 'It's the light! It's the *light!*'

Al Mackey wasn't the only one to spot someone familiar. Martin Welborn noticed a woman in a cluster of perhaps a dozen moguls around the bar at the far end of the tented garden. Occasionally someone with a more famous face would approach the moguls but would quickly disappear after only desultory conversation. It was a matter of paying respects, Martin Welborn decided. A few of these men were no doubt tremendously powerful in The Business, but the older ones, the moguls of yore, were the ones he recognized. Producers and directors with famous names and faces did *not* mingle with the actors and writers when they got involved in serious conversation.

At first the ash blonde who was chatting with a silver-maned mogul struck Martin Welborn'e eye because of her dress. It was a very simple India cotton gauze with a mauve and blue pleated front skirt and long sleeves. It looked as though it cost less than one hundred dollars and wasn't really suitable for evening wear. But she didn't seem the least bit self-conscious and unflinchingly stood eye to eye with her mogul, until he seemed to dismiss her when a legendary producer came in and kissed him on the cheek. The woman in the India cotton waited a discreet moment after being ignored, and drifted toward the bar, where she got a champagne refill.

He wondered if she had capped teeth. He wouldn't have thought such things if it hadn't been called to his attention by Al Mackey, who was frantically jumping from group to group noting that there were enough face-lifts, dental caps, transplants, and tummy tucks in this place to convince him that the plastic surgeons and dermatologists and dentists constituted the power behind the throne.

'Just think how *many* the doctors could get if they banded together in a show of strength!'

'How many what?' Martin Welborn asked.

'Blow jobs! Whadda ya think, dummy! Blow jobs!' Al Mackey giggled. He was more than half bagged, and all excited from having spotted a World Famous Singer and Songwriter who usually sang and wrote of angst and despair in Los Angeles, but also included the rest of the world.

Finally, Martin Welborn had had enough vodka to walk up to the woman in the cotton gauze dress and say, 'This is the second time I've seen you.'

'Pardon?'

'I saw you last week at the skating rink. You're a lovely skater.'

'Oh, do you skate?'

He'd expected her to thank him and walk away. 'No, I was just there on business.'

'And what business are you in?' Her eyes were lilac!

'I'm afraid I'm not in show business.' He smiled.

'And what business are you in?' She looked him directly in the eye and required an answer. She seemed genuinely interested.

'I'm a policeman,' he said.

'I've never met a policeman. Are you *here* on business?'

'We're investigating the Nigel St Claire murder and his nephew invited us to pop in tonight.'

'The movie line would be: "It's not official then?" '

'No.' He smiled.

'Herman St Claire doesn't invite just anyone to a party like this. He must be impressed by you.' She looked at him over the rim of the champagne glass. He had never stood face to face with a woman this beautiful in his entire life. He was starting to get the feeling he'd seen this in a movie somewhere. Several times, in fact. But the vodka mist was warm and reassuring.

'Perhaps you can point out some likely suspects for me?' He smiled, edging just an inch closer. This near, he was sure she was at least forty. It made her all the more attractive. Unlike Al Mackey, he preferred picking on women his own size.

'Suspects? I could point out a hundred or so. Let's do!' He could see that she wasn't entirely sober either. Looking for suspects with a beauty on his arm? He *had* seen this movie before.

'I'm Deedra Briggs.'

'I'm Martin Welborn,' he said, shaking hands as they strolled.

'Are you a captain or what?'

'Sergeant.'

'Well, Sergeant, do you see that group over there?'

'The ones you were talking with? I recognize some of them.'

'That's the royalty. The contract-player days are over, but there's still a lot of power around and a lot of it is in that group. Power at least as far as actors are concerned.'

'Are you an actress?'

He thought she flinched for a split second, but he could have been wrong. She said, 'I work at it. And I model a bit.'

'I probably should have known you're an actress. I don't go to movies often.'

249

'I don't play in movies often,' she said. 'Mostly television commercials. It's a living.'

She had a trained voice. She sounded like the prep school headmistress he saw in a television film one night. A headstrong member of the Eastern Establishment who had come to Hollywood to defy her father. Something like that. The television heroine had ridden to hounds.

'You're not what I would have expected from a policeman. An elbow-patches kind of mellow fellow. How long have you been a policeman?'

'In a few more weeks I'll have my twentieth anniversary.'

'Is that retirement time?'

'It could be. I'll be eligible for my pension.'

'Are you married?'

'Not exactly. Are you?'

'Not anymore.'

The music started and a few couples began taking to the floor. The music this early in the evening was obviously tailored to the tastes of the older moguls at the rear of the tent.

'Do you dance?'

'Well, I've seen you skate,' he said. 'I'm a little intimidated.'

'Good. I'm a lousy dancer. Let's go find a suspect.'

They walked to the fringe of the mogul group and listened.

'They don't invite actors to intimate parties,' she explained. 'Unless they need a court jester or two to amuse the frau of somebody important. Actually, they despise actors. We're unstable, immature, hysterical. Those are *deal* makers. Some of them have never read a book. But they read all *about* the book. Ditto with a script. They have people read the books and people read the scripts and then they use their unerring instincts and spend corporate millions on the tripe you see on the screen these days.'

'I don't see much on the screen these days.'

'Lucky,' she said, glaring toward the mogul group. 'To me they're the most despicable of the lot.' She finished her champagne and staggered a bit. 'Sorry.' She took his arm in both of hers and leaned against him.

'I saw you talking to one of them. The tall fellow with all the silver hair.'

'I was in one of his hit movies ten years ago. He's riding a string of losers. I believe he's on his way out. I can hardly bear to talk to him, but at least he *knows* he's a deal maker. Some of the others think they're *artists*.'

'Tell me,' Martin Welborn said suddenly, 'under any circumstances would anyone in . . . *this* world,' and he waved at the big top to encompass the whole circus, 'ever under certain circumstances be involved in making any kind of . . . porn films?'

'Making porn shows? Lord, no. Why do you ask?'

'Oh, we have a suspect who might have some connection and . . . well, it's remote.'

'Pornography's legal these days.'

'Yes, but I was thinking of kiddy porn, that sort of thing.'

'Sergeant, have you been to the movies lately? Don't you know that naked teenagers are hot commodities this year?'

'I mean *real* kiddy porn. The illegal kind.'

'See that man talking to Herman the Third?'

His name and even his face were instantly recognizable. He was a distinguished producer of some of the most enlightening and uplifting documentaries of our time.

'I recognize *him* all right,' Martin Welborn said.

'He owns the largest collection of porn, including kiddy porn, of anyone in the world, they say.'

'He does?'

'Despicable, isn't it?' She laughed wryly. 'Talk about lying down with the beasts. Everyone in The Business knows that little tidbit.'

'Really?'

'It's *very* common knowledge. I suspect even your policemen who work that specialty must know about his collection. I imagine his tastes encompass just about

251

anything macabre that could be put to film. Probably has the original sixteen-millimeter prints of Hitler's strangulation of the Rommel conspirators. I heard him discussing that at another party one time. His eyes lit up.'

'Unbelievable.'

'But he wouldn't *make* kiddy porn, though he loves it dearly. In fact, little Herman is probably trying to persuade him right this minute to make and distribute his forthcoming feature at Herman's studio. He somehow cadged the rights to a South African epic they're *all* interested in. I don't even know the name of it, but these boys know. They have paid informants at the New York publishing houses to steal and Xerox the potential blockbuster manuscripts.'

'Fascinating,' he said, noting that Herman III's eyes shone like mica.

'You've been a cop twenty years. I've been in this business as long.'

She wasn't ashamed to hint at her age. He liked that.

'But I do believe that those gentlemen aren't interested in any cinematic genre unless it's *safe* and profitable. They're screaming cowbirds. Do you know that species?'

'No.'

'The screaming cowbird waits for another bird to build a nest and then appropriates it. They're parasite birds.'

Meanwhile Al Mackey was nearly on his ear from his tenth double whisky, without having stopped for a bite to eat. He was reeling from one group to another, waiting for sultry girls to strip down and dance on the piano. He'd seen a few films too. So far, nothing much had happened, although he thought he'd stumbled on an orgy in the making. He saw a very intense group of men and women who turned out to be producers or something, making deals. It was the euphemism that threw him.

'Listen, do you think you could get in bed with us?' a man with a suntan like Herman III asked a woman who was dressed like a nineteenth-century German lampshade.

The lewd proposal stopped Al Mackey dead in his tracks.

She said, 'Well I could get in bed with your group, but not until the deal was sweetened.'

Jesus Christ! They have to pay for their orgies? Here on this freaking yellow brick road? But then when she quickly turned to talk to another man, the one with a silver mane said to a sweaty little guy, 'Miriam says she could get in bed with us if we sweeten it. I frankly think that it's as sweet as it's gonna get. Remember, Mort, we could get in bed with Merv. He's only asking half a mill and five points after two and a half times negative.'

As bagged as he was, Al Mackey wasn't drunk enough to think *anybody* would pay half a million for a blow job from a *dozen* Mervs and Miriams. He figured out that all this lewd and dirty talk that had him all excited simply involved business. The Business. What a letdown. They mixed their metaphors of sex and money like a horde of hookers.

And another thing: Nobody said good-bye. It was as though a sign of farewell would split these tenuous relationships forever. Upon parting, everyone touched cheeks, bussed the air, and said, 'Let's have lunch.'

But there were acres of tits! Tits around here must grow bigger and faster, like mushrooms in a cave. It must be the climate around Beverly Hills. He spotted Herman III talking to another mogul. Al Mackey staggered over and interrupted.

'Hi, Herman.'

'Hi, Marty. Having a good time?'

'Al.'

'Al, how's it going? Having fun?'

'Oh, yeah, Herman.' Then he took the baby mogul by the arm and dragged him aside. Herman III, who didn't drink, had to turn away. Al Mackey was blowing 100 proof.

'What can I do for you, Al?'

'Herman, can you introduce me to someone?'

'Who?'

'Anyone. You know what I mean?'

'A bimbo?'

'Yeah. A bimbo.'

'Look, Al,' Herman III said apologetically. 'I can make an introduction, but, uh, you gotta do your own moving. I mean, I'm not a pimp.'

'Of course not, Herman! The very idea!' Al Mackey cried. 'But can't you just point me in the right direction?'

'Okay, Al.' Herman III smiled, and Al Mackey vowed to get a suntan and have his teeth capped. Jesus, around here he felt like his old man must have felt as a bogtrotter at Ellis Island.

'Thanks, Herman, I'll be over there with *that* bunch. I like to listen to the actors.' At least they *really* talked dirty.

'Anything for L.A.'s finest. But remember, I'll just introduce you to a girl I think is gonna like you. I'm not a . . .'

'Whore. I know you're not.'

'Pimp.'

'That neither. Thanks, Herman.'

By this time, Martin Welborn had discovered that Deedra Briggs had lied to him. She was a wonderful dancer and made him look good. They were in each other's arms now, and he felt the thrust of breast and drumming of blood, and Martin Welborn was saddened to learn that this kind of party broke up earlier than police parties in Sherman Oaks. People in The Business went to bed early and did not abuse their bodies in the same way that police detectives did.

She had long since begun dancing with both arms around Martin Welborn's neck. 'A mellow fellow in elbow patches. You're what I've been looking for . . .'

'. . . all your life,' he said.

'Right.' She giggled.

'Deedra, could I . . . Would you like to see me again? Sometime? Not necessarily . . .'

'Will you take me home?'

He couldn't believe it. 'I should say so!'

'I don't have a car here. Jags just don't function well in California heat. I was warned.'

'Sure I'll take you home!' Martin Welborn said, and she buried her face in his neck as they swayed.

So, while Herman III was off being neither a whore nor a pimp, Al Mackey decided to make some small talk with the mogul crowd. He introduced himself to the tall mogul with the silver mane, who had been talking to the girl Marty was scoring with.

Making conversation wasn't easy with these people, since they all seemed to be intent on digits and numbers. Al Mackey quickly ran out of things to say. Then he thought about a novel he'd read lately.

'Have any of you read the novel about black fishermen in Bermuda who get caught in the typhoon and end up in Cuba? I just read it last week and I think it'd make an interesting movie, I mean, film.'

The three moguls looked at him suspiciously, but finally a fat mogul said, 'Blacks aren't in anymore. I wouldn't think you could cast it. Any white parts?'

'I wouldn't touch another hurricane picture,' a tall mogul warned.

'You wouldn't stand a chance with an all-male picture,' a thin mogul advised.

Al Mackey was delighted that they were talking at him and he turned to the one with the silver mane and said, 'How about you? Think it could make a good movie? I mean, film?'

And the tall mogul with the silver mane responded instinctively. A layer of egg white seemed to flow across his eyeballs from the upper regions. He seemed to be looking at Al Mackey through the wrong end of a telescope. He stared at Al Mackey with those oysterish unseeing eyes, and the words *slithered* out, all caked with mildew: 'All right, because you're a friend of Herman's. Messenger the script over to my office. I'll take a look and call you.'

Al Mackey, who was caught up in all of it, cried, 'That's

swell! Thanks!' And only while he was walking away did it occur to him. *What* fucking script?

There was only one way to straighten out his head: Have another drink. He found some actors at the bar. They were of course the most recognizable, and although the Famous Male Actors mingled among all groups, the Famous Female Actors seemed to withdraw into entourages.

Al Mackey preferred the younger up-and-comers. They had only three things to talk about: movies, drugs, and sex. Movies they almost got, exotic drugs that prolonged orgasm for days and days, and sex which was almost as good as the drugs that prolonged the sex. It was the conversation Al Mackey found most educational. He wished he'd brought his pencil.

He was all agog over a young actress he'd seen several times on television. She was talking about a private club where you could play backgammon and do dope, and Al Mackey learned that acid was back and the latest fad was sniffing Persian heroin. And in the private club's disco they had slide projectors synchronized by computers, and two motion picture systems, and an all-enveloping sound system, not to mention a multitude of lights and effects, and two machines, one for fog, one for multicolored bubbles.

A blond young actor, built like a running back, one they said was sure to be the next television superstar, jumped up with eyes like fiery hibiscus and yelled, 'Focus, focus, you asshole!'

Nobody but Al Mackey paid any attention to him so he sat back down. Somebody stuffed something under his nose and he shook his head, the bleached blond locks flying all over his face. He smiled. Apparently he was satisfied that they'd focused.

Then another actress, who Al Mackey was almost *sure* was the co-star of a series, said, 'That putz wanted me . . . get *this*! to play a part in his feature where I'm fucking my fourteen-year-old *son* and his estranged father is on the phone telling him how to make his mommy happy!'

'You see, that's how agents are!' another actress cried. 'Take your fucking spleen for ten percent. Who needs a spleen? You can live without a spleen!'

'Fucking your own son,' a young actor said, and then he grinned cagily. Would she?

'Focus, you son of a bitch!' the blond kid yelled again.

And somebody said, 'Call this little freak's manager and get him outa here or he'll be back to being butt-fucked by those bogus producers out front of Schwab's Drugstore.'

Then the outraged actress said, 'This movie, by the way, is supposed to slide by with a soft R rating.'

'Oooooooohhhhhhh!' they cried, sounding like the detective bureau the day Fuzznuts Francis 'impacted' for the twelfth time.

'Yeah, then the kid's daddy, according to this artful script, is supposed to ask the kid on the phone if he's playing with himself. All *that* kind of wonderful dialogue.'

'Jesus!' another actress cried. 'Are you going to *do* the film?'

'Are you crazy? I'm not *old* enough to have a fourteen-year-old son fucking me, you dumb cunt!'

The conversation was now so hot that Al Mackey was startled when Herman III tapped him on the shoulder and said, 'Al, I'd like you to meet somebody.'

He turned and was face to face with a twenty-four-year-old girl in the craziest onion-shaped pullover sweater he'd ever seen. It went clear to her thighs and hugged them. In fact it was worn like pants. How did she get in and out? Her matching green hat looked like a graduation cap. She wore tights underneath all of it. Funfinger was absolutely out. It was all or nothing in *this* costume.

'My name's Billie,' she said. 'Hi, Al. I hear you're a cop.'

'Hi, Billie.' The enchanted detective leered.

'I love cops. Before I got in The Business I wanted to *be* a cop,' she said.

'You kids make nice.' Herman III winked as he left them.

257

'What do you like best about cops?' Al Mackey was weaving like a punch-em doll.

'Gee, you're really bombed, Al.'

'Not that . . . that bombed,' he belched.

'Party's breaking up soon, Al,' she said. 'Wanna go for a walk out by the pool?'

'Do I? Do I? Do . . .'

'Let's go, Al,' she said. 'I used to go with a cop. Before I left Topeka.'

Al Mackey and Billie from Topeka were on their way for the garden stroll when Martin Welborn caught him by the arm and said, 'Al, I have to drive a lady home. She lives in West L.A. so I should be back pretty soon. Will you . . .'

'Yeah yeah yeah. Go ahead, Marty. Have a good one. Catch you later. Take your time. I'll be around. I'll . . .'

While Al Mackey was chasing after the sunflower in the onion suit, Martin Welborn delighted Deedra Briggs with the ride in the detective car.

'I love all that police talk on the radio,' she said as they drove toward Westwood Village.

'We usually turn it off. Detectives don't get that many radio calls.'

'Don't. I love it,' she said, and then she slid over close to him and put her head on his shoulder and said, 'Well, Sergeant Elbowpatches, I want you to know I had a very nice evening. And I was dreading this night.'

'Why did you come?'

'My manager insisted. Herman the Third needed some extra jesters, female type.' Then she touched the graying sideburns of the detective and said, 'I don't think I'll ever do that again.'

'Would you like to have dinner . . . sometime?' Martin Welborn asked.

'When?'

'Whenever you like. I'm very free and . . .'

'When?' she challenged. The champagne had made her voice torchy, and sweetened her breath on his face.

258

'Sunday?' he asked. 'Sunday evening?'

'Eight o'clock,' she said. 'I'll make pasta and a salad.'

'I didn't mean for you to . . .'

'Drive right over there and park in front of the door,' she said.

It was a high-rise condo, not far from the village. She kissed him on the right cheek twice and when he turned she kissed him on the mouth.

'Sunday. Eight o'clock. Number eight-three-nine. I'll buzz the door for you.' A flash of thigh, a hiss of satin undergarments as she slid across the seat, and she was gone.

Martin Welborn tried to think about Paula Welborn on the ride back to Holmby Hills. He switched off the radio, but that didn't help. He *couldn't* think about Paula for the first time in months. He didn't think about Elliott Robles or even Danny Meadows. He simply free-floated and thought of Deedra Briggs.

Meanwhile, Al Mackey was a rapt audience for Billie from Topeka.

'I was in a film with him,' she said. 'What a shit, I can tell you.'

'I'll bet!' Al Mackey said, almost falling off the chaise longue which was perilously close to the lighted Olympic-sized swimming pool.

'He's *always* loaded, Al. He's *such* a lude freak. You probably think he's in real good shape from seeing him in movies, right? Well, he also uses Mexican brown. And Persian by the *bead*! He whiffs it.'

Al Mackey had grabbed half a bottle of bourbon on the way out and was gulping it. Billie didn't drink, but she had spooned two loads of coke into her raw and dripping little nose while they talked.

'I didn't know he was a doper,' Al Mackey belched, without the faintest idea who was a doper or what they were talking about. He was too busy trying to figure how anybody could get out of that onion suit once they got into it.

'He can be an on-time guy sometimes. This was a German picture. Lots of tax shelter money there. We always said he was flying over Germany more than the Red Baron. And horny? We always said he'd eat anything before it ate him.'

'Really?' Al Mackey liked that. The conversation was getting off movies and drugs and onto sex where it belonged.

'You married, Al?'

'Not anymore.'

'I don't think I'll ever get married,' she said. 'I live with a guy now. You're married, everyone starts to get all bothered about everything. Was your wife jealous?'

'The first one was,' he belched. 'Caught me with a collapsible container once, and almost killed me over it.'

'What's a collapsible container?'

'A rubber. That's what we called them when we worked vice. In any police report when you refer to a collapsible container, it's a rubber.'

'Really? Did vice cops fuck girls for evidence?'

'Of course not, Billie! We used the collapsible container to put illegal booze in when we were working liquor violators. Better than balloons. Big opening. You can stash them easily in your pocket.' He took another pull of the whiskey, thinking of the bad old days. 'That bitch. She finds one in my pocket one night and instead of giving me a chance to explain, she gets my gun. And God or *something* wakes me up just in time to roll off the bed while she fires one for effect. Right in the pillow where my head was!'

'Gosh, she *was* jealous. All for finding one little collapsible container! Imagine that!' She took another hit from her tiny gold coke spoon and imagined it.

'Of course we'd been having problems before that.'

'Dipped your dick in a few stray dishes, eh, Al?' Billie said, wiggling her inflamed nostrils, sniffling back the mucus.

Beware the devil's dandruff, he'd heard an actress warn. Stick some Tampax up your nose, honey, or you'll leave here a coke freak. 'Just a few stray dishes, Billie.' Al Mackey leered. Not any more, God knows!

'Gosh, that musta been the old old days. I never even fucked a guy with a rubber.'

'You haven't?' Al Mackey felt a magnificent semi beginning to engorge!

'No way. My doctor keeps me on an IUD. I don't like the pill, cancer and all. You can get an IUD from a goddamn ophthalmologist around here. It's not like Topeka. All the doctors around here're pussy probers, seems to me. You go in with a tennis elbow, they stick their fingers up there looking for your phone number.'

'Uh huh,' the detective sighed. He loved this! Hollywood dirty talk!

Then she said, 'Al, when Herman told me you were a cop, I just *had* to meet you. You're nice. And you're not too old, neither.'

'Not at all!' He was swelling like a pigeon. This girl knew how to talk to a man!

'Al, let's go in that dressing room for a while. I'm feeling, a little . . . you know?'

It almost ended then and there when Al Mackey jumped up and pitched forward several feet. She saved him from going for a swim, and later he wondered if he was always being spared or *tortured* by a whimsical God.

The dressing room was almost as large as Al Mackey's apartment. It had a carpeted floor, a separate bath, and a dressing table. Billie from Topeka showed Al Mackey how she got in and out of the green onion suit. She undressed much quicker than he did.

As Al Mackey heaped blessings on Herman III and struggled out of his suit and shirt and gunbelt and necktie and underwear, and sat on the carpet trying desperately to pull his pants over his shoes, she said, 'Wow, Al, it's stiff as a bat already!'

And it was! 'Help me outa these freaking pants, Billie!' Al Mackey cried.

And the girl, flying at the Red Baron's altitude by now, easily slipped off Al Mackey's shoes and socks and pants, and finally the bony detective was as naked as she.

'Stiff as a bat! You don't mess around, Al! Where's your gun?'

'On the floor!' Al Mackey said, kissing Billie on the neck and shoulders and arm and fingers, getting the preliminaries moving while he worried about the terrible thing that happened at The Red Valentine Massage Parlor.

'Where's your handcuffs, Al?'

'On the floor!' he cried, running his face down her hip and feeling the fuzz on her delicious young thigh.

'Get your handcuffs, Al,' she said.

That stopped him. 'What for?'

'You gotta handcuff me to something.'

Al Mackey raised up, got dizzy, caught himself, but still fell back on his ass. 'Why should I handcuff you?'

'Al, for chrissake, ever since Herman told me to . . . told me that you were a cop, I been looking forward to this. Get the fucking handcuffs, will ya?'

'Okay, okay,' Al Mackey mumbled, feeling around the floor in the dark until he found them. He hoped his keys hadn't gotten lost. Houdini couldn't get back into that onion suit while handcuffed.

'Put them on me, quick!' she panted.

'Lemme see,' he said, fumbling with the ratchets.

'Gimme the fucking things!' she commanded, expertly slipping into the cuffs and tightening them down, handling them better than a twenty-year cop.

'Now,' she cried. 'Handcuff me to something!'

'Like what?' he said. The room was starting to spin.

'That stool! The little stool!' she cried. 'Lift it up and slip the chain around the leg. Make me feel helpless!'

'Yeah, but Billie,' he said, picking up the stool. 'This stool only weighs about a pound and a half. You could easily pull away from . . .'

'Get something for my face! Quick!' She was really whiffing wind now. He'd never heard such panting.

'What can I *get* you for your face, Billie?' Al Mackey was holding his dizzy head in both hands.

'Anything! A towel! Get a fucking towel!'

'A towel,' he said. 'Will my T-shirt do?'

'Yeah, quick! Put it over my face!'

God, he hoped his T-shirt wasn't too rancid. Then he looked at his erection. He was starting to lose it! 'Okay, how do you want me to do it? What am I supposed to do?'

'Over my face. Wrap it around. Fold it under my head. Quick!'

But while he was fumbling, she couldn't wait, and lifted her chained hands from under the stool and wrapped the T-shirt around her face like a blindfold. Then she lifted the stool and placed her manacled hands back in place.

And during all this, Al Mackey was trying to kiss her flat little belly and get things going again but she kept screaming obscenities. And the obscenities *scared* him!

'I don't get it!' he cried, finally. 'I don't know what I'm supposed to do!'

'Now!' she yelled. 'Now! I'm blindfolded! I'm chained to this table! I'm helpless, you filthy gorilla of a rapist! I can't stop you! I can beg, I can plead. Please don't rape me, you raping bastard!'

'I won't!' Al Mackey bleated. He was sitting on the floor holding his forlorn cock in his hand.

'I'm as helpless as a baby!' she screamed. 'I'm like a ten-year-old child!'

'Stop it!' Al Mackey cried. 'You're just making it worse!'

Then Billie from Topeka said, 'Huh?' and threw Al Mackey's T-shirt off her face, and saw him sitting there with yet another round that failed to fire.

'Jesus, Al, you're supposed to ravish me now! What the fuck's wrong with you!'

'I don't know!' he cried. 'All that talk. The handcuffs, and my T-shirt over your eyes. I don't know! It just . . . died!'

263

Billie from Topeka sat up disgustedly and said, 'Just my luck! I was looking forward to this ever since Herman said you were a cop. TAKE THESE THINGS OFF ME!'

They fumbled in the dark for three minutes until he found the handcuff key and unfettered her. She put on her onion suit and graduation cap in record time while the mortified detective struggled into his clothes, all the time enduring righteous and withering insults.

'You know, Al, I thought cops were macho and sexy.'

'I'm sorry, Billie.'

'You're about as sexy as Mother Teresa of Calcutta.'

'I'm sorry, Billie.'

'You're about as sexy as a bucket of saltpeter, Al.'

'I'm *really* sorry, Billie.'

But before storming out of the dressing room, Billie from Topeka got hold of herself, and took another little toot of cocaine and remembered that this putz was a pal of Herman III's. Yet she wasn't actress enough to keep *all* the edge out of her voice when she turned those brittle eyes on him and said, 'It's not the end of the world, Al. Maybe some other time. A finished movie's never as good as the dailies, or as *bad* as the rough-cut. Remember that.'

'Good-bye, Billie!' he cried.

The cinematic philosophizing didn't help. It was a disheveled Al Mackey whom Martin Welborn found waiting in front of the Holmby Hills mansion, clutching the red rose that a sympathetic valette had given him.

Al Mackey refused to discuss his evening all the way home. He said a brisk farewell to his partner upon being dropped off at his apartment and was too despondent to kick the cat out of bed. This seemed to confuse and infuriate the animal, who responded by clawing the silk border from the blanket.

On Sunday night, while Martin Welborn was keeping his date with Deedra Briggs, Al Mackey knew he had only one hope for surviving all this, and it was to be found not sitting at the bar of The Glitter Dome but in the *pocket* of

Wing himself. He dressed grimly for a momentous journey to Chinatown while Martin Welborn lay nude beside Deedra Briggs, on floor pillows, looking out at the lights of Westwood Village.

'And you can cook too,' Martin Welborn said, running a finger down her buttercup hip.

She laughed and said, 'You've got a few talents yourself, Sergeant Elbowpatches.'

'I can't believe you're real,' he said. 'It's like a . . .'

'A dream,' she whispered, kissing him gently.

'No, I was going to say a prayer.'

'That's an odd way to put it,' she said, kissing him again. 'You're a peculiar policeman, Martin Welborn.'

'You're the most beautiful woman I've . . .'

'And you're a divine gentle lover,' she said, putting her face on his bare chest.

'I'm decidedly out of practice. And never had much practice to begin with.'

'Divine gentle lovers like you are born, not made, pardon the pun.'

'Why do you stay in show business?' he asked, 'if you hate it so much.'

'Because I never met someone like you.'

'That sounds like a line from a script.'

'It is,' she chuckled. 'A bad script. I loved to act at one time. Never mind if I was good or wasn't. I wanted it more than I can explain. But I'm older now, and a little wiser, I hope.'

'Then get out of it,' he said.

'Will you come and be my love and let me make pasta for you?'

'I could be persuaded,' Martin Welborn said.

'So could I, Sergeant Elbowpatches,' she said. 'So could I.'

And while Martin Welborn was busy talking to Deedra Briggs about her going over a bigger wall than he vaulted when he left the seminary, Al Mackey was stalking somberly into The Glitter Dome on a quiet Sunday night.

Wing was extremely depressed. He hadn't had a single customer all evening who wasn't sober. He hadn't stolen a dime. He hopped around gleefully when he spotted Al Mackey. All was not lost!

'A free one to start the evening!' Wing cried, pouring Al Mackey a one-ounce shot of Tullamore Dew. No sense being *too* grateful.

'I gotta talk to you *privately*, Wing,' the detective said.

'Look around,' Wing said, pointing to a couple at the far end of the long bar. 'This is about as private as it can get.'

Al Mackey tossed back the Tullamore Dew, smacked the glass on the bar, and said, 'Make the next one a double.' Then the detective opened his wallet and placed a twenty on the bar in front of him.

Wing chuckled as he glided over to the cash register to break down the twenty. His antenna hairs came unglued when he bounded back with the pile of money. He always broke bills into lots of ones and lots of silver to facilitate his moves. Al Mackey didn't care. In fact, to keep Wing's little eyes all agleam, he opened his wallet and laid two more tens on top of the pile.

'Staying for a while tonight, eh?' Wing giggled. He pulled his hands from his sleeves and rubbed them together and poured *another* double.

'I don't know how to begin. I need help. I heard you can help guys with my problem.'

But Wing couldn't keep from sliding back and forth. Toward the money pile. This had been his longest day.

'Goddamnit, Wing, pay attention to me,' Al Mackey whined. 'I'll let you steal some money after I get drunk.'

'How about another double?'

'I haven't finished this one. Goddamnit, pay attention!'

'Okay okay,' Wing said, pulling himself together and smoothing down the antenna hairs on the side of his oily little head. 'So I'm listening.'

'I've been having this . . . problem lately and . . .'

'Yes yes,' Wing said. 'Yes yes.'

'Goddamnit, stop with the yes yes! You sound like some Jap I know in a massage parlor.'

Wing quickly reached below the bar and brought up *another* glass and poured a second double. Now Al Mackey had two drinks in front of him. 'You *gotta* drink,' Wing explained. 'Makes you talk easier.' Then Wing grabbed a ten off the bar and slid to the cash register, where he slipped two ones up his loose emerald sleeve before hopping back with the change.

'Okay, I'll drink,' Al Mackey sighed, polishing off the first double of Tullamore Dew and picking up the other one. 'I think I need . . .'

'Acupuncture? I can fix it up. Cures headaches, bad backs, athlete's foot, gonorr . . .'

'I don't need any freaking acupuncture! I need a : . . a broad!'

'A broad? Is that all? I thought all you detectives fucked left and right?'

'Wing, I'm not even fucking in and out!' Al Mackey cried. 'That's the problem!'

'You're just not getting enough?'

'None! I got a limp noodle,' he whispered.

'Absence makes the cock grow harder.' Wing grinned slyly.

'Stop it with your fortune cookie philosophy! I got a limber whang, Wing! I don't get straight I might as well become a priest!' Al Mackey took the double down in two gulps. Where was Marty's old seminary?

Wing clucked sympathetically and stole two quarters before Al Mackey put the glass back down. 'I might be able to help you.'

'You *gotta* help me, Wing!'

'How long's it been?'

'Almost four months!'

'Well, it's not something you forget,' Wing said, wiping

267

the bar with a towel, sweeping a stray quarter right into the emerald sleeve.

'I've almost forgotten already!'

'Naw, it's like painting by numbers. Anybody can do it. Wish there was a chicken or two around tonight. I'd show you.'

'Chicken! Vulture! Anything! Just take away this fucking albatross!'

'Okay, I don't do this for everybody,' Wing said, removing a little ivory box from his pants pocket.

'That's the aphrodisiac?' Al Mackey whispered.

'Keep your voice down,' Wing hissed, glancing quickly at the couple drinking quietly at the end of the bamboo long bar. 'You want *them* to hear us?'

When Al Mackey turned to look at *them*, Wing got another quarter into the sleeve. 'This never fails,' he said, taking a blue tissue-wrapped bundle from the ivory box. As Al Mackey leaned over the bar, Wing opened the tiny bundle and showed him perhaps a quarter of a gram of pearly powder. Then he folded the tissue carefully.

'That'll be fifty bucks. Wholesale because you're a good customer.'

'Fifty bucks!' Al Mackey cried.

'That's genuine ground-up elk antler. Put it on your Master Charge.'

'Fifty bucks! Why so much?'

'You think it's easy to find a goddamn elk in Chinatown these days?' Wing said testily, palming two quarters while Al Mackey reached for his credit card.

16

The Performers

When Al Mackey drove by Martin Welborn's apartment
to pick him up for work Monday morning, he found Marty
waiting in front. As dapper as always, in a gray three-piece
worsted and a blue silk tie.

'Don't tell me, you had a successful date with Deedra
whatser name.'

'She's a great cook.' Martin Welborn smiled.

'A great cook. What time did you get home last night?'

'I was in bed by eleven-thirty.'

'Whose?'

'Mine. What did you do last night?'

'Went to The Glitter Dome.'

'Have a nice time?'

'Don't ask. I spent almost a hundred bucks.'

'On what?'

'Don't ask. In fact, let's change the subject.'

'Okay. On to Nigel St Claire,' Martin Welborn said.
'Let's do some thinking this morning. I've got renewed
vigor.'

'I can see that.'

'We have to review all our information. And we have to
do some calling. I made a mental list on Saturday.'

'Don't you ever take a day off?'

'An idle mind . . .'

'Yeah yeah.'

It was a day to slog through it. Martin Welborn had
made a mental list, all right. They called the studio
security people and started them checking their logs for
three weeks prior to Nigel St Claire's death, to get a list of
every visitor who signed in with the St Claire office as his

destination. Ditto for Sapphire Productions. All this tedious research was okayed by Herman III, who could think of no one in Trousdale Estates who might be a close friend of Uncle Nigel's, or who might loan him his house as the need arose.

Nor could Herman think of anyone in or out of Trousdale who drove a black Bentley. The Beverly Hills P.D. promised to check with all officers of the night shift who worked the six square miles of Trousdale Estates and may have had any calls during the past several weeks reflecting strange comings or goings, or a black Bentley. One officer thought he'd seen a dark-colored Bentley parked by one of the homes on the upper streets of Trousdale, but couldn't remember which house.

'*If* Bozwell's even connected with the murder,' Al Mackey moaned at two P.M. that day, his finger sore from dialing. 'Do you realize we don't have a shred of evidence connecting Bozwell with Nigel St Claire? Just *speculation*, that's all.'

'It's time to sort out the troubling things,' Martin Welborn said after he'd been making notes for more than an hour. He had taken his coat off but otherwise looked as fresh as he had in the morning. Al Mackey, on the other hand, was a wreck, what with all these calls, and paper shuffling, and getting nowhere, and dying to get off duty and down to The Glitter Dome to find some chicken and test the goddamn elk antler potion. If that didn't work it was acupuncture. After that? He shivered, thinking about the night in the apartment chewing on that off-duty gun.

'Do you know what troubles me most, Al?' Martin Welborn asked.

'No.'

'Lies. I believe Peggy Farrell lied.'

'Hell, *all* whores lie. Which lie in particular?'

'I think a girl like Peggy would keep her eyes open when she was being taken somewhere by a guy she didn't know. Even if he was in a Bentley. She's obviously a bright, observant girl.'

'So?'

'So, she was *too* quick to say she couldn't find the house again. Remember, this is a girl who gets around. By car. By cab. She gives outcall messages, so she can read a map. She knows the West Side pretty well. In fact, she even had a few customers in Trousdale, remember?'

'Well, she's not going to tell us if she knows,' Al Mackey shrugged.

'But why would she *not* tell us? That's what bothers me. Unless Lloyd warned her. Or scared her?'

'Or Mister Silver?'

'I'm convinced she told part of the truth. As much as she thought was safe to tell.'

'Speculation,' Al Mackey said.

'I know someone else who lied, and it isn't speculation.'

'Who?'

'The old skating flash himself. Griswold Weils.'

'What did he lie about?'

'He said he was contacted by mail.'

'Yeah, a letter was sent to his guild.'

'The International Photographers' Union, Local six five nine. But it wasn't. I called them just to verify they had his address and forwarded his mail. They don't. He stopped paying dues about the time he got his first pornography bust. They show no forwarding address. He lied about how he was first contacted by Mister Gold.'

'Why would he lie about that?'

'I'm sure that's not *all* he lied about. If he'd lie about the little things . . .'

Al Mackey started rubbing the stubble of beard that was already starting. Hairy. A sure sign of middle age. You get hairy and ugly! 'You know, Marty, Peggy said that Mister Silver might have been wearing a wig. Griswold's bald.'

'Good lad.' Martin Welborn smiled. 'Now we tally debits and credits.'

'We don't have a damn thing but speculation.'

'We have lies,' Martin Welborn said. 'Thank God

271

people are such consummate liars or we'd never get things right.'

'But there's something still doesn't make a lick of sense. Why would a man like St Claire personally contact a loser like Griswold Weils, even if he *was* up to some kind of kinky filmmaking?'

'It doesn't seem likely that he would.'

'Why would Nigel St Claire get involved in kiddy porn?'

'It doesn't seem likely that he would.'

'What're we gonna do now?'

'Tell me, if Griswold Weils lied, and we know he did, and if he *is* Mister Silver in a wig, what would he be doing up in that house in Trousdale that night? That Just Plain Bill Bozwell couldn't do?'

'Peggy said he was making a deal.'

'Bozwell, or Lloyd to her, would make the deal. But Griswold Weils can do one thing that Bozwell and the Vietnamese friend can't do. He can operate a camera. If he was there, it was for that purpose and that purpose only.'

'Peggy Farrell didn't say she was photographed.'

'Exactly. I say she lied. And the last thing that I can't begin to handle is *why* the Vietnamese partner? What's he, a makeup artist? A porn movie stud? A gaffer or grip? A location man? A costume designer?'

'No, he's a thug,' said the Ferret, who was sitting at the next table with his bearded chin in his hands, listening to Martin Welborn theorize. 'He's a thug and a hoodlum. That's all he is.'

'Okay, Marty,' Al Mackey said. 'I think you're saying I won't be going to The Glitter Dome tonight. What're we gonna do?'

'Us? Nothing.' Martin Welborn smiled. 'I was hoping the Ferret and Weasel might do something for us.'

'Does it have something to do with the gook?' the Ferret asked, raising up.

'It might.'

'Count us in,' he said.

*

They didn't have to wait more than thirty minutes after twilight until Griswold Weils skated into the parking lot. Martin Welborn and Al Mackey were inside the office of the bowling alley manager with binoculars and a radio.

'Another lie.' Martin Welborn grinned. 'He said he'd never skate in that parking lot again.'

'Give him a break, Marty,' Al Mackey said. 'What a temptation for a fifty-two-year-old flash. Acres of asphalt, all that.'

'Six-W-three, go!' Martin Welborn said into the hand radio unit, and Al Mackey used his binoculars to watch as the Ferret who had exchanged his motorcycle boots for a rented pair of shoe skates with big nylon wheels and rubber stops, went pinwheeling across the parking lot. He looked none too ominous when he got on those skates and skidded and slipped and slid down that parking lot, arms windmilling, ponytail flying, in the general direction of Griswold Weils, who was skating backwards, his radio headset drowning out all the panicky, frantic cries of the Ferret, who bounced and skidded across the asphalt.

The Ferret was athletic enough to get the hang of it after ten minutes or so, and then he was at least able to skate forward in a reasonably straight line, while the parking lot filled with after-dark jiving skaters, a cacophony of music blaring from pocket transistors. As Griswold Weils was skating backwards, eyes closed, jiving to Pink Floyd, he dreamed of Thursday night at the rink, when he'd show up in his new skating silks and knock em dead. But suddenly he was jarred so violently that his headset went sailing off his bald head and rattled across the asphalt in three pieces.

Griswold Weils went flying one way, and the other skater, a bearded longhair, went flying the other way and hit the asphalt with a splat.

'Ooooowww, my arm's broke!' the hairy skater wailed. 'My fucking arm!'

A crowd of skaters gathered and two young men helped him up, and Griswold Weils, still dazed, searched for the batteries from his shattered transistor.

'He did it!' the hairy skater cried. 'Not looking where he's going! My arm! It's broke!' The arm hung at an odd angle from the elbow and did look broken, but the hairy skater wouldn't remove his leather jacket for anyone to take a closer look.

'You skated into *me*!' Griswold Weils cried.

'Oooowww!' the skater moaned. 'I was going frontwards. You were going backwards. It's *my* fault? Oooohhh, my arm!'

'He better get to a hospital,' somebody said.

'Who's gonna take me?' the hairy skater cried.

'Somebody oughtta call an ambulance,' someone said.

'I got a car,' the hairy skater moaned. 'But I can't drive like this. Somebody has to drive me.' Then he looked at Griswold Weils. 'You better drive me, Mister. I'll need your name and statement for my insurance.'

'Insurance?'

'You broke my arm!' the skater moaned. 'You don't wanna let me collect from the insurance company?'

And then the crowd of skaters turned on Griswold Weils. Not collect from a fucking insurance company! Insurance companies are part of Big Business! The Enemy! Boooooo! Mr Wheels, a friend of Big Business? Booooo!

Ten minutes later, a disgusted Griswold Weils, with his skates in the back seat of the Toyota, was driving the wounded skater in the general direction of Hollywood Presbyterian Hospital when the skater said, 'Mister, will you please make a right there in that alley so I can take a leak?'

'For chrissake!' Griswold Weils whined. 'I agree to drive ya to the hospital so ya don't sue me or something. I suppose with your broken arm I gotta take it out and shake it when you're through?'

'Please, Mister. If I don't take a piss I'm gonna faint!' the hairy skater groaned.

'For chrissake!' Griswold Weils whined, but he turned into an alley north of Santa Monica Boulevard and stopped.

And a moment after his passenger alighted and walked around the back of the car, the driver's door was jerked open and Griswold Weils' passenger, with *both* arms working extremely well, had his hand over Griswold Weils' mouth and a knife pressing his throat.

'Move and I'll cut you three ways: wide, deep, and forever,' he whispered, and Griswold Weils froze.

The skater said, 'Turn off the ignition,' and he was obeyed instantly. Then he climbed into the back seat of the Toyota and holding the knife point at the back of Griswold Weils' neck, said, 'Drive toward Griffith Park.'

'I ain't got no money,' Griswold Weils sobbed. 'I swear I ain't!'

'Drive, Mr Weils,' the hairy skater breathed, and Griswold Weils shut his mouth, started the car, and drove.

Ten minutes later they were on a dark and lonely road in the park. Griswold Weils looked around frantically. Why was there never a cop when you needed one! Then he spotted a large dark car in the distance. Maybe someone would help him if he leaped out and screamed.

They got nearer to the car and the headlights went on. The knife relaxed a bit and the skater said, 'Pull over and park.'

After parking the car, Griswold Weils sat and waited and squinted into the headlights. Then the lights went out and he blinked and saw it was a Rolls-Royce.

'Get out,' the skater said, and Griswold Weils stepped tentatively from the car. 'Lloyd wants to have a talk,' the skater said, and Griswold Weils peered through the night and saw that the big dark car was not a Rolly-Royce. It was a Bentley!

'I haven't told nothing!' Griswold Weils said. 'What's wrong with Lloyd? I haven't told nothing!'

'Shut your mouth!' the skater whispered, getting a handful of Griswold Weils' collar and pressing the knife against his ribs.

They stopped when they were still thirty feet from the car in the darkness. Griswold Weils could see Lloyd's silhouette behind the steering wheel, the familiar cap and glasses.

Griswold Weils called out, 'Lloyd! I didn't tell the cops nothing. They came, but I didn't tell them, Lloyd!'

The headlights blinked on, off, on. 'That's it. He don't wanna talk to ya,' the skater said, leading Griswold Weils back to the Toyota.

'But I didn't tell the cops nothing!' Griswold Weils sobbed. He was gushing tears now. 'Nothing! I swear!'

Then the passenger door of the Bentley opened and *another* leather-covered thug emerged and approached Griswold Weils as the Bentley started its engine, backed up, and drove away.

'Lloyd says to use our own judgment,' the second one said, as Griswold Weils wept and jabbered, 'I didn't tell the cops nothing! Please don't kill me!'

'Who said anything about killing ya?' the first thug said.

'You're not going to kill me?'

'No.' The first thug grinned, grabbing Griswold Weils' neck. 'I'm gonna hamstring ya. Only skating you'll be doing from now on will be on a little square platform on the sidewalk.'

And then, weeping brokenly, Griswold Weils was grabbed by each arm and led to the Toyota, where he was shoved into the back seat and down on the floor by the first one as the second one drove the Toyota deeper into the bowels of Griffin Park while Griswold Weils began wetting his skating pants but didn't even notice.

When it seemed they'd been driving for half an hour, but in reality had only been circling for five minutes, the one driving said, 'Goddamnit, I didn't see that stop sign!'

And the thug in the back seat with his knife pressed to the nape of the neck of Griswold Weils, able to dispatch him with one slice (as Griswold Weils had seen Laurence Olivier do to Woody Strode in *Spartacus*), said, 'You dumb shit! That's a cop car over there!'

Griswold Weils started hyperventilating, and spitting

up the bile of sheer terror. Suddenly he heard it: a police siren!

Had he not been practically catatonic by now, even Griswold Weils would have wondered why the hell the cop was hitting his siren in a quiet and deserted park at night when there wasn't another car on the lonely road. Griswold Weils had worked on enough cop shows to know that the siren is only used when there's heavy traffic to penetrate.

'Gud-damn, Buckmore!' Gibson Hand said to the grinning street monster behind the wheel, 'ain't that a little too much? The fuckin siren?'

But Buckmore Phipps said, 'Gibson, this ain't police work! This is show biz!'

Meanwhile, Schultz was blasting south in the maroon Bentley, which looked black in the moonlight, heading for Beverly Hills where his partner waited at the leasing agency with a very worried agency manager who wondered if he had made a mistake by being a 'good citizen' and loaning these cops a $100,000 machine.

When the street monsters approached the Toyota, one on each side, and the driver jumped out saying, 'Yes, Officer, what can I do for you tonight?' and the first thug kept his knife blade against the spinal cord of Griswold Weils, who kept thinking of poor Woody Strode, he heard one of the cops cry out: 'Watch out, partner!'

And then Griswold Weils felt the release of deadly pressure, and another voice cried out: 'Freeze!' And as he was drifting toward unconsciousness Griswold Weils thought, they *do* say Freeze! Just like on all the shows he'd worked.

Then he felt himself being lifted bodily from the back of the Toyota and he looked into the face of a huge black cop who said, 'Are you okay, sir?'

Later, Buckmore Phipps accused Gibson Hand of being the ham, because neither street monster had called anyone 'sir' since they were recruits in the police academy.

Then Griswold Weils was being propped up by a huge

white cop, and the huge black cop had the two thugs spreadeagled on the ground with their hands behind their ponytails, and the white cop was saying, 'What happened, mister? Were they trying to kidnap ya? Was it a robbery? Did they rape ya? What?'

Griswold Weils was periously close to slipping into shock and he lost track of time as the big white cop sat in the police car and called for assistance and had a hurried conversation with his black partner. He said something about getting Griswold Weils to the detectives while the other took the thugs to jail. Griswold Weils found himself being sped to Hollywood Station by the big white cop and helped up the stairs and into the detective squadroom while still too faint to recognize the two detectives on duty there.

'Mr Weils!' Al Mackey cried. 'What are *you* doing here?'

It was nearly ten o'clock when Al Mackey sat in the detective squadroom discussing the evening's performances with the actors: Schultz and Simon, the Weasel and Ferret, and the two street monsters, who were looking at their watches and thinking about The Glitter Dome but were nonetheless savoring the success of their dramatic debuts.

'I *loved* the way the little cocksucker turned gray!' Buckmore Phipps exclaimed. 'It was almost as much fun as the real thing. I think I could make it as a character actor in the movies. How much they charge you to join SAG?'

'I think you'd be a little tough on leading men,' the Weasel said, massaging his arm that Buckmore Phipps had nearly jerked loose from the socket.

'I'd like to see how you guys can use any of this information in a court of law,' the Ferret said. 'If it ever comes to that.'

'We're not *that* nimble and inventive,' Al Mackey said. 'We never thought Griswold was a killer, just a liar.'

'Whadda ya suppose he's doin now?' Gibson Hand grinned.

'Still on the toilet, I bet,' Buckmore Phipps said. 'When I dropped him off at his apartment, he said he had to take one more crap. He told me he was gonna write our captain a letter about us savin his life, but I think I talked him out of it. Told him we was too modest, and let's just keep our heroism a secret between him and us and the detectives.'

'What's he gonna think when he don't get a subpoena to go to court and testify against the two guys that tried to cut his throat?' Gibson Hand asked.

'He's going to be told they pleaded guilty at their arraignment,' Al Mackey said. 'He's going to be thrilled to get out of it with . . .'

'. . . with his life.' The Ferret grinned. 'Bet he'll never skate backwards again, long as he lives.'

And as the applause was shared by the evening's performers, Martin Welborn sat alone in the captain's office and analyzed the tape he'd made of Griswold Weils' statement to Al Mackey in the interrogation room.

The first part of the tape wasn't very useful, what with Griswold Weils admitting that he'd lied to the detectives, and how he shouldn't have, but how surprised he'd been to have the detectives link him with the dead body of Nigel St Claire, and how he had just started ad-libbing. And how much of what he'd told them had been in a script he'd shot five years earlier when cop shows were hot.

Martin Welborn punched the stop button when the tape counter reached the part he wanted to hear again.

Al Mackey's voice said, 'But why did you have to lie to us?'

'The first part was true,' Griswold Weils' voice said. 'I didn't know how much you knew or didn't know. I just wanted to say enough to get rid a you guys. I didn't want no more a Lloyd *or* his project.'

'Then you don't know for certain if Nigel St Claire had anything to do with your movie?'

'Not for sure.'

'And the only time you realized he *might* be involved

with Lloyd was when you read the newspaper the next morning about him being found dead in the parking lot?'

'That's it. Lloyd and his Oriental pal that never talked showed up at my apartment one night and Lloyd told me he heard I'd been busted for kiddy porn and he had a job and it paid five grand for two days' work.'

'And you agreed,' Al Mackey said. There was a hum on the tape and then Al Mackey said, 'If you tell us one more lie, Griswold, we will *not* be able to protect you from Lloyd, and won't take responsibility for your safety.'

'I agreed,' Griswold Weils said. 'But I'm making a comeback in legit work! It was just . . . Jesus! *Five* grand for two days in Mexico!'

'So you put on your Mister Silver disguise and went to the Trousdale house with Lloyd and auditioned the performers?'

'Lloyd gave me that dumb wig and beard. I could see he touched up his hair under that cap to make it gray. He never fooled me with his phony moustache and glasses and I don't think I fooled any a those kids that came for the audition. But what the hell, they probably expected phony names and disguises, the kind a movie they were gonna make.'

'But they *weren't* kids, you said. Or are you lying again? Were *some* of them kids?'

'Not kids like you mean,' Griswold Weils said. 'There was the blond girl with the wonderful complexion. She was Lloyd's favorite. Or his producer's favorite.'

'What producer?'

'I don't know! It was easy to see that Lloyd and the Oriental guy weren't in The Business. They were working with someone else who was packaging this thing. You think I asked questions? I just lit the bedroom and taped the auditions and that's it.'

'Who was the director?'

'For *this* audition? What director you need? Lloyd would tell the actors to strip down, get on the bed, roll around a little bit, and get dressed and out. It was quick. No one ever auditioned with another performer. It was just so someone *else* could get a close look at the performers on tape. That's one reason I know Lloyd musta worked with someone. Also, let's face it, Lloyd's not in The Business. Lloyd's a . . .'

'Thug.'

'Yeah, but I didn't know he was *that* dangerous. After the night in the bowling alley parking lot, I never saw or heard from him again till tonight up in Griffith Park. We still had the male performers to tape. They said there was some young marine, and a kid who works parking cars, and another one or two. Christ, I only *made* the ten percent he paid me in advance!'

'There's only one thing I can't understand, Griswold,' Al Mackey said. 'Why did you back out?'

'It worried me that he insisted on shooting it in Mexico. They were paying me for *two* days' work and I heard Lloyd give that little blond girl an offer for *three* days' work. That's when I figured it out! I'd told Lloyd no *little* kids and no animals. But I decided they were gonna take me and the equipment down there in Baja and get the place all lit and I was gonna shoot two days of *ordinary* porn with those young people. And then I was gonna get a ride back to Hollywood and someone *else* was gonna shoot the last day, which was probably the kind a stuff I said I *wouldn't* do. Little Mexican kids maybe? More likely, animals?'

'Who would operate the camera on the last day?'

'Lloyd maybe? He knew a little about photography. And he was asking a million questions when we were auditioning those girls in that house. He already knew something about sound mixing. He had good equipment. Hell, after I got the place lit and showed him how things work, I imagine he figured he could photograph the *rough* stuff by himself. The last *act* a their movie, so to speak.'

'So now, Griswold, you've told *most* of the truth. But you haven't told the truth about why you backed out. You don't expect me to believe that your conscience started bothering you.'

'The animals. The little Mexican kids. I . . .'

'All right, get out!' Al Mackey's voice said. 'Forget about police protection.'

'You gotta catch Lloyd!' Griswold Weils cried. 'He might try again!'

'He *will* try again,' Al Mackey said.

'Okay! I got a phone call,' Griswold Weils said quickly. '*Somebody* told me to get out of the deal with Lloyd or something bad was gonna happen.'

'Who phoned you?'

'I dunno! I panicked and called Sapphire Productions like I always did, and the same old geezer said Lloyd would phone me and when he did I told him I got a *warning*! And I was backing *out*!'

'What did he say?'

'What you'd expect. He didn't believe it. Thought I was getting cold feet. Reminded me he gave me an advance a five hundred. I told him I already *earned* that much, what with two trips up to that Trousdale house and photographing six girls for him. I just apologized and said I was out and hung up. When the phone rang after that, I didn't answer. And then . . . then he found me skating in the parking lot the night a the murder and tried to talk me into it and I said no way, and he *almost* made a threat. But finally he left and I saw his big Bentley parked over on the far side of the parking lot and it looked like someone was in it. I just figured it was the Oriental guy. I skated straight to my apartment. Next morning I hear on the news that Nigel St Claire was found shot dead in that parking lot! I say to myself, what would Nigel St Claire be doing there? Skating? No way. Only one skates there that time a night is *me*! So I figured he had to a been hooked up with Lloyd. I just hoped and prayed I'd never hear from Lloyd again. And then you guys came one day and scared the shit outa me and I made up a cockamamie story because I knew you didn't pick my name outa the phone book. And then tonight. You gotta *catch* this guy! He figures I might tell you about the night in the parking lot and he's trying to shut me up. He *must* be the one that killed Mister St Claire!'

'Why do you suppose Nigel St Claire ever became involved with Lloyd?'

'You ask *me*? I can't figure it. He coulda bought himself every animal flick ever made. If he was some kind a big-time porn lover, he coulda had his own library from every porn producer in Europe and South America, not to mention the States. I ain't gonna believe Nigel St Claire was trying to package an illegal porn show for *profit*. Just as soon believe he was importing Mexican brown from down there in Baja. It just don't make sense unless . . . unless maybe Lloyd was blackmailing him.'

'Blackmailing? For what?'

'How do I know? Maybe Nigel St Claire got loaded and ended up at one a those videotape parties one night? I done a few jobs like that. People lay around sucking and fucking in piles. And they want to videotape it for later so they can enjoy their performances. Celebrities like Mister St Claire would be dumb to attend those little gatherings, but who knows? Maybe he got loaded some night and ended up on tape. It's happened before. Or maybe Lloyd set him up with a cute sailor and took his picture on the sly. Then threatened to turn it over to some Hollywood scandal sheet? Maybe like that?'

'You've been thinking about this a *lot*,' Al Mackey said.

'You kidding? That's *all* I think about. My skating's getting so bad, that's why I let that killer run into me tonight. I never woulda gotten hit if I was still skating the way I was before I met Lloyd.'

'Can you think who the person might be who called and warned you to get out of the deal?'

'No idea. It wasn't the geezer at Sapphire Productions. I talked to him enough times to know. It sounded like a youngish guy. Lloyd would *not* believe I got the call no matter what I said. He just thought I was getting cold feet and welshing.'

Then the taped conversation was interrupted by the

door to the interrogation room being opened, and Martin Welborn heard his own voice on the tape saying, 'Excuse me, but I have a question or two. Griswold, were you driven each time to and *from* the Trousdale taping sessions by Lloyd?'

'Once I took a taxi back to my apartment. Lloyd said he had a busy night and he called the taxi for me.'

'Was it the night you photographed the little blonde with the beautiful complexion?'

'No, she was one a the first. I think it was the very next night, though.'

'Do you think your taxi could have been followed?'

'How should I know? I wasn't looking for things like that.'

'As I recall, your name's on your mailbox?'

'Yeah.'

'Is your phone number listed or unlisted?'

'Listed. I can't afford luxuries. Besides, I don't get many calls. But I'm making a comeback and . . .'

'How young was the guy's voice who warned you *not* to go forward with your Mexico film?'

'How young? I dunno. I just know it wasn't an old geezer's voice like the guy at Sapphire. It just wasn't a real old voice and it wasn't a real deep voice.'

'A tenor, more or less?'

'I didn't hear him sing.'

The night that had begun with such promise ended in bitter disappointment. At midnight, the address in Trousdale Estates given to the detectives by Griswold Weils was surrounded by eight policemen, four with shotguns. The shotgun wielders were, of course, the Ferret and Weasel, Buckmore Phipps and Gibson Hand. Schultz, Simon, Al Mackey and Martin Welborn had their revolvers drawn and it was Al Mackey and Martin Welborn who stood one on each side of the front door of the darkened house on the very top of the hill. Where, if one were in The Business, one would overlook all of Baghdad. And *dream*.

Martin Welborn tried the key that had been dropped at the waterfront in San Pedro by the man the Ferret was now praying would try to climb out the window. This time he wouldn't have to throw rocks at the assassin.

Buckmore Phipps and Gibson Hand were hoping to get Just Plain Bill Bozwell in their sights if he tried to help his pal battle it out. He made a bigger target than a little gook, and they figured to get more television coverage if they blew away a white hoodlum.

Martin Welborn and Al Mackey were hoping that the Vietnamese assassin wouldn't try to fight or run, so they could capture him alive and perhaps solve the mystery that was driving them all bonzo.

The key fit perfectly, and the detectives got their flashlights and guns ready when Martin Welborn turned it as quietly as possible. He entered the darkened house first, followed by Al Mackey, followed by Shultz and Simon, who looked like dancing Disney elephants tiptoeing across the marble portico into the foyer of the mock Roman digs.

There was no one in the house. After three minutes of creeping down carpeted corridors, and dripping sweat on marble floors, the detectives had checked all five bedrooms and the servants' quarters. Al Mackey began turning on lights and calling the others inside.

The street monsters were disappointed, and asked the detectives to give them a chance to kill Just Plain Bill some other time. Al Mackey promised he would, and they got into their black-and-white and drove back to Hollywood. The Ferret was beside himself, tearing through the house looking for any clue to the 'houseboy' he wanted on the wrong end of his shotgun.

There wasn't a single lead. On the off chance that they might pick up some lifts around the bar, they called for a latent-print specialist.

It was a lavish, expensive, ugly house. The owners were obviously in parts unknown. There wasn't a single article of clothing in the closets. But there was something interesting in the garage.

'The Bentley!' Al Mackey cried, when Schultz called him.

'It's been hotwired,' Schultz said. 'We can have it dusted, maybe get that gook's fingerprints.'

'Maybe get Nigel St Claire's fingerprints,' Martin Welborn said. 'I'd love to be able to prove *he* rode in this car.'

The latent-prints specialist found the bar area clean. So was the car. So was the bedroom described by Griswold Weils as the audition room. They found a realtor's card by the telephone in the kitchen.

'There won't be a single long-distance call charged to this phone,' Al Mackey sighed.

'And that realtor's going to tell us the owners are in England making a movie and he leased the house to a nice fellow named Lloyd. You pick the last name. And Lloyd paid cash and wore a cap and had glasses and promised he'd watch the house and see that the plants were watered and that nobody disturbed the owner's Bentley and . . .'

Martin Welborn was exactly right. Except that the owners were in *Spain* making a movie. There was one puzzling discovery in the house that night. The leaded glass by the side door had been broken. Someone had smashed the glass in order to reach inside and unlock the door. The glass had not been replaced and had been only halfheartedly swept away, probably when Lloyd moved out. Someone had broken into this house before Just Plain Bill Bozwell vacated the premises.

17

Danny Meadows

The first order of business the next morning was to reinterview Peggy Farrell and try to persuade the little hooker that honesty was the *only* policy, or she could wait for her eighteenth birthday in Juvenile Hall, because the police still had a missing persons' report signed by her father, Flameout Farrell. And, if they wanted to be really horseshit, a case might be made against Lorna Dillon for contributing to her delinquency.

Before they left the office for the house in Benedict Canyon, Martin Welborn tried to call Deedra Briggs to explain that he had been too preoccupied with Griswold Weils to call last night as promised. Only two days and he longed for his woman terribly.

Al Mackey guessed who Marty was calling from that boyish expectant look as he waited. Then the look faded and Marty hung up.

'Calling your friend?'

'Yeah.'

'Actors get up at four o'clock to go to work, you know.'

'That's probably it. She's working on a television commercial this week.'

'You can see her tonight maybe,' Al Mackey said.

'Sure.'

'This one might be good for you, Marty,' Al Mackey said. 'She seems okay.'

'She *is* okay.' Martin Welborn smiled.

'Well, let's go make the little hooker bawl.'

And bawl she did, as soon as she opened the door of the Benedict Canyon cottage. Peggy Farrell had been used and abused by men for a good part of her young life and the detectives only had to utter a portion of their catalogue of threats before she was lying on the couch crying her eyes out and begging them not to put her in Juvenile Hall. And offering to do *anything* for them, an enticement which had gotten her out of lots of temporary trouble but into lots of deep degradation these past two years on the streets.

'Try telling the truth,' Martin Welborn said, and the two detectives waited until the frail and wan and troubled child wiped her eyes on the sleeve of Lorna Dillon's large sweat shirt and gained some control.

'I didn't want to get Lorna in trouble. It's the last thing I wanted.'

'Then you have to tell us the truth this time, Peggy,' Al Mackey said.

'What time will she be home today?' Martin Welborn asked.

'About six, six-thirty.'

'Let's start with the audition,' Al Mackey said. 'You were videotaped that night in Trousdale by Mister Silver, weren't you?'

'Yes.'

'Sometime later you were told that you had the job?'

'I knew I had the job that night,' she said. 'Lloyd said the other girls couldn't compare to me and he was just going through the motions for his partner, but I was gonna be picked.'

'And how much were you going to get?'

'*Eight* thousand for three days in Mexico!'

'And how many others would be picked?'

'Just one boy, Lloyd said. He hadn't been picked yet.'

'And how did Lorna find out?'

'She . . . she was waiting up when I got home. She thought I was turning tricks again but I promised her I wasn't. And we had a fight, and . . . well, she hit me and I cried. And then she said she was sorry and we drank a bottle a wine and I hardly ever drink wine or anything and I got pretty high and . . .'

288

'You told her about Lloyd and the offer?'

'I didn't mean to, but I was excited and scared. Eight thousand bucks for *three* days!'

'And what happened?'

'She asked for the address and I gave it to her.'

'You'd memorized the street and the house number?' Al Mackey said.

'Yeah, I was nervous going up there with Lloyd even if he *did* drive a Bentley. It was scary.'

'Of course,' Martin Welborn said. 'Did Lorna do anything else?'

'At first she just made me promise to call Sapphire Productions and tell them I wasn't going to take the job, but . . .'

'But what?'

'I think she knew I would. I mean, I was getting antsy around here in the house all the time, with her working so much and all. I wanted my own money and it seemed better than going back to those gnarly massages. *Eight* thousand for *three* days?'

'What happened then?'

'Nothing. I decided I was gonna call Lloyd and take it. Then I changed my mind. Several days passed and I didn't call. Then I go . . . I go, fuck it! I'm *gonna* do it. And I tell Lorna I'm gonna do it, but she doesn't hit me this time. She gets *real* serious and she told me that Lloyd's been to my dad's restaurant looking for me. He's that anxious for me to be in the show. And then she tells me that the show in Mexico isn't gonna be some ordinary fuck movie between me and some boy, like I was told by Lloyd.'

'What did she say it would be?'

'She said it was gonna be something real kinky where I could get hurt.'

'How did she know that?'

'She's in The Business. She says nobody gets paid the kind a money I'm being offered to go to *Mexico* for three days and do an ordinary porn show. She said Lloyd was lying to me, and she said she was positive it was *dangerous*.

She said she called my dad and told him not to tell Lloyd nothing about me if he came there looking for me.'

'She *knows* Flameout Farrell?'

'Only on the telephone. When we first got together she called my dad and told . . . *almost* everything. That she takes care a me and likes me and is trying to get me off drugs and off the streets. And she even gave him her name and phone number. So you see? I'm not really a runaway no more. He knows how to get in touch with me if he really wants to.'

'That's interesting,' Al Mackey said, looking at Martin Welborn. Flameout hadn't told the Weasel and Ferret *everything*. No one was telling *everything*.

'Did Lorna tell your dad about the . . . *danger* you were in?' Martin Welborn asked.

'I don't know,' she said. 'She wouldn't tell me any more about what her and my dad talked about.'

'Did you ever hear from Lloyd again after those two times?' Martin Welborn asked.

'No, and I never called Sapphire Productions again. Lorna said not to even call him. Maybe that's how come I let the nurd in the pickup truck tempt me. I figured I lost the eight thousand and maybe I was mad and wanted to make some bread. Lorna just can't understand me wanting to have something a my *own*.'

'Have you ever heard the name Nigel St Claire?' Al Mackey asked.

'No.'

'Did you see on television or read in the paper about a big movie producer getting killed?'

No. I just watch *Laverne and Shirley* and *Happy Days*, stuff like that.'

'Did you ever hear Lorna mention that name?' Martin Welborn asked.

'No.'

'I want you to go somewhere this afternoon,' Martin Welborn said.

'Where?'

'Anywhere. Go visit your dad or something. We want to wait for Lorna and talk to her privately.'

'Can I go to a movie?' Now her eyes were like sun-filled amber. She looked twelve years old.

'Yeah. Do you have any money?'

'Not enough for popcorn *and* a movie,' she said.

Martin Welborn took ten dollars out of his pocket and said, 'Go to a movie and buy some popcorn, Peggy.'

'Well, we've got the rest of the afternoon to kill,' Al Mackey said when they got back in the car. 'May as well go to the station. Maybe someone's slipped another load of dope in Woofer's pipe. We should be there to get rousted like everyone else.'

'It'll give me a chance to call Deedra,' Martin Welborn said absently.

'Maybe she has a friend,' Al Mackey said, driving south, out of the canyon. 'I'm ready for a hot date. Wing's given me a few . . . pointers.'

'There's still something . . . *wrong*,' Martin Welborn said. 'It smells *all* wrong.'

'There you go again with the bird-dog bullshit. The case *stinks*, is what it does. I'm getting so I don't give a damn *who* wasted Nigel St Claire. I just wanna clear the case before Woofer whacks our balls.'

'It's still not right. Why film in Mexico?'

'Because Peggy's co-star was gonna to be a goddamn burro, or an iguana, that's why. And they're more plentiful in Mexico.'

'Maybe,' Martin Welborn said.

'And I don't think the Tijuana vice squad, if there *is* such a thing, is quite as diligent as ours, so there isn't much chance they'd get caught during production.'

'Maybe,' Martin Welborn said. 'Maybe.'

When they got to the squadroom Al Mackey reported their progress to the Ferret, who by now had all but given up his drug cases, so obsessed was he with the search for the Vietnamese assassin. Much to the displeasure of the

Weasel, who had to deliver a bagful of lies to Captain Woofer about a big dope case they were about to crack which would bust the seams of the county jail with drug traffickers and make Hollywood as dopefree as Spearfish, South Dakota, to which the Captain intended to retire.

Martin Welborn again received no answer when he called Deedra Briggs.

'Actors work long hours, Marty,' Al Mackey said.

'Yeah.'

'How about going down on Melrose for some Mexican food? I'm starved.'

'I'll come along,' the Ferret said. 'Maybe some food'll take my mind off finding the gook. I think I'm going bonzo.'

'I might as well come,' the Weasel said. 'Only work the Ferret's willing to do anymore has to be with you guys. I'm getting tense waiting for Woofer to knock our dicks down.'

'I'm not hungry,' Martin Welborn said, 'I'll see you when you get back. Take your time. Lorna Dillon doesn't get home till six.'

After the others had gone, Martin Welborn dialed Deedra Briggs' number yet another time just in case he had dialed incorrectly. He *had* to see her tonight.

Then he got an idea. The more he thought of it the more shape it seemed to take. He made another phone call, this one to Sergeant Gabe Samson of Administrative Vice Division, the department's pornography expert, who had been comparing the mug shots of Just Plain Bill Bozwell with performers in recent porn films. Martin Welborn talked for a moment with Samson, then hung up and wrote on the sign-out sheet, listing his destination as Parker Center, Administrative Vice Division.

He still hadn't returned when the others came back from lunch smelling of beans and burritos and salsa and chile verde. Al Mackey noticed the sign-out and was surprised when Marty wasn't back until everyone else was going end-of-watch.

When he came in Martin Welborn looked pale and tense and troubled.

'I saw you went to Ad Vice,' Al Mackey said. 'Samson able to make Bill Bozwell?'

'No,' Martin Welborn said. 'Excuse me, Al, I have to make a call.'

Al Mackey knew who he was calling, so he walked away from the homicide table and said his good-nights to the Ferret and Weasel, who were signing out. He saw Martin Welborn hang up, again having received no answer. Then Martin Welborn picked up their plastic briefcase and said, 'It's time to talk to Lorna Dillon.'

Martin Welborn didn't talk much on the ride to the cottage except to say he might be making a mistake. He stared a lot and Al Mackey didn't press him. They were sitting in front of her cottage when she came in the driveway in her Fiat. She didn't look terribly surprised to see them, but she seemed surprised that Peggy wasn't home.

'We sent her to a movie,' Martin Welborn said when they were inside and seated in the tidy living room.

'So it's me you wanted to see.'

'You don't look astonished,' Al Mackey said.

'I thought you might discover that Peggy hadn't told you . . . everything.'

'And how about you?' Martin Welborn said. 'Have you told us everything?'

'Everything I'm going to,' she said calmly. 'I don't have to talk to you at all, do I?'

'No,' Martin Welborn said. 'But I have to advise you of your rights.'

She sat quietly during the reading of her constitutional rights and then said, 'You think *I* killed Nigel St Claire.'

'Possibly,' Martin Welborn said. 'And you might actually *want* to talk about it.'

'And why would I have wanted to kill him?'

'I think you suspected what Lloyd and his Vietnamese friend were going to do in Mexico. I think after Peggy had

293

her audition you were outraged, and went to the house in Trousdale the next day and found no one at home. I think you broke the glass of the side door and went inside and saw enough to satisfy yourself as to what they were *really* going to make in Mexico.'

'And what's that?'

'A snuff film,' Martin Welborn said.

'A snuff film? How interesting. Have you ever seen a snuff film?'

'As far as the Los Angeles Police Department knows, there's never been a snuff film actually verified. There've been simulated snuff films from South America where they use animal guts and tricks they use in regular movies. But no police agency has yet confiscated a real snuff film despite all the rumors of their existence.'

'And how did I know they were going to use Peggy for a snuff film?'

'You found something in the house. Something that spelled *more* than S and M, which you probably suspected at first. Something that told you they weren't just going to physically abuse Peggy in their movie. They were going to *kill* her. On camera. A genuine snuff film.'

'And then what?'

'You waited at the Trousdale house and followed Weils' taxi right to his apartment. You looked at his name on the mailbox. You found him in the phone book. You finally decided to call and warn him to change his plans. You have a deep voice. You wanted to sound like a man.'

'And then?'

'And then you found out from Flameout Farrell that Lloyd was still coming around looking for Peggy. You were furious, but still all you had was the suspicion of a snuff film in another country. There was nothing you could even report to the police. You decided to tell Lloyd that you were onto him and he'd better leave Peggy alone. You took a gun for protection and . . .'

'I don't have a gun.'

'. . . and you waited at Griswold Weils' apartment for a

night or two until you saw that Bentley drive up across the street in the bowling alley parking lot.'

'And then?'

'And then you waited until you saw Lloyd go to the apartment to talk to Griswold Weils. You walked to the Bentley to wait for him. You were shocked to see a man in that car whom you knew.'

'I didn't know Nigel St Claire.'

'You know his face. You were *shocked* to think he was part of this. You were more than shocked. You were *furious*.'

'Why would Nigel St Claire be part of it?'

'I don't know. To have something no one else has? Or perhaps Nigel St Claire was simply a victim of blackmail and was helping Lloyd the blackmailer *put together his package*, as they say in your business. Maybe he didn't know that Lloyd was planning to make something more than kiddy porn, or animal porn, or something more than S and M.'

'In other words, Nigel St Claire might have been a *victim* after all? A *victim* of an extortion? Wrongfully killed by an outraged lover of a little girl he was *only* going to exploit in an ordinary way by letting a dog or a donkey fuck her brains out? Or maybe let her be whipped and burned and savaged a little, with eight thousand dollars to salve the wounds?'

'Something like that,' Martin Welborn said.

'Yes. Maybe Nigel St Claire thought it was *only* to be kiddy porn with Mexican kids and they don't count for much anyway? In any case, he didn't know it was a *snuff* film because he wouldn't countenance *murder*, no matter how sinister and perverted he was, correct? Or how frightened he was of a blackmailer?'

'Something like that,' Martin Welborn said.

'Well then, a piece of filth like Nigel St Claire *should* be killed. And I'm delighted that someone performed the public service. May I borrow a piece of notebook paper?'

Al Mackey looked at Martin Welborn and tore off a sheet of yellow lined paper.

'Your pencil, please?' she said.

Then they watched her write a name and telephone number. When she was finished, she said, 'This is *not* a signed confession. I want you to save yourself further embarrassment. I want you to call this man tomorrow. He's the production manager on a show I just finished. I want you to ask him where I was for three days *before* and four days *after* Nigel St Claire was killed. I want you to question him thoroughly and then question *every* witness he gives you. I want you to be absolutely satisfied that I was on location in Wyoming. Far from a commercial airport, at *all* times in the immediate presence of a cast and crew of more than one hundred people. I'd like you to do all that, and I don't require an apology. But I do want you to promise not to bother Peggy and me ever again or I'll call my lawyer and bring a lawsuit against you for police harassment.'

When they were driving back to the station, Al Mackey said, 'She wasn't bluffing, Marty.'

'Damn it, I know I've got *most* of it right,' Martin Welborn said. 'I *know* I do. The snuff film. It makes sense. Bozwell and his friend are thugs, hoodlums, *killers*, if there's enough money in it.'

'What if you've got it correct up to the point of St Claire's murder?' Al Mackey said. 'The snuff film makes some sense. More, if St Claire was a blackmail victim ond didn't know what Bozwell was really up to. In other words, St Claire was a filthy cowardly pig, but not a killer. How about St Claire just gets sick of being leaned on? And when Bozwell came back to the car from Weils' apartment, St Claire has it out with him and says he won't give him any more help or money. And Bozwell shoots him. Then Bozwell goes out of the movie business, gets rid of all his equipment, and goes back into the armed robbery business, which he does best anyway. Something like that?'

'Plausible. But I just can't see Bozwell killing his meal ticket.'

'What if St Claire went bughouse and attacked him?'

'Plausible,' Martin Welborn said. 'If we ever catch the Vietnamese partner, he might verify that theory.'

'He's about our *last* hope. Because when Bozwell shows up for his preliminary hearing on the goldbug robbery he's not going to give us the time of day.'

'Not the time of day,' Martin Welborn said.

'Who came up with the snuff film idea? You or Ad Vice?'

'I did. It *has* to be that. I was sure of it after spending the afternoon at Ad Vice. I saw kiddy porn. I saw S and M films. It *has* to be that.'

'How do you feel after a day at the sewer cinema?'

'I feel like seeing Deedra tonight and talking about retirement.'

'Whose?'

'Mine. Hers.'

'You've only known this woman for a few days!'

'She hates the movie business. She's getting out of it. Not because of me, of course.'

'Marty, don't depend too much on this new . . . friendship.'

'Sometimes you have to take a chance, Al,' Martin Welborn said, and his long brown eyes had dropped at the corners and Al Mackey got nervous because they were starting to drift in and out of focus again.

One of the children in the kiddy porn looked exactly like Danny Meadows. Of course he knew it wasn't, but he looked like Danny Meadows. Perhaps it was the glazed look in the child's eyes when the man was sexually abusing him for the camera. The child was drugged and his mouth made the word, 'Daddy?' Maybe that's what made him think of Danny Meadows.

'Marty, I'm talking to you,' Al Mackey said.

'Huh?'

'Marty, you had that look again.'

'What look?'

'Were you thinking about Elliott Robles?'

'No.'

'It wasn't your fault, Marty. Elliott's death wasn't your fault.'

'Yes,' he said, ambiguously.

'What're you gonna do tonight?'

Martin Welborn stared past Al Mackey and said, 'I'm going to see Deedra. We'll talk about painting. She's a wonderful painter and she wants to teach me to skate. Think I'm too old?'

'You're not too old, Marty,' Al Mackey said, hoping that Martin Welborn could see Deedra Briggs tonight. And that they'd talk about painting and roller skates.

At 7:30 that night, Deedra Briggs was home and answered the phone.

'Sergeant Elbowpatches!' she exclaimed. 'I was hoping you'd call *last* night!'

'I wanted to, Deedra, but we were . . .'

'I'm so excited! I was busting to tell somebody! Do you remember the tall man with the silver hair who was talking to Herman's mogul group?'

'Yes.'

'He called my agent yesterday. Personally! I'm getting the third lead in that South African picture I told you about!'

'He's one of the men you despise,' Martin Welborn said.

'And third billing, Martin! Do you know what that means?'

'A lot of money.'

'The hell with the money! I'd pay them! Do you know what it means to my career at this point? Martin, I'm no kid. I thought it was over. The South African picture. God, I don't even know the working title. Everyone's talking about it!'

'The other producer who owns the rights,' Martin Welborn said, 'is the one with the world's largest porn collection.'

'They've become partners. God, I'm so excited I can't come down off the ceiling. I have to *tell* people!'

'When will you be leaving?'

'They start shooting at the end of the summer if the script's in shape.'

'I was wondering if you'd like some dinner tonight.'

'Oh, I can't, Martin. I've been invited to discuss the project with them. Over dinner. I'm so sorry. Maybe tomorrow or the next day?'

'Sure. I'll call.'

'I'm so excited!'

'Good-bye, Deedra.'

'Let's get together for lunch, Sergeant Elbowpatches!' she said merrily.

When Martin Welborn hung up the phone he went to the kitchen and poured himself a tumbler of vodka. His lower back had begun hurting during the conversation with Deedra Briggs. Now the pain was getting unbearable. He gulped down the vodka like water, and it burned so much he gagged. Still, he poured another. He drank it the same way. The pain of the vodka didn't dull the other. He was hammered with bolts of pain. He limped into the bedroom and stripped off all his clothes. He was in too much agony to satisfy his compulsion for neatness and order. He stepped out of his clothes where they lay and limped to the device in the corner of the bedroom. He groaned as he strapped himself into position. Then he let himself down until he was suspended upside down with his spine perfectly straight and his head three inches from the floor.

But the pain was not subsiding. He moaned again. It was hurting so much he started to weep. The tears were running the wrong way, into his eyebrows and hair instead of into his mouth. He wept like the little boy in the film he had seen today. The little boy was drugged, but still the pain had made him weep. When he wept he looked just like Danny Meadows.

*

It wasn't as though it was a big deal homicide, Captain Woofer had said. It wasn't any kind of homicide.

And it wasn't often that veteran homicide detectives rolled on an all-units call unless it was code three. This was only a code two broadcast. The next-door neighbor who heard the boy whimpering on the service porch had been too hysterical to respond hysterically. She had simply told the communications operator that someone had been cut and to send the police and an ambulance. Then she hung up and couldn't stop screaming even after the police arrived.

Martin Welborn remembered exactly what he and Al had been talking about when they heard the radio call. They had been discussing Paula's agreement not to seek a divorce, thus remaining his spouse and heir as far as the Department was concerned. He was willing to pay her far more than she could have gotten in spousal support. A marriage was not dead without an official seal. Not in the eyes of man. God no longer mattered. But a bitter call from Paula for more money had precipitated a night of haunting loneliness.

Perhaps if Paula hadn't called the night before. It had exhausted him physically as well as spiritually. He was in no condition to accommodate the meeting with Danny Meadows.

Perhaps if the radio call hadn't been broadcast at that precise moment. Two minutes later they'd have been back at the station. Martin Welborn distinctly remembered what he had said when Al Mackey asked if he wanted to respond to the call since they were so close. He'd said, 'I'm tired, Al. Do what you like.' The words were etched like a steel engraving. He remembered precisely.

If he hadn't said the last part. If they'd been two blocks closer to the station. If the neighbor had responded more predictably, the call would have been code three, and a radio car would have arrived first.

Is that finally it? It's all an accident? Coincidence? A series of tiny vagaries?

Mr and Mrs Meadows were clearly not evil people, the public defender had said. And he was clearly right. They hadn't the dignity for evil. Wouldn't that be the last laugh on all failed seminarians: There's no evil. No good. No choices. Only accidents.

They arrived long before the first radio car. The screaming woman stood in front of Danny Meadows' house. She never said a word. She didn't even point. She looked at the house and screamed. A

300

Mackey took hold of her and she tried to talk. They couldn't make sense of it. Martin Welborn drew his revolver and walked toward the house. He remembered distinctly what Al Mackey said: 'Be careful, Marty.'

Al was coming up the steps when Martin Welborn stepped very cautiously into the ominous wood-frame house. There were three mottled puppies in the house. Urine and defecation from the puppies was everywhere. The house was rank with it. And with the smell of spilled beer and port wine. Martin Welborn was proceeding very carefully through the stink and debris when Al came through the door, gun in hand. They didn't know what they were looking for.

Al Mackey nudged open a bedroom door and they both ducked back on either side. Al went into the bedroom first. The mattress was without sheets and stained with menstrual blood and urine and semen. The slipless pillows were as mottled as the puppies. As far as unfit homes go, this one wasn't bad enough, not by legal definition. There was no broken and jagged window glass. No cans of toxic paint or chemicals, no vials of sedatives or other deadly substances.

The radio broadcast had called it an ambulance cutting. But who was cut? And where? Then they heard the whimpering from the service porch.

Martin Welborn walked through the befouled living room as the fat puppies squealed happily and bit at his pants cuffs. At first he thought the sound was from another puppy. Then he knew better. It was human whimpering. Then Martin Welborn met Danny Meadows.

He was lying on the service porch, huddling like a ragbag beneath the free-standing washtub. There was a pool of blood on the grimy linoleum in front of the washtub. One of the prancing puppies pattered through the puddle and hopped on Martin Welborn's leg with bloody little paws when the detective knelt to peer at Danny Meadows.

Danny Meadows was eight years old. His face was ghostly. He was in shock. He stared with enormous blue eyes and said 'Daddy?' to Martin Welborn.

Danny Meadows wore a filthy green T-shirt, socks, sneakers. He held his blue jeans in front of him as though he was ashamed. The jeans were blood-soaked. He looked Martin Welborn in the eyes and said, 'Daddy?' The fat puppy splashed through the blood and scampered around Martin Welborn, trying to play with him.

Martin Welborn reached and gently took the bloody jeans away from Danny Meadows. The boy whimpered, but released his hold. Martin Welborn gasped and dropped his gun into the blood. It struck the puppy's toe and the puppy yapped and ran crying into the living room. Danny Meadows looked at Martin Welborn and said, 'Daddy?'

There was a yawning hole where the penis should have been. Most of the bleeding had coagulated and the gaping vertical wound oozed and drained, but was not pumping.

Al Mackey heard the siren first. His voice was unrecognizable. He said something to Martin Welborn about the ambulance.

'Who . . . hurt you?' Martin Welborn asked.

Danny Meadows said, 'Daddy?'

Then through the storm of horror, it struck Martin Welborn! Where? Where?

'Son!' he said. 'Where . . . where did . . . where . . .'

Martin Welborn started crying. The ambulance was pulling up in front of the house. Martin Welborn leaped up and began searching frantically. He tore at piles of dirty clothes. He ran to the sink. He stuck his hand in the garbage disposal. Martin Welborn slipped in the blood and fell down when he lunged into the living room.

He didn't see the paramedics enter the house. He didn't hear Al Mackey's frantic instructions to them. He had to find it! He ran into the bedroom and looked first for the knife. He looked for more blood. He never heard Al Mackey yelling at him. The toilet!

He ran to the bathroom. He plunged his hand into the yellow water. Al Mackey was yelling at him.

Martin Welborn pushed his partner out of the doorway and surged back into the living room while the paramedics were running down the sidewalk with Danny Meadows wrapped in a blanket.

Martin Welborn found it in the living room. It was in an ashtray covered with cigarette butts. It had been burned. He was crying brokenly when he took it out of the ashtray. He went reeling into the bathroom and washed it in the sink. Al Mackey was shuddering and screaming in his ear.

'For God's sake, Martin! Stop! For God's sake!'

Martin Welborn wrapped it in a handkerchief and took it to Children's Hospital. A surgical team worked for five hours reattaching it. They weren't certain for ten days. Then they admitted that the operation was a failure. A second amputation was finally performed to save Danny Meadows' life.

It was determined that both parents had played important roles in the six-month ordeal of their middle child, Danny Meadows, a chronic bed-wetter. Their other children had been neglected but never abused. The final act was in response to his final warning for bed-wetting. It was never precisely determined which one actually wielded the knife. They blamed each other.

And their son, Danny Meadows, met Martin Welborn and became an unrelenting little specter, among a host of other specters, who rose up to torment Martin Welborn in the night.

At last the blinding pain had begun to ease. He stopped weeping from the agony of it. He released the buckle and fell onto the floor of his bedroom. His naked body was drenched with sweat. He tried to sit up but had to lie down again. He tried a second time. He felt that all the blood in his body was surging and sloshing in his skull. He was too nauseous to get up. He pulled the blanket off the foot of the bed. The hardness of the floor offered some relief from the pain. He drew the blanket over him and fell asleep on the floor. He was terrified that the pain would return, but it didn't.

The Crimson Slippers

The next afternoon they would get the biggest break in the Nigel St Claire murder case they they could possibly get. The break was so sudden and so dramatic it virtually assured Al Mackey that he would never have to make an arrest in the Nigel St Claire case. And that was the biggest break of all.

In the morning, Al Mackey arrived as usual at Martin Welborn's apartment. Martin Welborn was not waiting out front so Al Mackey went to the door and knocked. He waited only a few seconds before reaching for the laminated police identification card. He thought of Marty hanging like a dead marlin, and started to panic as he struggled to slip the lock.

Then the door opened. Martin Welborn said, 'You taking up housebreaking, Aloysius, my boy?'

He was showered and shaved and brushed and tailored. As neat as ever. But he was exceedingly pale, and dark under the eyes, and there was a wisp of a tremor in his voice when he said, 'Well, my son, do you like my new suit? Do I glitter when I walk?'

Al Mackey didn't like the way Martin Welborn glittered *in the eyes*. And he didn't like the way Marty walked, or talked, or did anything else that day. Marty was out of focus most of the morning, which was devoted to playing catch-up on the mountain of paper work. They both shuffled paper until noon. Al Mackey was a wreck, and looked at Marty's work for telltale lapses of coherence or continuity.

During his twenty-two years Al Mackey had known too many who succumbed to the Ultimate Policeman's Disease. He had had a radio car partner in 1968 who, during a roll-call harangue on firearms safety which warned that twenty percent of the nation's policemen shot on duty had been accidentally shot by other cops, had startled the assembly by crying out: 'But what percentage shoot *themselves*?' He had that glittering, thousand-yard stare. Two weeks later, in the station parking lot, he shot himself and became part of the fearful statistic which the Department *didn't* keep.

Just after noon Schultz and Simon invited the other team of homicide detectives to go for a bout of dysentery at their favorite burrito stand.

'Come on, Marty, let's go. I haven't done the chili cha-cha since yesterday,' Al Mackey said.

'You go, Al. I'm not hungry.'

'Come on, Marty. Get a bite to eat.'

'I'm not hungry, Al. You go ahead.'

Al Mackey reluctantly accompanied the behemoths, and got sick watching them consume four burritos each.

It was after one o'clock when they got back. Martin Welborn was not in the squadroom. Al Mackey checked the sign-out sheet and saw that Marty had listed his destination as personnel division. What would Marty be doing at personnel? But before he had time to give it much thought, The Big Break came.

The Ferret received a call from robbery downtown. When he hung up the telephone he screamed 'SON OF A BITCH!' so thunderously that Gladys Bruckmeyer came up out of her typing chair, ripping the knees of her pantyhose clear off her varicosed old wheels.

'What the hell is *wrong* with you, Ferret?' Schultz demanded.

'They shot the gook! And Just Plain Bill! They shot them both!'

There was no time to wait for Marty to return. There was no time for anything but for Al Mackey and the Ferret to drive code-three in a black-and-white radio car out the San Bernardino Freeway to the county hospital, where two robbery detectives met them at the elevator. On the way to the intensive care unit they learned that Bill Bozwell and his Vietnamese companion, whose California driver's license showed his name to be Loc Nguyen, had experienced an even worse run of luck than usual when, at ten minutes past noon, they had held up a diamond merchant in a parking lot on Hill Street in downtown Los Angeles. After slugging the merchant, who fought for his goods, they ran smack into three detectives from bunco-forgery who were screwing off in a department store looking for a sale on golf balls. In a one-sided gun battle the detectives put seven ·38 rounds into Bill Bozwell and Loc Nguyen. Just Plain Bill Bozwell was D.O.A., and Loc Nguyen was not expected to survive the afternoon.

The robbery dicks said that there was a wise-ass young doctor in I.C.U. who knew that if a suspect doesn't truly *believe* he's going to die, and if he doesn't *in fact* die, then a dying declaration is no good, legally speaking. Hence, he felt that detectives hovering over deathbeds giving a patient the Final Word was very bad for the prognosis of survival, however slim.

Al Mackey was nearly bonzo when they arrived at I.C.U. He was ready to throttle any young croaker who tried to prevent him from getting them out of this case so that they might go on a goddamn fishing trip or something, and get Marty some rest.

The doctor was not a problem. He was in the corridor writing on a chart when he saw the four detectives. 'Have at him,' the doctor said, with a toss of his perm toward the flattened figure at the far end of I.C.U. 'You can't hurt him now.'

'Is he dead, goddamnit?' Al Mackey exclaimed.

'As good as,' the doctor said, glancing up curiously. 'He's in a coma.'

'Could you guys wait here?' Al Mackey asked the robbery dicks, who nodded and headed for the coffee machine as Al Mackey and the Ferret strode toward the little man breathing the last oxygen he'd ever consume.

306

Two nurses left them and walked into the corridor, and Al Mackey drew the curtain around the bed.

'Well, is it him?' he whispered to the Ferret.

Suddenly the Ferret discovered something extraordinary. Seeing him lying there with the I.V. and the plasma, and the oxygen mask, and the spurious expression of repose, he looked so *different*. The Ferret didn't, couldn't *hate* him. 'He looks so small,' the Ferret said. 'He looks like a little kid.'

'Goddamnit, Ferret, don't say they all look alike! Is it him or not?'

'He looked so different when he was grinning at me.'

'Do you want me to rip off that fucking oxygen mask and make him grin?' Al Mackey said, and the Ferret looked at him and shook his head.

'It's him,' the Ferret said. 'I think.'

'Now get outa here so I can take his dying declaration,' Al Mackey said.

'A statement from *him*?' the Ferret said incredulously.

'Get the fuck outa here!' Al Mackey said.

The Vietnamese assassin made quite a complete dying declaration, according to Al Mackey's report. After expressing a clear understanding that he was going to die, the assassin told the detective that he and Just Plain Bill Bozwell did indeed shoot Nigel St Claire to death that night in the parking lot. It happened after they'd spontaneously kidnapped the hapless mogul from a street in Hollywood where Nigel St Claire had apparently stopped to buy a newspaper. The team of robbers simply seized an opportunity, overpowered the obviously wealthy victim, took him to a lonely parking lot near Gower in Bozwell's car, and shot him dead. They were frightened off by a passing car before they had a chance to rob the corpse.

The assassin barely got the story out before he expired. But he managed. And the Nigel St Claire case was cleared. The sister of Loc Nguyen later told police through the translator that she knew her brother would come to no

307

good, but she'd certainly misjudged his potential after having the police report translated for her. She'd always thought he was a dumb little thug who'd never learned more than a few words of English, yet look how beautifully he'd confessed his crimes at the end. And all in English! It just goes to show that all people have potential, she said.

There were lots of huzzahs and backslapping around the squadroom that afternoon. The captain had borrowed poor old Cal Greenberg's electric shaver and was getting himself all gussied up for a report to a television news team on the happy ending to the Nigel St Claire murder case. He was rehearsing several phrases upon which to end his formal statement regarding the sudden break in the murder investigation. He settled on: 'He works in mysterious ways.'

And he-who-worked-in-mysterious-ways was at that moment sitting in the squadroom wondering where the hell Martin Welborn went after he returned from personnel division. Al Mackey was dictating the dying declaration to Gladys Bruckmeyer when Martin Welborn came in the door.

'Well, my son, congratulations on clearing the case.' Martin Welborn smiled.

'Where the hell you been? Why'd you go to personnel? Where'd you go after that?'

'First, I went to personnel to tell them to process my retirement papers. I'm taking a two-week vacation until my twentieth anniversary, and then . . .'

'You're pulling the pin?' the Ferret said.

'Yeah, twenty years is enough.'

'I figured you for a lifer,' the Weasel said.

'Anyone who doesn't change his mind doesn't have one.' Martin Welborn smiled.

'Where'd you go the *rest* of the afternoon?' Al Mackey wanted to know. 'You called in and were told about Bozwell and his pal. And you *still* went somewhere else!'

'Oh, I had to go see someone. The last piece of business in the Nigel St Claire case.'

'Where?'

'I had to see Flameout Farrell.'

'For what?'

'Nothing important. To tell him that I thought Peggy would be safe from the movies now. That she'd helped us a lot. That sort of thing.'

'I'll be damned!' the Ferret said. 'Here we are, big-shot detectives, wrapping up the year's hottest homicide and you're dicking around with that little bookmaker?'

'Fathers worry about their children,' Martin Welborn said. 'I wanted to reassure him.'

'I wouldn't know,' Al Mackey said, 'not having been a father.'

'Let's go out tonight and celebrate your retirement,' Simon said.

'Hell, maybe I'll pull the pin too. We'll both get out of this evil place,' Al Mackey said.

'What evil place?'

'Hollywood, U.S.A.'

'Al, my son, Hollywood, California, is no more evil than Hannibal, Missouri. There's no evil. No good. It's all an accident.'

'Let's go celebrate at some silk-stocking restaurant,' Schultz said. 'Where all the movie stars go! Is there any place we can dance?'

'How about the dress in those places?' the Weasel asked.

'You can wear one if you want. I still won't dance with *you*,' the Ferret answered.

'Come on, Marty. Come with us,' Schultz said. 'The Ferret's got the post-investigation poorlies. We gotta cheer him up. We'll celebrate the clearing of the case *and* your retirement.'

'You guys go and have a drink for me,' Martin Welborn said. 'I have to pack. I'm renting a cabin in the mountains for the next couple of weeks.'

'What mountains?' Al Mackey asked.

'Lake Arrowhead. I'll come back for my retirement party. You *are* having an official party for me, aren't you?' Martin Welborn smiled.

'The biggest and best,' the Weasel said. 'Come on, let's get started. I say we oughtta begin with martinis at the Polo Lounge! Ferret, can we wear our Hell's Angels jackets at the Beverly Hills Hotel?'

Martin Welborn did not give the phone number of the Lake Arrowhead cabin to anyone. When Al Mackey went to Marty's apartment the next morning he had already gone. Al Mackey did something no one thought possible during the next two weeks. He lost *more* weight, thinking about Martin Welborn all alone in the mountains. And then he did something *he* didn't think was possible: He screwed his socks off the night after payday.

She was Schultz's forty-five-year-old widowed sister, Hilda. She didn't look *too* much like Schultz, thankfully, but she had eaten more than her share of strudel and wiener schnitzel in her day, and she was twice the size of Al Mackey. It had started out as a favor to the big detective, whom she was visiting from Milwaukee. Schultz didn't know what the hell to do with her after showing her Disneyland and Knott's Berry Farm.

The remarkable thing was that Al Mackey only intended to take the dumpy dame to Busch Gardens (all expenses paid by Schultz) and they somehow ended up drinking lots of beer and necking by the aviaries, which led to Al Mackey's apartment, where she made him stiff as a bat with all her good-natured hugging and kissing and flattery. She said he was the best-looking man she'd ever dated (her late husband being the *only* other one). She said he was sexy and fun and manly. And it straightened his whanger out. He banged Hilda *three* times that night even without consuming the powdered elk's antler! He couldn't wait for Marty to get back from his vacation so he could tell him how things were looking up.

*

310

Two days after his twentieth anniversary as a policeman, when his pension was secure for a surviving spouse, and one day before his lease expired at his cabin in the mountains, Martin Welborn arose after lying in bed through the twilight. He showered and shaved and dressed himself as though he were going to work. He wore gun, badge, and handcuffs. He drove his car toward the coil of mountain road leading down from the lake.

Clouds veered. The wind screamed. As he sped toward the most perilous curve on that road, one marked by a great darkling pine and a cliff plunging one thousand feet to the canyon below, Martin Welborn began thinking of the time so long ago when a young policeman sat in St Vibiana's Cathedral and listened to a Gregorian choir. Though most of the others in the congregation were derelicts of skid row, where the cathedral loomed in the deadly smog, it mattered not. The old cardinal was still alive, one of the last of his breed.

As Martin Welborn pressed the accelerator he thought of that day in the cathedral when he had kissed the cardinal's ring.

The mountain road glittered like steel in the frosty moonlight. The serpentine curve and the black void veered.

The Faith was impregnable then. There was peace and Perfect Order in the cathedral that day.

A hawk shadow on the moon. A sable pine loomed at the knife edge of darkness. The black needles hurtled toward him.

How perfect that moment in the cathedral had been. The majestic old cardinal wore lovely crimson slippers.

19

Flameout Farrell

Al Mackey still had not wept by the day of the funeral.
He hadn't wept when Captain Woofer woke him in the
middle of the night to tell him about Marty's car accident.
He hadn't wept when he telephoned personnel division
the next day and discovered that Marty had increased his
insurance to the maximum on the very day they cleared
the Nigel St Claire murder case. Marty named his two
daughters as beneficiaries of the double indemnity clause
for accidental death, and each girl would receive one
hundred thousand dollars.

He didn't even weep when he thought of Paula Welborn
getting Marty's pension for the rest of her life. *Her* delayed
compensation for *his* stress.

But then, he knew that Marty wanted it that way. He
was never one to *stop* loving anything once he started.

He didn't weep when the Department's firing squad,
and the bugler blowing taps, devastated Marty's two
pretty daughters sitting at graveside, at the hideous circus
that is a police funeral.

He didn't weep when everyone said all the platitudes to
him after the funeral.

'He must've fallen asleep at the wheel.'

'Yes, he must've fallen asleep,' Al Mackey would answer.

'He never knew what hit him after he went off the road.'

'No, he never knew what hit him,' Al Mackey would
answer.

'At least he didn't suffer.'

'No, he didn't suffer,' Al Mackey would answer. 'Marty
didn't suffer.'

Al Mackey saw someone at the graveside, however,

whose presence came as close to making him weep as anything could. It was a man with a wan and gossamer look, and skin that was like old ivory in its translucence. A peculiar wisp of a man. Al Mackey guessed immediately who he was. And his mind swerved. He realized that he had probably known who'd killed Nigel St Claire since that last day he'd seen Marty alive.

Later, Al Mackey waited alone for that man when he opened the door of the restaurant. The man was in his only suit, which he had respectfully worn to the funeral. Al Mackey charged through the door and, grabbing him by the necktie, dragged him back into the kitchen and spread him across the sink, knocking a pile of dishes on the floor.

'Don't hurt me,' Flameout Farrell said.

'You *dare* to come to his funeral, you son of a bitch!'

'Please. Please!' Flameout Farrell said.

Al Mackey realized there was only one person who would have possessed the necessary outrage after being told of the snuff film conspiracy by Lorna Dillon. One person desperate enough to wait with a gun in the big parking lot by Griswold Weils' apartment house. But when the black Bentley finally appeared, Bozwell/Lloyd had a stranger with him, and Bozwell/Lloyd was not a man to have been intimidated by such a pathetic gunman. Then, two frantic shots. But it was the *stranger* who got hit. No doubt by accident.

'Fathers worry about their children,' Marty had said that day.

'I wouldn't know,' Al Mackey had answered, 'never having been a father.'

But he *had* known. He'd repressed it. He could never have proved *any* of it. He couldn't prove it *now*.

'Please, Mr Mackey,' Flameout Farrell said.

'How do you know my name, goddamn you?'

'*He* told me, Mr Mackey. He told me you might come.'

Al Mackey slapped the unresisting bookmaker across the face. 'You're lying!'

'He gave me something for *you*, Mr Mackey,' Flameout

Farrell gasped. 'He said to give it to you if you ever came. He . . . he was so . . . *decent* to me when he came that day.'

That stopped Al Mackey. He released his hold on the bookmaker, whose ivory flesh bore the imprint of the detective's hand.

Flameout Farrell hunched before Al Mackey and took his tattered wallet from his pants pocket and removed a folded note, offering it to the detective. Then the little bookmaker began weeping more brokenly than he had wept before the astonished Weasel and Ferret the night he first mentioned his daughter, Peggy.

'He . . . he told me . . .' the bookmaker sobbed, 'that . . . killing that man wasn't an . . . *evil* thing.'

It was unmistakably Marty's handwriting. And finally Al Mackey wept. He wept when he read it, and when he ran out of the restaurant. He wept all the way back to Hollywood Station. He could hardly see the street for the tears. The note said:

Aloysius, my boy:
    You've already cleared the case. Go home. It's *over*. Have a drink for me sometime.

Luv,
MARTY

20

Apple Valley

By the time Al Mackey got himself sufficiently pulled together to enter the squadroom, the others had returned from the funeral. Some were already back to police business. Some were not. Schultz was sitting at the homicide table with his head down. He looked up and his eyes were raw.

The giant detective looked at Al Mackey and said, 'Marty was a *nice* man.'

Captain Woofer strode out of his office just then, all business, and shouted, 'Ferret! You and the Weasel get in here!'

Captain Woofer didn't even bother to close the door of his office as he railed at the two narcs, who were still wearing the ill-fitting suits and greasy neckties they'd donned for the funeral.

Captain Woofer was bitching and moaning about all the dopers and dealers the Ferret and Weasel *hadn't* arrested all the time they'd been screwing around on the Nigel St Claire case where they hadn't *really* been needed anyway. And there was an implied threat to whack their balls and knock their dicks down if they didn't produce some results up on the boulevard. Pronto.

The Ferret and Weasel were grim and determined when they came out of Captain Woofer's office. The narcs immediately began stripping off the neckties and suit coats and they whispered furiously as the squadroom settled back into the routine of the day.

Captain Woofer, ever since the sabotage of his briar pipe, was very careful what he smoked around here. In fact, Lieutenant Fossback, a nonsmoker, had gamely taken up pipe smoking upon the captain's recommendation. Captain Woofer was careful to observe Lieutenant Fossback's symptoms before *he* ever lit up a load of his own from the same humidor. So far, Lieutenant Fossback was only intermittently chartreuse, like the cookie bandit. They all said that Captain Woofer and Lieutenant Fossback were like the Borgias at dinner. It would have been impossible for anyone to slip another load of dope into Captain Woofer's pipe without going through his lieutenant.

But while Gladys Bruckmeyer busied herself with a fresh pot of coffee to help Captain Woofer out of his bad mood, she received some unexpected help from the friendly Ferret, who wiped the captain's cup and helped her pour.

It was Gladys Bruckmeyer herself who took the captain's afternoon coffee to him, and trembled when he took a sip saying, 'Goddamn, Gladys, this coffee's bitter! I told you it's not economical to make it too strong!'

'I'm sorry, Captain,' the old dame said. She was only six months from the pension and Apple Valley. She trembled at *everything* these days.

While the captain grumbled and drank his bitter coffee, the Weasel and Ferret went to their lockers and switched back to their street garb before returning to the squadroom.

Even as the two narcs reentered the squadroom the rest of the detectives knew that something was very wrong with Captain Woofer. He had begun a loud and angry conversation in his office. And he was *alone*.

All the detectives and Gladys Bruckmeyer stopped doing business and listened as the captain cackled hysterically at a joke the nonexistent visitor just told.

'Something's wrong with the captain!' Gladys Bruckmeyer cried out.

'Frankly, my dear, I don't give a damn,' said the Weasel, sounding just like Clark Gable.

'Round up the usual suspects,' said the Ferret, sounding just like Claude Rains.

Then the Weasel and Ferret exited, not even bothering

to stay for the finale, when the captain got sick and tired of arguing with his phantom friend and walked unsteadily out of his office and glared, with pupils like double-aught buckshot, at the roomful of expectant detectives.

Just before he pitched forward into the lap of poor old Cal Greenberg, who was waiting this time like a catcher for a knuckleball, Captain Woofer pointed a wrathful finger at quivering Gladys Bruckmeyer and said: 'YOU, GLADYS BRUCKMEYER. YOU LET THE LADYBUGS LOOSE IN THE CASTLE!'

This time Gladys Bruckmeyer didn't even bother to admit her guilt and ask for another chance. She just sat back and trembled and was grateful that she hadn't jumped up reflexively and torn her pantyhose again. She was down to her last pair. Apple Valley seemed an eternity away.

THE BLACK MARBLE
Joseph Wambaugh

Detective Sergeant A. M. Valnikov is a Los Angeles cop who has just seen too much killing. Now he's lost in a haze of vodka and bitter memories.

Natalie Zimmerman is given the job of pulling him back together. A tough, attractive and uncompromising policewoman, she's not keen to share a beat with a man she despises — and one she thinks is half insane.

Together, the ill-assorted couple stumble into a bizarre and brutal extortion case that hurtles the reader through Joseph Wambaugh's most ferociously comic, explosive and surprising novel yet.

THE CHOIRBOYS

Joseph Wambaugh

A profane, brutal, bitterly funny account of ten cops, working the nightwatch out of Wiltshire Division in Los Angeles. Off duty they attend 'choir practice', a euphemism for the orgies of drink, food and sex that help them to escape the emotional torture of police work. Until one night the wild brawl leads to a tragedy that puts an end to choir practice forever.

'A stark, unrelenting, orgiastic black comedy . . . brilliant work of fiction and Wambaugh's finest book to date.' *Los Angeles Times*

'A wildly inventive picaresque novel . . . outrageously funny.' *Sunday Times*

All Futura Books are available at your bookshop or newsagent, or can be ordered from the following address:
   Futura Books,
   Cash Sales Department,
   P.O. Box 11,
   Falmouth,
   Cornwall TR10 9EN.

Alternatively you may fax your order to the above address. Fax No. 0326 76423.

Payments can be made as follows: Cheque, postal order (payable to Macdonald & Co (Publishers) Ltd) or by credit cards, Visa/Access. Do not send cash or currency. UK customers: please send a cheque or postal order (no currency) and allow 80p for postage and packing for the first book plus 20p for each additional book up to a maximum charge of £2.00.

B.F.P.O. customers please allow 80p for the first book plus 20p for each additional book.

Overseas customers including Ireland, please allow £1.50 for postage and packing for the first book, £1.00 for the second book, and 30p for each additional book.

NAME (Block Letters) ....

ADDRESS ....

....

☐ I enclose my remittance for _____

☐ I wish to pay by Access/Visa Card

Number ⬚⬚⬚⬚⬚⬚⬚⬚⬚⬚⬚⬚⬚⬚⬚⬚

Card Expiry Date ⬚⬚⬚⬚